Praise for

THE
WRONG
GIRL

'Wilson is one of our most **original** and
sensitive crime writers'
Sunday Express

'Brilliant mystery, with **untold twists and turns**
. . . will definitely leave you thinking about the book and its
characters even after turning the final page'
Book Addict Shaun

'With **stunning writing**, vivid characters
and **bags of suspense**, THE WRONG GIRL is
a **must read** for fans of psychological thrillers'
Crime Thriller Girl

'Sensitive and **thought-provoking**'
Shiny New Books

'**Brilliant characters** built layer by layer and a
plot which comes ingeniously together. **A great read**'
The Book Bag

Laura Wilson's acclaimed and award-winning crime novels have won her many fans. Her novel *Stratton's War* won the Ellis Peters Award, while *The Lover* and *A Thousand Lies* were both shortlisted for the CWA Gold Dagger. Laura is the Guardian's crime reviewer. She lives in Islington, London

Also by Laura Wilson

A Little Death
Dying Voices
My Best Friend
Hello Bunny Alice
The Cover
A Thousand Lies

DI Stratton series:

Stratton's War
An Empty Death
A Capital Crime
A Willing Victim
The Riot

THE
WRONG
GIRL

LAURA
WILSON

Quercus

First published in Great Britain in 2015 by Quercus Publishing Ltd
This paperback edition published in Great Britain in 2016 by

Quercus Publishing Ltd
Carmelite House
50 Victoria Embankment
London EC4Y 0DZ

An Hachette UK company

A CIP catalogue record for this book is available
from the British Library

PB ISBN 978 1 78206 312 4
EBOOK ISBN 978 1 78206 311 7

10 9 8 7 6 5 4 3 2 1

Typeset by CC Book Production

Printed and bound in Great Britain by Clays Ltd, St Ives plc

To Florence and Gemma

PROLOGUE

He wasn't going anywhere, just driving. That's what he kept telling himself. There was a half-bottle of Teacher's on the van's passenger seat, mostly full, and he could hear a couple of empties clinking and rolling about underneath. He thought, although he wasn't sure, that they'd been there for some time.

Heat haze on the road. Where was he, anyway? All fields round here, far as the eye could see; not a building in sight. Quiet enough, though. He could stop and lie down on the plastic sacks of compost and bark chips in the back. He'd be happy to sleep forever – he'd not been able to manage more than two or three hours a night these last months, and it was killing him. In desperation, he'd tried manufacturing dreams for himself, consolatory fantasies to help him drift off, but he'd used them too often and they always went wrong.

Everything had gone wrong, too many times. How he'd prided himself on being Mr Fix-it, back in the days when he was a roadie – and the habit was still there, forty years later. What a joke that was.

Fix *this*, you fucker. But he couldn't fix entire lives, his own or anyone else's, any more than he could bring the child back.

He kept on driving. His back was aching and he was sweating like a pig, despite the open window, but he didn't know what else to do. He knew how he'd look to Jeff, if he ever got there: the gut, the bad teeth, the hangdog folds of the face. If he let his beard grow, he'd never have to look at himself in the mirror again. Except, he'd probably manage to mess that up, just like everything else.

He reached over to the passenger seat and, deftly opening the whisky bottle with his left hand, raised it to his mouth.

He'd tried not to remember things – or one thing, at least – and then found that he actually couldn't. Like the letter Pa had written. He'd lost that about six months after the old man had died, and now, seventeen years later – time accelerating away from him – he couldn't remember what it had said. An apology, yes, but not the *words*.

He ought to have asked while Pa was still alive, or asked his mother while he'd still had the chance. Now, he couldn't remember what had held him back. He'd stopped even trying to make himself think about it.

But – he took another swig from the bottle – he wasn't responsible for what had happened, not at the beginning. He'd just got lumbered with it. *Because*, jeered a voice in his head, *you're Mr Fix-it, aren't you?*

At the time, he'd pushed it away, disbelieving because he didn't want to believe. That wasn't 'fixing it'. Had he known the worst all along, or only suspected? He couldn't remember. The booze, he thought. What it does.

That whole business of knowing and not knowing. The tricks we play on ourselves. Honesty-lying, he'd heard someone call it. What alcoholics do.

Then this new thing. When he'd tried to fix that, he'd just made it worse. And if he did talk to Jeff, and managed to get some answers, would it make any difference?

He'd been afraid for such a long time. At first, he hadn't realised that what he was feeling *was* fear – and when he had realised, he'd tried to deny it. The booze had blotted it out, but never for long enough, and now he was full of fear, all the time. The first drink helped with that, and sometimes the second, but not the rest.

He'd made a mess of everything.

He took another drink and glanced at his watch. Past seven o'clock, now – time playing tricks on him. How long had he been driving? Longer than he'd thought. Several hours longer, in fact.

Janice would say he ought to talk about it – trying to be kind, but not having a clue . . . Or, if she did, that would make it unimaginably worse. And what if Jeff realised what he was really getting at? He'd have to be careful how he asked the questions. He'd be casual, pretend he was just passing through.

If he got there. He could still go home.

Except, this was his only chance, while Suzie and the others were away. Otherwise, she'd want to know where he'd been. They all would, and he couldn't face that.

No, he certainly didn't want to talk to anyone about it.

He was way beyond that.

Soon it would be dark.

ONE

How was she supposed to know? She'd thought he was just really, really asleep, like when he'd been in the pub with Mark and them, and they all came in late and made a noise downstairs. He was still in his daytime clothes and the curtains weren't pulled, but that was how he always slept when he'd been out the night before, and no one would want to get under a duvet when it was so boiling hot all the time, would they?

That's why she'd gone to get her coloured pens, because he'd thought it was funny last time when she did *Dan the Man* in a heart on his arm and he'd woken up and seen it. She'd just started on the words, doing it really carefully because it was the hairy bit of his arm so it was quite difficult to make the letters neat. Then Mum had come in and started shouting, and slapped her hand away so hard that the pen flew right across the room.

It wasn't fair. Mum was always shouting, and she didn't have the right because she wasn't even Molly's real mum. She was just Suzie, like Dan was just Dan and not her great-uncle or whatever he was supposed to be – except that he wasn't even that anymore, because he was dead. At least Suzie's latest boyfriend, Mark, didn't pretend to be her real dad. He'd have been rubbish, anyway. He wasn't even a good boyfriend: Suzie was always angry because he never came round when he said he would.

Her real mum wouldn't have shouted, or hit her. *She* wouldn't have sat in the kitchen for hours, drinking wine and yelling at Molly to go away. Or thumped up the stairs in the middle of the night and fallen over and woken her up. Or stayed in her bedroom all morning and refused to unlock the door or even say anything.

It wasn't Molly's fault that Dan was dead. Mum – no, she was *Suzie*, not Mum – had said she should have known, but she didn't see how she could have. He hadn't gone cold and hard like the squirrel they'd found in the garden. Tom had said that it was because he hadn't been dead for long enough. It was a shame Tom wasn't her real brother: even though he was loads older and out a lot, he was always nice to her when he was there. He'd found her hiding in Dan's shed after Suzie had started shouting, and he'd taken her roller-skating in Norwich. They'd gone in Dan's van, and afterwards they went to a nice café. Tom had said she could have anything she wanted. He hadn't even minded when she'd taken ages to decide, and after that they went to see *Maleficent*.

On the way home, Tom had told her it wasn't anyone's fault that Dan was dead. Molly didn't believe him, but she didn't say so because he was saying it to be nice and make her feel better. It *was* someone's fault, because things always were. Like the reason she was here in this big old messy house with Suzie and not at home with her real mum and dad.

Anyway, now she knew whose fault *that* was: Dan's. She knew because of what she'd discovered in his shed before Tom had found her and taken her roller-skating and everything.

She'd have to think what to do about that. First, though, she had to go back into Dan's room and get her coloured pens. Tom had told her that some people came to take Dan away while they were out. Molly'd kept telling herself that was true, and Dan wasn't in his room anymore, but now that she was actually standing at the top of the stairs, hanging on to the banister with both hands and staring across a few feet of landing at the closed door, she didn't feel so certain.

Perhaps Dan was still lying on his bed, only his body had gone flat because he wasn't breathing. Or he might be standing, propped behind the door or in the wardrobe, with unmoving eyes, his face like plasticine when all the colours mixed up, and sort of melted-looking and shiny in a horrible way, like the waxworks she'd seen last year in the museum at Great Yarmouth. She'd had to sleep with the light on and the door open for ages after, in case she woke up and found one of them in her room.

All she had to do was get across the landing, open the door, go into Dan's room, grab her pens off the table by his bed and run back out, and then everything would be all right. She could go and sit on her own bed for a bit and practise writing her real name in different colours.

First, though, she'd got to make it safe, and that meant working out how to do it in the right order, so Waxwork Dan couldn't get her if he was there. Molly squeezed her eyes shut to make the image go away, then opened them and stared down at her two hands, side by side, clutching the banister. As long as she was touching something all the time, it would be OK. If she worked her way around the landing anticlockwise, she could avoid the gap at the top of the stairs. Then, once she'd managed to open the door, she'd have to hold her breath and sort of shrink into herself so she was as small as possible, and not touch *anything* except the pens. The one Suzie had hit across the room was Molly's favourite – purple – but she mustn't stop and look for it in case it took too long and something bad happened.

Heart pounding, Molly lifted one hand off the banister. The putty-coloured, lumpy-featured waxwork faces inside her head crowded nearer as she took the first tiny step towards her goal.

TWO

The combination was 0570, the month and year of her daughter's birth. Ordinarily, this would have been a very bad idea, because – like the date of your wedding anniversary or something obvious like 1234 – it was easily guessed, but as Janice had never told anyone, husband or friend, that she had had a child, she reckoned it was safe enough. She used to it access everything, sometimes together with the name she'd given the baby: Suzanne. Janice assumed she was called something else now. They'd had a week together before the adoption officer – heather twinset and one front tooth flecked with lipstick – had said that she was going to show Suzanne to her prospective parents, and taken her away. Nineteen-year-old Janice had waited for the woman to bring her baby back so that she could say goodbye, but she hadn't come.

Unit S0356 was near the end of one of dozens of identical corridors lined with heavy metal doors in a self-storage facility just off the Purley Way, Croydon. Boxy and, but for the name written on the primary-coloured sign, virtually indistinguishable from its neighbours, it had strip lighting and air that hummed. Apart from that, and the occasional metallic clang or rumble of a trolley, it was silent.

Ten years ago, before she'd cleared her house prior to renting it out, Janice had attended a workshop in a converted barn in Devon. 'De-cluttering: How to overcome the practical and emotional challenges of the sorting process' had been very helpful. Not for Janice the jumbles of exercise bikes, foot spas, digital photo frames and pasta-making machines she'd glimpsed in other people's lockers, although she hadn't entirely managed to embrace her inner minimalist, getting seriously hung up on the clothes bit of the process. The facilitator had told the group that women either kept stuff because to throw the clothes away would be an admission of shopping failure, or because to get rid of them would be to admit that they'd never again be a size ten.

There was also the hope that the clothes might come back into fashion or acquire vintage status, and quite a lot of Janice's stuff from the late sixties and the seventies came into this category. The clothes from Biba, Bus Stop and Thea Porter and the pricey painted silk creations from Granny Takes a Trip were definitely worth a bit. Although no longer able to wear them – they were a tiny size eight and nowadays, she was a bit larger than that – Janice hadn't felt able to part with them. In any case, she didn't need the money. The divorce from her first husband in 1978 had left her with a dilapidated four-bedroom Victorian house in the then not-particularly-desirable area of Notting Hill Gate. Now it was worth a fortune, and she rented it out for an embarrassingly large sum, splitting her time between travelling, a pretty cottage on the Suffolk coast (courtesy of her second divorce, in 1993) and an occasional night or weekend staying with friends in London. That she could do this was entirely due to chance – right time, right place, right people. Apart from the money she spent on travel, Janice lived unostentatiously, trying to disguise her good luck.

Between overseas trips, she had decided to rearrange the furniture in her cottage. She was trying to work out the easiest way of retrieving a Victorian chest of drawers from behind a pair of art deco mirrors when her phone rang.

The name *DAN* appeared on the screen: her brother, who had moved back to the family home in Norfolk during their parents' last years. They'd grown apart and didn't speak often. 'Hi, how's it going?'

'Not well, I'm afraid.' It was a woman's voice. 'That's why I'm calling. Am I speaking to Janice Keaton?'

'That's right.' Janice forced herself to speak slowly. 'And you are . . . ?'

'Suzie.'

'I'm sorry?'

'Suzie. Short for Suzanne. I'm your daughter.'

THREE

Unbalanced, Janice lurched sideways, banging her elbow painfully on the edge of the metal door frame. 'I'm sorry, what did you . . . ?' Her voice felt remote, as if someone else were controlling her larynx.

'I'm your daughter,' repeated the voice, matter-of-factly. 'You're my mother.' The accent was southern English and slightly husky – a smoker, perhaps.

Her daughter – here, now. Suddenly everything, including the background hum, was silent, as though the air itself were holding its breath. 'You're . . .' It was no good – nothing more would come out. Gripping the phone tightly, Janice slid down the wall until she was sitting on the cold concrete floor. *My daughter. Suzie, my daughter. She has the name I gave her.*

Suzie's voice came from the other end of the line in waves, like the sea. '. . . afraid he's dead.'

'What?' said Janice. 'Who's dead?'

'Dan. Your brother. I'm sorry.'

'I don't understand. Why are you . . . ? I mean, how . . . ?'

'How do I know? I'm in Norfolk. I've been staying here.'

'Where?' asked Janice, stupidly.

'At the Old Rectory. I'm really sorry about Dan. We found him this morning. In bed.'

'We?'

'Molly. My daughter.'

'Your daughter?'

'Yes. She's ten.'

I have a granddaughter, thought Janice. Molly. *Suzie and Molly*. 'I'm sorry, this is all a bit . . . You're saying that Dan is dead?'

'Yes, this morning.'

'How did he die?'

'Well, obviously his heart stopped beating, but we don't really know yet.'

'Has he – *had* he – been ill?'

'He seemed OK. Or if he wasn't, he hadn't said anything to me. When did you last talk to him?'

Catching an undertone of accusation, Janice said, 'I'm sorry, I can't remember.' When had it been? She didn't know. She remembered sending him a postcard, back in May, when she was in Yangon. She'd written *Happy Birthday* across the bottom. 'We weren't particularly close, I'm afraid.'

'Yes, I know.'

Dan and Suzie must have discussed her. Ignoring the prick of resentment, Janice said, 'He was only sixty-six.' Three years older than she was.

'I know. The G.P. said there'd have to be a post-mortem because he hadn't seen him for ages.'

'Yes, I suppose there would be. Dan didn't tell me about you. That you were there, I mean.'

'I asked him not to.'

Janice felt as though someone had punched her in the chest. 'You didn't want to meet me?'

'I just wanted to get used to the idea of another family first, you know?'

'Yes,' said Janice automatically, although she didn't know at all. 'How long have you been staying with him?'

'Since February.'

Six months. 'And you didn't . . . He didn't . . .' Janice clutched at the information, trying to secure it, but it seemed too much to grapple with, let alone land. She gulped in some air and said, 'I'm sorry, I don't understand. How did you meet Dan?'

'I had an address for you – the one in the file – so I wrote a letter and he phoned me.'

'So you wrote to *me* and *he* opened the letter?'

'Yeah, by mistake – with it being his surname and everything. That's just how it worked out. Look, when can you come up?'

Just how it worked out . . . 'Come up?'

'Here. I'm not really part of the family and there's the funeral and everything, so . . . you know . . .'

'Shall I come tomorrow?'

'All right.'

'Well, it's . . .' Janice groped for a word. *Astonishing? Amazing?* 'It's lovely to talk to you at last.'

'Yes.' This was said flatly, with no discernible emotion. 'You sound posher than I expected. Posher than Dan, I mean.'

'Do I? Sorry.'

'No, just saying. Anyway, see you tomorrow, OK?'

'Yes, I—' Before Janice could get any further, the dial tone buzzed in her ear.

How extraordinary, she thought, that the most important occasion of her life to date – the first conversation she'd ever had with her only child, after forty-four years and three months – should have taken place in a self-storage facility in Croydon. Four hours later, she was a few hundred yards down the Purley Way, sitting on the side of a double bed in a bland, budget chain hotel. She hadn't felt capable of driving any further.

She'd walked into the lobby, checked in, and then stood staring, dazed, at the rows of Twixes, Anadin tablets, condoms and soft drinks in the bank of vending machines before purchasing, with some difficulty, a plastic packet containing a toothbrush and toothpaste, and a cardboard cup of caffè latte. Now, in the late afternoon, she was sitting on the bed, bracing herself with her palms flat down on the burnished copper and purple bedspread, and staring at the print on the wall in front of her. She'd phoned Liz and Bob, the friends she'd been going to have an early dinner with, and made an excuse. She couldn't face talking to anyone, and especially not Liz, whose daughter, Saffron, was on her third cycle of I.V.F.

Tomorrow, she was going to see her daughter. The baby who had been taken away forty-four years ago had returned as a woman on the end of a phone line. Although the line itself had been perfectly clear, Janice had felt as though they were shouting across a vast distance of missed years and unshared experiences. She didn't even know Suzie's full name yet.

Over those years, she'd rehearsed many variations of that first conversation, but it hadn't been remotely like any of them. She'd never imagined her first meeting with her daughter taking place in her childhood home either, and tomorrow, it would.

Would Suzie have even phoned if Dan hadn't died? Perhaps she wouldn't. Yet Suzie had been looking for her, hadn't she? She'd said so. That was how she'd found Dan. And why *had* Dan died, suddenly and for no good reason?

FOUR

What the hell was going on? Janice sat very still, head down, feeling as if everything around her might suddenly fall apart – a cartoon fissure appear in the floor and the bed be swallowed up, taking her with it, or the entire room disintegrate into smithereens. She got off the bed and sat on the carpet instead.

It felt safer, but not much.

After some time, she pulled herself up on the bed, where she lay, fully clothed, for several hours, staring at the ceiling. Too much emotion – Dan, Suzie, Molly, the past, the future – had pushed her rational brain into neutral so that she couldn't think, but two or three times she wept helplessly, big, heaving sobs that left her barely able to breathe.

At nine p.m., she cleaned her teeth, then took off her jeans and got under the bedspread, but she couldn't sleep. She tried television, flicking, unseeing, around the channels, then took her novel, a Booker shortlister from the year before last, out of her bag and flipped over the pages. At quarter past four in the morning, she gave up, got dressed and checked out.

By the time she arrived at her cottage in Walberswick, it had been light for an hour or so. She got out of the car, ducking behind the hedge to avoid the neighbour walking his spaniels, and, creeping indoors, went into the utility room to retrieve her suitcase. Staring blearily out of the small window, across the marshes at the stump of disused windmill in the distance, she thought: I haven't got a big brother anymore. Some time on Monday night or in the early hours of yesterday morning, I stopped being a sister.

There must have been something wrong. Healthy people didn't die in their sleep for no reason. Dan, she knew, had never gone near a doctor if he could help it, and he certainly wasn't the type who'd self-diagnose on the internet – even if he'd had a computer, which, as far as Janice knew, he hadn't. Once, when she'd said something about the online community, he'd said it wasn't a community but a bunch of socially retarded compulsive wankers, so she seriously doubted that he'd acquired a laptop since she'd last spoken to him – which, she now remembered, was four or five months ago.

Had Suzie been fond of Dan? Janice mentally replayed as much of their conversation as she could remember. She'd sounded detached, as though she were merely passing on information. But then, she – Janice – had probably sounded like that herself – shock would do that to you.

Dan had been the last person in Janice's immediate family who'd known her from a child. Upstairs, she put the case down on her bed and started opening cupboard drawers and pulling things out. How long was she going to stay in Norfolk? More to the point, how long would Suzie want her there? The Victorian rectory in Repshall might now belong to her, since she was Dan's next of kin, but it was Suzie who lived there, and Molly. 'Molly,' said Janice, aloud. 'My granddaughter, Molly.' The words felt unusual in her mouth, as though she were trying out an obscure foreign language.

What should she wear? She leant over the dressing table to peer at herself in the mirror. God, the bags under her eyes! She'd resisted the urge to have herself stitched and injected into line-free immobility, but now she wondered if, perhaps, a small amount of work mightn't be a good idea. But, for now, she still had her summer tan, and her hair, tinted the week before, looked all right.

Who would Suzie look like, her or Jeff? She couldn't really remember what Jeff looked like, beyond a general impression of narrow blue eyes and high cheekbones. She must have a photograph knocking around somewhere. Ten to one it was in Croydon, in the big box with all the letters and things. Stupid! If she'd thought, she could have gone back and fetched it to show Suzie.

Janice didn't even have a baby picture of her daughter. Her only keepsake – referred to by Ma as a 'souvenir', as if Janice had been on a trip to Torquay or Benidorm – was the pale yellow cot blanket she'd knitted during her pregnancy. She'd wanted it to go with the baby, but the non-reappearance of the adoption officer had put paid to that. Ma, whose primary emotion surrounding Janice's pregnancy had been embarrassment, had told her not to make a fuss.

All the books Janice had read about adoption reunions indicated that contact was best initiated by the child, which was why she'd never tried: she'd winced too many times at stories about over-needy mothers who'd never got over the pain of parting with their babies, when what the now-adult children wanted was to have their curiosity satisfied and the questions about their identity answered. Or – and potentially worse, Janice thought – now-adult children who'd constructed a fantasy mother which no real person could hope to equal.

Stop trying to analyse everything, Janice told herself. She chose a floaty top to wear with her jeans and shoved on the bangles she'd bought last year in Cambodia, finished packing and put her stuff in the car.

She walked down to the harbour to try and collect her thoughts, because there was no doubt about it: she was nervous – no, actually frightened – of meeting her daughter. I wish I had her letter, she thought. I'm her mother. I should have met her first. *That's just how it worked out* . . . Pretending not to have noticed another neighbour, this time with a black Labrador in tow, who was waving from the beach, she wrenched her thoughts away from Suzie and on to Dan. She had no idea who his friends were – who would she invite to the funeral?

Since their parents had died, she'd spoken to her brother a few times a year on the phone, but that was it. It had always been difficult getting information out of Dan. He never talked about himself or other people, so if you asked it felt like prying, and whenever she'd suggested coming up to see him, he'd always have some excuse to put her off: he was too busy, she ought to wait until the weather improved, or – once – a lorry had overturned and deposited several hundredweight of manure in the driveway. Could he have had cancer, and not told her? If that were the case, he hadn't told Suzie, either, or been to the doctor. Perhaps he'd just felt worse and worse and been too afraid to tell anybody. I should have insisted on coming to see him, she thought, or simply turned up without warning.

It was going to be another hot day; already, the air was moist and sluggish. There were still a few summer visitors about, but, it being almost September, the children would soon be back at school. Janice started walking down the row of beach huts; they weren't candy coloured here, like neighbouring Southwold, but a uniform, sombre black. Dan hadn't mentioned any lovers in recent years, although there had been plenty in the past, and he'd been married, once. There hadn't been any kids. Janice couldn't remember Dan ever actually telling her, but she assumed he must have got divorced. She bloody well hoped so: Marietta, though undeniably beautiful, had been a cow.

She stared at the flaking paint on the hull of an upturned boat and wondered if Dan had kept up with any of his school friends. She could remember some of these: Jonno (fat and funny), Roger (whose face was so pitted with acne that it might have been the surface of an angry planet) and Simon (the dishy one, who, on the rare but heart-stoppingly wonderful occasions when he'd paid her any attention, had made her blush and giggle) . . . Then there were the people on the music scene that Dan had introduced her to when she'd come down to London, aged sixteen. Some of them had become famous. Surely he'd have mentioned it if he'd been in touch with any of them?

Hearing someone call out, she looked round, but the only person she could see was a woman standing further down the row of beach huts, hand above eyes, scanning the horizon. Suddenly, a little girl, sticky, sandy and already full of sun, ran out from behind one of the fishing boats and flung herself at the woman, clasping her round the legs. The woman bent over to stroke the child's hair, and the tenderness of the gesture made Janice want to cry. There was a fierce, wrenching pain inside her chest as if her heart, thawed, was bursting out of its casing, and when the tears did come, she couldn't stop them. She turned away before either mother or child saw her and, still weeping, hurried back through the village to her car.

FIVE

Coming off the Norwich bypass, Janice started to wonder if Suzie had tried to find Jeff as well as her. His name wasn't in the adoption agency's records, but Dan could have told her what it was. She'd read that, for a variety of reasons, far fewer people looked for their fathers than for their mothers. Perhaps Suzie had discussed it with Dan, and he'd explained what had happened before she was born.

Janice tried to imagine this conversation, and failed. She had no idea where Jeff might be, or even if he was still alive. What if Suzie already had looked on Facebook or something, and found him? What might he have told her? That it was all a mistake? Because that was the truth: getting pregnant had been a mistake. She hadn't been in love with Jeff and she'd certainly never intended to stay with him, but she couldn't tell Suzie that. Still less could she tell her that she'd been planning to have an abortion before Jeff talked her out of it, or that Ma had told her later that that's exactly what she should have done, rather than end up with what she'd referred to as 'this mess'.

In the conversations she'd rehearsed, she now realised, these details had been quickly skated over, the emotional ice being too thin to bear any weight. How could she tell Suzie that she'd felt as though she were drowning, that Ma had come to visit her in the hospital and, having hovered momentarily over the crib like a bad fairy, had averted her face and never once mentioned the baby, then or afterwards.

They'd made it quite clear what they'd thought of Jeff though – or rather, Ma had. Pa was like Dan, not much given to expressing himself. She'd never been sure what Dan had thought about any of it. In fact, the only time she ever remembered him saying anything was when Ma and Pa had brought her home after Suzie was taken away. He'd been working as a roadie then, and he'd put his arm round her shoulders, said he was sorry about the baby, and had given her a carton of duty-free cigarettes from Hamburg.

Now the memory of his kindness made her weep again. Forty-four years of no tears at all, she thought as she leant over to claw a packet of tissues out of the glovebox, and now I can't seem to do anything except cry. It was true: two divorces, numerous break-ups, the deaths of both parents and of friends and, last year, of a lover, as well as umpteen smaller tragedies, and she hadn't shed a single tear. Now, with the shipwreck of her life groaning to the surface and breaking apart, she couldn't stop.

She'd always managed to steer clear of the subject of adoption, even in a general way. When women said things like, 'I don't understand how anyone can give away their baby,' it made her shrivel inside. Suzie was a mother. She'd be bound to say that, especially if she was a single mother, because attitudes were so different now.

She must hate me, thought Janice. That's why she hasn't been in touch, why she told Dan not to say anything. She hates me, and it's my fault. She could already hear Suzie's voice in her head: *If you'd really loved me, you wouldn't have let me go.*

'I did love you,' she said, desperately. 'I did. I do.'

Almost blinded by tears, she pulled over and rested her forehead against the steering wheel. Suzie's voice came again, accusing: *Then how could you do it?*

'I was nineteen,' Janice croaked, 'and everything was different then.' The truth, but how lame it sounded, how pathetic. She could try and explain to Suzie that she'd been young and hadn't known what the hell she was doing and that Jeff, who'd been all for it at the beginning, had decided six months in that it wasn't his scene, and split. She could try and explain that everyone had told her that adoption was the best thing, and that the most important decision of her life had, effectively, been taken out of her hands.

She looked up, blinking, and saw that she had stopped outside a petrol station. Closed now, with a ridge of concrete around it to deter caravans, Janice remembered it from childhood, when her father had gone there to fill up his Austin Cambridge. The canopy was still there, and the pumps in the centre of the forecourt, but the boarded-up shop was tagged with graffiti, and dandelions were pushing their way through the asphalt. Wondering when it had closed, she realised, with a shock, that the last time she'd been to Norfolk – and the last time she'd actually laid eyes on Dan – had been Ma's funeral, in 2008. That had been after an eleven-year gap – Pa had died in 1997.

Janice had been in regular contact with her parents in the years directly after Suzie's birth, but as time went on and her anger against them, and against herself for not being more assertive, had increased, she'd felt less and less inclined to visit or even phone.

Suzie had been their only grandchild. If Molly was ten, she must have been born in 2003 or 2004. That meant that Ma, at least, could have known her great-granddaughter if things had been different.

She had to pull herself together. She owed it to Suzie not to arrive a wet, weeping mess. Bad enough that Dan was dead, without her falling to pieces as well.

Wiping her eyes, she looked across the road and saw a pair of high, solid gates with a sign: *LAND SELECTED FOR QUALITY DWELLINGS BY PORTWAY EXECUTIVE HOMES*. Underneath, in smaller type, it said, *No unauthorised admittance. All visitors must report to site office.*

Of course: Crowhurst Psychiatric Hospital. In the era of the big bin, the Victorian cod-Gothic pile had served most of the county. When it was still in use, it had been hidden from the road by tall hedges, but now, spiked fences had been erected around the perimeter and there were security cameras, boxed in metal grilles, on poles. A great deal of land had belonged to it, including a forest – now, presumably, all sold. Janice could just see, over the gates, the sharp gables of the gatekeeper's lodge, and the chimneys of the big house in the far distance. She pictured missing tiles, broken windows and leaves, blown in, gathered in the corners of the rooms, flaking murals left over from the sixties and seventies – self-expression for the mad. She'd never been in there, or known anyone who had. A memory popped up, startling her, of Pa saying that they used to use something called paraldehyde to sedate the patients, and that it made your breath smell and rotted your teeth. Thinking about this now, Janice wondered how it was that Pa, who had been a Professor of Theoretical Physics, not a doctor, had come by this information.

She did some more nose blowing and applied some make-up, then stared for a moment out of the car window at the vast sweep of the fields beyond the garage forecourt, wondering if the secrets – whether intended to be such, or not – and lack of discussion about important things mightn't have had something to do with the landscape. Maybe, being big and empty, with its flat land and huge sky, it made you keep things close.

SIX

Phoebe Amanda Piper.
Phoebe Amanda Piper, aged ten.
Love from Phoebe xxx.

All the way down the dull mauve page of her scrapbook. Pink looked best, Molly thought, then turquoise, then orange. Purple would have been best of all, but she wasn't ready to go back into Dan's room and find the pen, even though she'd managed to get the others. She'd done it all properly, going round the landing and holding her breath and everything, so Waxwork Dan wasn't in the room and it was OK, but it might not work for a second time.

Suzie was still shut up in her bedroom, so Molly couldn't ask her to help with the pen, and Tom hadn't come home yet. Sighing, she put the scrapbook aside and lay down flat on her bed, clutching the sides of the mattress and staring at the ceiling. It was high – much further up than in the last place they'd lived – and it had a brownish stain on one side, shaped like a rabbit's ears, from where the roof had leaked.

When she imagined the meeting with her real parents, it was always in the same place: a pink, satin-lined marquee like the one Ellie's mum and dad had hired when it was Ellie's big sister's wedding. There wouldn't be a big cake or any of that stuff – well, *duh* – but there'd be flowers and those goldy chairs with thin legs. Molly would have a dress like the one Ellie'd had for being a bridesmaid, only it would be pink, not blue.

She didn't know if it would be exactly like that, but she knew she'd be in the middle, with her real dad, David Piper, sitting on one side and Melissa Piper, her real mum, on the other. They'd be behind a long table covered in a white cloth, and there'd be lots of people with microphones, cameras clicking and phones held up, flashing. Outside, there'd be people waving and yelling and holding up posters they'd made, like the ones on *Big Brother*, only these ones would say *Welcome Home* and *We Heart Feebs* and have her photo really big.

David and Melissa would say how happy they were, and how much they loved her, and there'd be a cuddle for the T.V. cameras. She'd have to remember not to blink, because that made you look funny.

They'd want a photo of her with Snuggle Pup as well, because everyone knew about Snuggle Pup. There'd been lots of pictures in the papers of her holding him, from before she'd been stolen, when she was really little, and Melissa had been photographed with him loads of times and cuddled him on television and everything. Molly thought she could remember the feeling of him, floppy ears and plush orangey-brown fur, tucked under her arm while Melissa read her a bedtime story. She couldn't remember any of the stories, but it had been when she was three, so nobody would expect her to . . . Would they? Molly was a bit worried that they might, or that her not remembering might upset Melissa.

She never wanted to upset Melissa, or David. Ever since she'd realised who she really was, she'd loved them more than anything in the world. Course, she'd loved them before, only she hadn't known it, because she hadn't known she was Phoebe Piper. Molly wasn't sure if she ought to be sad about this, or if it was just interesting.

She'd never do anything bad. Melissa and David loved her so much. They'd been looking for her for *seven whole years*. Seven was an important number – Molly knew that. It was lucky, and there were seven days in a week and seven colours in a rainbow and seven Harry Potter books and James Bond was 007. There was lots of stuff with sevens in it in stories, too. Molly was too old for books at bedtime now, but perhaps Melissa would read her one sometimes, to make up. Melissa would be glad to, if she asked, especially once she had explained that Suzie had never read her a bedtime story, not even once.

It would be funny being called Phoebe again. She'd had to practise spelling it for ages before she got it right. Phoebe meant 'bright and shining'. When they'd done about names at school, and everyone had to find out what their name meant, she'd looked it up first, because it was her real name. Then she'd looked up Amanda, because that was her real middle name, and it meant 'deserving to be loved'. After that, she'd looked up Molly and found out that it wasn't even a proper name, just a different way of saying Mary, and Mary meant 'bitter'. It was a rubbish name.

She'd have to get used to calling Melissa and David Mum and Dad, too. She didn't think that would be too difficult. And she'd be famous, one of the most famous girls in the world. Really, she was already – it was just that nobody knew it yet. Soon, it would happen. Molly whispered it to herself as she stared up at the rabbit-ears stain on the ceiling. *Soon.*

The first time she'd been recognised was when she was six, only she hadn't realised till afterwards. She'd got lost when they were out shopping and a security guard had taken her to a nice place where they'd given her orange squash and an ice cream and everyone wanted to talk to her. Two policemen came, and when Suzie came to get her they'd taken her off into this little room for ages and ages. When they'd all come out, and they were in the corridor so Molly could hear, Suzie had said, 'That bloody picture.' Molly didn't know what it meant then, only later, when Suzie had explained about the little girl who was missing, and how they'd made up a photograph of what she might look like now she was six, and she looked just like Molly. She'd been too young to understand, but people had kept on looking at her in a really starey way, and sometimes they'd said things, but to each other, if there was two of them, not to Suzie. Then it stopped for a bit and Molly forgot about it, and then it started happening again just before they came here, because they did a new picture and it *still* looked like Molly. A woman had noticed when they went to see the Christmas lights in London, and she told a policeman and he came and talked to Suzie when they were just standing on the pavement with all the people there who could hear what he was saying and everyone was looking. Molly could tell Suzie was embarrassed because she'd undone her scarf and her neck was all blotchy red. And still Molly hadn't known, not really, but afterwards she'd thought about it a lot and got Tom to show her all the stuff about Phoebe Piper on his laptop – things from the newspapers. Then, when she'd been looking at them, she'd started remembering about what it was like when she was Phoebe. She'd known it was right because she could feel it inside. And she'd noticed people looking even more, this time, if they were in a bus or on the Tube – *really* staring, so that Suzie had to pretend she hadn't seen them doing it. And when they'd lived in the B & B, one of the women there had even called her Phoebe, instead of Molly.

After she'd been at the new school in Norfolk for a bit, Molly'd told Ellie about it, except she'd left out about the woman in the

B & B being mad and smelling of wee. Ellie agreed that she did look like Phoebe Piper, but after that she'd started going round with Jasmine. The two of them were always talking about Molly, laughing behind her back. Ellie'd never been to London. Nor had Jasmine. They were stupid and horrible and didn't know anything.

> Still praying, still searching.
> Think abt u all the time.
> Never give up.
> Phoebe, our princess.
> Sending our love.
> God bless u.

She'd seen the messages on the website when Tom let her go on his computer. There'd be even more, now, because people put new things up every day. It was nice thinking about them, especially after what happened with Dan.

It would be good if Tom could carry on being her brother when she was Phoebe again. Of course, the Pipers would want her all to themselves, but they didn't have any other children so she wouldn't have new brothers or sisters to replace Tom, and maybe they'd let her keep him.

> Light a candle 4 Phoebe 2nite.
> Lost angel.
> Stay strong.
> Never 4get u.
> All our prayers.
> Come back soon, baby girl.

Soon, Molly told herself. Because she really *did* know, now, and it *was* true. What she'd found yesterday in Dan's shed proved that it was.

Now we'll see who's stupid, Ellie Roberts. Now we'll see, Jasmine Burnside. We'll see who's stupid now, won't we?

SEVEN

The villages Janice passed through were tidier than she remembered. The bungalows with flat-roofed sun lounges that she'd seen being put up in the sixties and seventies now looked shabby and forlorn, but nothing else did. The gardens were neater and prettier, and the paint – an awful lot of which, on doors and window frames, seemed to be sage green – looked fresh. There were new houses, too, in brick and flint, carefully built in the vernacular style. They made Janice think of being the new kid at school, painfully aware of the thick stiffness of your new blazer and desperate to fit in.

The pond at Gorleigh Green was definitely cleaner, and there were geese and ducks waddling across the surrounding grass. The Methodist Chapel at Yelton had been converted into an antique shop, and further down the lane, a boutiquey place called The Old Forge had Cath Kidston products draped over bits of driftwood in the window. It must, she supposed, be the same on the coast, with gastro pubs, and fishermen's cottages turned into second homes for Londoners.

When had it all become the stuff of colour supplements? Perhaps, thought Janice, the gentrification had already begun six years before, when she'd come for Ma's funeral, and she'd failed to notice.

She drove past the ruins of the priory and the now-disused R.A.F. Ventham, and then the road dipped down into Repshall, the gentle incline the nearest thing to a hill for miles around.

The sage-green paint was everywhere here, too, and the village sign on its pole in the middle of the green – a man harvesting with a scythe – had been picked out in bright colours. The village shop, however, still looked as Janice remembered it: the faded advertisement for the *Eastern Daily Press* above the window, and a few moribund spuds and carrots in boxes on a bench outside. The only things that seemed different were the newspapers, also displayed outside, but now in an individually compartmentalised case under plastic lids.

That familiarity, at least, was reassuring. The Lord Nelson was still there, too, and open for lunch. Slowing down, Janice saw a succession of burly young workmen stooping to step through the low door and, through the open window of her car, heard snatches of conversation in Polish, or perhaps Bulgarian or Romanian.

Rounding the corner, she took a deep breath. The Old Rectory was just about to come into view, and . . . Oh, God. There it was, at the bend of the lane, the gates open, two pairs of Dutch gables clearly visible above the unkempt hawthorn hedge.

Janice stopped the car in the lane. She needed time to think. Should she have called to say when she'd be arriving? Perhaps she ought to phone and warn Suzie. She felt trapped, sick with expectation. What if it all went wrong? A horn sounded behind her and Janice saw, in her rear-view mirror, a tractor pulling a load of straw. The huge rolls, sticking out of the open trailer on either side, were brushing the hedgerow, and there was no question of it being able to overtake. Automatically, she restarted the car, and before she knew it, she'd driven the few hundred yards up the lane, turned off and pulled up in front of the porch.

A child's bicycle was lying on the gravel, but there were no vehicles other than her own in the drive. With flaking paint and weeds around the porch, the house, Janice thought, had a weary look, as though it had resigned itself to the depredations of the weather. The front door was slightly ajar. Janice got out of the car, hesitated for a moment, and then gave the wood a slight, non-committal push with her fingertips.

It was almost as hot inside the house as it was outside, and the coconut mat was askew on the chequered tiles of the passage floor, a child-size denim jacket lying next to it. The rest of the coats and boots, Janice saw, hung where such things always had, in the small room off to the left-hand side, but the hall had a neglected appearance, scratches and scrapes on the wooden panelling, scuffs on the skirting and doors.

No sound from anywhere. 'Hello!' Janice called out, and then, attempting to inject a cheerful note into her voice, 'Anybody home?'

Nothing. She went into the sitting room, which ran the length of the back of the house. This looked messy and neglected, too, with the tall French windows so dirty that the garden beyond was a greenish smear. On the mantelpiece, amidst a jumble of glasses and ashtrays, stood a framed photograph of her parents on their wedding day. Pa in uniform, not yet demobbed, had his arm round Ma in her best jacket and skirt, both shyly proud. Janice leant forward to blow dust off the glass. Had it always been there? She couldn't remember. Maybe Dan had brought it out to show Suzie. She wondered what her daughter had thought, looking at it, especially if Dan had told her that Ma, at least, hadn't wanted her to exist.

At the other end of the room, the baby grand piano that Ma had played still stood, but now, its lid down and covered in clutter, it was no longer an instrument but just another surface. Janice knew, without testing, that it would be out of tune.

She went through to the kitchen. Like the sitting room, it was big, and almost unchanged: flagstones, a Belfast sink and wooden draining board in front of the window, and a long table where they'd eaten their meals when she was a child. Now, there were two empty wine bottles standing on the table beside a saucer full of cigarette butts, and the scarred wooden surface was stained and strewn with ash. Only one wine glass, though, which presumably meant that, the previous night, at least, Suzie had been drinking alone. There was a smell – something rotten – coming from an overflowing plastic bin beside the back door. Cardboard pizza boxes were piled up beside it, next to more empty bottles: wine, mostly, and supermarket brands of vodka and whisky. Crockery was piled precariously in the sink, and the floor felt sticky underfoot.

In Janice's memory, her childhood home was tidy, well kept. Now, it was neglected, a place with a history of carelessness, not love or pride. She shrank back, sensing recrimination and disappointment – lives gone wrong – then told herself not to be stupid. Dan had just died, for God's sake. Suzie – *her daughter* – would be in shock. What had she expected? A tea party?

Standing in the doorway, she called out again, and, after a moment, heard movement above her head.

'Hang on!' It must be Suzie's voice. It sounded weary, as though dredged up from the nadir of a hangover, which, Janice thought, eyeing the bottles on the table, might very well be the case – but who was she to pass judgement? She hadn't been here, or found Dan dead. And even if she had, it still wouldn't give her the right to criticise.

'In the kitchen!' she called. Perhaps Suzie would like a cup of tea. Spotting a calcified kettle, she took it over to the sink, acutely aware, as she turned on the tap, of the noises above her head and then on the stairs. It was no use. Her hands were shaking and water was going everywhere. She put the kettle down on the draining board and turned off the tap.

'Janice.'

She turned. Her daughter was standing in the doorway, clad in a grimy cream-coloured bathrobe.

EIGHT

Afterwards, Janice asked herself what she'd expected. Had she thought that Suzie was going to run into her arms and call her 'Mum' and weep on her breast? She hadn't expected that, had she? *Had* she? A connection: it's *now*, it's *you*. My daughter. My baby.

Except that Suzie wasn't a baby. Of course she wasn't. She was a woman on the verge of middle age, a stranger.

She was tall, like Janice, and slim, but her face was sallow and queasy looking, with smudges of yesterday's make-up under her eyes and hair stuck sweatily to her cheek.

It had soon become clear that Suzie wasn't up to making eye contact, let alone having a conversation. She'd responded to Janice's suggestion that she go back to bed with a murmured, 'I know, I look like shit – I'm sorry,' before returning upstairs, leaving disappointment, like a vapour trail, in her wake. Telling herself that any charge between the two of them had been effectively earthed by Suzie's hangover, Janice finished filling the kettle, lit the gas and set about tidying the kitchen. As she opened the windows to get rid of the lingering smell of smoke, the awful thought occurred that perhaps the prospect of meeting her birth mother was the reason that Suzie had drunk so much . . . But it couldn't have been just that, surely? There was Dan, as well.

That must be it – Suzie had become fond of him, of course she had. Now, as well as feeling grief for him, and probably appre-hension about their meeting, the poor girl would also be feeling remorse and shame, as well as dehydration, nausea and a headache.

Janice had wanted to ask about Molly – who was, presumably, the owner of the bicycle she'd seen outside – but it hadn't seemed appropriate.

Better, thought Janice, not to go looking for her. She didn't want it to seem as if she were nosing around and taking over.

She added the bottles from the table to the ranks round the bin, then started looking around for dustbin liners. The kitchen didn't seem particularly well stocked with either food or cleaning products – not entirely surprising, as she couldn't imagine that Dan had been much of a housekeeper – and she resolved on a major shop at the first opportunity.

The kettle was boiling. Janice found a box of P.G. Tips and was opening cupboards in search of mugs when she heard a slight scraping noise coming from the doorway. Turning, she saw that she was being stared at by a girl of about ten years old with a face that was oddly – in fact, eerily – familiar.

'Hello,' said Janice. 'Are you Molly?'

The girl didn't seem alarmed, but she didn't speak, either. Skinny, lightly tanned and dressed in a green T-shirt and denim shorts, she was undoubtedly pretty, with a tangle of long, fair hair, a pair of enormous hazel eyes and a light dusting of freckles.

'My name's Janice.'

The girl looked at her blankly, shuffling her feet as though about to flee.

Janice tried again. 'Do you live here?'

A nod, then, in a whisper, 'I'm Molly.'

'I thought you must be. You're Suzie's daughter, aren't you?'

The girl frowned, as though she knew something was wrong, but wasn't sure what, and looked round the room. Perhaps, thought Janice, she was just very shy. 'Yes.' Another whisper.

Janice wondered if Molly had even been told she was coming. Perhaps Suzie had felt that Dan's death was enough of a shock without the addition of an unknown grandmother. Perhaps Molly wasn't even aware that Suzie was adopted.

'Your dad – is he here, too?'

Molly's look – bafflement combined with scorn – suggested that this was a question she couldn't reasonably be expected to answer. Perhaps, thought Janice, not having a father is simply a fact to her, like a Manx cat having no tail. 'Do you know who I am?' she asked.

'You're Janice,' said Molly, patiently. 'You just told me.'

'Has your mother told you about me?'

Molly rolled her eyes. 'No.' Clearly, thought Janice, it wasn't particularly unusual for the girl to find complete strangers wandering round the house. She wondered if they were Dan's friends, or Suzie's friends, or both.

'Well . . .' Janice thought for a second, then decided to go for it. Molly would have to find out sometime, wouldn't she? 'This may come as a bit of a shock, especially if your mum hasn't mentioned it, or anything, but . . . I'm your . . .' Here, she realised she hadn't settled on a word for what she was – grandmother? Grandma? Granny? Gran? Plumping for the first because the others seemed presumptuously informal – the shortened title ought, surely, to be bestowed and not insisted upon – she finished, 'I'm your grandmother. I'm Suzie's – your mother's – mother.'

As she was saying this, Molly's face seemed, just for a moment, to light up, but then the girl's jaw stiffened and her eyes narrowed to slits. 'No, you're not,' she said. 'You're telling lies.' Before Janice had time to deny it or try to explain, Molly had charged upstairs and a door – presumably the one to her bedroom – had slammed.

Shit. Janice sat down at the table, knuckles against forehead. What a minefield. At least she hadn't made some appalling gaffe about Dan ... *Hang on.* If Suzie hadn't told her daughter about being adopted, then who on earth did Molly think Dan was? A boyfriend?

Janice closed her eyes tightly. Don't go there, she told herself. She must concentrate on practical things and not let her imagination run away with her. Suzie would come down and talk to her when she was ready, and, in the meantime, poor Molly must be starving. By the look of it – a bowl with a few flakes of cereal clinging to the sides, left on top of the claggy pile in the sink – she'd got herself some breakfast, but no lunch, and it was past two o'clock. A further search of the kitchen revealed two hoar-frosted pizzas and a bag of sprouts in the chest freezer, and the last few slices of a white loaf, some butter and a pot of blackberry jam.

Sandwiches, then. Better than nothing, anyway. Spreading butter, she wondered why it was that Molly had looked quite so familiar. A visceral pang of recognition of one's own flesh and blood was a lovely idea but, much as she'd like to believe in such a thing, Janice suspected that it only happened in bad novels.

It wasn't because she thought she'd seen a family likeness – but there had definitely been *something*. It was as if she'd seen Molly dozens of times before, but how and where?

Janice shook her head. She'd take the sandwiches up to Molly and try for a fresh start.

NINE

'I thought you might like something to eat.'

It was even hotter upstairs, and Molly was sprawled across her bed, her legs at strange angles, like a marionette dropped from a height, surrounded by felt-tip pens and scraps of paper. She was colouring something in, and didn't look up. 'I'm not hungry.'

'I'll leave it, shall I?' Janice addressed the top of the girl's head.

'I don't want it.'

'You might later.'

'I won't.'

'You never know.'

'Yes, I do.'

Janice put the jam sandwiches and a can of Fanta on the desk. 'This was my room when I was your age.' The bed beneath the window was the same, and so were the desk, the matching plywood chair, the shelves and the clothes cupboard with the two drawers at the bottom. In fact, apart from the bedclothes, the only thing that seemed to have changed was the colour of the walls, which, previously papered with a design of little spriggy flowers, were now painted a greyish pink. The framed Morland print – setters under a tree – still hung at the head of the bed, and apart from some stickers – smiley faces, cartoon monsters, Hello Kitty – dotted about the walls, Molly seemed to have made no effort to personalise the place. 'And that was my favourite plate.'

Molly's head came up sharply. 'Which one?'

'The Spanish dancer.' Janice gestured at the sandwiches. 'No one liked it apart from me. My mother . . .' Janice almost added, 'your great-grandmother,' but stopped herself in time. 'She used to use it to feed the cat.'

'What was the cat's name?'

'Freddy.'

'I wish we could have a cat.'

'Perhaps you can. After all,' Janice thought of the mess in the kitchen, 'they don't take much looking after.'

Molly shook her head. 'Suzie doesn't like them.'

Not 'Mum', then. Janice wondered if that had been Suzie's decision, or Molly's, or both.

'It's my favourite plate, too,' Molly said. 'Was this really your room?'

'Yes. Can I sit down?'

'If you want.'

Janice moved some of the papers and pens and sat down on the bed. The duvet cover – sailing boats on a washy blue background – was grubby and marked with streaks of felt-tip pen. Molly eyed her critically. 'It must have been ages ago.'

'It was.'

'Dan was here, too.'

'Yes, he was,' said Janice, remembering that it was Molly who'd found his body. 'Dan was my brother.' Molly frowned, then bent her head and picked at a scab on her knee. 'Don't do that,' said Janice. 'You'll make it bleed.'

'No, I won't. It's ready to come off. Hang on.' Molly picked carefully for a moment, and then said triumphantly, 'There, see?'

and pointed to an area of pinkish, shiny skin. 'I've made it more tidy.'

'I suppose so,' said Janice, 'but you still shouldn't. If you pick at things, they don't heal.'

Molly stared at her again, head on one side in appraisal. 'Are you really my grandmother?'

'Yes.'

'Then you ought to have some baby pictures of me.'

Caught off guard by this, Janice felt herself falter, as though she'd stepped suddenly off the kerb into traffic. 'I'm afraid I haven't.'

'Then you're not really, are you?'

'I'm sorry. I wish I did have some pictures.'

'Suzie hasn't got any either.'

'Oh, I'm sure that's not true.' Janice heard herself give a brief, uncomfortable laugh. 'I bet she's got lots. The reason that I haven't got any is that I didn't know about you until yesterday. I mean, I didn't know that you existed.'

'Why not?'

'Because,' said Janice carefully, 'your mum hadn't told me about you.' Quickly, in case Molly thought this was a criticism of Suzie, she added, 'It wasn't her fault. She was looking for me, you see. That's how she found your Uncle Dan, because she had the address of this house, and Dan was here.' *That's just how it worked out*, Suzie's voice echoed, matter-of-fact, inside her head.

'Dan's not my uncle,' said Molly.

'No, you're quite right, he's not. He is – I mean, he *was* – your *great*-uncle: your mother's uncle. Anyway, she found him because this is where I used to live when your mum was born. With *my* parents – and Dan's, of course. You've probably seen the photo on the mantelpiece downstairs.'

Molly looked doubtful. 'Why did Suzie have to look for you?'

'Because—' Janice was suddenly and uncomfortably aware of how hot she was, 'she was adopted. I wasn't able to look after her, and I had to give her to somebody who could, and those people became her parents – and your grandparents.'

Molly stared at her. 'Do you mean Gamga?'

'Yes . . . I suppose so.'

'She's dead.' Molly's tone was severe.

'Oh. I'm sorry. Well,' Janice added lamely, 'I'm here, anyway.'

Molly's eyes narrowed. 'Do you mean you gave Suzie to somebody when she was a baby?'

'Yes.'

'Somebody you didn't *know*?'

'Yes.'

'And they just took her away?'

'Yes.'

'And you never saw her again?'

'Not until now, no.'

'And you never knew where she was?'

Janice shook her head.

'Didn't you want to know?' Molly's eyes were round with accusation. 'Didn't you even *care*?'

'Yes, I did, but I'd given her up, so . . .' Janice turned slightly and stared out of the open window at the back garden. The trees and shrubs were overgrown. A rusty wheelbarrow stood beside the shed, and there was a patio chair – white moulded plastic – on its side in the middle of the scrubby lawn. 'It was a better life, with a mother and . . .' She'd been going to say 'a father' but, remembering that Molly didn't appear to have one, changed it to, 'a proper home.'

'But her mother was *you*.' Molly's voice was stern. 'You just said.'

'Yes,' said Janice. 'But it wasn't like now.'

'Why wasn't it?'

'It was ... different. The way people thought. If someone was having a baby, and they weren't married, it was bad.'

Molly considered this for a moment. 'It wasn't the baby's fault.'

'No, of course not.'

'But it would still end up in the wrong place.' Don't cry, Janice told herself. Do anything, say anything, only don't cry. 'So, then, it would have the wrong life.'

'But now,' Janice cleared her throat, 'this is the right place, isn't it? The right life. For your mum, I mean.'

Molly looked unconvinced. 'She's already had quite a lot of the wrong one, though, so it might not work. She might be somebody else by now, so she couldn't get into the right life even if she wanted to.'

Even if Janice had been able to speak, she wouldn't have known what to say. After a moment, during which Molly carried on looking at her with unblinking attention, she said, 'Do you like it here?'

'It's OK.'

'Does your mum like it?'

'Don't know.'

'Does she have a job here?' Janice wondered if it wasn't a bit underhand, getting information about Suzie from Molly, but as she was bound to find out anyway, she decided it probably didn't matter.

'Not really. I think she helps Mark a bit.'

'Who's Mark?'

'Her boyfriend. He works in the pub sometimes. When it's busy.'

What the hell? thought Janice. 'Does he live here, too?'

'No, but he stays sometimes.'

'So it's – it was – just you and your mum and Dan, was it?'

'And Tom.'

'Who's Tom?'

'My brother.' And my grandson, thought Janice. I have two grandchildren. 'Half-brother, really,' Molly corrected. 'He was at college in London, only he couldn't get a job after, so he came to live here with us.'

'How old is he?'

'Twenty-four.' Different fathers, thought Janice, wondering if Tom knew about her. 'He's been helping Dan, doing the things,' Molly added.

'What sort of things?'

Molly sighed. 'Things for people here. Cutting down trees and stuff.'

So Dan had been the local odd-job man. It sounded right: he was always a fixer. Like when he was on tour with the bands – solving logistical problems, scoring drugs. Doing the impossible on the road.

'Tom might have some baby photos of you,' said Janice. 'You should ask him.'

'I did, but he doesn't even remember when I was a baby, because he was living at his dad's.'

'Where's Tom now?'

'Don't know. He went out, so he might be at Megan's.'

'Is that his girlfriend?'

'Not his proper one.' Molly looked scornful. 'She thinks she is, because he goes there sometimes, but she's not. He's got a real one in London. He told me. But he might not be at Megan's,' she added. 'He's got other friends as well.' This was said defensively, as if Janice had accused Tom of being a Billy-no-mates.

'I'm sure he has. What about you? Do you have any friends in the village?'

Molly shook her head. 'All the people here are old – older than you, even – like the Rocklins. They're over there.' Following Molly's pointing finger, Janice could see a small segment of shaggy-looking garden in the corner of a field, and a pair of French doors at the rear of a whitewashed cottage.

'I remember the Rocklins. They lived here when I was young.' Janice recalled Mrs Rocklin's face, burnt on one side – the lash-less eye, its involuntary glare half glimpsed behind artfully arranged curls, the shiny pink patch of skin on the cheek and one corner of the mouth pulled sharply upwards, as if by an invisible thread. She also remembered Mrs Rocklin saying that she had 'let herself down' by getting pregnant and that no one would want to marry her. She didn't remember seeing either Mr or Mrs Rocklin at Ma's funeral, and it had never occurred to her that they might be still alive – Mrs Rocklin had been older than Ma, so now she would be well over ninety. 'They must be getting on a bit.'

'They are. They're as old as –' Molly screwed up her face, trying to think of something that old – 'dust. Really old dust. Her face is funny, and he's all scrunched up in a wheelchair.' Molly demonstrated, hunching her shoulders and turning her hands into claws.

'You must have some friends at school, then.'

Molly stared at her, wordlessly. Surely to God, thought Janice, she's not being taught at home – stuck out here with no friends of her own age? She glanced round the bedroom for some evidence of education and her eye lighted on a small photograph pinned to the corkboard above the desk: Molly, her long hair neatly brushed, wearing a navy blue school sweater. The picture looked as familiar as Molly herself had – more so, even – but Janice couldn't for the life of her think why. She must be imagining it, or it was subliminal – a similar-looking girl used to advertise insurance or yoghurt or something.

'I did have a friend at school,' said Molly, 'but she doesn't like me anymore.'

Janice's recollections of her own time at school were, nowadays, little more than blurred impressions, with only a handful of names and incidents, but she knew, with painful exactitude, what was behind Molly's few words: the shifting allegiances, the whispering and giggles behind the hands, the rejection. Being an outcast, with no one to talk to or play with. Last to be picked for the team. The teacher having to find you a partner for the crocodile.

'There must be lots of people in your class.' Janice tried to sound encouraging.

'Yes,' said Molly impatiently, 'but they've got friends already. They've all been there for ages. Ellie and me were new at the same time.'

Janice looked at Molly's hurt face and felt a strong urge to hug her, but thought she might not like it. 'I'm sure you'll make some new friends soon,' she said.

Molly shook her head. 'It doesn't matter, anyway. I don't care about them. And,' she added, in a so-there voice, 'you can't have a baby picture of me, because there aren't any. Not even one.'

'That's a shame,' said Janice, thinking this wasn't the moment to pursue the subject. 'Do you think – if you don't want to eat your lunch right now – you could help me unload my stuff from the car? I'm going to be staying here for a few days.'

'OK. But I will have a sandwich first.' Molly jumped off the bed and stuffed a whole sandwich into her mouth. After a moment, her cheeks bulged and her eyes began to water and she began to cough, spewing out bits of bread and jam.

Seeing no tissues, Janice nipped across the landing to the bathroom – green stains below the massive Victorian taps, silverfish on the woodblock floor – and fetched some loo roll. 'There you are.'

'*Mmmpf*.' Molly finished what was still inside her mouth and wiped the rest off her chin and the front of her green T-shirt. 'Thanks. Will you do something for me if I help you with your stuff?'

'What's that?'

'Go into Dan's room and get my purple felt-tip. I dropped it on the floor.'

TEN

Molly waited until she heard Janice step on the creaky board just outside Dan's room, then leant down and, from under her mattress, pulled out the things she'd found in his shed. She'd found the envelope on the shelf, propped against a tin of the smelly stuff he'd used to paint the fence. Even though she didn't understand all of it yet, the letter was part of the proof that she really was Phoebe, but – for the time being, at least – it didn't matter half as much as the photograph she'd spotted lying in the dust and mouse poo at the back of the workbench underneath the shelf. It was small, dog-eared and black and white, and she'd turned it over to find a message staggering across the back in uneven capital letters:

ASK HER WHO YOUR MOTHER IS

Poised on the edge of the bed, ready to stuff everything back into its hiding place, Molly looked at the photo of two women, arm in arm, shown from the waist up against a blur of bushes. Even if the photo hadn't been black and white, she'd have known it was old from the women's clothes and hair. Both were slim, and Molly thought they were quite young, but the old-fashionedness made it hard to tell. They looked as if they were only smiling because of the camera. Molly didn't think they'd wanted to link

47

arms, either. Maybe the person who'd taken the photo had told them they had to.

Dan must have left the photo for *her*, but the envelope had *Joe* written across it. It had *Private* on it, too, but that didn't count if you were dead, and when she'd looked at the letter inside, it didn't say *Dear* anyone. It mentioned the picnic they'd been on, her and Melissa and David, just before she'd been taken away. There was a bit about a hair ribbon, too, that Dan had, and it would be good if she could find that because then it would be evidence. First, though, she needed to find out who the women in the photo were and talk to both of them, because Dan had forgotten to tell her which one she had to ask.

Molly stared hard at the photo. Neither of the women looked like Janice, but Janice was old, and – unless they were really fat or something – old people didn't really look like anyone except other old people.

She didn't want to ask Janice if she knew who the women were, in case she told Suzie. She didn't want to show the letter to Joe, either. She knew who he was and everything, and it wouldn't be difficult to show him, because his house was only about five minutes' walk away, but he was a bit funny in the head so he might not understand it. The letter said something about how Dan had persuaded Joe not to tell anyone about the picnic, but she bet Joe wouldn't even remember any picnic. Worse still, he might not even read the letter, but just throw it on the bonfire in his garden like he did with all the other stuff people gave him.

There was a special phone number you could ring to say if you'd seen Phoebe Piper. She'd seen it when Tom showed her the things about Phoebe on the computer, and had written it down when he wasn't looking, but she'd never phoned because of what had happened with Suzie, before, at the shopping centre and when they went to see the Christmas lights. The police would believe *her*, not Molly, and she'd be angry and Dan wasn't here anymore so they might have to go back to London again and live in the B & B with the mad woman who smelt of wee and the horrible people who shouted in the night.

Even if it meant she couldn't be Phoebe just yet, anything was better than *that*. She'd got to be careful. Slithering off the bed, she knelt on the rug and pushed the letter and photograph back into their hiding place.

ELEVEN

Like her old room, Dan's looked as if it had hardly been altered at all. Alone – Molly'd said she'd wait in her own room while Janice found the pen – it was a relief to feel only the single pain of losing him. In fact, she was almost glad of it because, unlike with Suzie and Molly, the pain wasn't on account of anything that she'd done wrong.

The first thing she did was to open the windows. That would allow Dan's soul to be released – Janice had read somewhere that this was important – as well as dispersing the lingering odour of dope and stale sweat, which, she reluctantly admitted to herself, was a whole lot stronger than any spiritual presence.

On the windowsill, surrounded by fly corpses, was a framed black and white photograph of her father with Dan, aged about six, holding his hand. She picked it up without knowing why and sat down on the cover that had been hastily pulled over the unmade single bed – by Suzie, she supposed, or the people who'd come for Dan. She felt solid with grief, as though her body had been filled with cement.

The room was depressing, and it looked – and certainly smelt – as though Dan had stopped caring about himself and his surroundings some time ago. The only piece of furniture that she didn't remember was a desk that looked like a 1970s office leftover, cluttered on top with papers and ancient-looking electronic equipment, more of which was jumbled along the skirting in a tangle of leads and plugs. A pair of jeans, the last he'd worn, perhaps, had been stepped out of and left – two collapsed denim legs and the lolling tongue of a leather belt. A guitar, propped in a corner, mute strings slackening out of tune, was surrounded by a phalanx of empty beer bottles, and mugs were clustered on the bedside table, blooms of mould floating like tiny water lilies on half-drunk tea.

There was a framed poster on the wall, its volcano of colours long faded by the sun. The words *Free Festival '69* were written across the top in a bubbly hippie typeface. Janice found herself reading the names of the bands: Armadillo, The Pobbles, Electric Village, Psychedelic Pandas . . . and, at the bottom, in larger letters, the band who'd really, *really* made it: Weather Ship Tango Delta. Dan must have been working as a roadie for one of them at the time – not the Weather Ship, she thought, that had been earlier on. Electric Village, perhaps, or The Pobbles.

Deliberately, Janice turned her head away. The last thing she needed was to start thinking about those days. Instead, she stared down at the photo in her lap. The two figures, with their carefully slicked-down hair and solemn expressions – Dan in his lumpy, hand-knitted jumper and Pa in a three-piece suit, pipe in mouth – looked impossibly remote. Pa especially. I was always afraid of him, Janice thought, and then, No, not afraid – in awe. He'd always given the impression that everything he said was carefully weighed, each decision considered and thoughtful. Thinking about this now, Janice decided that at least some of it had to do with his being a pipe smoker. That way he'd had of holding the pipe at a downward angle while it was in his mouth, which made him look as though he were exercising enormous restraint and tolerance by not saying something incredibly clever and utterly crushing . . .

He'd certainly done a lot of that when Janice had told him she was pregnant. He'd never said as much, but she'd felt that his disappointment in her was deep and irrevocable. She wondered, now, if this had also been true of his feelings about Dan. He, after all, had been *the boy,* and Pa couldn't have approved of the fact that he'd gone off to hang out with bands and become a roadie instead of going to university and getting a 'proper' job.

Really, she supposed, she'd never tried very hard to see it from her parents' point of view. They'd had a war – excitement, yes, but fear, loss and scars of mind as well as body – before settling down to bring up their children in the world they had saved for them, only to find that their son and daughter rejected what they had to offer, hightailing it to London at the first opportunity in search of something else.

'Have you found it?'

Janice looked up to see Molly standing in the doorway.

'Sorry, I got distracted.' She returned the photograph to its place. 'Maybe,' she said, getting up and bending over to look under the bed, 'it's under here somewhere.' Seeing only the dusty glint of more bottles – spirits this time, she thought – she gave a hasty downward tug on the cover. After a few minutes, during which Molly inched her way into the room, Janice managed to locate the pen underneath the wardrobe.

'Thanks.' Molly snatched it and dashed back to the safety of the landing. 'Shall we get your stuff now?'

The spare room – a single bed in the middle of a jumble of mismatched furniture, with curtains Janice remembered from childhood – was at the front of the house, with a window overlooking the drive.

'I like your car,' Molly said.

'Maybe we can go out somewhere.' Janice finished stuffing the duvet into the cover she'd found in the airing cupboard and edged past a stack of cardboard boxes to join Molly, who was staring down at the Fiat 500.

'Maybe.' Molly didn't sound at all sure.

A small group of what looked like teenagers were walking down the lane, towards the pub. 'I thought you said everyone here was old,' Janice said.

'Those people don't live here.' Molly sounded dismissive. 'They're *weirdos*.'

Surprised by her tone, Janice said, 'What makes you say that?'

Molly looked uncomfortable. 'I'm not supposed to talk about it.'

'About what?'

'Those people.'

The group were closer now, and Janice could see that they were quite a bit older than she'd first thought, with new-agey looking clothes. Neo-hippies. She'd met lots of them in Goa. 'Why not? They look all right to me.'

'They're not. They're a nuisance.' An obvious quote. It must be from Suzie, Janice thought. Dan wouldn't have said something like that. At least, she didn't think he would – they'd grown so apart over the years that she was no longer sure.

'Why?'

'They hang around and make a mess. We don't talk to them.'

'Who's "we"?'

'Nobody.'

'Well, if you're all so unfriendly, I don't understand why they hang around.'

Molly sighed, a parody of a put-upon adult. 'I suppose I'd better tell you if you're going to stay here. You mustn't tell anyone else, though.'

'I promise. Cross my heart and hope to die.'

'It's not funny; it's *important*. They come here because of Joe. Not just those ones, but loads. Whole coaches, even. They won't leave him alone, and we hate them.'

'Who's Joe?'

'He lives here. He was in that band that's on the poster on Dan's wall. Weather something.'

'Weather Ship Tango Delta?' Janice felt a flutter, like a small, trapped bird, inside her ribcage.

Molly nodded. 'It's silly. A weather ship isn't even a thing.'

'Yes, it is. They sort of park them in the sea to give information about the weather. Stuff like which way the wind's blowing.' Molly looked disbelieving and Janice added, defensively, 'Well, they used to. It's probably all done by satellites nowadays.'

'Anyway,' said Molly, 'I thought you'd know about them because you're old. Joe was really famous. When Dan told me, I didn't believe it because he's fat and his teeth are all horrible, but it was in the olden days. He's on YouTube – Tom showed me.'

'Are you talking about Joe Vincent?'

Molly nodded. 'He lives here – on the other side of the village, before the houses start properly. It's always got things on the fence – flowers and stuff.'

'I saw those on the way here. I thought there'd been an accident.'

'No, they're for him. The weirdos leave them.'

Janice felt breathless. 'Are you sure about this, Molly?'

'Well, *ye-es*.' A twangy, scornful whine.

'How long has he lived here?'

'I don't know. Ages. Dan went to see him sometimes. He helped him in the garden and stuff.' Molly made a face. 'You look all funny.'

'I feel all funny.' Janice sat down on the bed.

'You're all right, aren't you?' Molly looked uneasy. 'I mean, you're not going to . . . you know . . .' She's scared, thought Janice. Because of Dan. 'When Gamga died,' Molly continued, 'it was OK, because she was in the hospital and everything.'

Janice could see what she meant – Gamga had, so to speak, given notice. 'Don't worry. I'm fine. It was just a bit of a shock, that's all. I know – knew – Joe. We were . . . friends.'

'But you mustn't go there.' Molly's voice had risen an anxious semitone. 'He hates it when people knock on the door or try and talk to him. That's why we don't tell them where he lives, if they ask. The weirdos think they're his friends, but they're not.' Her eyes narrowed in sudden suspicion. 'You're not a weirdo, are you?'

Janice shook her head. 'Really, I'm not. I used to know him, that's all – same as Dan.'

'I suppose that's OK.' Molly's tone was grudging. 'But you still have to promise you won't go to his house.'

'OK.' Janice put her hand over her heart. 'I promise.'

'Really?'

'Yes,' said Janice, firmly. 'But if Dan was Joe's friend, Molly, someone needs to tell him. Otherwise, he might think Dan doesn't want to see him anymore.'

'*You* can't tell him.' Molly sounded panicky again. 'If you were really his friend, you'd have known he was here. Anyway, Joe doesn't have friends. Not properly. He doesn't want to.' Janice wondered if that were really true or if, like Molly, he was pretending. 'That's why,' Molly finished, 'you have to keep it secret.'

TWELVE

So that was what had happened to Joe. Gorgeous, talented, fucked-up Joe. She knew he'd gone crazy and left the band, but all she'd known about him after that was by elimination: he hadn't fitted either of the two rock-star templates available, neither dying young nor effecting a rags-to-riches comeback later on. He'd simply walked away without saying a word – but why on earth had he ended up here, of all places, and why hadn't Dan told her about it?

Molly'd said Joe had been here for ages, but time was different when you were ten, so 'ages' might mean anything over a month. Presumably he'd been here before she and Suzie had, though, or she'd have mentioned his arrival.

Molly'd said he was fat, too. Janice couldn't imagine that. For so long, it had been as though his face was tattooed on her eyelids, filling up the spaces between her thoughts. Of course, he wouldn't look the same as back when they'd had their scene, any more than she did. *Had their scene*. Janice grimaced. If you said that now, she thought, people would think it meant being in a play, but everyone had said it back then. Molly had called it 'the olden days', hadn't she? That was a sort of generic past, thought Janice, where Roman centurions coexisted with hansom cabs and people writing with feathers, and medieval princesses in tall pointy hats stood cheek-by-jowl with Hitler and the first men on the moon.

That had been 1969, hadn't it? Neil Armstrong and the rest of them, sometime in the summer. Janice remembered Joe talking about it one night after they'd made love, lying side by side on their backs, on grass as thick and glossy as the fur of a healthy animal, looking up at the stars, and Joe saying, 'I've run out of thought.' By that time, he'd already begun to drift, not turning up to gigs – sometimes not even being informed of them by the rest of the band – and Ray Greene standing in for him. Odd, thought Janice, that she couldn't remember anyone saying much about the gradual transfer of personnel, or about Joe's mental state, even though everyone in the know must surely have recognised that his days with the Weather Ship were numbered. But then, Joe was a rock star, and they were expected to take drugs and be crazy. Madness – provided it was suitably flamboyant – was part of the deal. Pointing it out would have been uncool.

That must have been one of the last conversations she'd had with Joe – although, thinking about it now, 'conversation' wasn't really the right word because, as far as she could remember, he'd done all the talking. She hadn't said much, partly because she hadn't really understood what he was on about and partly because she'd been happy and mellow and hadn't wanted to risk spoiling the mood. A few days later, he'd disappeared for the first time and she'd been frantic. Then, after three days, he'd returned, apparently unable to say where he'd been. She'd tried asking, but one of the others – not from the band, she thought, but someone else – had told her not to be so uptight. *Joe doesn't have problems. If you're bothered, that's your hang-up.* But it was after that the stories had started, from that last tour, of how he'd stand on stage, mute, his arms at his sides and the Fender Esquire, with its mirror discs, hanging untouched across his body.

By the time the rumours really got going and the rest of the group had decided he was out for good, she'd been back here with Ma and Pa, seven months pregnant with Suzie. Dan had come home for the odd couple of days before he went off on tour, and, being a roadie, he'd heard all sorts of things. Joe had taken so much acid he'd blown his mind, he was living with people who spiked him, he'd stopped talking entirely, he'd attacked a sound engineer at the studio, and he'd walked the length of Britain to get his head together. Dan had had no idea if any of the stories were true. He hadn't seemed interested in talking about it, and it would have been uncool to be too inquisitive – Joe was simply doing his thing. Besides, Janice hadn't believed it – or not much of it, anyway. She'd known people who'd taken acid every day, and they were OK. As for the reports of violence, the Joe she'd known was a gentle person and she couldn't imagine him attacking anybody.

She'd gone to live in Ibiza for a while after that, and she'd hear things from people who came out: *Joe's too much, man. L.S.D., Mandrax. Like his mind's burning up right in front of you. Totally freaked me out. That stare. The guy's just gone.* By the time she came back, it was the whole rock 'n' roll myth: fans repeating outrageous stories in hushed, reverential tones. People believed those things because they wanted to, maybe even needed to. Perhaps, Janice thought, the stories had been true, after all. Joe had not, so far as she knew, ever bothered to deny anything; he'd simply withdrawn, which had fuelled the rumours all the more, until he was more famous for being mad than for his music.

Knowing he was at the other end of the village was disconcerting. *I shouldn't feel anything after all this time,* Janice told herself. *Mild curiosity, nothing more. It shouldn't jolt me like this.*

She felt the unfairness of it keenly: the past ought to be dealt with one person, and one piece, at a time, not all in a rush.

This wasn't the time, though. Right now, she needed to concentrate on unpacking. She gazed around the room, wondering where to put her stuff. The wardrobe was crammed full of women's clothing. Spotting the heavy pelt of a fur coat, smelling of mothballs and hanging like a headless creature at the end of the row, she realised that the things must have belonged to Ma. The chest of drawers was full, too. Thermal underwear, the dull beige balls of rolled-up tights, crumbling eye shadow, a half-full bottle of 4711 . . . Dan seemed not to have thrown anything away, but transported it wholesale, armfuls of the past, across the landing.

Next to the chest of drawers was a carrier bag crammed with shoes. On the top was a pair of brown lace-ups that Janice recognised as the ones Ma had worn for gardening. On impulse, she picked one up and saw, in its shape, the ghost of Ma's foot – the slight bulge made by her enlarged toe joint, and the heels, worn down on the inside by the way she'd stood and moved. My shoes are like that, thought Janice. My feet have grown into the same shape as hers. Perhaps Suzie's are doing the same.

Sitting on the narrow bed with the shoe in her lap, Janice felt as though she were realising Ma's death for the first time, and realising, too, her own death that was to come. She wept again, fruitlessly, over mistakes made and time squandered, and was still crying several minutes later, when she heard a noise on the landing and looked up just in time to catch a blur of flying hair and a glimpse of green T-shirt before Molly thudded away down the stairs.

Listening to her go, Janice suddenly remembered that the family cat hadn't been called Freddy at all, but Charlie. Freddy was the cat in the Fabulous Furry Freak Brothers comics. No, the cat's owner: Fat Freddy. The cat was just 'Fat Freddy's cat'. It was disconcerting, being quite sure about something then finding out you were wrong.

THIRTEEN

Pointless, Janice told herself, to sit about getting emotional. She needed to do something useful – preferably something that would get her out of the house. It wasn't likely that Suzie would be up and about for a couple of hours yet, so she might as well go shopping. If she got bin liners and cleaning stuff, she could finish sorting out the kitchen. She wondered if Molly might like to come along for the ride, but the child seemed to have vanished. Anyway, it wasn't as if she was leaving her by herself.

Following directions to the supermarket from a woman in the village, Janice found herself slowing down as she drove past the house Molly'd said was Joe's. The tributes on the picket fence were still there – different coloured ribbons tied round the posts, cards and photographs bagged in polythene. Looking more closely, she could see C.D.s in bags, too, and something that looked as if it might be a scroll of parchment. Slightly further down was a lifebelt – stolen, Janice supposed, from some seafront – propped against the palings, a red ribbon dangling forlornly from its safety rope.

The house – a Victorian cottage, by the look of it, with pointy gables, standing by itself between two fields of wheat stubble – was hidden almost to the roof by foliage, but she spotted, between the cankered limbs of apple trees, a solitary upper window, its frame a dull, peeling blue.

For a second, she was tempted, but then, remembering her promise to Molly, she changed gear and drove past. It wasn't the only reason, of course, but she pushed the other one – safeguarding her memories from the catastrophe of his not having a clue who she was – quickly away. Then, he'd had the world at his feet, whereas she was . . . Well, looked at from this distance, she'd been just a girlfriend, really – a *groupie*, even – but, in her mind, it had been more, much more, than just wanting a piece of him because of his talent, his fame. They'd had a connection, something real, something that formed part of who she *was*. If Joe were to be indifferent, then, whatever the cause, she didn't think she could bear it, especially at the moment.

At the supermarket, she completed a major shop, loading the trolley with all the staples, trying to second-guess tastes and flavours, wanting to please. She added a bar of chocolate and a bag of Haribo for Molly – unashamed bribery – and a case of wine, some vodka and a bottle of tonic for Suzie. Hair of the dog or icebreaker: either way, she hoped it would show that she was being understanding and not judgemental.

She wondered about buying cigarettes for Suzie or whether that was going too far. In the end, she decided to get the cigarettes and pick up a box of nicotine patches at the pharmacy on the way out, for some appropriate, and less fraught, future occasion.

There were rows of magazines next to the cigarette kiosk and, waiting her turn, Janice was wondering whether children of Molly's age still read comics, and, if so, whether Molly might like one, when she spotted her granddaughter's photograph on the front page of the *Eastern Daily Press*. It was identical to the one she'd seen in Molly's bedroom, with the brushed hair and the navy blue sweater – except that the headline beside it read, *NEW HOPE FOR PHOEBE*.

With a murmured excuse, Janice stepped out of line momentarily to pick up a copy. *That* was the reason Molly's face was so familiar: she was the dead spit of Phoebe Piper, missing since Easter 2007, her case so well publicised that she no longer needed a surname. Or rather, Janice corrected herself, Molly was the dead spit of the computer-generated, age-progressed image of Phoebe. No one actually knew what Phoebe now looked like – assuming that she was still alive – because she'd not been seen since she was abducted, aged three, while on holiday with her parents in Suffolk.

Janice could see quite clearly, in her mind's eye, the last real photograph of Phoebe, taken a matter of hours before she'd disappeared: the big round eyes, the mop of blonde hair, the fluffy pink sweater, the delighted smile. She was childhood innocence personified and in 2007, and for several years afterwards, her image had been everywhere you looked. Her parents' faces were familiar, too: a smooth-skinned, expensively groomed professional couple, photogenic and articulate, the mother frequently snapped carrying Phoebe's favourite soft toy like a talisman. Quickly, via well-publicised meetings with government ministers, senior churchmen, famous sports personalities and Richard Branson, and with appearances on television shows – ultimately *Oprah* – they had joined the extended celebrity family. There was merchandising – posters, wristbands and T-shirts – available from the official Find Phoebe website, a charity had been set up and rewards for the little girl's discovery had been offered by newspapers and wealthy, high-profile individuals.

Of course, Molly hadn't actually told Janice that it was her photograph, had she? But then, why have it pinned up in her room? Unless – and the thought struck Janice as unbearably sad – Molly, having no photos of herself, had appropriated an image that looked like her in an attempt to demonstrate that someone cared enough about her to take her picture.

It's my fault, thought Janice. I failed to cherish Suzie, and Suzie, in her turn, has failed to cherish Molly.

'You all right there?'

Janice realised she'd reached the head of the queue and that the girl on the till – huge false eyelashes and hair scraped back into a high ponytail – was staring at her. 'Yes, sorry. Twenty Marlboro Light, please, and this.' She put the paper down on the counter.

The girl glanced down. 'Them travellers – that's where they ought to look.' Janice made a non-committal noise and concentrated hard on getting the right change. 'Don't know why they call them that – never go anywhere, do they? And the way they treat their dogs . . .'

Travellers, thought Janice, hoisting bags-for-life out of the trolley and into the car. Caravans on bricks, mounds of rubbish, children with impetigo in dirty clothes. People on the margins.

She got into the car and, leaving the door open, propped the *Eastern Daily Press* against the steering wheel and skimmed the article. Despite the headline, it wasn't really 'new hope', or even news at all, just some stuff about a chap the police had interviewed who'd recently died. The piece said that he'd lived on the 'notorious Brenner Farm site' for several years. Travellers had been evicted from the site after a long battle, Janice remembered. She'd read about it on the internet a couple of years ago, while she was travelling in Nepal. That must have been what the girl on the till was talking about. The story's become self-perpetuating, she thought. Phoebe's face sells papers.

The Pipers had been staying in a National Trust cottage on the edge of a nature reserve when Phoebe was abducted from its car park. Janice had a clear memory: rain on the camera lens as it panned across dozens, even hundreds, of garage-forecourt bou-quets with semi-literate notes attached, and soft toys that formed a memorial blanket of bedraggled nylon pelts on the asphalt.

Thinking about it now, it occurred to Janice that most of the people who'd left things at the impromptu shrine and wound yellow ribbon round the nearby trees must have made quite a journey, since the nature reserve was over half an hour's drive from the nearest town. Within twenty-four hours, though, the place had been heaving, with every room-for-hire in the vicinity snapped up by journalists, camera crews, private detectives acting on spec, clairvoyants and psycho-geographers. Anyone who had ever had anything to do with the Piper family had been inter-viewed by the police and, subsequently, the media. There had been fingertip searches, forensic investigation, sniffer dogs. Lakes, rivers and reed beds had been dragged. Appeals had been made to the public, and there was a televised reconstruction of Phoebe's last known movements. Janice recalled it from a dozen viewings – the giggling, gap-toothed moppet, stomping through shallow car-park puddles in her fun-coloured Boden mac and matching wellies, while her parents were unloading picnic things from their hatchback, their outing curtailed because of the rain.

Janice imagined the sequence of events as precautionary anxiety about Phoebe running in front of a car turned to real, stomach-chilling fear. The shouts getting louder, the car standing unheeded, its boot wide open, and the controlled run becoming flat out as Melissa and David Piper searched the car park from end to end . . .

When days became weeks and Phoebe was still missing, the

tabloids had taken against Melissa, claiming that, since she had not shed public tears, she must not care about her daughter, and must, therefore, have had a hand in her disappearance. The broadsheets had carried opinion pieces written in Melissa's defence, stating that self-control implied neither lack of feeling nor guilt, and bemoaning the fact that stoicism in the face of calamity was nowadays viewed as suspicious rather than praiseworthy.

Weeks became months. The tabloids forgot that they'd ever suspected Melissa and she'd reverted to her default position of 'tragic mum'. Months became years, and the interest continued, but, despite an occasional flurry of media excitement, Phoebe remained as ineluctably missing as if a wicked fairy, cackling and waving a wand, had caused her to vanish into thin air.

FOURTEEN

Janice slammed the car door and poked the key into the ignition, wanting to remove herself, physically, from the thought, but it wasn't so easy. Driving along the lanes back to Repshall, it kept nagging at her. Suzie could be anyone. Janice had only her word for it that she was her daughter, or that Molly was her granddaughter – or, for that matter, that Dan was dead. The latter, of course, could be easily verified by a call to the G.P. As for the rest, though . . . Birth certificate? Corroboration from the adoptive parents, assuming they were still alive?

This was absurd. People didn't go about claiming to be related to complete strangers, and in any case, if Suzie wasn't genuine, how could she have got hold of the address on the adoption agency's form? And, given the existence of D.N.A. testing, why would anyone bother to assert something that could be so easily disproved? Besides, Suzie looked like her, didn't she?

Did she?

Not *un*like, anyway. And surely it was over-elaborate for a con trick? After all, Suzie – assuming that actually was her name – could simply have wormed her way into Dan's life and tried to get him to marry her, or change his will. Which he might, of course, already have done without Janice's knowledge – but in that case, she'd have the house, which she could sell, if she liked, so why bother to pretend to be Janice's daughter? That would only make sense if she was after Janice's money as well; if so, she was playing a long game – and she certainly couldn't have known that Dan was going to die so suddenly. Unless, of course . . .

No. Now she really *was* being ridiculous. There was no 'unless' or 'of course' about it. If Molly and Phoebe were one and the same – which was what had started off this idiotic train of speculation in the first place – then nobody in their right mind would choose to bring her back to a spot so close to where she was taken, even after seven years.

Janice had made a silly assumption, and she'd been wrong. Simple as that. Nevertheless, with no actual proof that Suzie was her daughter . . .

This was insane. The reason Dan hadn't told her about Suzie was because Suzie had asked him not to, and the reason for that – and for her not telling Molly – was that she wanted to take things slowly, which was quite natural and entirely sensible. She'd met Dan, and she wanted a bit of time before she met Janice. *That's just how it worked out. I wanted to get used to another family, you know?* But I don't, thought Janice. I don't know anything.

She stopped the car in the rutted entry to a field, opened the window, and, closing her eyes, began practising her yoga breathing. After several minutes, she had begun to feel calmer, even serene, when she heard a cawing, raucous and horrible, and, opening her eyes, saw crows gathering in the rows of yellow stubble, stabbing the ground with sudden, vicious movements.

Instinctively, Janice pressed the button to close the window. There was something primeval about them – the jabbing beaks, the beady little eyes, the claws. Not a flock, she thought, watching them hop and peck. A different word, something sinister. A murder

– that was it. A murder of crows. But, Janice told herself, it's only a word, and they are only birds. They don't *mean* anything. She started the car and drove away, but the feeling of unease lingered and she could not shake it off.

FIFTEEN

Telling herself that this was a good opportunity to get reacquainted with the area, Janice drove around for a while, turning left and right at random, getting lost deliberately. After about twenty minutes, she remembered that, distracted by the newspaper, she'd forgotten to buy the nicotine patches at the supermarket or fill up the car.

Not wanting to retrace her steps, she drove on towards Cromer and found a petrol station with a small supermarket attached. They didn't sell nicotine patches, but she spotted a Weather Ship Tango Delta C.D. – virtually the only name she recognised amongst the rows of music – and bought it on impulse. Examining it in the car, she saw that it was a reissue of their first ever L.P. – *Song of Sixpence* – with extra tracks. These days, Janice really only listened to classical music; she hadn't heard any of the Weather Ship's stuff for years. Turning the box over, she read:

Joe Vincent – Vocals, guitar
Roger Maynard – Vocals, keyboards
Keith Petrie – Vocals, guitar (bass)
John Blackmore – Drums, percussion

Presumably, she thought, the others – and Ray Greene, who had replaced Joe about six months after the L.P. had come out – must now live in ageing-rock-star splendour in places like L.A.

Janice listened as she drove, immediately recognising 'Ribbons in the Wind': '*All the colours are running away / Streamers on the wind, one step ahead of me / See, round the corner, behind the tree / You're here, you're not here . . .*' She was pleasantly surprised at how many of the words she remembered, not just to that song, but to lots of them. There was 'You'll Never Learn', which had been their second single; 'Take A Joke', with its creepy chanted chorus of '*Doesn't matter, doesn't matter*', and 'Come Out to Play' with the '*All fall down*' stuff at the end like the nursery rhyme, and the children's laughter. Then 'Alchymy', which Janice remembered them playing at the UFO Club, dappled in the colours of the light-show as the music swirled and throbbed. It occurred to her that this was probably the first time she'd heard it when she wasn't stoned or tripping. People used to say it was the sound of consciousness expanding. *She* might have – no, she *had* – said it. The thought made her take a mental step back, embarrassed by her former self.

'Takkeney Green' was coming to an end as she drove back down the gentle incline to Repshall. '*I know it was real / Even if some things aren't real / I've seen the pictures in my head . . .*' As the car rounded the bend, the roof of Joe's house came into view between the leafy upper branches of the trees, the tiles patched green with lichen. After a few seconds, Janice caught a glimpse of a battered lean-to with moss-streaked glass panels and a figure on the path dismounting from a bicycle.

It was a man. Janice had an impression of bulk and a mop of silver hair before the hedge hid him from view. Passing the front gate, she slowed without meaning to, and the man, now pulling a plastic bag from the bike's wicker basket, turned and looked, blank and uncomprehending, towards her.

Right then, as if the moment had been engineered by some malevolent spirit, she heard the opening chords of 'Not Me Anymore', and Joe's voice, singing, '*Let me borrow your eyes . . .*'

Was that him? The scruffy T-shirt and baggy shorts, the thick waist, the stiff, lumbering motion?

'*Let me borrow your eyes . . .*' Janice stamped on the accelerator harder than she meant to, and the car shot down the road. It was too much. To hear Joe now, singing the phrase he'd used so many times when he'd wanted her kohl pencil to encircle his beautiful eyes, when he'd grinned at her in the mirror with that impish, knowing charm – the boy couldn't help it – so slim, so sexy, in his hippie finery with his wild black hair . . .

He'd shown no sign of recognising her, but why would he? It was over forty years ago. She was an entirely different person. It was absurd to expect him to have remained the same. Besides, he didn't look so bad. Molly's description of 'fat' was unfair. 'Solid' would be more accurate.

'*I don't know / Who it is anymore / And you don't know why . . .*' The lost look she thought she'd seen in his eyes was probably just absent-mindedness, not medication or madness. He was just getting on with his day, and she was being ridiculously overdramatic. '*Say anything and I'll believe it / I want to believe it . . .*' What on earth had he been singing about, anyway? Janice had always been so busy enjoying the sensation the music produced in her that she'd never taken much notice of the lyrics. What had he meant?

Not much, probably. People were always finding stoned significance in things. That was what it had been about in those days – fucking with your head in order to see the world differently. And, said a spiteful little voice in the back of her mind, Joe had probably said 'Let me borrow your eyes' to dozens, perhaps even hundreds, of other women besides her. After all, there'd been beautiful girls everywhere, just waiting for their chance.

Pulling up in front of the Old Rectory, Janice remained in the car to listen to the last couple of songs. Not recognising the music, she picked up the cover of the C.D. and saw that they were the bonus tracks. Both were dated 1971, two years later than the original album, and were credited to and sung by Joe. He sounded off-key, as though he'd somehow lost control of his voice. The lyrics weren't always easy to hear, either. Janice thought that the first song, 'Offshore', was about a man who was floating in the sea and possibly drowning but didn't mind very much. The second, 'Look at Yourself', initially sounded like someone saying cute things to a girlfriend, and then seemed to turn into something weird about flies and not being able to recognise his own face.

Janice remembered one of the very last times she'd seen Joe: he'd been standing in front of the bathroom mirror, covering his entire face with shaving foam. When she'd asked him why, he'd said, 'So I don't have to look at myself.'

The song ended abruptly, with a thud, as if Joe had fallen over. Janice wondered why they'd bothered to include the later offerings, because they weren't a patch on the others.

Look At Yourself. Janice adjusted the Fiat's rear-view mirror and stared at as much as she could see of her own face. It was recognisable, but still – as was always the case these days – the crêpey eyelids and the lines that radiated outwards gave her a mild sense of shock.

How long would it be before a complete stranger stared back at her from the mirror? Unlike her parents, whose youth had been swallowed up by the war, Janice's generation had been young with a capital Y, and were never going to grow old. Our trouble, she thought, was that we could never imagine not being young.

SIXTEEN

Janice had just finished putting the shopping away when Suzie appeared. Still pale, but with her hair brushed, she was dressed in jeans and a T-shirt.

'Sorry about before.' Sounding more weary than apologetic, Suzie pulled a chair out and sat down, elbows on the table, head between her hands. Her hair, Janice saw, hung down with a slight natural wave, like her own, and her fingers were long and elegant. It's *now*, Janice thought. It's *you*. You're my daughter, in this room, just a few feet away from me. Surely she ought to feel more?

Suzie raised her head fractionally. 'What are those?'

'I bought them for Molly.' Janice picked up the chocolate and the bag of Haribo. 'I can put them away if you don't want her to have them.'

'No, it's fine. You've met her, then?'

'Yes, we had a chat. I'm not sure she believes me, though.'

'How do you mean?'

'About being her grandmother.'

Suzie lowered her arms and looked at Janice for the first time. She had, Janice saw, made some effort with make-up, but her eyelids were red and swollen by tears. 'I suppose that's my fault,' she said defensively. 'I probably should have told her, but . . .' She shook her head, then lowered it again and started massaging her temples.

But what? thought Janice. Suzie had had plenty of time, hadn't she? Say nothing, she told herself. Let her come to you. 'I got these for you,' she said, sliding the cigarette packet across the table. 'And some more wine and things.'

'Thanks.' Suzie's voice was flat.

'Would you like a cup of tea?'

'Please.'

As she turned away to fill the kettle, it occurred to Janice that perhaps the reason Suzie had put off meeting her for so long was to avoid disappointment. She imagined Suzie taking out her imaginary birth mother, as it were, and looking at her, delaying the decision to meet an actual person as a way of keeping her options open.

'It's strange being back here, after so long.' Janice assembled mugs and milk on the table and leant against the sink, waiting for the kettle to boil. 'Especially like this.'

'I suppose it must be. Look, sorry about the mess, OK?' Suzie's tone was more truculent than apologetic.

'That's all right. I know what it's like, keeping on top of things.'

'Yeah? I should have thought you could afford to pay someone to do that.'

Dan must have explained my circumstances, thought Janice. It had never occurred to her that her brother might have resented her money. She'd offered, from time to time, to help with the upkeep of the house, but he'd always refused. 'I'll get you an ashtray.'

'Thanks.'

The kettle rumbled to the boil and Janice turned off the gas and filled the mugs. 'Sugar?'

'Just milk.' Suzie was fiddling with the foil from the cigarette packet. She's nice looking, Janice thought. High cheekbones and large eyes, brown, like her own. She could be beautiful if she took more care of herself.

The doubts she'd had when she'd read the newspaper in the car flitted through her mind. The books she'd read about adoption said that most people didn't experience an instant bond, but shouldn't she be feeling more of a connection? At the moment, her mental and emotional engines seemed to have stalled, flooded by the enormity of the situation.

'There you are.' She sat down opposite Suzie.

'Thanks.' Suzie stared down into the mug and Janice saw, with a small shock, that she was crossing and recrossing the first two fingers of her right hand, with the thin strip of folded foil from the cigarette packet between them.

'I used to do that when I smoked.'

'What?'

'Fiddle with the bit of foil between my fingers.'

'Did you?'

'Yes. Exactly like you're doing now.'

Suzie, evidently unaware of what she'd been doing, shook the strip of foil free and pushed it away from her. Watching her, Janice felt a pinprick of hurt.

'It's rather a lot to take in,' she said. 'Your call, coming out of the blue like that . . .'

Suzie nodded, but said nothing.

'I mean, I don't even know what your name is. Your full name, I mean.'

'Suzanne Armitage.' Suzie's tone was deadpan, as if identifying herself to authority.

'Is that who adopted you? Mr and Mrs Armitage?'

Suzie shook her head. 'My married name. Before that, it was Peel.'

'I called you Suzanne,' said Janice. 'I'd always assumed they'd give you a different name.'

'They did. I was christened Sandra.' Suzie made a face. 'Sandra Joanne. I changed it.'

'When was that?'

'When I was eighteen, I applied for my original birth certificate. I didn't know before – the name, I mean. I've always known I was adopted – for as long as I can remember, anyway.' Suzie reached for the foil strip from the cigarette packet and fiddled with it for a moment before realising what she was doing and pushing it away. 'If I'm honest,' she said, 'it was more because I didn't want to be someone called Sandra Joanne than anything else, although there was a bit of me thinking, well, obviously that's what I'm meant to be called. Suzanne, I mean, not Sandra. And when I was twenty, I married Andy, so then I got rid of the "Peel" bit as well.'

Janice thought of what Molly had said about having the wrong life, and of her daughter's old name discarded, like a husk, while she became another person. It would live on only in fading ink on old school registers and the backs of photographs, and as a semantic attachment to a bundle of impressions and emotions in the memories of relatives and childhood friends.

If Suzie had had the right life, with Janice, then those memories would be hers: the first tooth, the sports days, the tears over homework, the first period, rows over staying out late . . . All of it.

Seeing Suzie staring at her with a matter-of-fact expression and feeling, once again, the treacherous prickling of tears, Janice told herself to keep to the safer ground of practicalities. Everything else could come later, when they'd got more used to each other – there was no need to rush. Nodding in a way that she hoped signified that she'd taken this on board and was about to change the subject,

Janice said, 'Did the G.P. tell you when we'd get the results of the post-mortem?'

'He didn't know.' Suzie seemed unfazed by the question. 'I should think it takes a few days.'

'I know you said Dan was OK – not ill, I mean – but what about mentally? Did he seem depressed or worried or anything like that?'

'No, just normal.'

'And he was still fit, was he?'

'Yeah. Out working, a lot of the time.'

Janice remembered what Molly'd said about her brother, Tom, helping Dan to do odd jobs for people. He had once mentioned something to her about mowing people's lawns but, as with most things in his life, he hadn't been forthcoming and attempts at questioning had just made him clam up even more. 'That was the gardening, was it? Molly said that Tom was giving him a hand.'

'Yeah, he was.'

'Do you think he'll be back soon? I'm looking forward to meeting him.'

'Not sure. He's probably out with his mates or something.'

'Does he know?'

'About you? Yes. He's fine about it.'

At least someone is, thought Janice. 'Molly told me he'd been at college in London.'

'Yeah. Didn't do him much good, though.' Suzie rubbed the area under her left eye with her knuckle, leaving a smudge of mascara. 'He's from my marriage. Actually, he was the reason for it.' This was delivered in a no-nonsense tone that didn't invite comment. 'Lasted eleven years.' Before Janice could say anything, Suzie returned to the gardening theme. 'The two of them were working for a guy who does landscaping. Digging ponds and stuff. People buying second homes, want their gardens done up. Either that or retired people who've moved out of London. There's hardly anybody under fifty here, except at weekends.'

This, Janice realised, was the most she'd heard Suzie say about anything. 'I didn't realise it was that bad. Molly said everyone was old, but I thought she just meant there weren't any other children.'

'There aren't, not round here.' Suzie lit a cigarette. 'It's been rough on her, but we were in a B & B and Tom was couchsurfing, so when Dan offered, I thought, why not?'

'When was that? I mean, after you'd written the letter to me and he opened it, what happened then?'

'Like I said, he phoned me. We had a chat, and he came to see us.'

'Where were you living?'

'In London. He came a couple of times, and then he said, why didn't we come and live here?'

'I don't understand why he didn't tell me,' said Janice. 'I mean, I know you said you'd asked him not to, but *before* that. When he realised the letter you'd written was meant for me, not him.'

Suzie nodded. 'I was a bit surprised about that, but when I asked him he said you'd gone away and he couldn't get hold of you.'

'When was this?'

Suzie thought for a moment. 'End of January, beginning of February, something like that.'

She'd been in the Andaman Islands. Admittedly, it had been difficult getting a signal on her phone, but it wasn't impossible.

'Maybe he didn't want to do it over the phone,' said Suzie.

'Maybe.'

'Anyway, he's been really good to us, letting us stay here.'

'Yes,' said Janice. Even if he hadn't been able to get through on her mobile, he could have left a message on her landline in Suffolk for when she got back, but he hadn't. Had he tried, but put the phone down, not knowing what to say? He could have just told me to ring him, she thought. He didn't have to say why.

'Do you want to see him?'

'See him?' Janice echoed, confused.

'You know. To say goodbye. I'm sure they'd let you if you asked.'

Janice pictured the slovenly museum of failure that was Dan's room and thought of the distance that had grown between them. It wasn't just because she'd travelled; he'd retreated – the endless excuses, postponing her visits – and, on their rare phone calls, there'd been silences after the pleasantries had been exchanged, neither one knowing what to say. He'd holed himself up here when he was in his late forties, ostensibly to look after Ma and Pa, and she had been grateful to him for taking the onus off her, but now she found herself wondering how much looking after her parents had actually required, except at the end. 'I don't think so,' she said. 'I'd rather remember him as he was. What were you doing before you came here?'

'I used to manage a pub and we had a little flat upstairs. That was in Leytonstone. But when the pub closed, we lost our home as well as my job – that's how come we ended up in the B & B. We were on a list for rehousing, but it takes ages and anyway, they want to clear all the poor people out of London, don't they?'

'Weren't you able to get another job?'

'Yeah, but there was still no way I could afford to pay a private landlord.' This was said with something like a challenge, and Janice toyed with her mug, not meeting Suzie's eye. 'I could barely make ends meet as it was.'

'I'm sorry. Couldn't your parents—' Too late, Janice remembered what Molly had said about her grandmother dying. 'I mean, the family home . . .'

'What family home? Mum's dead and Dad's got dementia. My

brother got power of attorney and he sold the house to pay for the care home. I used to visit when we were in Leytonstone – not that Dad knew who the hell I was – but when we came here I couldn't afford the fare, and anyway, what's the point?'

'I can see it's a difficult situation,' said Janice carefully. 'I didn't know you had a brother.'

'No reason why you should.'

'Is he older than you?'

'Younger. They adopted because they thought they couldn't have any, then a couple of years later, he came along.'

Recognising warning signs and desperate to avoid confrontation, Janice said, 'Do you have any other siblings?'

'Just him.'

Stop asking questions, Janice told herself. Find something – anything – neutral. 'I understand Joe Vincent lives down the road.'

'Molly tell you that, did she?'

Shit, thought Janice, remembering what Molly had said about it being a secret. She shook her head. 'I think it must have been Dan.' Suzie looked disbelieving, so Janice thought she'd better embellish a bit. She didn't really think that Molly would get into trouble, but she certainly didn't want to give her granddaughter any reason not to trust her. 'He told me he'd been helping him out a bit – that's how I knew about his gardening work.'

Suzie seemed to accept this. 'He never charged Joe, though. I think it was because he felt sorry for him, really.'

'Have you told him about Dan?'

'Not yet. I was going to go tomorrow, when I'm a bit more together. I know they go back a long way.'

'He was a roadie for the Weather Ship in the very early days.' Had Dan told Suzie about her and Joe? Janice thought he probably hadn't. Even if you were a hundred times more garrulous and indiscreet than Dan, it wasn't exactly tactful to discuss the sexual history of someone's mother with them, especially given the circumstances.

Suzie nodded. 'He told me. To be honest, I'd never even heard of Joe Vincent. I mean, I know the stuff they did later, after he'd gone – the hits, anyway – but I've never been a huge fan. Loads of people are, though. They come from miles away. In the time I've been here, we've had Germans, Swedes . . . a whole coach full of Japanese, once. They come up here looking for him and drive everyone mad. Nobody's going to tell them where he lives, but it's not hard to spot because of all the crap people leave outside his house. Every so often, Joe collects it all up and burns it in the back garden.'

'He'd have a job with the lifebelt,' said Janice, remembering the one propped against the fence.

'You saw that, did you? God knows what that was about. There's quite often mirrors and bicycle wheels – Dan says it's all stuff he sang about – but I hadn't seen one of those before.'

'I think,' said Janice, remembering the C.D., 'that it might be something to do with a song called 'Offshore', about someone who's drowning. At least,' she added, 'I think that's what it's about.'

'That's probably it. They want to save him or something. You wouldn't believe some of the people who come here – trying to climb into his garden and take photos through the windows. If he goes to the village shop, it's ten to one there'll be some idiot trying to take a photo or get his autograph.'

'I suppose that's par for the course if you're famous.'

'Yes, but he doesn't want to be famous. He still gets the money from the songs he wrote – Dan told me – but he doesn't do that stuff anymore and these people just don't get it. Dan said he doesn't even understand why they're there, and he's afraid of them.'

'Just because you're paranoid,' said Janice, lightly, 'it doesn't mean they're not out to get you.'

'It isn't funny,' snapped Suzie. 'I bet if any of those people had a brother or a father who was mentally ill and people kept on hounding him and spying on him, they'd be disgusted. But they're fascinated by the idea of Joe being famous, and what happened to him, so they have to come and be near him – as if they're going to, I don't know, absorb the myth, or something. There's a couple of old trampy types who hang about – leftovers from the sixties – like those Japanese soldiers you hear about, who've been in the jungle for years and don't know the war's finished. One bloke's there practically every day. We think he must live near here, because he won't leave Joe alone. Dan had a word with him a couple of times, but it didn't make any difference. He wants to be near Joe, so he thinks that makes it OK. They all do – they think Joe belongs to them.'

Like I did, once, thought Janice. Pushing away the image of herself as one of a clamouring crowd, she said, 'Is that what the trouble is, mental illness?'

'I suppose it must be – or it was in the past, anyway. Now, I think it's more that he finds it hard to cope with things, but I should think anyone would find it hard to cope if they had a bunch of weirdos hanging round outside their house all the time. Dan said he doesn't even remember that much from the past, except when he gets these weird sort of flashbacks from all the stuff he took back in the sixties.'

'Acid flashbacks?' Janice had read about these, but she'd never really believed they existed. She'd taken her share of trips – more than her share – and she'd never had one.

'I suppose. But it's not like he's a total recluse – he goes to the shop and the pub and for bike rides and stuff, if there's nobody about. He just doesn't talk much. Why are you so interested in Joe, anyway? I'd have thought you'd be more interested in your own family.'

'Of course I'm interested!' Janice was appalled. 'It's only that I've waited so long for this – to meet you, I mean – and now it's happened . . . I mean, I'm sorry for the *way* it's happened, but I'm delighted it has and I don't want to mess it up, but you seemed so . . . I don't know, I just felt that anything I said was going to be wrong, so I thought it would be easier to talk about something that was at one remove, I suppose. Give you some space.'

'*Space*.' Suzie ground out her cigarette and levered herself away from the table. 'Yeah, man.' She stood up, apparently to leave.

Now what had she done wrong? Janice stood up in her turn. 'Look, I'm sorry. I don't understand what's going on here – I mean, I do, but it's a lot of emotions all at once for everybody, and I don't want us to get off on the wrong foot. I'd like us to be friends, Suzie. I'd love it. It's just that this is a weird situation, that's all.'

'No shit, Sherlock.' Suzie stared at her for a moment. 'I don't know about you, but I could do with a drink.'

SEVENTEEN

Janice wondered, when they were both seated again with glasses of red wine in front of them, if she ought to propose a toast, but she wasn't sure how to frame it. 'A new start', so soon after Dan's death, seemed callous, and 'a new family' was not only presumptuous but also showed disregard for Suzie's adoptive father. 'Here's to us' seemed unpleasantly self-congratulatory, and she was racking her brain for something that was suitably diffident when Suzie said, abruptly, 'Cheers,' and then, bashing her glass against Janice's, drained half its contents. 'That's better.'

Now, Janice told herself sternly, was not the time to start worrying about how much Suzie drank. For all she knew, it might just be a reaction to Dan's death and her arrival – after all, if the bottles she'd seen under her brother's bed were anything to go by, he'd probably been responsible for the majority of the empties she'd cleared out of the kitchen.

'I don't know Joe that well,' said Suzie conversationally, as if the previous fraught exchange hadn't taken place. 'I'm not sure there's anyone who does. Even Dan. He said that half the time he had no idea what Joe was thinking.'

Thankful that the conversation had been steered back to the safe ground of what must be – at least from Suzie's point of view – a neutral topic, Janice said, 'How long has he been here? Do you know?'

'Not sure. Fifteen or twenty years, I think. Dan told me it was after his mum died. He'd lived with her, and before that he'd been in Crowhurst for a couple of years, I do know that . . . You know what I mean by Crowhurst?'

Janice nodded. 'I came past it on the way here. Being turned into luxury homes, now.'

'It *was*, but not anymore. Dan told me the N.H.S. sold off most of the land when the place closed down in the early nineties, and the big house was derelict until a developer bought it to turn into flats. It was an Irish company and when they went bust that was that – no one else wanted to know.'

'Odd that he wanted to come back here,' said Janice, 'unless it makes him feel safe or something, being near Crowhurst . . . Although, I suppose he does come from somewhere round here, doesn't he? So—'

'Do you know him, then?' Suzie's eyes were shrewd.

'I did. Back in the old days.'

'Before I was born, you mean.'

'When I lived in London. It was different then, with bands. People – fans – had more access to musicians. There wasn't a whole industry of management and P.R. people and security making it impossible.'

'Was that when Dan was there?'

'Yes. He'd been there for about a year by the time I arrived. That was 1967. I was sixteen, I wasn't doing well at school and I was really fed up, and every so often Dan would write to me telling me how great it was in London, so one day I just thought, why not?'

'You ran away?'

'Yeah. It was in the summer. I left a note telling Ma and Pa I was going to stay with Dan. He was pretty freaked out when he found me on the doorstep. Wanted to send me straight back,

THE WRONG GIRL | 87

but I wouldn't go, and in the end his girlfriend told him to stop hassling me.'

'Didn't your parents come and get you?'

'They tried – there was a lot of stuff about my not being old enough to make my own decisions, but I pointed out that if they forced me to go back to Norfolk with them, I'd only run away again. Dan's girlfriend had done a really good job convincing him by the time they arrived, so he took my side, and in the end they gave up. Dan introduced me to all his friends – you know, guys in bands and people like that – and I went to the Speakeasy Club and the UFO Club and all the places that were cool at the time, and—'

'What's the You-Foe Club?'

'Oh, sorry – U.F.O. Club. That was how people said it. It was the place to be, if you liked the psychedelic stuff.'

'I thought it was all psychedelic back then.'

'God, no. There were some groups who were really into it all, and a lot of others who looked the part but were only doing it because they thought it was their best chance of success. Dan was a roadie by then, and he seemed to know everyone, and some-body in the Weather Ship – not Joe, I don't think – asked me if I wanted to go on to some party or other with them, and everyone got stoned, and . . . Well, I liked the scene, so I hung around, and Joe was there, and . . .' Janice faltered, feeling uncomfortable. It had occurred to her recently, reading the articles about the whole Jimmy Savile business, that back in those days she'd been a useful asset to Dan. Not that he was pimping her or anything like that, and she hadn't done anything she didn't want to do – or not much, anyway – but that had been the unspoken and, certainly on her part, unconscious trade-off. After all, she'd owed Dan for sticking up for her with Ma and Pa, hadn't she? Anyway, she'd liked being in that scene, and, after all, no one was harming anyone, so . . . A warning instinct told her that these thoughts were just the consciously 'thinkable' part of a very large and dangerous mental iceberg and if she didn't want her narrative of her own past to be holed below the waterline, she'd better move on quick. It was just the time, she told herself. What people did, that's all.

It occurred to her then that Dan must have done it, too – or at least been on the receiving end. Some of the groups he'd worked for were getting pretty important, and there were always plenty of girls who'd blow a roadie to get to the band.

'What?' Suzie was staring at her. 'You look like you've seen a ghost.'

'Not literally.' Janice took a sip of wine. Suzie's glass, she noticed, was almost empty. 'I was just remembering, that's all.'

'You slept with him. Because he was in the band.'

Surprised by her directness, Janice said, 'Yes,' and hastily followed it with, 'but it was more than that. We had a relationship.'

'Were you in love with him?'

'Yes, I was.'

'Was he in love with you?'

'I don't know,' said Janice, taken aback. 'That's not really a question you can answer on behalf of somebody else.'

'Wouldn't he have told you if he had been?'

'Not necessarily.'

'Didn't you ask him?'

Janice blinked. 'I don't suppose it ever occurred to me to ask.'

'I thought it was all about peace and love in those days.'

'Well, yes, but that was more of a universal thing.' Seeing Suzie's raised eyebrows, she added, 'In any case, actions speak louder than words. A lot of people say "I love you" when they don't mean it.'

For a horrible moment, Janice could feel the question of whether she'd ever said it to Suzie's father shoulder its way between them like an ill-bred dog, but, after what seemed an age, Suzie said, 'Was Joe faithful to you?'

Relieved, Janice drank some more of her wine. 'It was a bit more complicated than that.'

'How? Either he was or he wasn't.'

'It was difficult.' Janice toyed with the stem of her glass to avoid having to look at Suzie. 'He was gorgeous looking, and he was in a band, and there were a lot of girls after him, and of course that was part of the attraction, to be with someone like that. But at the same time, it was impossible not to get jealous, and that wasn't cool – you know, getting possessive and being clingy and all of that.'

'But if you were his girlfriend . . . ?'

'I know. But I don't think it's ever a good idea to be overly possessive.'

'No,' said Suzie sardonically. 'And you haven't been, have you?'

'I didn't mean that!' Janice stared at her, mortified. 'I meant about relationships – with men, I mean.'

Suzie leant over to refill her glass. 'It's all right. I can take it. Are you in a relationship now?'

'No. I was, but he died last year.'

'Oh.' Suzie lowered her eyes. 'I'm sorry.'

'He had cancer,' said Janice. 'We'd been together for a couple of years – we never lived together or anything, it was more . . .' She stopped, unsure, now, how to categorise what she'd had with Jim.

'Friends with benefits?' supplied Suzie.

'A bit, I suppose, but we liked the same things, so we used to go to places together and have holidays and things. It wasn't just, you know, convenience – although I suppose there's a bit of that in all relationships, isn't there? Neither of us wanted to move in with the other, and we wanted to be free to do our own thing, as well, so . . . well, you know.'

'Would you have brought him up here with you? If he'd still been alive, I mean.'

Janice shook her head. 'I don't think it would have occurred to me. He was a lovely guy, but we were pretty semi-detached, really.'

'So you hadn't told him about me?'

'No.' Janice thought it better not to say that she hadn't told anybody else, either. It occurred to her then that maybe she had a habit of secrecy, like Dan – or just didn't like to lay herself open by mentioning painful things, anyway. Was that, perhaps, why Dan hadn't liked to talk about the past?

'You don't have to be defensive about it.' Suzie grinned. 'Anyway, it's none of my business, really.' She drank some more wine, then asked, 'What did you do for money when you first went to London?'

'I had a job in a clothes shop for a while, and I worked at some of the clubs, taking the money and that sort of thing. It was easier then, if you wanted to rent a place, and a lot of students had grants, so . . . But, going back to what I said about not being possessive, it wasn't that I didn't love you,' Janice said. 'It's just that it was different then – the money thing was easier, but—'

'That's the second time you've said it was different,' said Suzie.

'Is it? Sorry. But it's true. And it's hard to explain about the past because it makes everything sound so cut and dried. You know, people like to tell themselves that they thought it all through and reached conclusions and made decisions, but life isn't like that – not on a daily basis, anyway. Most of it's just reacting to things that happen to us – making it up as we go along – and I'm no different.'

'Making it up, like giving me away, you mean?'

'No!' Janice recoiled. This was like walking through a minefield – words blowing up in her face.

'So then it was – what was it you just said? A conclusion and a decision.'

'Neither. I wasn't in a position to make decisions, and I certainly didn't give you up because I didn't want you. I did it because everyone told me it would be best for you, and I felt – I was *made* to feel – that there was no option. It wasn't just Ma and Pa, but the matron and everyone at the hospital – all saying it was selfish to want to keep you. Everyone was against me.' Janice stopped, blinking back tears. 'Look, this isn't how I wanted to say any of this, and it's probably coming out all wrong, and, anyway, it's not fair to burden you with it.'

Suzie's eyes were as hard as her voice. 'Like I said, I can take it.'

'I'm sorry. I know I keep saying I'm sorry, but I don't know what you want me to say.'

Suzie's brow creased in a deep frown, and she stood up once more, picking up her glass and the packet of cigarettes as she did so. 'You know what? Neither do I.' Scooping up the bottle of wine, she said, 'Mind if I take this?' and left the room without waiting for an answer.

EIGHTEEN

Phoebe Piper.

PP 4 Ever.

This is Phoebe Piper's pen.

It was good having the purple felt-tip again. Janice was OK, Molly thought, even though she couldn't trust her yet. It was nice of her to fetch the pen. She'd looked sad when she was in Dan's room, so perhaps she was telling the truth about him being her brother, even though she'd told a lie about being Suzie's mum. Gamga was Suzie's mum, everyone knew that, so what Janice had said wasn't even a good lie. There wasn't any point to it, either, because if Molly hadn't known that, and wanted to check, she could just have asked Suzie. Molly was trying to cure herself of telling pointless lies, but she still did it sometimes, like telling Ellie she'd been to Disney World last year or when she'd said to Suzie that someone had pushed her off the little kids' climbing frame at school.

This summer, Molly'd noticed something about lying. When children told lies, even if they were quite good ones, everyone said, 'You're lying,' and, 'I don't believe you,' and things like that. When grown-ups told lies, like when Suzie told Dan that she'd had a job in a pub and they'd lived there and then the pub got closed so they didn't have a home anymore, people just listened politely and nobody said they didn't believe it. It wasn't fair.

Molly put the scrapbook down on her bed and knelt up so that she could look across the back garden. Suzie had told worse lies than that, about her – and the letter and photo Dan had left must mean she'd lied about not knowing him before they'd come here, as well as everything else. Molly didn't want to think about that too much, because then she'd have to hate Suzie and Dan, and she didn't want to. Especially not Dan, because he'd been nice to her and she was – really, *properly* – sorry he was dead.

The problem was not knowing what to do. She needed to find the hair ribbon, she knew that much, but what about after that? What if she couldn't work out who the woman in the photo was? Suzie was really good at lying, so the police would always believe her, not Molly. Even if she showed them the letter, Suzie could always say she knew nothing about it. And supposing the police made them go back to the B & B? Dan had said they could stay here as long as they wanted, but Dan was dead. There'd been a girl at her school in London and she and her mum were living at her aunt's flat and her aunt got hit by a car, so then the landlord told them to get out and they didn't have anywhere to go. They'd ended up having to sleep in someone's garage for three days and Kayleigh said she was really scared. That sounded worse than the B & B, even, and Molly didn't want it happening to them.

Suzie hadn't said anything about Janice being her real mum, and not telling was a way of lying, sort of. Thinking about this made Molly wonder if Janice might be telling the truth. When Janice had gone out, she'd had a look inside her suitcase to see if she had any baby pictures of Suzie. There weren't any, but that might be because they were in her handbag. And she'd said about the plate, hadn't she? The one that was her favourite. And about it being her room, and having a cat . . . Those things had sounded true, but Janice *might* have been making them up, and Dan was dead so she couldn't ask him. It occurred to Molly then that if you were so old that you were the only one alive who knew about something, you could say anything you liked and no one could say it was a lie. That would be good – apart from having to be really old, of course, which would be rubbish.

In any case, Molly thought, it didn't really matter to her who Suzie's mum was, because Suzie wasn't *her* mum, was she? So, even if Janice *was* Suzie's real mum, she wasn't Molly's real grandma any more than Gamga was. That was a pity, really, with Janice being so nice and talking to her and fetching the pen and everything, but Molly knew that she did have at least one real grandma, because she'd seen a photo in the paper with all the Piper family together. It was taken when she was a baby, and she was sitting right in the middle, on Melissa's knee.

If it *was* true about Janice, then that made it OK for Suzie, because she'd found her real mum, hadn't she? She'd spent a long time with the wrong family, though, being the wrong person. Forty-four years was a lot. Suzie won't be able to change back, Molly thought, because she's too used to being Suzie. And if *she* didn't do something soon then she might have to spend that long being Molly and not Phoebe, and then she wouldn't be able to be Phoebe properly when the time came.

She'd missed enough of being Phoebe already. Seven birthdays, seven Christmases, seven summer holidays – lots and lots of things. It was, Molly thought, a bit like on sports day, when she'd been thinking about something else and missed the start of the sack race. She'd only started a teeny-weeny bit after the others, but she couldn't catch up, so she'd come last. Mrs Kelly'd kept saying, after, that it didn't matter, but it obviously did, or why would they even bother having a race? At least Mrs Kelly was trying to be nice – Suzie hadn't even cared enough to come along to watch. Afterwards, she'd told a lie to Mrs Kelly about having to go to a meeting and not being able to change the day, and Mrs Kelly had listened politely and said, 'What a shame,' and 'Never mind, there's always next year.'

Except there wouldn't be next year, because by next summer she'd be Phoebe again. She had to be. Not being able to catch up with the life you were supposed to have was a lot worse than coming last in the sack race, because if you couldn't do that, then you'd never be able to belong anywhere. It would be like when everyone in the class except her was invited to Jasmine's party, but for your whole life. Afterwards, Jasmine's mum had said sorry to Suzie and told her that Jasmine had forgotten to tell her that there was a new girl, but Molly knew that Jasmine hadn't really forgotten; she was just being spiteful. Ellie was a new girl, and she'd remembered *her*, hadn't she? Now Courtney was having a party, and Molly wasn't invited to that either, and she bet it was because Jasmine told Courtney not to.

She'd decided to concentrate on finding the ribbon for now, because she could do that by herself. She'd hoped it might be in Dan's shed, but she'd looked everywhere and it wasn't, and now she was beginning to think it must be somewhere in his room. That meant she'd have to go in there and close the door, in case anyone saw, and closing the door meant she wouldn't be able to get out fast enough if something bad happened. It also meant she'd have to look in the wardrobe, and Waxwork Dan might be in there, waiting in the gloom, staring glassily at her from between the shoulders of empty coats.

Molly closed her eyes tight and shook her head violently, but the image wouldn't go away. I've already done it once, she told herself, to get the felt-tips. She'd got the pens – all except the purple one, anyway. And nothing bad had happened when Janice went into Dan's room and looked underneath the wardrobe, so it might be all right . . . In a way, she thought, it was quite exciting. Like something in a story, except that people in stories always had friends to help them, like Harry Potter did, and it was a lot easier to read about stuff like that than actually having to do it. But if she didn't do it, she'd be the wrong girl for the rest of her life and she'd never, ever be happy.

NINETEEN

Janice glanced at her watch: 6.15 p.m. She might as well go and finish sorting out her room. She'd only need to clear out the top drawer in the chest – that would be plenty of space for her few things. Opening the broom cupboard, she retrieved the plastic shopping bags that she'd stuffed inside a bucket and went upstairs.

She'd intended to dump all the stuff into the supermarket bags without looking at it, but things kept catching her eye: the silver cup from a long-ago sports day, engraved *A. J. Stephenson, 1934*, and underneath, *Long Jump & 440 Yard Dash*; the unlikely sapphire-coloured bri-nylon shortie nightdress – here, she had to struggle with the accompanying mental snapshot of Ma and Pa in a staticky middle-aged coupling – and, at the bottom of the drawer, a shoe box. Opening it, she discovered a stack of black and white photographs: men in collars and ties and women in cloche hats sitting in deckchairs, milling around at church bazaars, arranged in a smiling line in front of a charabanc . . . Underneath these was a pile of letters on flimsy paper, written by Ma during the war, when she'd still been Audrey Stephenson, and kept, neatly folded, by Pa. Having glanced at the top one – *Darling Frank . . .* – Janice closed the lid firmly. The last thing she needed, especially now, was to meet her parents as the young people they'd once been, she in the A.T.S., he in the R.A.F., with neither Dan nor herself imagined, let alone born.

Given how badly it was going with Suzie, perhaps she shouldn't bother to unpack at all. Suddenly weary, Janice sat down on the bed. Her suitcase was open on the floor and now she noticed that the contents had a tumbled look, as though someone – probably Molly – had been searching for something. Photographic evidence of love, perhaps?

Not such a stupid idea. Why shouldn't Molly be looking for reassurance that she was thought of and mattered? People did it all the time, even if they pretended otherwise.

Janice twisted round to stare out of the window. She could just about make out Joe's house across the fields. What wouldn't she have given, back then, to hear him say 'I love you'?

She bent down and unearthed her laptop from amongst the confusion of clothes. If only he *had* said it, just once. Placing the computer on the small table beside the bed, she plugged the lead into the wall and sat, side on, staring at the icons as they popped up on the screen, and remembering. You weren't supposed to be jealous or paranoid or get hung up on people, but just enjoy sex – although, Janice thought, conforming to nonconformity had, in many ways, been just as difficult as conforming to the old, repressive rules, and however much everyone pretended other-wise, it had caused just as much heartache. Also, however much she resisted saying so out loud, there was no getting around the fact that she had definitely, on more than a few occasions, con-fused feeling that she ought to with actually wanting to. It was that thing of not wanting to but wanting to be the kind of person who wanted to, because it was cool. That must apply to so many people so much of the time that there really ought to be a word for it, Janice thought.

It was also true that on more than one occasion she'd gone to bed with somebody because they'd wanted to and she'd felt it would have been rude to refuse. That wasn't true with any of the guys in the bands, of course, because they *were* cool, and being with them had made her cool by association. That had definitely been the case with Joe at the beginning – why she'd wanted him – but then she'd fallen head over heels in love. The idea that something that meant so much to her might have meant nothing to Joe – that he might not even *remember* it – made her feel actually sick.

Janice had meant to check her emails, but found herself looking for Joe on YouTube instead. She found black and white footage of the band on stage – all flashes and starbursts and silhouettes and droning guitars – and a scrappy, badly cut piece of film showing them all looning around in a wood somewhere, to the soundtrack of 'Come Out to Play', which hardly showed Joe at all. Further down the list of clips, the majority of which were of Weather Ship Tango Delta's later performances, after Joe had left, she found an interview from 1967 with Joe and Keith Petrie. The elderly interviewer, besuited and bow-tied, treated the pair of them like schoolboys, asking querulously why the music had to be so loud and, when they answered, finding fault with their reasoning. Joe, with his kohl-rimmed eyes, tousled hair and a Chinese jacket embroidered with dragons, looked every bit as skinny and gorgeous as she remembered. What she'd forgotten, in the intervening years, was quite how much of a nice middle-class boy he had been. Janice played the clip several times, marvelling at the thoughtful sincerity of what he said, and at how politely he and Keith listened while the bloke – a classical music reviewer, obviously chosen deliberately – patronised them. That, she thought, was how people ought to remember Joe. Not all the other stuff, but at his best: charming, courteous, intelligent.

There was a later interview with Joe, played over a series of photographs – including one of his room in the flat in Earls Court, the bed a mattress laid on floorboards he'd painted in different colours. He seemed to be talking about how words complicated everything, but his speech was so slow and disjointed that it was hard to tell. The interviewer, an American who sounded as stoned as Joe did, tried to prompt him with halting questions, but the gaps between phrases, and eventually between words, got longer and longer, until all that was left was the hiss of the tape recorder. Janice muted the volume and concentrated on the string of pictures. He'd been *so* handsome . . .

Right at the end there was a tiny clip, in colour, from a set the Weather Ship had played at the UFO Club, droning guitars and pink and green amoeba blobs swirling over the band and the bobbing heads of the audience. Janice was wondering if perhaps she'd been there, when, for a moment, one of the faces in the crowd turned away from the stage and towards the camera and with a shock she realised she was looking at her younger – impossibly younger – self: enormous dark eyes and a halo of hair, backlit by trippy trails of colours. What had she been thinking? Had she gone home afterwards with Joe, to the room with the multicoloured floor?

She'd forgotten so much. Why hadn't she kept a diary? If she had, it would show that they'd had a relationship – that she hadn't just been some groupie. Even if Joe didn't remember, she'd have real, actual evidence.

Remembering, suddenly, what Molly had told her about Joe not wanting to have friends, she wondered if perhaps he, like Suzie, had told Dan not to tell her he was here. This, she thought, offered at least a crumb of comfort: to be remembered and betrayed, in however small a way, was preferable to the catastrophe of being forgotten altogether.

TWENTY

Almost seven o'clock. It was a bit cooler now, and Janice decided she'd have a shower and go for a walk through the village before it got dark. She wasn't going to Joc's, she was just taking herself for a walk, and if she happened to pass his house, then so be it. After all, she hadn't been back to Repshall for six years, so why not?

As she stopped to pat a couple of ponies in the field next to the church, it occurred to her that she'd not laid eyes on her parents' grave since her mother was buried.

She found it easily enough – a grey granite headstone with plain lettering – and stood guiltily, head down, to read:

In Loving Memory Of
Francis Richard Carthy-Todd
22.03.1914 – 18.11.1997

Added, below that, was:

And His Beloved Wife
Audrey Jane
14.06.1920 – 11.09.2008

Was that what they'd agreed? She couldn't remember discussing it, and wondered if they'd actually done so. She was pretty sure that Dan hadn't mentioned the space left beneath their mother's name for another one – presumably his own.

She stood for a further moment, awkwardly reverent, and then, with a feeling of being generally at fault, as though the surrounding dead were rebuking her for not being a better person while she had the chance, muttered, 'Sorry.'

Except, she thought, as she walked across the green, it's all too late. Her relationship with Ma and Pa had broken, irrevocably, the moment she told them she was pregnant – and giving Suzie up had simply meant that she'd lost her baby as well as her parents.

She went past the shop – now closed, with the dismal vegetables carted inside to moulder overnight – and down the lane. The descending sun cast bands of shadow across the surface of the road and in the fields on either side the crows wheeled and cawed. Ahead of her, a black cat slipped out from beneath the hedge and paused for a second to glare at her with malevolent yellow eyes before merging with the shadows in the gateway on the other side of the road. Looking beyond it, Janice thought she saw a larger shape disappear around the bend in the road, and had the impression of something ragged trailing behind it. It's nothing, she told herself. Her pulse had accelerated and the back of her head was tingling. A trick of the light, that's all. Her scalp felt sweaty, too, and her heart was banging in her chest. As a child, she'd never felt uneasy running around these lanes at dusk – probably because she wasn't viewing the world through the prism of too many horror films.

This wasn't just a few gothic special effects provided by nature, though. It was something more: it was *her*. Standing stock still in the lane, it came to Janice that all her life she'd conformed one way or the other to something or other, because you had to. You didn't have a choice, except in deciding what to conform to. Freedom was an illusion, and all of it was meaningless. An impression of Ma's face, hollowed and waxy in death, appeared at the edge of her mind: all anyone amounted to in the end. How had she not realised this before? It was just a lot of egos, hers and everyone else's, all separate, with everyone desperate not to be ordinary . . .

Did that even make sense? Christ, she couldn't breathe. She gulped air, each intake knife-like. What was happening to her? She was trembling all over and her hands felt stiff, like flippers. Panic, causeless and terrifying, overwhelmed her. Clamping one palm over her mouth for fear that she might actually howl, she stumbled the fifty-odd feet to the gateway and leant over the metal bars, clinging to the mud-smeared top rail with both hands, trying to control her breathing.

How long it lasted, she didn't know, but when she opened her eyes she found that she was repeating, between snatches of air, 'It's all right, it's all right, it's all right . . .'

It really was all right, Janice told herself. Just a dizzy spell – hardly surprising, what with the shock of Dan's death, and Suzie and Molly, and not having lunch and then the glass of wine on an empty stomach. Could happen to anyone. She just needed to pull herself together, that was all. She stood up straight, ran her hands through her hair and shook her head violently. Time to go back, she decided. She'd eat something and get an early night: everything was bound to look better in the morning.

Turning, she spotted a skein of smoke coming from behind a stand of trees at the far side of the field. Remembering what Suzie had said, she wondered if Joe was having one of his bonfires, getting rid of the tributes that had been left for him . . . No, thought Janice. Not for him – for the person he used to be.

*

Back in the kitchen, feeling sheepish for the speed – not exactly running, but a lot faster than ordinary walking – with which she'd returned, Janice found a note from Molly on the table.

Thank you for getting my pen and for the sanwitch, it was nice. Suzie said to tell you she has gone out. It is to see Mark so I got my dinner and going to bed now, Molly xxx

P.S. Thanks for the sweets

The note was written in the purple felt-tip, and decorated with a drawing of an improbably solid-looking flower. Glancing round, Janice saw that there were crumbs on the breadboard and a plate and knife with smears of butter and jam in the sink. Mark, she remembered, as she washed them up, was the boyfriend Molly had mentioned, who worked in the pub sometimes. Janice opened the fridge door and stared inside, feeling that she probably ought to eat something and trying to decide what, wondering if Suzie often went out with Mark and left her daughter by herself.

After a minute, she closed the fridge door and, putting Molly's note in her pocket, made a cup of tea to take to bed. At least, she thought, trudging wearily up the stairs, one person seems to want me to be here.

TWENTY-ONE

After a poor night's sleep, Janice woke, sweaty and uneasy, at half past nine, showered, and went down to the kitchen. She was making toast when three loud thuds on the stairs announced Molly, who bounced in with what looked like a scrapbook tucked under her arm, a teddy bear holding a bunch of balloons decorating its cover. She was wearing the same clothes as she'd had on the previous day.

'Want some breakfast?' Janice asked.

'I can get it.'

Janice watched as Molly gathered together a box of cereal, a bowl, a spoon and a carton of milk, clutching the precarious pile to her chest and anchoring it with her chin, without unclamping the scrapbook from her side. 'What's that?'

'Nothing.' Molly leant forward and deposited everything on the kitchen table, then quickly picked up the scrapbook again, holding it flat to her chest. 'It's for school.'

Homework, left until the last minute, Janice thought, because term started in September, didn't it? She hadn't seen much evidence of preparation for a new school year. Ma had stitched Cash's name tapes into socks and sports kit when Janice was at school; even if no one did that anymore, there must be other things that Molly needed. 'Do you need help with it?'

Molly shook her head vehemently. 'I have to do it myself.'

'OK.' Thank God, thought Janice, turning back to the toaster in order to hide her relief. She was fairly certain she wouldn't have the first clue about whatever it was that modern ten-year-olds were expected to do for homework. Remembering what Molly had said about Ellie not being her friend anymore, Janice thought, *She's probably dreading going back*, and then – remembering her own childhood, how timeless and present it had seemed – *Perhaps she hasn't realised it's going to happen, yet.*

'I saw you yesterday.' Molly spoke indistinctly, through cornflakes.

'Oh?'

'In the evening. You said you wouldn't go to Joe's house.'

'I didn't.'

'Yes, you did. You *promised*.'

'I didn't go to Joe's house.'

'I saw you.'

'I was going in that direction,' Janice admitted, 'but I didn't get that far. I think he might have been having a bonfire.'

Molly nodded. 'He does that a lot.'

A thought struck Janice. 'That wasn't you following me down the road, was it?'

Molly shovelled in more cornflakes and made an exaggerated pointing gesture at her mouth, shaking her head at the same time.

'Not you?'

'Mmph. Probably the Sneaky Man. He's there a lot, hanging around.'

'Who's the Sneaky Man?'

'Don't know his real name – that's just what I call him. Joe's always hiding from him. Dan kept telling him to leave Joe alone,

but it didn't make any difference. I used to be quite scared of him,'
Molly admitted, 'but that was really because he looked a bit like
a wizard. I'm not scared anymore, though. Well, not much, but I
don't like him, anyway. He comes here sometimes, too.'

'To this house, you mean?'

'No, he walks up and down the road. He smells, and he's got
this sort of necklace made of horrible things.'

'Does he live in the village?'

Molly shook her head. 'No one knows where he lives, I don't
think.'

'So . . . if it wasn't you in the road, how did you see me?'

'From the window.'

'Of my room?' She'd been right about the suitcase, Janice
thought, pretending not to notice Molly's sheepish expression.
'Have you seen your mum this morning?'

'No. She's probably still at Mark's.'

'Does she stay there often?'

'Sometimes. Sometimes he comes here.'

'Do you like him?'

'He's OK, I suppose.'

'Only OK?'

'Yeah.' Molly shrugged. 'Doesn't really matter – it's not like he's
going to be my new dad or anything.'

'Isn't he?'

Molly rolled her eyes, bolted the last of her cornflakes and then,
swivelling in her chair, grabbed a can of something out of the
fridge before running off upstairs.

Janice sat at the kitchen table, feeling unsure what to do. After
what had happened last night in the lane, she needed to regain
her equilibrium.

She could do her yoga in the sitting room – more space there than upstairs. Then, if Suzie still wasn't back, she'd make a start clearing out Dan's room.

The yoga practice was unsuccessful, mainly because, at floor level, no matter how much she tried to focus on her breathing, she kept getting distracted by the quantities of dust she could see beneath the furniture. After she'd slipped and bashed her knee on the parquet, she gave up and, dragging the ancient Electrolux hoover from its place under the stairs, set to work. Half an hour's vigorous activity later, the room was not only clean and tidy, but it looked pretty much as Janice remembered it from her childhood. Standing in the doorway, surveying the order she had created, she felt relaxed and benevolent. None of it was Suzie's fault, after all. She'd lost her job, lost her home, she'd got a child to look after – two, really, because Tom obviously wasn't fending for himself – and she'd come to rely on Dan in the last six months and now he was dead . . .

Primed with rubber gloves and a roll of bin liners, she lugged the hoover upstairs to Dan's room. The door was closed, as it had been all the time she'd been there, and, opening it, she was astonished to see Molly standing in the middle of the room, looking guilty, a length of pink ribbon hanging limply from a snarl of hair at the side of her head.

'I thought you were doing your homework.'

'I was.' Molly, fiddling with the end of the ribbon, didn't meet her eye. 'I just came in here, that's all.'

'That's all right. Do you want me to tie your ribbon?'

'OK.'

'If you fetch your hairbrush, I can do you a French plait.'

'What's that?'

'Sort of like a cornrow – right from here.' Janice tapped the top of Molly's head.

'Can you really?' Molly grinned up at her. 'That would be great!' As she charged out of the room, Janice wondered if Suzie ever spent any time with her. The pang of sadness she felt on seeing her granddaughter's evident delight was, she knew, sadness for herself, too – for all the time she hadn't spent with Suzie, the mother–daughter things they had not done.

Looking around, she spotted a pocket mirror in a pink, plastic casing – obviously Molly's – propped up on the solitary bookshelf above Dan's desk. The books – *Jonathan Livingstone Seagull*, *The Electric Kool-Aid Acid Test* and the *Fender Amp Guide* amongst them – were fuzzed with dust and looked as if they hadn't been opened for a long time, but Molly had obviously been having a poke around, because the wardrobe door was ajar and a pile of old newspapers and colour supplements had been pulled out on to the floor. Perhaps the letter Suzie had written to her was somewhere here, if Dan had kept it. He should have done, she thought – it was hers, after all, and not his. The desk seemed more likely, but a cursory inspection of the two drawers yielded nothing. Turning back to the wardrobe and seeing a rack full of L.P.s inside, stuck between two cardboard boxes, Janice squatted down for a closer look, walking her fingers across the tops of albums. In between *Trout Mask Replica* and *Odgens' Nut Gone Flake*, she found, not a letter from Suzie, but a black and white photograph of a young woman, her face framed in the upswept curls of the 1940s, dressed in the uniform of one of the services. A relative, she guessed, seeing something familiar in the cast of the cheeks and nose. Someone called – according to the signature scrawled across the bottom right-hand corner and followed by two kisses – Marguerite.

That was the problem with family photographs: if they weren't labelled, then, within two generations, no one had any idea who the people were. We don't realise how soon we are forgotten, she thought, how soon our names part company with our faces. With a vague idea of seeing if she could find a match in one of the family albums, she laid the photograph on top of the mess on Dan's desk.

'I brought a comb, too.' Molly bounced back into the room. 'And an elastic band. What are you doing?'

'Just having a look. Why don't you sit on the chair? It'll be easier.'

'OK. What's that?' Molly twitched the L.P. Janice had been holding out of her hand and danced across to plonk herself down on Dan's desk chair.

'You need to keep still.' Janice positioned herself behind Molly, put one hand on top of the girl's warm head, untied the pink ribbon and set to work with the comb. Molly maintained a stoic silence as Janice concentrated on tugging out the tangles, only once giving a muted yelp. At least, Janice thought, dirty hair, even if less pleasant to handle, was easier to plait. 'I was surprised,' she said, 'to find you in here, when you wouldn't come before – not by yourself, anyway.'

'I made myself. So I could do it and I wouldn't be scared.'

'That's a good idea. That's me, look,' Janice pointed over Molly's shoulder with the comb. 'On the cover.'

Molly stared intently at the photograph of Janice and two other girls, naked, covered in paint and writhing around on a huge canvas. 'Electric Village,' she read. 'What's that?'

'The name of the group. That's a sleeve for an L.P. A record,' she clarified, in case Molly didn't know.

'It's *vinyl*,' Molly corrected. 'From the olden days. Dan told me. Which one is you?'

Carefully, Janice extracted one set of fingers from the plait and pointed at the image of herself on her knees with her back arched, breasts streaked red and green, and her long hair a flying slick of blue. 'There.'

Molly wriggled around and eyed Janice. 'It doesn't look like you.'

'Hardly surprising.' Janice pushed Molly's head round to face forwards again. 'It was a long time ago.'

Molly turned the cover over. 'Nineteen seventy-two. That's a really long time ago.'

Suzie would have been two, Janice thought. One or two, depending on the month. There was another photo on the back, showing the four members of the group standing against a backdrop of the smudgy imprints, in paint, of breasts, bellies and thighs, with the song titles and credits listed off to one side.

'I didn't really look like that then either,' said Janice, wishing she hadn't brought the subject up in the first place. 'I mean, I wasn't stripy. Or blue.'

Molly ignored the feeble joke and wriggled round again to stare at her. Janice, uncomfortable, shuffled sideways and concentrated hard on the plait.

'Did you have to do it?'

'Have to?'

'Did they make you?'

'No . . .' Disconcerted, Janice laughed. 'Course not. It was fun. Took ages to get the paint off, though. I was finding bits for weeks, every time I had a bath.'

Molly said nothing.

Why *had* she done it? She'd been having a thing with the guitarist – she remembered that. Noel something. She peered over Molly's shoulder, but without her glasses the small type was impossible to read. He'd been into threesomes. They'd had one with one of the other girls in the photo, hadn't they? What had her name been? Janice couldn't remember. She hadn't wanted to, and the girl, whatever her name was, had said she was uptight. The relationship with Noel hadn't lasted very long after that. She couldn't remember how it had finished. Maybe he'd ended up with the other girl, if she liked threesomes – or said she did.

'Did they pay you a lot of money?'

'We didn't get paid.'

Molly's head whipped round again. 'What? Nothing?'

'No.' Janice put the flat of her free hand against the girl's cheek and pushed her head round. It hadn't occurred to them – well, certainly not to her – to ask for any money.

'Can I get down now?'

'Almost finished.' I shouldn't have said anything to Molly, Janice thought. Now she thinks I'm some sort of weirdo, and it's my own fault. 'There you go.'

'Did you put the ribbon on?'

'Yes. Take that,' Janice indicated the pink-edged mirror propped on the bookshelf, 'into the bathroom, and you'll be able to see what it looks like.'

The L.P. fell to the floor as Molly propelled herself from the chair, and, grabbing the mirror, disappeared.

Stop worrying, Janice told herself. Molly's far more interested in what her hair looks like than some old album cover – and who can blame her? She picked the record up off the floor and squinted at the names on the back. Noel Stillman, that was it. Outlaw clothes, shoulder-length black hair, Zapata moustache. He'd been very hairy all over, in fact. Chest, shoulders, bum like a monkey's . . . It occurred to her that no one had thought to credit her, or the other two girls. They were anonymous – bodies with no names attached.

Oh, well. Bit late to make a fuss now. Unwrapping a bin liner from the roll, Janice began shovelling the newspapers into it when Molly came lolloping back, in a happy buzz of excitement. 'It's brilliant! Can you teach me how—?' She stopped, her smile gone, staring at the lumpy black plastic sack. 'What are you doing?'

'Clearing up,' said Janice, surprised. 'I was going to throw these away.'

'You can't!'

'I can put them out for recycling if you show me where the—'

'You *can't*!' Molly's voice was shrill with panic. 'They're Dan's things. You can't just throw them away.' Molly grabbed the bin liner and upended it so that the newspapers slid out on to the floor.

Taken aback by her vehemence, Janice said, as gently as she could, 'I know, love, but Dan isn't going to have any use for them now, is he?'

'You can't just come and take his stuff! And I'm not your love.'

'I'm sorry. I was just trying to tidy up.'

'You're taking things!' To Janice's horror, Molly began to cry, her face bright pink as enormous sobs pumped her chest. 'They're – not – *yours*!'

'OK, I won't if you don't want me to. Look, why don't we leave everything where it is for the time being?'

'You're – not – even – meant – to be here. Suzie – doesn't – want you here – and nor do I!'

'Molly, calm down. See, I'm putting the things back in the wardrobe.'

'No! I hate you! You can't have any of it! Nothing! You leave it – all of it – you leave it alone!'

Janice turned, putting her hands up in a gesture of surrender. 'I promise—'

Too late. Molly was off, footsteps thudding down the stairs.

Janice heard the shuddering crash as the front door slammed behind her, then nothing. It's no use, she thought, as she sat down on Dan's bed. I don't understand anything. I had a second chance, and I've already blown it.

TWENTY-TWO

Molly ran. She didn't care where, just *away*. Away from stupid Janice, who was messing up Dan's room and trying to take all his things away before she'd had a chance to see if there was any more stuff about Phoebe in there. That was probably why she was doing it, Molly thought. Janice *knew*. She wasn't that clever, though, or she wouldn't have left that photo right where Molly could see it. It was definitely one of the women from the other picture, the one she'd got from Dan's shed. It had a name on it, too, but the writing was hard to read.

Molly'd just had time to stuff it up her T-shirt when Janice was pretending to put Dan's things back in the wardrobe. When she'd seen the hair ribbon, she'd pretended to be all friendly and nice, plaiting her hair and everything, and all the time while she was going on about that stupid record-cover thing – serve her right if she got paint up her bum, thought Molly grimly – she was plotting how to remove any stuff about Phoebe from the room. But she hadn't got the ribbon, because Molly had beaten her to it. That was lucky, because Dan had put it in a really obvious place – all squashed up inside a funny little plastic bag, in the wooden box where he kept his dope.

The impetus had gone by the time she'd got to the bend in the road, and she slowed and wandered forlornly down to the edge of the village green, where she slid the photo out from under her T-shirt and stood trying to work out the word scribbled across the corner. She thought it was *Margaret*, but she wasn't quite sure. It was the sort of name an old person might have, but she didn't know anyone called Margaret, so it wasn't much help.

She was thirsty, but Dan had told her that the pump hadn't worked even when he was a kid, and she didn't have any money. She dawdled in the direction of the shop, wondering if she were brave enough to ask Mrs Garner for a glass of water. Suzie and Tom spent enough money in there, buying cigarettes and beer and things, and Dan had, too, but Mrs Garner wasn't a friendly person. She was old in a really horrible way, with a hairy chin, and when people asked where things were or if she had them in stock, she huffed and puffed as if they'd asked her to climb a mountain.

Molly hovered by the display outside the shop, hoping against hope that some kind passer-by might offer to buy her a Coke or something, but there was nobody around. Now she was away from the house, she didn't know what to do with herself. If she went into the woods, it would only remind her of how, a couple of months earlier, before Ellie went off with Jasmine, the two of them had played at stables there and galloped down the grassy slope to the stream, whinnying. In any case, that was something that Molly did, not Phoebe. Phoebe wouldn't wander around the lanes by herself either, because only saddos did that – and anyway, Phoebe'd have loads of friends, so she wouldn't have to.

Even someone really stupid wouldn't want to eat a carrot that had gone black at the end. Molly turned her back on Mrs Garner's rubbish vegetables and stared listlessly at the row of newspapers that were displayed under plastic lids to stop them getting wet if it rained. Even the papers with big capital letters looked boring. One had a photo of people kissing, but she didn't know who either of them were, so that was boring, too, and so was everything else. Her gaze was sliding past the different typefaces and dull photographs of men in suits when *PHOEBE'S PARENTS TO DIVORCE* leapt out at her. Gasping as if she'd been drenched with icy water, Molly flipped up the lid and grabbed the paper. It said *Daily Mail Exclusive*, and underneath there was a photograph of Melissa and David Piper with a big white zigzag between them, like a tear. Melissa, carrying Snuggle Pup, looked sad, and David had his head down as if he didn't want anyone to see him.

Her parents were getting divorced, because of her. As she stared at the page, numb with shock, the words and phrases seemed to rear up at her: *looked strained . . . very sad . . . taken its toll . . . We'll always be there for Phoebe . . .* If she were with them, this wouldn't be happening. They'd stay together and they'd be happy because *she* would make them happy.

'Hey!' Mrs Garner was standing in the doorway of the shop. 'Unless you're going to pay for that, you can put it back. This isn't a library.'

'Sorry,' Molly muttered, ducking her head. Shoving the newspaper back inside its plastic box, she ran. She had to get home as fast as possible. She'd have to pack, but just the scrapbook, the letter from Dan's shed that proved everything and the photos as well, even if she didn't know who the people were. She'd take her toothbrush, and her jacket for if it got cold, but nothing else because she wouldn't need Molly's stuff once she was Phoebe again. In any case, Melissa and David would want her to have new clothes, wouldn't they? Melissa would be dying to take her shopping, and then they'd go home and she'd do a fashion show for both of them, like on a catwalk, skipping and twirling in her new things with music playing, while they clapped and clapped and clapped. But that wouldn't happen if she didn't stop them before they'd got divorced and everything was ruined. Compared to such a calamity, the threat of what Suzie might say or do, or of the B & B – or even the thought of poor Kayleigh, sleeping in the garage – evaporated into nothing at all.

She'd got to be quick, though. Janice didn't know about the note and the photo she'd found in Dan's shed, and nor did Suzie, but Janice knew about the photo in his room, and it wouldn't be long before she realised Molly had taken it. She'd tell Suzie, and then they'd try to stop her . . . What she'd got to do wouldn't take long, though. She'd change into her best skirt, then she'd pack up the things – not in her backpack, because that had *Molly Armitage* written on the inside, for school, so she'd have to get a plastic bag – and she ought to do something about Janice, to stop her suspecting anything. And then what? As she hurtled back to the house on frantic legs, her chest feeling as if it might actually burst, Molly tried desperately to think of a way that she could get to Melissa and David. She knew where they lived – not the actual address, but the village and where it was – because it had been in one of the papers, and she'd stuck the cutting into her scrapbook. There'd been photos, too, not of the actual house, but of the place: a duck pond; cricketers, with the church in the background; people smiling in a pub garden. Molly'd looked it up in the map book from Dan's van, and it was miles away. You'd have to get to London first, and then it was the same distance again, measured with a finger and thumb, before you arrived. She had nearly thirty pounds saved – it should have been more, but Suzie had borrowed five pounds two days ago and she hadn't given it back yet.

How could she get there? When she'd thought about Melissa and David before, she'd never really tried to figure out the difficult bits – not properly, anyway. She'd tried, loads, but she'd always got bored and started thinking about the good bits, instead. Don't stop, she told herself, as the sudden, sharp pain of a stitch made her clutch at her side. Keep going – you have to.

'I must get to them,' she gasped. 'I must. I must.' Somehow she'd do it. If they got divorced, it would be her fault because she hadn't tried to get back to them. If they got divorced, she'd be stuck being the wrong person and everything would be wrong forever and ever.

TWENTY-THREE

Janice looked at her watch – five past one – and realised that she must have been sitting on Dan's bed for over half an hour, the sprawl of newspapers round her feet. The solid feeling had returned, with all the dull heaviness of despair. She went downstairs, opened the front door and looked around, but Molly was nowhere to be seen. Spotting the *Eastern Daily Press* through the window of her car, she retrieved it from the passenger seat.

She'd thought of reading the paper over a sandwich, although she wasn't particularly hungry, and perhaps making extra sandwiches in case Molly or Suzie returned, but once in the kitchen she found she had neither the energy nor the willpower to do more than sit at the table and leaf, uncomprehending, through pages of local news.

Molly was upset about Dan's death, she told herself. That must be it. She just needed time – that was all. She'd soon forget about a bunch of old newspapers and magazines – after all, Dan'd had dozens of things she could choose a keepsake from, if she wanted one. I'll go back and finish clearing up later, Janice thought, once she's calmed down a bit. Apart from anything else, she needed to find Dan's will, if there was one. She doubted Molly would understand that. Worse, she might get the idea that Janice was about to turf them out, which might, of course, be at the back of Suzie's mind, too. She'd have to reassure them. But, Janice thought with guilty irritation, where the hell *was* Suzie? She ought to be here, looking after Molly, not going off to spend the night with her boyfriend and leaving her daughter with someone who was – let's face it – a virtual stranger.

After ten minutes fruitlessly trying to concentrate on articles about road closures and the lack of local swimming pools, she gave up and went to stare listlessly into the fridge, trying to decide what to eat. The more Molly's frantic, angry words echoed in her mind, the more confused she felt, with a creeping sense of shame that became almost physical, as if someone were trickling cold water down her back. If only Molly would return, then they could—

'Hello.' Molly was standing in the doorway.

Wondering how long she'd been there, Janice took the first things to hand – butter and sliced ham – out of the fridge and closed the door. 'Hello.'

'I'm sorry I shouted.' Molly's voice was small and she did not meet Janice's eye but looked down at her jelly bracelets, which she was pushing up and down her arm. 'I just wanted his things to be there for a bit longer, that's all. I didn't want them to just go because then there wouldn't be anything.'

Light with relief, Janice, even before she realised she was doing it, bent forward and planted a kiss on the top of Molly's head. The girl jumped slightly, banging Janice's chin, and they both stepped back, Molly rubbing her crown.

Embarrassed, Janice laughed. 'I do understand. We can leave things for a while, if you want. I'll have to tidy up a bit, though.'

'S'OK.' Molly stopped rubbing her head and, flipping her plait forward over her shoulder, started fiddling with the pink ribbon. She looked as if there was something else she wanted to say, or wanted Janice to say.

'Would you like a sandwich?'

Molly shook her head.

Janice thought she looked wistful. Perhaps she just wanted comfort. After all, Suzie wasn't back (*still* – what was she playing at?) and Molly had nowhere else to go for consolation. The kiss had been a mistake, because unexpected. What she should have done was to ask first. 'How about a hug?'

Molly frowned, then said, 'OK.'

She didn't relax in Janice's arms, but stood still and stiff, as if she wasn't quite sure what was expected of her. 'That better?'

Molly's answering smile was, Janice thought, more conscientious than anything. 'Well, I'm going to have a sandwich.' Rummaging in the drawer for a breadknife, she added, 'I'll make you one for later on, shall I?'

Hearing no reply, she turned round to repeat the question, but Molly had gone.

She was a few bites into the ham sandwich she'd made when she heard tyres on the gravel outside and, going to the window, saw a young man getting out of a battered-looking white van. Seeing her through the glass, he gave a brief, unsurprised wave. There was no sign of Suzie, so presumably it wasn't Mark. A closer look told her that, unless her daughter was in the habit of cradle-snatching, he was quite a bit too young. He was tall, slim and certainly nice looking: the sort of chiselled, rectangular face common amongst male models, with tanned skin and a mop of black hair.

Tom, presumably. Her grandson, come back from the girlfriend-who-wasn't-a-proper-girlfriend. He was much darker than Molly, but then they'd had different fathers. Uncertain of what to do, Janice sat back down again until he barged in through the side door, lugging a bulging army kitbag behind him.

'You must be Janice.' He dropped the kitbag on the flagstones, wiped his hand on his skinny jeans and held it out. 'Tom. Mum told me about you.'

'Really?' Janice shook his hand. 'What did she say?'

'That you're her mum.'

'She didn't say anything else?'

'Only that you're Min's sister.'

'Min?'

'Sorry – Dan. That's what I called him.'

'Oh.' Janice couldn't think of anything to say. *Min*. It was unsettling, as if Tom had created a new person, made up from scratch.

'From those comics – Desperate Dan, Minnie the Minx . . . you know?'

'You're not old enough to remember the *Dandy* and the *Beano*, are you?'

'Yeah, from when I was a kid. I was talking to M— to Dan about it once, all the characters, and we had this sort of joke.' Tom grinned, embarrassed. 'Stupid, really.'

Janice willed herself to smile in return, but knew that she'd only managed to stretch her mouth as if she were humouring a potentially troublesome stranger. 'Was that everything your mother said?'

Tom looked nonplussed, as if he couldn't imagine what other information might have been required. 'Yeah.'

At least, thought Janice, there's one member of the family who's straightforward.

'Mum in?'

'No. I'm not sure where she is.'

'Probably round at Mark's.'

'Molly was here a minute ago, but she's disappeared, too.'

'She'll be back when she's hungry. Any tea going?'

'I can make you some. And lunch, if you want. Only a sandwich, but—'

'Great! Anything, I don't mind.' He turned his back on her and, loosening the top of the kitbag, started pulling something out. 'Friend leant this to me, for the festival. Thought I'd better make sure it's OK.'

Janice paused, kettle in hand. 'What festival?'

'Chipfest. I know . . .' Tom looked sheepish. 'Timing and everything. But staying here won't bring him back, so . . . I promised I'd give a mate a lift, and the tickets cost a fortune.' Tom unrolled the sleeping bag on the floor and patted it in several places. 'Looks all right, doesn't it? And it's not wet or anything.' He sat down in the middle of it, arms round his knees. 'Dan would have understood.'

Janice ran the tap. *What he would have wanted.* So easily said to justify some piece of selfishness – although, in this case, she thought, Tom was probably right. 'I'm sure he would,' she said. 'Who's playing? Anyone I might have heard of?'

'Seasick Steve, Lucinda Williams, Arcade Fire . . . Hang on . . .' Tom scrabbled in the kitbag and produced a tattered flyer with *CHIPFEST 2014* in block letters across the top. 'Kasabian, Johnny Marr, I Am Kloot, Cat Power . . . There's a few more, but I haven't heard of them. Well, barely.'

'I've heard of some of them,' Janice said. 'The more famous ones, anyway. Where is it?'

'Wiltshire. Chippenham, down near Devizes.'

'How lovely. Would you like cheese and pickle, or ham?'

'Can I have both? If you wrap one lot up, I can eat them on the way. I promised to pick my mate up at three.'

'How long will it take you to get to Chippenham?'

'About five hours, I think. Min – I mean Dan – hasn't got satnav, but there's a map in the van, so we should be OK.'

'That's Dan's van, is it?'

'Yeah. It's OK, though. I'm insured.'

'How does Suzie manage? I haven't seen a car here.'

'Dan gives her – gave her – lifts to the shops and stuff. Or Mark, sometimes. There's a bus service, but it's rubbish – once a week or something.'

Cuts, thought Janice. It had been once an hour except Sundays when she was a kid. Pretty isolating, being stuck here with no transport.

'You know,' she put the finished sandwiches on a plate and placed it on the sleeping bag, 'it's years since I've been to a music festival. How much does it cost nowadays?'

'A hundred and seventy-five pounds.'

'Whoo! When you said "a fortune", I thought you meant about fifty quid. Do they charge by the vehicle?'

'No, that's for one person. Parking's fifteen pounds extra.'

'Crikey. When I went to the Isle of Wight festival in 1969, it was about two pounds ten. Old money, that is. God, sorry – you must have got sick of Dan telling you stuff like that.'

'No, because he wouldn't talk about it. I kept asking him – about being on the road and the bands he was with and all that – because I was really interested, but it was like, I don't know, he'd forgotten or he didn't want to think about it or whatever. If I kept asking, it used to piss him off. Who was playing at the Isle of Wight?'

'Mmm.' Janice pretended to think. It had just been a throwaway remark, made for something to say. She hadn't expected Tom to be actually interested. 'Well, the ones you'd have heard of are Bob Dylan, The Who, The Moody Blues . . .' The Weather Ship. *Joe.* That was why she'd gone – why she'd persuaded Jeff to go. Images jostled in her mind: the crowd and the marquees bathed in acid afterglow, sleeping on the beach on the Saturday night and being woken by the rain on her face in the morning . . . Jeff saying, after he'd seen her talking to Joe in the V.I.P. enclosure, *I'm really a come-down for you, aren't I? Not even a roadie, let alone a musician.*

'Can you remember any others?'

'I think Pentangle might have been there – they were a folk group – and there must have been some others, but I can't remember who.' *It's where your mother was conceived.* The words formed in her mind so clearly that she wondered, for a panicky second, whether she'd said them aloud.

'Was M— Was Dan there?'

Had he been? Janice had an image of him in profile, half sitting, half lying on the grass, leaning on his elbows and blowing smoke at the sky, but that might have been from another festival. Glastonbury, perhaps. That had been a couple of years later, well after Suzie was born, so Jeff couldn't have been there – or not with them, anyway. The Weather Ship were supposed to be there, but they'd cancelled. Was that because of Joe, or had he left by then? Was he already in Crowhurst? Janice pictured him, tame and blank-eyed, wired up to some science-fiction electrotherapy device.

'Are you OK?'

'Sorry, I was miles away.' Janice shook her head. 'Trying to remember, but it's no good.'

'You were pretty cool, though, weren't you?'

'I don't know about that,' said Janice, feeling pleased.

'Did you know Joe, too?'

Janice nodded. 'It was a long time ago, though.' Remembering her panic attack the previous night, she thought: Be vague, keep it at arm's length. Safer that way.

'You don't have to tell me. I mean, I'm interested, but . . .' Tom shrugged and leant back, resting his weight on his palms.

'There's not much to tell, really.' Janice finished smoothing the tinfoil around Tom's remaining sandwich, then concentrated hard on wrapping the one she'd made for Molly.

'It's just, I always thought . . .' Tom's tone was measured, as if this was something he'd thought about quite a lot. Janice didn't look at him. 'I thought Dan was, you know, bottling things up about stuff that happened in the past – that's why I said that before, about him getting arsey, but it was more than that. It was like he was going to explode or something, and I used to think, if he ever does, he's going to take the whole village with him.'

'Really?' Janice made herself stop fiddling with the tinfoil; she turned round, leaning against the worktop. 'Doesn't sound like the Dan I knew.'

'Yeah, well . . .' Tom sounded less certain now. 'A lot of the time he was fine, but then other times it was like he was trying really hard to stop himself going postal, you know?'

'Not really, but people change, don't they?'

'Actually,' Tom stood up and started rolling up the sleeping bag, 'I don't think he was like that with Mum or Moll, so perhaps it was just me, asking him stuff.' He glanced at his watch. 'Better pack, or I'll be late. Thanks for this.' He put the now-empty plate on the table and, dropping the wrapped-up sandwich into the mouth of his kitbag, strode off upstairs.

Janice stared at the remains of her own sandwich for a moment, then threw it in the bin. She took the plates to the sink and stood in front of it, staring out of the open window at Dan's van. An angry Dan was hard to imagine, but people did change, didn't they? I didn't know him anymore, she thought sadly. He turned into someone else while I wasn't looking.

Too much. She closed her eyes and stood listening to Tom bumping about upstairs. It was a shame he was going straight off to the festival. Having him around when she talked to Suzie might have made them both a bit more relaxed.

A sudden tapping and fluttering near her face, as if a bird had somehow got into the room and was blundering about, made her rear back, momentarily panic-stricken. Opening her eyes, what she saw was not frantic wings, but fingers, rapid against the glass, and then, suddenly, like a jack-in-the-box, a head popped up and leant through the open window. Shocked, Janice recoiled from the bloated features that wagged, puppet-like, in front of her face; then, collecting herself, she said, 'Joe? Is that really you?'

TWENTY-FOUR

'It's Janice.' Now he'd stopped wiggling his head about, he looked all right – or, anyway, not grotesque – but just abstracted, as if his thoughts might be elsewhere. Then, as if noticing her for the first time, he said, haltingly but quite without surprise, 'Oh, yeah. Right.'

As she leant over the sink towards him, Joe tilted his head and looked past her, as if he expected someone else to be in the room. His hair is still beautiful, she thought, looking at the thick silver curls, and so are his eyes – they're just a bit puffy, that's all. After a moment, he smiled at her and said, 'Can I speak to Dan, please?' It was a flash of the charming middle-class boy he'd once been, with the scrupulous politeness that would be accorded a friend's mother.

Taken aback, and responding in kind, Janice said, 'It's lovely to see you. How about a nice cold drink?'

'Yes, thanks.'

Wherever Suzie had got to, she obviously hadn't yet told Joe about Dan. 'The thing is,' Janice said, once Joe was standing in the kitchen, where he'd refused a chair with the wariness of one who expects a trap but accepted a glass of Coke, 'Dan died a couple of days ago. I'm sorry. I know you were friends.'

The ghost of a frown creased Joe's forehead. Please, please, let him have understood, Janice thought.

'We were going to come and tell you. It's just that it happened very suddenly, so—'

There was a crash from above, followed by the noise of something heavy being bumped down the stairs, and then Tom stuck his head round the door, eyebrows telegraphing a question when he caught sight of Joe. Janice mouthed, 'Dan,' then said, aloud, 'Are you off?'

'Yeah. I'm going to Chipfest,' he told Joe. 'Down in Wiltshire. They've got some really good bands.'

Joe blinked at the flyer Tom handed to him, then returned it. 'That's nice,' he said, his tone polite but indifferent.

When Tom had left the room, dragging his kitbag behind him, Janice laughed encouragingly and said, 'I haven't heard of half of them, either.'

'Is Marie here?'

'Marie? I'm sorry, I don't—'

'Sorry.' Joe shook his head. 'Molly. About the ribbon.'

'Ribbon?'

'Hair ribbon.' A flicker of irritation crossed Joe's face.

What on earth did he want with Molly's hair ribbon, anyway? thought Janice. How did he even know she had one? Had she gone to his house and shown it to him or something? 'I'm not sure where she is at the moment. Wait a sec and I'll see.'

Janice went to the kitchen door and called upstairs. Getting no response, she climbed up to the half landing and called again. 'Molly? Someone here to see you!'

No answer. Janice lingered, both hands on the wooden newel post, staring through the big window at the back garden. She could be a Swingball set at the edge of the lawn, its punctured yellow sphere dangling forlornly from the plastic pole, there was no sign of Molly. Janice heard the van drive off.

Heading back downstairs, she thought, *But you never see girls wearing ribbons in their hair nowadays. Not like when I was Molly's age.*

'She was here,' Joe said. He'd put the glass down on the table and was standing, staring out of the window at the drive.

'What, just now?'

'No, before. When I came up the road.'

'Well then,' said Janice, painfully conscious of the artificial brightness in her voice, 'she can't have gone far. She'll probably be back in a minute.'

Joe made a small noise in his throat, which might have been agreement or protest. Surely I can connect with him, she thought. Surely I can get him to remember me. 'What was that lovely song you wrote about ribbons?' she asked, then quoted, '"*All the colours are running away | Streamers on the wind, one step ahead of me | See, round the corner, behind the tree | You're here, you're not here . . .*" Do you remember?'

For a second, Janice thought she saw something of the old Joe in his eyes – a sudden, impish gleam – and she leant forward in anticipation. Then it was gone, replaced by wariness. 'I don't do that anymore,' he said, flatly.

Janice breathed out again. 'I'm sorry.'

'Yeah, well.' Joe shook his head in dismissal. 'Look, about Dan . . . I'm sorry.'

'Yes, it's a shame. He hadn't been ill, so . . . Well, it's just one of those things.'

'Yes.' Joe lowered his eyes.

'Yes . . .' Janice couldn't think of anything to say. What she really wanted was to remind him of something they'd done together, and for him to remember too, and then it would be something they could share and perhaps even laugh about, but she couldn't think of anything. On impulse, and wishing she could take the words back almost before they were uttered, she said, 'Do you remember me?'

Joe's answering smile was polite but provisional, as though he were nervous of saying something wrong. After a moment, he touched her arm with his fingers so lightly that she could barely feel it and said, 'It's nice to see you again.'

He had excused himself straight after, brushing off her suggestion that she could bring Molly round to see him later in the day. He'd seemed suddenly tired, which Janice supposed you would be if you didn't engage with people much, because you'd get out of practice.

He doesn't have a clue who I am, she thought, standing at the front door and watching him walk away down the road. For a split second she'd thought that he had, but then she'd realised that he was being polite in the way that polite famous people tended to be – even, apparently, when they'd lost their marbles. But, she thought, apart from the business of the hair ribbon, he hadn't seemed mad, despite what everyone had said. And why should he remember her? She hadn't reminded him that she was Dan's sister, had she? That was the problem with being someone like Joe: people knew all about you and assumed that, by some weird reverse osmosis, you would know all about them . . . *But I was part of your life*, she thought. *We shared things. I loved you so much.*

For a moment she considered running after him, but what would she say? Please remember me? I'm here? I exist? *Better to say nothing at all*, she thought, and closed the door.

TWENTY-FIVE

Janice stood in the doorway of Molly's empty bedroom. The child's obviously used to wandering about alone, she thought, and she can't have gone far. It was what she and Dan had done as children, after all. On fine days in the summer holidays, Ma had sent them out with packets of sandwiches and told them not to come back until teatime. Now, it sounded absurdly Enid Blyton-ish, but it was what people had done – and as Suzie obviously thought it was OK for Molly to wander about by herself, who was she to interfere?

In Dan's room, she switched on the radio beside the bed: a play about a woman having a mid-life crisis while running a seaside café. Since when had Dan listened to Radio 4? Moving the bed away from the wall to strip off the sheets, she found more empty bottles. Peering over the edge of the mattress at the lumps of dusty glass, Janice imagined Dan sitting on the edge of the bed, miserable, angry and alone, pouring booze down his neck as the light faded behind him. What had gone wrong?

Having dumped the bundle of dirty bed linen on the landing and clanked two bin liners full of empties down the stairs, Janice turned her attention to the newspapers and magazines left slewed across the floor, which Molly had been so keen to keep. All were Sunday papers – mostly *The Times* or the *Observer*, with a scattering of *Mail* and *Express* – and all from the last two or three years. Why had Dan saved them? Perhaps it was simply that he'd got into the habit of reading them in bed and hadn't bothered to throw them away afterwards. She shook each one – Suzie's letter to her might have got shoved inside the pages – and scanned the headlines for a clue to her brother's lost happiness, but found nothing.

She stacked the colour supplements separately, glancing briefly at the cover images: Barack Obama, Nigella Lawson, Miranda Hart . . . And there was that photo again, the one she'd seen in Molly's bedroom: Phoebe Piper, as she might look aged ten, in a school sweater. Against it, in white type in the bottom left-hand corner, Janice read MISSING and, underneath, *The Families Who Have Never Given Up Hope*. Flicking through the magazine, she came across a double-page spread of children's faces. Most of them were school portraits in black and white: a montage of freckles, grins held for too long, fierce partings, dodgy fringes and pairs of National Health spectacles, all frozen in time. There must be pictures of Suzie like this, thought Janice, imagining her daughter at six, gap-toothed in a wobbly cardboard frame, smiling across the years into the senile face of her adoptive father.

There was a string of captions running across the bottom of the two pages: *Steven Lorimer, last seen aged eight in 1962; Marcus Bewlay, aged five, 1964; Sabrina Mortimer, aged nine, 1966; Duncan Renshaw, aged seven, 1970; Lisa Wynn, aged five, 1967* . . .

They'd all be in their forties or fifties now, and – assuming that any of them were still alive – unidentifiable, thought Janice. None of the names rang a bell, except for Lisa Wynn, although she had no idea why it should be familiar. The photograph was of a round-eyed, snub-nosed child with a worried expression and dark hair in two tightly woven plaits. Turning the page to a drawing unsettlingly like a criminal photofit that attempted to show how Lisa might look now, she discovered that the girl had wandered away from a family picnic in 'a well-known beauty spot' on the Norfolk–Suffolk border, never to be seen again. Janice recognised the place. She'd been there on picnics as a child, and later with Dan and Joe and some of the others.

The journalist who'd spoken to Lisa's seventy-nine-year-old mother, Winifred, at her home in Bury St Edmunds, noted,

> Your eye is drawn to the framed photograph of Lisa, aged five, in the centre of the mantelpiece. Despite the net curtains, the bright, definite colours are slowly fading to a pastel ghostliness . . .
>
> 'She wanted a kitten. Kept on at me about it, but I'd put it off because I didn't want the bother. My other daughter, Barbara, said to me, "But Mum, you weren't to know," but I felt terrible about that. I used to argue with my husband, too, before he was taken [Robert Wynn died in 1995, aged sixty-five]. He'd say, "You've got to accept that Lisa's not coming back," but I couldn't. I felt, if I gave up hope, that I was turning my back on her. I'd feel as though I was abandoning her, and I'll never do that.'

Janice skimmed the rest of the interview.

> 'I don't feel bitter, but when I see the money the Pipers have been given for publicity and private detectives and the rest of it . . .' Winifred shakes her head. 'Obviously, the internet wasn't there in 1967, but I wish we'd had some of that for Lisa . . .
>
> 'I wouldn't want to talk to Melissa Piper, for her sake. Nobody wants to think there's a possibility that their child might still be missing after nearly fifty years, do they? I wouldn't wish that on anybody. It was awful, reading about it. I tried not to, because it brought it all back . . .'

Janice could picture herself and Dan as children, playing hide-and-seek amongst those stands of trees, running across the grass with their arms outstretched, yelling themselves hoarse and rolling down the hill. The picnics in later years with Joe and the others hadn't been that dissimilar, really: plenty of looning around, giggling and silly games, but with wine, dope and acid instead of Ma, sandwiches and travel sweets.

The lower half of the page was taken up by a family photograph from the Christmas before Lisa had vanished. Robert Wynn, flanked by his grinning daughters and wearing a paper hat from a cracker, looked contented. Only Winifred looked uncertain – as if, Janice thought, she sensed the catastrophe to come. Easy to see significance after the event; in all probability, called in from the kitchen, she'd been worrying about the pans left on the stove.

> 'I was told I ought to have another child, but I didn't want one. The way they were saying it was like it would be a replacement, and I didn't want that.'
>
> 'Dad never really talked about it,' says Barbara. 'I think there was a great weight on him, that it was his fault because he hadn't protected his family, and he felt helpless. It was too much, so he just sort of submerged himself in the routine of going to work, washing the car, gardening. Trying to make life normal again, when it couldn't be. That was one of the hardest things for Mum, him doing that, but it was his way of managing.'

Janice closed the magazine, shaking her head at the sadness of it, and the quotidian heroism of Robert Wynn, kept up because there was nothing else he could do.

'You OK?'

She looked up to see Suzie standing in the doorway, at the same time becoming aware once more of the seagull noises and crashing waves from the radio.

'What's that you're listening to?' Despite the dark circles under her eyes Suzie looked, Janice thought, better than she had the previous day.

'A play.' Janice reached over and turned it off. 'I wasn't really paying attention.'

'Thanks for doing this.' Suzie flapped a hand in the direction of the pile of sheets on the landing. 'I'll put them in the wash. Where's Molly?'

'I'm not sure. She was here earlier.'

'Oh?'

'When Joe came. Joe Vincent. He wanted to speak to her.'

'To *Molly*? Why?'

'I'm not entirely sure. Something about a ribbon, I think.'

'A *ribbon*?'

'As I say, I'm not sure – he wasn't very clear. Anyway, she wasn't here. Joe said he'd seen her, though, so she must have been somewhere around.'

'How bizarre.' Suzie shrugged. 'She's probably off somewhere on her bike.'

'I told Joe about Dan. Tom was here, too, getting his things for the festival.'

'What festival?'

'It's called Chipfest. In Wiltshire. He's taken the van.'

'Oh, yeah. He did tell me.' Suzie picked her way between the piles of papers and magazines, pulled out the chair from Dan's desk and sat down, elbows on knees, hands dangly limply between her legs. 'God, look at all this stuff.'

'Molly's OK, is she, riding about by herself?'

Suzie stiffened, and glared at her. 'If you're that concerned, why didn't you keep an eye on her?'

'I'm sorry,' said Janice. 'I probably should have, but I wasn't sure where you were, and . . .' She tailed off, fearful that Suzie would take this, too, as a criticism. 'She did get a bit upset about me clearing up in Dan's room, but she was fine afterwards.'

'No, I'm sorry.' Suzie leant forward once more, rubbing her eyes. 'And I'm sure Molly is fine. I'm just shattered, and I needed to get out of the house for a bit. It's all so . . .' She shook her head in dismay.

'Complicated?' supplied Janice.

'Yeah.' Suzie's expression was rueful, but at least, Janice thought, it was something approaching a smile. 'I mean, holy fuck.'

'You can say that again. In fact—'

The sound of tyres crunching on the gravel at the front of the house made her break off.

'Tom's probably forgotten something.' Suzie got up and went through to the spare room to look out of the window. A moment later she was back, white-faced. 'It's the police.'

TWENTY-SIX

'Oh, thank God for that!' Suzie gave a little bark of relieved laughter. 'I thought you were going to tell us Molly'd been run over or something.'

'Molly?' D.S. Calvert was round-faced and, Janice thought, about Suzie's age, with reddish hair going grey.

'My daughter. She's off riding her bike.'

D.S. Calvert frowned. 'There's a girl's bike leaning against the side of the house.'

'Oh.' Suzie looked nonplussed for a moment, then said, 'Well, she can't have gone far. She's pretty sensible. Sorry, do come in.'

Janice felt a prickle of anxiety, like static electricity, as she followed the others into the kitchen.

When they were seated around the kitchen table, and D.S. Calvert had refused tea, he cleared his throat. 'As I said, I need to ask you a couple of questions about Mr Carthy-Todd.'

'I'll do my best,' said Janice, 'but I hadn't seen him for—'

'Sorry, you are?'

'Janice Keaton. I'm Dan's – Mr Carthy-Todd's – sister.' Janice glanced at Suzie, who was staring down at the table. 'This is Suzie Armitage, my daughter.'

'And it was you who reported the death, Mrs Armitage? You phoned the G.P.?'

'Yes, that's right.'

Now that the rush of relief about Molly was over, Janice thought that Suzie seemed wary, like a cat that senses danger. 'Is there a problem?' she asked.

'Were you here when Mr Carthy-Todd died, Mrs Keaton?'

'No, I came when Suzie phoned to tell me Dan had died. I live in Suffolk.'

'And you, Mrs Armitage?'

'I live here.'

'I see. And you were the one who found him, were you?'

'Yes.'

'Did he have any history of drug use?'

'Phhh . . .' Suzie puffed out her cheeks. 'Not that I know of.'

'Mrs Keaton?'

'I don't think so, but I haven't really seen him in the last few years, so . . .' She tailed off, apologetic. 'I did find quite a lot of bottles in his room, though.'

'When did you last see him?'

'I haven't seen him since we buried my mother.'

'And that was?'

'Two thousand and eight. He didn't want me here,' Janice added, feeling the need to justify herself. 'He didn't even tell me about Suzie.'

D.S. Calvert frowned again. 'Tell you what?'

Janice's vocal cords suddenly felt as though they were paralysed. She'd not spoken about this for so long that saying it to someone official felt next to impossible. She looked at Suzie, who was staring down at the table, and thought, *It has to be me. I have to be the one to say it.*

'That she'd written to me,' Janice said. 'I'm Suzie's – Mrs Armitage's – birth mother. She was adopted, and we met yesterday for the first time – the first time since she was born, I mean.'

'But . . .' Calvert's brow wrinkled in perplexity. 'If Mrs Armitage was staying here . . . ?'

'I didn't know,' said Janice. 'That's what I was trying to explain. I've been away, you see. Travelling. Dan didn't tell me she was here.'

Calvert's expression said all too clearly that Suzie could have told her herself, but he contented himself with, 'I see. You weren't close.' Turning to Suzie, he said, 'And you've lived here how long?'

'About six months.'

'And you haven't seen anything unusual about Mr Carthy-Todd's behaviour? Mood swings, erratic behaviour, increasing dependence on alcohol, anything like that?'

'Not really.' Turning to Janice, Suzie said, 'Honestly, I'd say if I had. But Dan was never that communicative, and . . . well, he was just Dan. The Dan I knew, anyway.'

'Anything on prescription?'

'If he had, he never said. And I know he hadn't seen the G.P. in ages, because that's why there had to be a post-mortem. Dr Bird explained that when he came after Dan died. Why do you want to know?'

'The post-mortem showed a very high level of alcohol in the bloodstream – you mentioned the bottles, Mrs Keaton – and the pathologist says there's a strong possibility he may have taken drugs, although obviously we'll have to wait for the results of the toxicology screen—'

'Hang on,' Suzie cut across him. 'Are you saying you think he committed suicide?'

'We're not sure, Mrs Armitage. As I say, we'll have a better idea when we've seen the test results, but obviously I need to ask you—'

'He didn't leave a note,' said Janice.

'That's not indicative, Mrs Keaton. Many people don't. Well,' D.S. Calvert stood up and, producing a card, said, 'if there's anything else you think of that may be relevant, perhaps you could let me know.'

TWENTY-SEVEN

'I'm glad he didn't ask to see Dan's room,' said Janice, as D.S. Calvert's car went through the gate and into the lane. 'I know he smoked dope, because I could smell it, but I never thought to see if there was any left.'

'He couldn't go into Dan's room without a warrant. And don't tell me that *you* never smoked dope.'

'I wasn't going to. But he might have been taking other things as well, stuff you didn't know about. It's not impossible, is it?'

'I suppose, but I didn't see anything in his room, and it would have been obvious, wouldn't it? By the bed or on the floor or something.'

'I don't know. I had a quick look in his desk, but I didn't see anything either. Do you think we ought to have another look?'

Suzie sighed. 'Yeah, come on.'

'Dan kept his dope up there, by the way.' Suzie indicated a wooden box on the bookshelf. 'Not exactly hard to find.' She lifted a tangle of cables and headphones from the clutter on the top of the desk and looked underneath it. 'There's nothing here,' she said. 'It must have been an accident.'

Janice stood up from rummaging in the wastepaper bin. 'I'd

have said that, too, but now I feel I don't know anymore. Shall we pull the bed right out? I only moved it a bit when I stripped it and got rid of the bottles.'

Several minutes' pushing and shoving yielded nothing more than a wire coat hanger, a few odd coins and a great deal of dust. *Dan's skin*, Janice thought, as they moved the bed back into place. *Soon we'll be hoovering up the last of him.*

'If it'd been something the G.P.'d given him ages ago, and he'd saved them and taken the lot, surely we'd have found the packaging.' Suzie lowered herself on to the carpet and sat, leaning against the desk, thunking one arm down on to a pile of newspapers. 'And they'd know about it at the surgery, wouldn't they? I mean, D.S. Whatsit's going to ask, isn't he?'

'I suppose so – and if it was a prescription thing, they'll know to look for that first, won't they? But you can buy stuff off the internet, and—'

'Dan didn't have a computer.'

'There's Wi-Fi here, though. I know, because I was looking at emails. Have you or Tom got one?'

'Tom has.'

'Then perhaps—'

'Perhaps what?' Suzie's eyes were blazing. 'Perhaps Tom bought drugs for him off the internet, is that what you're saying?'

'No, I'm not saying that. What I'm saying is that Dan might have borrowed Tom's computer and found out how to buy things.'

'He wouldn't even have known how to switch it on.'

'Are you absolutely sure?'

'Yes! You'd know that if you'd ever bothered to keep in touch.'

'Yes,' said Janice quietly. 'I probably would. I'm just trying to understand, that's all.'

'Bit late for that, isn't it?'

'Look . . .' Defeated, Janice levered herself off the bed. 'I know what you must think of me, and—'

'No, you don't,' said Suzie, adding, in a voice Janice hadn't heard before, low and thick, 'How dare you tell me what I think? You don't know anything.'

It took a moment before Janice felt able to speak. 'I know I'm not perfect. I know I've done things wrong. But – and I know that this isn't much of an excuse – Dan wasn't exactly forthcoming to me about how he was feeling.'

'Yeah, well.' Suzie bit off the words in savage staccato. 'You didn't *exactly* volunteer to help him, did you, when your mother lost her marbles? You were too busy running away to *find yourself.*'

Janice felt as if she'd been punched. 'Lost her marbles?'

'My God.' Suzie folded her arms. 'You didn't even know, did you?'

Janice swallowed. 'No.' She heard the word, a tiny, fearful thing, creep out of her mouth.

'He told me,' said Suzie. 'When he first came back – when your dad was still alive – he found all these Post-it notes scattered round the kitchen. On the drawers – *Knives and Forks*, *Tea Towels*, stuff like that. When he asked your mum why she didn't just open the drawers to see what was inside if she couldn't remember, she made a joke of it, but then he realised it wasn't just that, it was because she was forgetting what the things were called. He said she was still pretty much OK then, but after your dad died she started doing things like going down to the village shop and forgetting the way home, so she'd wander off in the wrong direction and he'd have to fetch her back. She'd forget what she was doing halfway through doing it. How to drive, how to work the washing machine, how to cook. Everything.'

'He told me she was getting forgetful,' said Janice. She couldn't actually remember Dan saying any such thing, but even this little bit of knowledge seemed preferable to an admission of total ignorance. At what point, she wondered, had Ma's symptoms ceased to be just a worry, and become her destiny? Had she been aware that she'd slipped her mental moorings and was drifting away into the darkness?

'Bit more than just forgetful,' said Suzie. 'It took a few years, but the way Dan told me, it was a complete wipeout. He said it started with the Post-it notes all over the place, and then she stopped knowing when things were funny, and then it went downhill until she just wasn't *there* anymore. There's a photo here somewhere . . .' She stood up and started scrabbling through the contents of the top drawer of the desk. 'He showed me. Here it is.'

Janice stared at the dog-eared snapshot of Dan and Ma, together at the kitchen table, the remains of a meal in front of them. Dan was smiling tautly at Ma, who looked not so much vacant as actually *vacated*, as though the person behind the eyes had nipped out for five minutes, leaving her body empty. The date *30/10/06* was scrawled on the back. 'I wish he'd told me,' she said bleakly, imagining Ma, blank-eyed and babbling by turns, while Dan, stoic, tried to coax her to eat, wash, get into bed . . . 'I could have done something, or just – I don't know – just *been there* for him.'

'He obviously didn't think so.'

'No, he didn't.' Wanting the photograph out of sight, Janice returned it to the drawer, recalling, as she did so, how, at the funeral, a few of the neighbours had murmured things about 'a blessing in disguise'. The vicar, who'd given the eulogy, had glossed over Ma's last years, leaving an impression of eccentricity rather than mental decay, so that Janice hadn't thought much more about it.

'Can you imagine,' asked Suzie, 'what that must have been like, stuck here, day after day, with someone who didn't even know who he was anymore? And before that she used to tell him that she hated him because he was keeping you away.'

'He wasn't keeping me away.' But even as she said it, Janice thought: *He was, by not telling me*. Yes, she could have asked – or asked more, and more urgently – but he could have told. Why didn't he? Why hadn't he said anything about all this? Was it because men don't, or was there another reason?

'In her mind,' said Suzie, 'or what was left of it, he *was* keeping you away. You weren't there, were you? And there had to be a reason why you weren't, so . . .' She shrugged. 'I suppose you're going to tell me that the real reason was me, aren't you? Because – you know what? – and yes, I do realise that this sounds like a stroppy teenager – I didn't ask to be born.'

'I know, and none of this was your fault. None of it *is* your fault. I'm sorry.' Tears came and, not wanting to provoke further accusations of self-pity – the stuff about running away to find herself had hit a nerve – Janice turned away, towards the window. I wasn't forthcoming to Dan either, she thought. Just as it had simply never occurred to her that she might open up to Dan about the significant events of her adult life, it obviously hadn't occurred to him that he might talk to her.

Blinking, she noticed a house on the other side of the field beyond the garden. Even from this distance it had a new appearance, its edges somehow raw, and she was fairly sure it hadn't been there when she'd come for Ma's funeral six years ago. There'd been a different structure there in her childhood, but she couldn't remember what it had looked like, or even what it had been. House? Bungalow? Nissen hut? All that was left was an indeterminate building-shaped hole in her mind. Was that how Ma had started? Little things like that and, yesterday, not remembering the name of the cat.

Six months earlier, Janice had turned on the radio and, after a couple of intelligible words, ceased to be able to understand anything. Now she remembered the instant spike of horror – something terrible had happened to her brain – and the giddiness of the few seconds' sheer panic before the words had become comprehensible once more, and she realised that the speaker had, momentarily and for illustrative purposes, broken into Welsh.

Ma had been older when it had started, of course, because she'd been in her seventies when Pa had died . . . What if Dan had begun to notice the symptoms in himself, and feared he was going the same way? That would explain what Tom had said, about him getting angry when he'd asked him about stuff from the past – if Dan wasn't actually *able* to remember, but couldn't bring himself to admit it. And, unlike Ma, he'd had no one to look after him.

She could see why he might have felt he couldn't ask Suzie, but he'd had *her*, hadn't he? Except he hadn't known it . . . Turning back to Suzie, who was now rummaging about in the bottom drawer, she asked, 'Did Dan seem to have any of the symptoms himself? Forgetting people's names or anything like that?'

Suzie considered this for a moment. 'Can't think of anything. I mean, no more than anyone else.'

'So he never said he was worried about . . . ?' Janice raised an arm and made a vague circling gesture at her temple. 'Going the same way?'

'Nope.' Suzie shoved the drawer closed. 'And there's no pills or anything in here either.'

'He obviously opened up more to you than he did to me.'

'Yeah, well . . .' Suzie shrugged. 'I was here, wasn't I? And,' she added, 'sometimes it's easier to say things if the person doesn't really know you that well.'

The kindness of her tone, with its implied excuse, jolted Janice into looking at her properly. As their eyes met, she felt the mutual acknowledgement of common ground. The 'complete wipeout' might have been Dan's fate. It might, still, be hers, or Suzie's, or, when it came to their respective turns, Tom's or Molly's.

There it was. Not positive, certainly not promising, but a connection nonetheless.

'I'm going to have a bath,' Suzie announced suddenly. As she left the room, Janice had a sudden wild desire to call her back and give her a hug. Instead she glanced at her watch and saw that it was nearly six. How had it got so late? She gazed at the jumble of cables, headphones and scraps of paper on Dan's desk. She was fairly sure she'd put the black and white photograph of 'Marguerite' on there too, but she must have been mistaken because it was nowhere to be seen.

Anyway, it didn't matter. Having missed lunch Molly must be starving, and she needed to go and find her and make sure she got something to eat.

TWENTY-EIGHT

Molly wasn't in the garden. Janice crossed the lawn, skirting the fallen plastic chair, and opened the door of the shed. She wasn't there either. Janice looked round at the wide shelf beneath the murky window, with its scattering of earth, paint-splashed radio and china mug full of nuts and bolts. Squinting at the faded picture on the side, Janice saw that it was the 1972 'Penthouse Pet', whose pert breasts and blonde hair were now, after forty-plus years, barely visible. She looked round at the cobwebby rows of tins and sprays, at the hoe and spade leaning against the wall beside towers of plastic flowerpots, the sacks of compost and sand. In the middle of it all stood a decrepit Lloyd Loom chair, its legs unravelling – clawed, perhaps, all those years ago by the cat whose name was Charlie, not Freddy – and, underneath, a couple of empty beer cans.

The single cushion on the seat looked far too small and thin for comfort. Janice imagined Dan sitting there, by himself, doing . . . what? Staring into space? Worrying about what was going on inside Ma's head and then, as time went on, worrying more and more about what was going on inside his own?

Janice bent, mechanically, to pick up the empty cans and, twitching up a folded newspaper beside them, left, shutting the door with more force than necessary. Molly'll be back when she's hungry, she thought. All the same, it wouldn't do any harm to wander down the lane a bit. She left the beer cans and newspaper on the kitchen table before heading off in the opposite direction to the village.

How often had she and Dan hurtled up and down this stretch of road on their bikes? Whole summers, fearless and light as air.

Dangerous Dan. That was what Pa had started calling him after he'd been given a lift home by the motorist he'd swerved to avoid, shooting straight over the handlebars and landing, head first, on a pile of hardcore by the side of the road. Dangerous Dan. That was from a poem: something to do with the gold rush, and a 'lady that's known as Lou'. Janice had an idea that it hadn't ended well.

Nine or ten, he must have been, when that happened. Suddenly he'd been 'Dan', and no one, not even Ma, was allowed to call him Danny anymore. Dangerous Dan, afraid of nothing.

Janice could see what Molly had meant: the Rocklins did look impossibly old. Newly decanted from an ambulance in the driveway of their whitewashed cottage, he was in a wheelchair, blanketed and strapped in, while she hovered, looking almost as frail, beside the overgrown hedge.

'Can we help you?' Despite the heat, Mrs Rocklin was wearing a guernsey sweater. Janice noticed immediately that the damage to her face, surrounded by the scores and creases of old age, was less shocking than before, although now she had no way of hiding it, having only slightly more hair remaining than her husband, who, with his tufted pink head, open mouth and closed eyes, looked like an oversized baby bird.

'I'm looking for my granddaughter.' Again, the words felt strange in her mouth, so that for a split second she wondered if she'd pronounced them correctly. 'She's ten.'

'Didn't see anyone on the road,' said the paramedic. 'And this is the only house for quite a way. On foot, was she?'

'Yes,' said Janice. 'At least, I think so.'

'Sorry, can't help you.' He turned back to his patient and began pushing him up the concrete ramp that ran alongside the front steps.

'Are you Audrey and Frank's girl?' Mrs Rocklin's rheumy eyes were shrewd. 'Thought you lived abroad. Come to see your brother, have you?'

It hadn't occurred to Janice that she'd have to explain about Dan. 'Unfortunately, he died.'

'But I saw him last week, and he was perfectly all right,' Mrs Rocklin said, as if that meant that Janice must be lying.

'It was very sudden.'

She'd expected this to be greeted with polite condolence, but Mrs Rocklin put her head on one side and said, still in a tone of disbelief, 'Oh?'

'Yes,' said Janice. 'It was quite a shock for us too.' Surely, she thought, that would prompt the necessary words of commiseration or, at the very least, no further questions, but Mrs Rocklin just carried on staring at her. 'Two days ago,' she added, annoyed that she felt the need to elaborate. 'I got a message.'

'From that girl he lives with?'

So she didn't know, then. 'From my daughter.'

'Your daughter.' Now, the lips pursed in outright suspicion.

Feeling a sudden desire to grab the woman by her narrow shoulders and shake her, Janice said, 'Yes. Her name is Suzie and she is my daughter. The little girl is Molly and she is my granddaughter.'

'And now you've lost her.'

'Not exactly,' said Janice, stung by the implied *as well*. 'I just wondered if you'd seen her come this way, that's all.'

'Like I said, love,' said the paramedic, impatient now, on the front porch, 'if she had, I'd have seen her.'

'Not to worry.' Janice raised a hand in acknowledgement, murmured, 'Lovely to see you again,' and began retracing her steps. What a horrible old bag! Of course she hadn't lost Molly, any more than she'd lost Suzie. In all probability Molly'd gone to the shop, and if Janice had just gone in the other direction she'd have met her coming back. Shying away from the question of why she *hadn't* gone in the other direction – that, unconsciously, her discomfort at the thought of another meeting with Joe, after he'd failed to recognise her, was greater than her desire to find her granddaughter – Janice told herself firmly that Molly would be home by the time she got back.

TWENTY-NINE

'She not back yet?' On Janice's second fruitless circuit of the house Suzie appeared on the landing, drying her wet hair with a towel. 'What's the time, anyway?'

'Twenty-five past six.'

'Humph.' Suzie grimaced. 'Perhaps she's gone to Ellie's.'

'I don't think so.'

'Oh?' Suzie paused, the towel held against the side of her head. 'Why not?'

'I don't know how far away Ellie lives, of course,' said Janice, 'but if Molly hasn't got her bike . . .'

'That's usually how she gets there,' Suzie admitted. 'I suppose Ellie's mum might have come and collected her or something.'

'Wouldn't she have told you though? You know, phoned to say they were coming?'

'She probably thought Molly'd told me.'

'The other thing,' Janice began cautiously, fearful that it would seem like criticism of her daughter's mothering skills, 'is that, well . . . Molly told me that Ellie doesn't want to be her friend anymore.'

'When did she say that?'

'Yesterday. She was pretending it didn't matter, but she was obviously quite hurt.'

155

'I'm sure they'll make up. Kids always do, don't they?'

'Do they?'

'Yeah.' Suzie carried on rubbing her hair with the towel, brisk and dismissive. 'Why don't you go down and pour us a drink? I won't be a minute.'

Janice put the beer cans from Dan's shed in the bin. She was about to stuff the newspaper in after them when it occurred to her that Suzie might be some time. Feeling that she didn't have the energy to trudge back upstairs to get the year-before-last's Booker short-lister, let alone the concentration required to read the thing, she put the paper on the table and then – what the hell – opened a fresh bottle of wine and settled down to read.

Brushing earth off the front page, she saw that it was a copy of the *Eastern Daily Press* from the previous week, and that a quarter of the available space was taken up by a vaguely familiar-looking black and white portrait photograph with the headline *REMAINS MAY BE MISSING GIRL* next to it. *Tests are being carried out in order to establish whether the partial skeleton discovered in woodland near Thetford two weeks ago is that of five-year-old Lisa Wynn, who disappeared from a family picnic nearby in July 1967.*

Of course. She'd seen the photo in the magazine upstairs. *Lisa's father, Robert Wynn, died in 1995. Her mother, eighty-one-year-old Winifred Wynn, who was diagnosed with cancer last year, and her sister, Barbara Lacey, now fifty-seven, were unavailable for comment yesterday.* Hardly surprising, thought Janice. What on earth were they supposed to say? *The whereabouts of the rest of the skeleton is unknown, but searches of the surrounding area are continuing.*

Feeling uneasy, Janice went to stand at the kitchen window and stare down the lane. No sign of Molly. Soon it would start to get dark.

*

Hearing a noise behind her, Janice turned away from the lengthening shadows outside to see Suzie pouring herself a glass of wine.

'She not back yet?'

'No. Do you think you should phone Ellie's mum? I mean, on the off-chance?'

'Yeah. Good idea.' Suzie took a big swig of wine before digging her phone out of her jeans pocket and jabbing it into life. 'Hello, Nicky? It's Molly's mum, Suzie. Is she with you?'

'. . .'

'No, no, it's fine. Just not sure where she is, that's all. I don't suppose Ellie . . . ?'

'. . .'

'No, I see. Not to worry – she'll probably turn up in a minute. Thanks, anyway.'

'. . .'

'Yeah, OK.'

'. . .'

'Yeah, I will. Bye.' Suzie snapped the phone shut, shaking her head. 'Shit.'

Janice moved back to the table, wincing inwardly as she saw Suzie glance at the newspaper – REMAINS MAY BE MISSING GIRL – that lay between them.

'Looks like you were right about them falling out. Ellie's mum said she hadn't been round there for a while. She said Ellie was out at a birthday party – gone to see a film or whatever.'

Something else Molly'd been excluded from by her classmates, thought Janice. 'What about other friends?'

'No other close ones – no one she's talked about, anyway. It'll be dark soon.'

'I'm sure there's a simple explanation.'

'What, though? And a hit-and-run's a simple explanation, isn't it? Supposing she's lying in a ditch somewhere?'

'I'm sure she's fine,' said Janice firmly, picking up the newspaper and stuffing it into the bin liner with the cans and bottles. 'Why don't I go for a drive around and have a look? I can ask in the village if anyone's seen her. You stay put here – I bet she's back before I am.'

THIRTY

The white tail of a rabbit flashed across the Fiat's headlights and disappeared, swallowed up by a hedge grown dense in the dusk. Twilight was softening the edges of the landscape and making the gnarled trees at the edges of the fields look blighted, as if they had survived a nuclear blast. Janice thought of the soberly coloured pamphlets they'd been given at school about how to put a paper bag over your head while the earth became its own tomb. *Take cover and do not go outside again until it is safe to do so.*

Which would be never. Behind the hedge she could make out the forms of round straw bales, dotted at intervals across the stubble. Seeing movement she slowed, but it was only a deer, halting for a moment in the middle of the field before dashing towards the edge of the woods beyond. Soon, she thought, staring through the gloom at the mass of trees, it would be too dark to spot Molly, unless she was actually walking along the road or – in the places where there was one – along the verge. She thought of little Lisa Wynn, dead in the woods near Thetford, mouldering and flyblown, her clothes rotting and her bones pulled apart and dragged away down holes to be gnawed, until only a few were left.

Don't, she told herself. It won't happen to Molly. Molly's fine. In her mind's eye, Janice saw her granddaughter sitting in the passenger seat, asleep, the side of her head resting against the window.

As the car approached the village a dog began to bark, unseen, behind a fence. There were lights in a few of the windows around the green, but only the Lord Nelson was bright, with lamps outside and a string of coloured bulbs looped above its ground-floor windows.

Inside, the pub was smaller than she remembered and the few drinkers clustered around the bar turned to look at her, so that she felt as though she'd walked, brazen and uninvited, into someone's home.

'Evening.' A fleshy, balding man of about her age – presumably the landlord – rested his hands wide apart on the polished wood of his bar. With the beer towel in front of him like an altar cloth he made Janice think, momentarily, of a priest. His small congregation of drinkers – all male and, Janice thought, from the look of them, locals rather than second-homers – gazed at her curiously. 'What can I get you?'

'Nothing, thanks. I'm sorry to disturb you, but I just wondered if anyone had seen my granddaughter. She went out earlier and she's not come back yet . . . It's probably nothing,' she added. 'I mean, she's probably fine – she lives just up the road, at the Old Rectory – but she is only ten and it's getting dark.'

'You mean Suzie's kid?'

'Yes,' said Janice, remembering what Molly had said about Suzie's boyfriend, Mark, working in the pub sometimes and Suzie helping. 'She didn't take her bike, so I don't suppose she's gone far.'

One of the customers said, 'You're Suzie's mum, are you?'

'Yes, I am.' Digging her phone out of her bag, Janice turned back to the landlord. 'If you do see Molly, can you give Suzie a ring? I can give you her number.'

The landlord held up a big pink hand. 'That's OK. We've got Dan's number here.'

Oh, God. They didn't know. Suzie had – presumably – told Mark, but it hadn't got as far as the pub. 'About Dan . . . I'm afraid he's dead. He died. That's why I'm here, really.'

The landlord frowned. 'But I thought you said it was about your granddaughter.'

'No,' said Janice, wishing she hadn't attempted to explain. 'I mean that's why I came back.'

'Back to Repshall, you mean?'

Janice nodded. 'Look, if you do see her, please could you—'

'When did it happen?'

'The day before yesterday.'

'Came on sudden, did it? Heart attack?' This came from an older man, his face like a wizened apple, who spoke in a strong Norfolk accent. It was, Janice realised, the first she'd heard since she'd been back.

'We're not sure. He died in his sleep. He wasn't ill, so they're doing a post-mortem.'

'Ah. They'd need to do that, yes.' The row of heads at the bar nodded judiciously, mouths turned down at the corners. The landlord, however, was staring at her, eyes narrowed and mouth slightly open.

'You're Dan's sister.'

'Yes, that's right. Janice.'

'I'm Simon. Simon Curtis. I don't suppose you remember me – I was at school with Dan.'

Simon Curtis. *The dishy one.* To her horror, Janice felt treacherous blood surge into her face at the memory. 'Yes, of course,' she said, knowing, as she said it, that she was overcompensating for the shock of the bulging, pouched and pink reality of how he looked by her brightness of tone. 'Of course I do!'

'You think you're going to change the world, and you end up doing exactly what your parents did, including going bald . . . Actually, that was just Dad.' There was real regret, Janice thought, in the rueful laugh.

'Your parents didn't run this pub when we were kids, did they?'

'No, they were at the Jolly Miller at Gorleigh Green. They moved here in 1980, and I took over the lease when they retired you look wonderful, though.' There was no pause between the last remark and the previous one, and Janice blinked at him for a moment, wondering if she might unwittingly have tuned out for thirty seconds or so and missed something.

'Thanks. Look, I'd love to stay and chat, but I really do have to find Molly.'

'Of course. Tell you what, you give me your mobile number, just in case. We'll keep an eye out. I'm sorry about Dan. We'd lost touch over the years – he didn't come in much – but . . . Well, I'm sorry. It must have been a shock.'

'Yes.' Janice sighed. 'Although I suppose Dan and I had lost touch too, really. Thanks, Simon.'

The last of the light was fading as Janice left the pub and drove out of the village and along the lanes. Passing a defunct market gardening operation, she slowed to a halt and peered at dilapidated greenhouses and the dark humps of polytunnels where nothing grew except weeds, wondering if Molly was in one of them, immersed in some private game and heedless of the darkness gathering around her. She was about to get the torch out of the Fiat's boot and have a look around, when she became aware of something moving close by – very close, in fact. A scraping, rustling sound, and— No, it couldn't be . . . could it?

Breathing. Very close indeed. Janice switched on the car's inside light and turned round to look at the back seat.

Nothing there. Of course there wasn't. Molly couldn't possibly have hidden there without her knowing, Janice told herself as she twisted round to peer into the rear footwell. She could still hear breathing, though, louder now and laboured.

Unnerved, she lowered the window a fraction and, putting her mouth to the gap, called out, uncertainly, 'Molly?'

Abruptly, the noise stopped.

'Molly?'

No response. Janice imagined some shiny-eyed crepuscular creature slinking away into the empty, ominous darkness. Of course Molly wasn't here. She'd be at home by now, and the mistake or misunderstanding or whatever it was that had caused them both to think she'd gone missing would be resolved, with anger giving way to relief. Trying to ignore the ripple of fear that came with the question of why Suzie hadn't rung to tell her this, Janice scrabbled in her bag for her phone.

'Have you found her?'

'No. I was just about to come back – I thought she'd be home by now.'

'Well, she isn't. It's five to eight, for fuck's sake. This is just . . . Fuck! Where *is* she?'

Her voice was emotional and blurred, the words just starting to bleed into each other. Janice wondered how much more wine Suzie had drunk while she'd been gone. 'We'll find her,' she said. 'Don't worry. I asked them to keep an eye out at the pub.'

'You've been in the *pub*?'

'Only to tell them about Molly. I didn't stop for a drink. Apart from school friends, there's no one else round here whose house she might have gone to, is there?'

'No, nobody.'

'Anyone who might have given her lift somewhere, say, or maybe—'

'No!' Suzie's voice was shrill with panic. Janice imagined what she must be seeing, a series of disconnected sounds and pictures in vivid close-up: Molly's small body, violated and discarded in a ditch; the police officer's fatal knock, a fault line to break the world apart, the eyes at once sympathetic and suspicious. *Mrs Armitage? May we come in? It's about your daughter.* 'She'd never get in anyone's car.' Suzie said. 'I've always told her that, right from when she was little.' Vehement, telling it to herself as much as Janice.

'I didn't mean a stranger Suzie, I meant someone from the village, or—'

'She wouldn't do that either – I've told her – and anyway, she doesn't know anyone from the village. Oh, God, what if—'

'Wait,' said Janice. 'Just a minute. You know I said that Joe came round this afternoon, asking for Molly – what if that's where she is? If he'd wanted to talk to her about something and he'd met her in the road on the way back home . . . ? She might have gone to his house with him, mightn't she? I mean, even if she doesn't know him very well Dan did, so . . . Look, why don't I go there now?'

THIRTY-ONE

Janice looked round the studio. A storm of paint exploded from the walls, dribbling down to such bits of the skirting as she could see and splattering the radiators and the door. Beneath her feet was a mulch of newspapers, drop cloths and spent tubes of paint. Every surface, plus various tin plates and enamel pie dishes that were piled about the place, seemed to have been used as a palette, and thickets of brushes, stiff with paint, poked out of soup tins and coffee jars. The room was at the rear of the house, and a stack of canvases was propped against the French windows, their backs to the room. One of the curtains hung down loosely behind them, half off its rail. Other canvases, face out, were propped against pieces of furniture. None of the paintings were framed, and they seemed, apart from a couple of still lifes of fruit, to be blocky, almost abstract landscapes in shades of blue, green and grey.

'Where is she, Joe?'

When he'd answered the door and, in response to her question, wordlessly ushered her inside, Janice had followed, light with relief. Now he gave her the same polite but uncomprehending look she'd seen when he came up to the house.

She tried again. 'I'm looking for Molly. Did she come to see you?'

Joe frowned at her. 'I'm not sure,' he said warily.

'This afternoon?' said Janice, trying to keep the urgency out of her voice. 'Or this evening? Did she come here?'

'I don't know. I didn't see her.' Joe frowned again, then added, 'Sometimes she comes into the garden.' Janice imagined Joe looking out of a back window and seeing Molly's small form silhouetted against the line of trees and the vast empty sky

At the end of the hallway, which was lined with big tins of house paint – Joe obviously liked the stuff – there was a galley kitchen, a single-storey extension from the original building. Janice saw an old-fashioned cooker with a top-level grill, ill-assorted fitments inexpertly painted in different pastel shades, and a Workmate covered in clotted condiment bottles. Opening the back door, she leant into the darkness and called out, 'Molly? Molly!'

There was no response. When she turned around Joe was standing disconcertingly close behind her, forlorn as a lost dog under the bare bulb hanging from the ceiling. 'Is there an outside light?'

Shaking his head, Joe went to one of the drawers and extracted, with some difficulty, a heavy-duty rubber torch. Janice shone it around the garden, illuminating the remains of a bonfire, an upturned wheelbarrow and a jumble of bamboo canes, before venturing across the ragged grass to the big trees at the bottom of the garden.

Nothing.

'She's not out there.' Janice returned the torch. 'Can I look upstairs?'

Joe stood back, mute, acceding as though he had no choice in the matter. There were only two rooms and a bathroom upstairs. The first, with its single bed, was so spartan that it made Janice think of the way in which a former prisoner might live. Joe paints and gardens and gets along, she thought, but his life is a struggle.

There was something so irredeemably sad about this that for a second, she forgot about Molly. *This is how it ends*, she thought, looking round at the botched carpentry of the homemade bedside table, the stale sheets spilling from the tattered wicker laundry basket and the grey carpet tiles, some with stains. The mundanity of madness: no glamour, no heroism, nothing spectacular. *This is it.*

The sitting room at the back had only a little more furniture – a sofa with cushions scattered across it and an armchair. In the middle of the carpet – dark brown, this time – was a plastic toolbox and the plywood remains of some D.I.Y. project. *Joe keeping himself occupied*, Janice thought. *Things to make and do.*

'There's no one up there.'

Joe was standing in the middle of his studio. He looked guarded, as if afraid of giving something away.

Janice remembered what Suzie had said – *Anyone would find it hard to cope if they had a bunch of weirdos hanging round outside their house all the time* – and smothered the impulse to give him a hug. Instead, she said, 'Will you let me know if you see Molly? I am – I was – Dan's sister, and I'm staying at Dan's house. So if you see her, you can ring me there, on his number.'

Joe nodded.

'Well, I've got to find Molly, so I'd better go.' Still she stood there. Was he keeping something back, or was he just alarmed because she'd burst into his house asking questions? Or was it *she* who wanted something more?

Firmly squashing this last thought, she was turning to go when Joe said, 'I hope it's all right this time.'

'This time? I don't understand. Has someone else disappeared?'

Joe didn't answer, but his eyes strayed in the direction of the nearest painting. Somewhere in the region of two feet by three feet, it depicted a series of gentle green slopes dotted with trees. No flowers, except a single pink blob at the bottom. In the centre of the picture was a couple, lying side by side on the grass, and another figure was seated beside them, playing the guitar. In the bottom right-hand corner was a fourth figure, carrying some sort of bundle, who looked as if he – or possibly she – were about to walk out of the picture altogether.

Glancing around her, Janice saw that all of the landscapes were more or less the same. The figures in the middle of the paintings differed – sometimes sitting or lying on the grass, sometimes dancing or embracing – but the one in the corner was always the same. Trying not to let her impatience show, Janice bent down and looked more closely at the painting Joe had indicated. Apart from the small pink blob, the only spot of warm – or warmish – colour was a streak of pinky white on the bundle being carried by the person in the corner. Two thin streaks, in fact, hanging down . . . Legs? A child, perhaps?

'What? What am I looking at?'

Joe nodded, as if confirming something he'd just said. 'I hope it's all right.'

'I'm sorry, Joe. I'm not sure what you're trying to tell me, but I really do have to go.'

'Where is she? Have you got her?' The ashtray was three-quarters full, and Suzie was making inroads into a second bottle, her mouth stained with dark ridges of red wine.

'She wasn't there.'

'Then where the hell is she? I don't believe this.' Suzie gestured at the uncurtained window. 'It's pitch-black out there.'

'You don't think that Molly could have gone with Tom, do you?'

Suzie shook her head. 'I rang him. He didn't even see her. I rang up Beth and Anja, too – they're a couple of the mums from school – and I got some other numbers, but it's people who live miles away, so how could Molly have got there? Anyway, they're all at this poxy party – the one Molly wasn't invited to.'

'Is there anyone else who might know where she is?'

'Not that I can think of – it's not like she's on Facebook or anything. I rang Mark – he's on his way over.'

'Mark . . . Does he know? About me, I mean.'

'Jesus,' muttered Suzie. 'I *told* him, OK?' She looked as though she was about to say something sarcastic, but after a second her expression changed to one of anxiety. 'Oh, God.' She stared at Janice intently. 'You don't think one of those weirdos who hang around Joe's place took her, do you?'

'I shouldn't think so – they're there for Joe, aren't they?'

'Yes, but they might have done something to her. Anything might have happened.'

'Joe said something about how he hoped it would be all right this time.' Janice dumped her handbag on the table. 'It made me think that another kid might have disappeared.'

'Not while we've been living here. Forget it, Janice – he doesn't know what day it is half the time.'

She's probably right, Janice thought. Suppressing the feeling – too vague to be helpful – that there was something else going on and she didn't understand it, she said, 'Molly wouldn't . . . I mean, her dad – does he live near here? Because she might—'

'Molly's dad fucked off six months after she was born and I haven't seen him since,' snapped Suzie. 'He couldn't deal with parenthood. Some people can't.'

'I'm sorry,' said Janice, inwardly cringing.

'I'm not. He was a waste of space.'

'And you're sure there's no one else who might have given her a lift somewhere?'

'I told you, she'd never get in anyone's car.' Suzie jabbed her cigarette at the ashtray and jumped up to stare out of the window into the darkness, with its infinite terrible possibilities, while Janice racked her brain for an alternative. There must be something obvious that they hadn't thought of, some safe and harmless explanation, but—

'She could be anywhere by now!' Suzie turned to face her. 'Why the fuck didn't you keep an eye on her?'

Pulling herself together, Janice said, as calmly as she could, 'You didn't ask me to, and you didn't seem all that bothered when I pointed out that she'd gone, either. And,' she added, seeing that Suzie was about to speak, 'as it's gone nine, I think we should call the police.'

THIRTY-TWO

Janice turned on her laptop and sat down on the bed. In all likelihood Molly would return before the police arrived, and even if she didn't, the vast majority of missing children were found within forty-eight hours . . . Here, Suzie's response to this point – 'Yes, and the majority of children who aren't found are killed within forty-eight hours' – popped back into her head and refused to budge.

Taking charge of the situation had stopped Suzie throwing out any more accusations, but Janice sensed this was likely to be temporary and, in order to avoid pointless arguments, had absented herself as soon as Suzie's boyfriend, Mark, had arrived. She'd gone upstairs and opened the door of Molly's room, half hoping to see her curled up underneath the covers, having somehow gone unnoticed before and slept, oblivious, through all the fuss.

She'd shaken out the duvet, which was bunched up, as Molly had left it, and smoothed it across the bed. The felt-tip marks she'd noticed earlier were on the pillows too, and the bottom sheet, and she'd wondered when the linen had last been changed. Then she'd gone to stare at the things in her own room instead.

Mark Bell had seemed OK, she thought. Perhaps ten years older than Suzie, and friendly enough, although something about him suggested a failed actor. Not the clothes – khaki chinos and a check shirt – but perhaps the mane of bronzy (and presumably touched-up) hair and the way he'd looked her in the eye with what she thought of as a salesman's intensity. Straight R.P. rather than actually posh, his accent had sounded acquired, although, as with the failed-actor business, she couldn't have said precisely why. Worry, she thought now, was making her suspicious when there was no cause for it.

When Suzie, tearful, had rushed into his arms, he'd aimed a look over her head at Janice that she'd interpreted as 'Suzie is being an overanxious mum' and 'Don't worry, I'll take over from here.' Obviously meant to be reassuring, it made her feel simultaneously relieved and angry, and after introducing herself she'd retreated.

Janice turned on her computer. Molly was going to be fine, she told herself. She had to be – not least because the thought of losing her granddaughter when she'd only just found her was unbearable. But it would not need to be borne, because it *wasn't going to happen*. They'd done everything they could, and the police had told them to stay put until they arrived, and what she needed to do now was to occupy her mind until they did. That business about Joe thinking Molly was called Marie and talking about hair ribbons, for instance . . . Janice checked her emails – nothing new except spam – and then, for want of anything better to do, she looked up Joe's Wikipedia entry:

English musician and composer Joseph Alan 'Joe' Vincent (2nd March 1946) was a founder member of the band Weather Ship Tango Delta. One of the most influential musicians in British pop history, he was the Weather Ship's lead guitarist during the years 1966 to 1969, writing most of the material. His influence continued to manifest itself years after he officially left the band in 1970 amidst speculation about his mental health.

I don't do that anymore. Remembering Joe's words and the finality of his tone, Janice realised that she'd seen nothing in his house that was a link to his musical past, or to any music – not even a radio. But then, what had she expected? A rock 'n' roll Miss Havisham, mouldering in a house full of cobwebby guitars and dusty L.P.s?

There was a lot more on Wikipedia about innovative guitar work and quintessentially English psychedelia and a unique talent destroyed by heavy drug use, which Janice skipped over, and then a biographical section.

Born in Bury St Edmunds, Suffolk, Vincent was the elder of two children. His father, Charles Joseph Vincent, was a solicitor. His younger sister, Marie Elizabeth Vincent (b.1948), died aged seven after being hit by a car. Her death is thought to have had a profound effect on Vincent, who was nine years old at the time.

Various lyrics from Joe's songs, especially the more whimsical, nursery-rhymey stuff, were advanced to support this theory, including, 'All the colours are running away / Streamers on the wind, one step ahead of me / See, round the corner, behind the tree / You're here, you're not here . . .' from 'Ribbons in the Wind'. There was a photo of the original cover of *Song of Sixpence*, showing a blurred photograph of a just-glimpsed young girl running around a corner, long hair and ribbons streaming out behind her.

There, and gone. Janice pictured Molly standing in the middle of Dan's room with the length of pink ribbon dangling forlornly from her hair. Was Joe's grasp of time really so hazy that he'd got confused and thought that Molly was his long-dead sister, or was there something else going on?

Janice couldn't remember Marie ever being mentioned, either

by Joe or anyone else. She supposed that was because no one ever talked about the past, or where they came from – those things weren't cool: the present was all that mattered.

Those paintings, though . . . If the bundle being carried by the person in the corner was Marie after her accident, that would make sense, although she hadn't spotted any vehicles or roads in the paintings and the Wikipedia entry said Marie had died after being hit by a car. If she'd been carried to a grass verge or there'd been a field nearby, that would make sense too – although the other people in the landscapes weren't taking any notice of her, or of the person carrying her, and he or she was walking *away* from them, not towards them.

Janice carried on reading until she came to a bit about how 'Look at Yourself' – the song she'd heard for the first time the day before – . . . *was inspired by his girlfriend of the time, model Janice Carthy-Todd*. Despite herself, she couldn't help feeling a thrill of pleasure at seeing herself officially linked with Joe. There, after all, was proof – her name in black and white on the screen – showing that she had had a small part in the story, at least, even though she'd known nothing about the song. Looking up the lyrics, she found:

> Your eyes, your nose, your mouth
> Girl in the mirror
> Out of place
> Beside her face
> She looks at me and says, 'Who's there?'
> You spoon-feed my thoughts
> I've heard reports
> But I don't mind

Look at the flies, baby
Look at the flies
See them multiply

And the mushrooms growing up the stairs
Spores in the air
More and more
More and more

Take me away
Take me away

Not quite so thrilling, after all. Janice couldn't imagine what any of it had to do with her. It wasn't exactly flattering to think that you'd inspired a song about flies and mushrooms – not that she had any recollection of an incident or a conversation involving either – and the spoon-feeding thing suggested that she was trying to control him in some way, which couldn't have been further from the truth. Like any hippie girlfriend, she'd done what was expected of her – kept quiet, rolled the joints and provided sex on tap . . . not that that had been any hardship with Joe, of course. It was obviously rubbish, part of the whole rock 'n' roll mythology thing, the obsessive picking-over and analysing, making connections on the merest shreds of evidence – exactly what she was doing with Joe's paintings, come to think of it. And in any case, you could hardly call one album cover and a couple of photo shoots for a friend who designed dresses 'being a model'. She'd certainly never referred to herself as one anyway, so God knows where that came from, and—

The sound of a car crunching across the gravel drive below made her jump up, snapping the lid of her laptop shut on the past.

THIRTY-THREE

'. . . vast majority of missing people *are* found within forty-eight hours of their disappearance. With children, it's usually much sooner.'

The air in the room crackled with anxiety. Mark Bell had his arm around Suzie. Her eyes looked raw, and the skin beneath them was shiny, troughed with tears. D.S. Calvert was back, this time with P.C. Wright, who was female, considerably younger and looked as though she were learning the ropes. The pair of them were sitting opposite Suzie and Mark at the kitchen table. Janice was relieved to see that someone – Mark, she guessed – had removed the wine bottles and glasses, and hoped that it had been done before the officers had arrived.

After D.S. Calvert had introduced her to P.C. Wright she made tea, glad to be able to concentrate on something peripheral. It was important that she make a conscious effort to remain calm, she told herself – getting into a state wasn't going to help anyone – but her chest felt constricted and her throat tight, so that it was difficult to breathe.

Suzie plunged into a tangled explanation about Molly's disappearance and Dan's death and the circumstances of their arrival in Norfolk and Tom going off to the festival, with Mark nodding in confirmation. She was still just on the right side of slurring, and

Janice hoped that the officers would assume that the escalating vehemence and repetition in the telling were down to her being upset and not to the empty Shiraz bottles by the bin.

P.C. Wright, with her big hazel eyes and air of trim competence, made Janice think of new prefects at school, given their first taste of responsibility and taking it very seriously. She looked barely out of school herself, although she was, presumably, in her twenties. Shaking her head at the thought that it was almost fifty (fifty!) years since *she* had been at school, Janice busied herself in locating the Duchy Originals biscuits she'd bought at the supermarket and fanning them out on a plate.

'Those look good.' Mark gave her an encouraging smile as she put them on the table. 'Thanks.'

Suzie interrupted her narrative long enough to mutter, 'For God's sake,' before pushing the plate in the direction of the officers. Calvert took a biscuit but Wright didn't, although Janice thought she looked as if she wanted to. She wished Suzie would have one – blotting paper for the wine, and carbohydrates were supposed to be comforting, weren't they?

She poured sugar into a bowl and added it to the mugs on the tray. It seemed such a little thing to do, so unimportant, and she wished she could do something more. Had Ma and Pa felt this almost physical ache, ever, about her and Dan? That was something else she'd never thought about from their point of view.

'. . . were you, Mrs Keaton?' D.S. Calvert was talking to her.

Janice turned, tray in hand. 'I'm sorry, I didn't quite . . . ?'

'I understand you were the last person to see Molly, is that correct? I mean,' he added hastily, 'to see her *here*. In this house.'

'Yes. Molly came into the kitchen while I was making sandwiches,' Janice said, distributing mugs.

'When I was here earlier to talk about Mr Carthy-Todd, I got the impression that neither of you were quite sure where she was,' said D.S. Calvert. 'But it was you –' he made a sort of abbreviated pointing gesture towards Janice – 'who was supposed to be looking after her, was it?'

There was a clear implication here, and Janice, who could feel the heat of a blush suffusing her face, didn't know what to say. It wasn't as if she'd actually been asked to look after Molly – Suzie had simply disappeared and left her to it. Taking the chair at the end of the table, she began, 'Well . . . yes, I was, but . . . she wasn't actually *missing* missing at that point, if you see what I mean.'

'You mean you weren't worried about her?'

'Yes. Well, I was a bit worried, but not . . .' Oh, God. Why didn't Suzie *say* something? Janice glanced at her daughter, who, hunched up against Mark's chest, was staring down at the table, as silent and unresponsive after her torrent of words as if someone had switched her off with a button.

'But you *were* babysitting at the time she went off?'

'I wouldn't say babysitting exactly, but I was here.'

'So it was just the two of you in the house, was it?'

'Yes. Molly'd left me a note to say that Suzie had gone to see Mark and she was taking herself off to bed, and—'

'Sorry.' P.C. Wright held up the neat silver ballpoint that she'd had poised over her notebook. 'You're saying Molly left a note? When was this?'

'Yesterday evening.'

D.S. Calvert looked puzzled for a moment, and then his brow cleared. 'Oh, yes, of course, you explained before. You'd just arrived, hadn't you?'

'Yes. I'm staying here.'

Before she could add anything else, P.C. Wright said, 'D.S. Calvert has explained the situation, Mrs Keaton – or some of it, at least.'

The situation that Suzie had left her daughter with someone who was, in effect, a complete stranger, thought Janice grimly.

D.S. Calvert gave P.C. Wright an almost imperceptible nod and she carried on. 'Molly's your granddaughter, is that right?'

'Yes.'

'And had you met *her* before you arrived here?'

'No.'

'You didn't know about her at all?'

'No, nothing.'

'Is this correct, Mrs Armitage?'

Mark, who had been staring at Janice with great interest, squeezed Suzie's shoulder and, as if operated by his touch, she lifted her head, blinked as though a bright light had been shone in her face, and said, 'Yes.'

After a moment – Suzie was now looking at the table again – Janice said, 'I'm afraid we're still getting used to each other. It's bound to be a little strange, after so many years apart.'

P.C. Wright, ballpoint raised, gazed at her shrewdly. 'Do you think that might be something to do with why Molly ran away?'

'I don't know. I suppose it's possible. I mean, she'd only just found out, but she didn't seem too concerned.'

'You mean she hadn't known before? Had you not told her about Mrs Keaton, Mrs Armitage?'

'No. I . . .' Suzie stopped, shaking her head. She had a look of bored exasperation that made Janice think of someone trying to explain something to a child who kept asking why. 'It was complicated – but it doesn't matter now, does it? We just need to get her back.'

'I see,' said P.C. Wright neutrally. 'And what about Mr Carthy-Todd? Could he have had something to do with her running away?'

'How? He's dead.'

'Before that.'

The air in the room seemed to stiffen, and Janice had a sudden wild fear that D.S. Calvert was about to announce that there'd been complaints about Dan hanging round playgrounds and schools. Rubbish, she told herself – anything like that would have been mentioned during the policeman's first visit. 'Absolutely not,' she said firmly.

'But you've told us you weren't here,' said P.C. Wright. 'Mrs Armitage?'

'No,' said Suzie. 'Molly's pretty savvy about all that stuff. She'd have told me.'

'Are you sure about that?'

'Yes,' snapped Suzie. 'Positive.'

D.S. Calvert and P.C. Wright exchanged glances and Janice read headlines in their eyes: *SUICIDE, PAEDOPHILE RING, GIRL TAKEN.* Had the objects of Dan's desire got younger as he'd got older? His wife, Marietta, had been the same sort of age as he was, but maybe, somewhere down the line . . . Oh, God. No, Janice told herself. Not my brother. It isn't possible.

'. . . about Molly's father?' P.C. Wright was speaking again. 'Is he here at all?'

'No. It didn't work out.' The waste of space who'd fucked off six months after his daughter was born, thought Janice, remembering what Suzie had told her. 'We're not in contact with him anymore.'

'So he's not in contact with Molly?'

'No. She was a baby when he left. I don't suppose she even remembers him.'

'He doesn't pay maintenance?'

'No. Even if he wanted to,' this was accompanied by a brief and wholly disbelieving lift of the chin, 'he doesn't know where we are.'

'Is that deliberate? Was his behaviour ever a cause for concern?'

Suzie shook her head. 'As I say, we lost touch.'

'And you're sure he's not in touch with Molly? You might not know about it, necessarily – if it's via social media. Does she have a Facebook account?'

'She's too young for all that – anyway, she doesn't have a computer.'

'Plenty of under-thirteens do have Facebook pages, though. Are you on the internet?'

'Yes. Tom's got a computer.'

'So it's not impossible. We'll check. What's the father's name?'

'It's got nothing to do with him!' Suzie's voice was loud, ragged. 'This is just wasting time – if you're not going to help—'

'Mrs Armitage –' P.C. Wright's voice was calm and slightly lower than before, and Janice had a mental snapshot of her in an airy classroom, role-playing disasters while a supervisor wrote notes on a clipboard – 'of course we're going to help. That's why we're here. We just have to get a complete picture, that's all.' P.C. Wright's pen hovered over her notebook.

Suzie gave a shuddering sigh. 'His name's Adam. Adam Northwood.'

'Last known address?'

'I don't know. He was staying with a friend when he left us – just, you know, on the sofa – but after that . . .' Suzie shrugged. 'It was almost ten years ago – he could be anywhere.'

'So you never pursued him for maintenance?'

'No!' Suzie's voice had risen an exasperated semitone. 'There was no point. He didn't have a job, just casual work.'

'So you didn't quarrel at all?'

'No. It's like I said – it just didn't work out.' She made it sound, thought Janice, as though the relationship had had an existence entirely independent from the two of them, as though she, Suzie, had had no control over it. But then, it had happened to her too, hadn't it, with Jeff? 'I don't know what else you want me to say,' Suzie finished, her voice shredded with the effort of holding back tears. 'It's nothing to do with him.'

'We have to ask.' Now P.C. Wright's tone was deliberately – actually rather pointedly, Janice thought – non-judgemental.

'It's OK,' said Mark soothingly, and squeezed Suzie's shoulder again. 'They've got to do their job, love.'

P.C. Wright looked as though she were about to say something else, but Calvert got in first. 'So – Mrs Keaton – what time was it when Molly came into the kitchen?'

'About one fifteen. She didn't want any lunch. She said she'd come to apologise for shouting.'

'Oh?'

'It was earlier. I'd been tidying up in Dan's room, putting some stuff in bin liners, and Molly got agitated because she didn't want me to throw things away. I was only getting rid of some old newspapers and magazines, but I think she thought I was going to get rid of everything. She seemed quite upset. Unsettled. Obviously I don't know her very well, not yet, but it wasn't surprising – it was a lot for her to take in.'

'So when did you realise she was missing?'

'Well, I suppose . . . Tom said he was picking a friend up at three and it would take twenty minutes to get there, and Joe was still here when he left, so—'

'Joe?'

'Joe Vincent,' said Suzie. 'He lives down the road.'

D.S. Calvert's eyes widened with interest. 'I've heard about him. He was with a band in the sixties, wasn't he? Was he friendly with Mr Carthy-Todd?'

Here we go, thought Janice.

'Weather Ship Tango Delta,' said Suzie. 'And yes, Dan knew him. He used to help him in the garden. Joe's lived here for years. He attracts a lot of weirdos, people who come up here looking for him. Molly knows not to talk to them, but one of them might have . . .' Suzie put out her hands as if to ward off her unspoken thought. 'I don't know, but they're obsessive, you know? There's one guy who just never goes away; he lives in the woods or something. And it's like Janice says, Joe was round here this afternoon, asking to talk to Molly.'

'Why was that?' Calvert looked at Janice.

'To be honest, I'm not entirely sure.' For a split second she thought of mentioning the ribbon, but then she remembered how bewildered Joe had looked. In any case, what did that have to do with anything?

'We'll make enquiries,' said Calvert. 'What time did you realise she was missing?'

'Well, about three fifteen, I suppose. I looked round the door of her room and she wasn't there, but I assumed that she must be in the garden or out on her bike.'

'Did you look?'

'No, not until later.'

'I arrived at,' D.S. Calvert consulted his notebook, 'approximately four o'clock, and the bike was here.'

'Yes,' said Janice, 'but as I explained, it wasn't until later that we became concerned.'

'How much later?'

'I suppose it must have been around half past five.'

'Almost two hours later.'

'Yes, but . . .' Janice looked at Suzie for help. What the hell was the matter with her? OK, she was upset, of course she was, and she probably felt guilty about her earlier complacency and was also – very probably – a bit pissed, but why the hell didn't she *say* something? Both officers had clearly interpreted her – their – lack of immediate panic as selfish unconcern, so it was pointless trying to justify it. 'I went up the lane to ask the neighbours, and I've been driving round looking for her.'

'So – before that – Mrs Armitage came back after you'd looked into Molly's room and found she wasn't there, did she?'

'Yes.'

'How long after?'

'I'm not sure. Half an hour, something like that.'

Turning to Mark, Calvert said, 'Were you with her?' The police officer's tone was bland, the expression in his eyes anything but. The mother's boyfriend, thought Janice. Of course they'd suspect him. The closet pervert, the clever paedo who targeted the lonely single mum with the prepubescent daughter, the straight-up ordinary guy who gave in to a sudden and inexplicable urge . . . Mark certainly didn't look like any of those, but then, who did? Instinct was telling her that he'd done nothing wrong, but instinct wasn't always right, and in this situation statistics were more important, and more telling, than mere hunches. Besides, she didn't know Mark any more than D.S. Calvert and P.C. Wright did. How well did Suzie know him? she wondered. But then, how well had *she* known her own brother?

It hadn't occurred to Janice to ask Suzie how she'd got home, although surely she'd have heard if a car had pulled up on the gravel, wouldn't she? She looked at Mark, who seemed to be sitting very still – not that he'd been moving about much before, but now, she saw, he had a watchfulness about him that was almost catlike in its intensity. 'Yes,' he said. 'I gave her a lift. I dropped her off in the lane.'

That explained not hearing the car, thought Janice.

'And you didn't come into the house?'

'No.'

'And you didn't see Molly?'

Mark shook his head with a slight smile, as if he couldn't believe what he was being asked. 'I'd have told Suzie if I had.'

'And you returned when?'

'Just before you arrived. Suzie called me at . . .' Mark took his mobile phone out of his pocket and pressed a button on the screen, 'eight minutes to nine, and I came over. I was at home.'

'Where do you live?'

'Just outside Sparthorpe. About ten minutes' drive.'

'OK. You can give the details to P.C. Wright. I'm going to call this in.' After a bit more about the vast majority of missing children being found quickly and the police taking it very seriously, during which Suzie put her head in her hands, D.S. Calvert went outside to the police car.

THIRTY-FOUR

Mark reeled off an address for P.C. Wright, who took it down in her neat, round handwriting.

'How long have you known Mrs Armitage?'

Mark thought for a moment. 'A couple of months, something like that.'

'June,' said Suzie, suddenly reanimated. 'It was the Summer Solstice Fair – my first time behind the bar at the Nelson, remember?' Turning to P.C. Wright, she said, 'Mark wouldn't do anything to Molly, if that's what you're thinking. He'd never hurt her.' Janice couldn't help feeling stung that Suzie hadn't leapt to *her* defence – but then, why should she? Suzie hardly knew her – not that that had stopped her assuming that she, Janice, would look after Molly without so much as a by-your-leave, of course . . . 'This really is a waste of time,' Suzie continued. 'You should be out looking for her, not sitting here going on about Molly's dad and then accusing Mark when there are all those weirdos hanging round Joe's place, and—'

'Nobody's being accused, Mrs Armitage.' P.C. Wright's voice went back into calm mode. 'My colleague is calling it in now, and we'll do everything we can. I'll need to take a few details about Molly, to help us. What's her full name?'

Suzie looked surprised. 'Molly Armitage.'

'No middle name?'

'No, just Molly.'

'How tall was she?'

Suzie opened her mouth and then closed it again, uncertain. 'She came up to about here on me.' She indicated her shoulder.

'About four foot five,' said Mark. P.C. Wright looked at him blankly. 'Oh . . . One point three metres, something like that?'

P.C. Wright wrote this down without acknowledging it. 'Weight?'

As neither Suzie nor Mark looked as if they were about to speak, Janice said, 'About five stone, I should think. Sorry, I'm not very good at metric.'

'Thirty kilograms?' offered Mark. 'Thirty-two? About that, anyway.'

'Hair?'

'Fair,' said Suzie. 'Blonde. And she's got hazel eyes.'

'Distinguishing marks?'

Suzie shook her head, and Janice saw that her eyes were squeezed shut and her mouth twisted with the effort of not crying.

'Freckles,' she volunteered. 'Just a few, on her nose.'

P.C. Wright didn't write this down. 'Braces?'

'I'm sorry?'

'Braces. On her teeth.'

'Oh. Sorry. No.'

'What was she wearing?'

'Denim shorts, green T-shirt . . .'

'Anything on it?'

'No, just plain.'

'Shoes?'

'Trainers, I think.'

'Pink,' said Suzie in a choking voice. She wiped her nose with her knuckle and tried again. 'Pink and white. And her denim jacket – that was in the hall, and now it's gone. It's the only thing that's missing.'

'Right. Now, if you could let us have a recent photo, that would be a great help.'

Suzie looked entirely blank, and Janice wondered if, after all, Molly hadn't been exaggerating when she'd talked about her mum not having any photographs. The Phoebe Piper picture upstairs would do as well as any, she thought, given the resemblance, but she could hardly suggest that – the two police officers must think the set-up was quite strange enough as it was.

'My phone doesn't take pictures,' said Suzie finally. 'It's too cheap. Mark's got a few, though, haven't you?'

Mark looked even more wary at this – as well he might, thought Janice. In this situation, any adult male looking through a camera at a child not his own must be instantly suspect. 'Only the ones I took in the garden, and they're mostly of you,' he said.

He fiddled with his phone for a moment, one-handed, then pushed it across the table, angling it so that P.C. Wright could see. Janice leant forward and saw, sideways on, a photo of Molly sitting on the grass next to Suzie, both of them in T-shirts and shorts. Mark swiped away this and several similar images with his thumb, until he came to a picture of Molly by herself, wearing the same clothes and straddling her bicycle, hands on the handlebars and leaning forward, grinning.

P.C. Wright took the phone between her thumb and finger and tilted it, frowning. 'You don't have a head shot? A school photograph, perhaps?'

'Not a recent one. It's like I said – we only moved here six months ago, and a lot of our stuff's still in London, in someone's garage.'

Of course, thought Janice. *That* was the explanation for what Molly'd said about not having any baby pictures. She'd just reached the age when she'd started to be interested in such things, and Suzie had left them in storage with a load of other stuff, and not yet got round to retrieving them, which – given that she had no transport of her own – was hardly surprising.

'It'd better be this one, then.' P.C. Wright slid the phone back across the table to Mark.

'Where do I send it?'

'My colleague will be able to tell you. Now, are you absolutely sure that you've looked everywhere – that there's nowhere else in the house that Molly could be?'

'No,' said Suzie. 'I *told* you, I've looked everywhere.'

Janice thought for a moment. 'I suppose there's the loft.'

'Oh, what?' Suzie's face was contorted, furious. 'Molly went up there and then pulled up the ladder and closed the hatch behind her? How was she supposed to manage that, for Christ's sake?'

'Thank you.' P.C. Wright spoke to Janice. 'We'll—'

'How was she supposed to do that? I mean, *how*?'

'Please, Mrs Armitage,' the policewoman tilted her hands, palms down, in a placatory gesture. 'This isn't helping.'

'No,' said Suzie, shoving her chair back so that Mark, his arm still round her shoulders, was caught off balance, 'and sitting here talking bollocks isn't helping either.'

'Which is why,' P.C. Wright rose from her chair, 'we're going to go upstairs now, to have a look. If you could stay here, please –' again the calming-down hands – 'I'm sure Mrs Keaton can show me to the loft.'

'I can't see how Molly could have got up here,' said Janice, casting around for the pole to open the catch on the trapdoor. 'Or, even if she did, how she could have shut it after herself, because they never lock from the inside, do they?'

P.C. Wright, her feet firmly planted, stood so still in the middle of the rug on the landing that she made Janice feel as though she were lurching about like a drunk as she looked round corners and opened doors. 'Best to be on the safe side.'

Safe side of what? Janice wondered, wishing she'd never suggested it. Some regulation or other, presumably. She ran the pole to earth beside the wardrobe in Tom's room, and succeeded, after a couple of minutes' fiddling about trying to position the hook correctly, in opening the latch and lowering the extending ladder.

Standing looking up the rungs and into the square of blackness, she remembered reading about a schoolgirl, Tina – no, Tia – something, a couple of years ago, whose body was found in the loft. That had been the mother's – or perhaps grandmother's – partner, she thought, remembering the crop-haired, rat-like face. Was P.C. Wright thinking of it too?

Janice felt a shiver of apprehension as, reaching the top of the ladder, she ascended, reluctantly, into a darkness that seemed as close and thick as if someone had put a cloth bag over her head. Some instinctive, purely physical memory made her left hand grope for the light switch. It was, as her body had remembered, fixed low down on one of the wooden uprights, and, flicking it on, she discovered she was standing on a small section of hardboard, surrounded by a sea of joists and the dense grey candyfloss of loft insulation. The roof sloped down on either side, in front and behind, the bare light bulb dangling in the centre, a couple of feet from her head. Behind it, she could see the grey rectangle of the cold-water tank, standing on its own platform, and a few other hardboard islands – a pile of suitcases, cardboard boxes and, under a sheet of dusty polythene, a white basketwork crib on a stand. Dan's and hers in turn, presumably, kept in reserve for legitimate grandchildren who'd never arrived.

Nothing else. P.C. Wright scrambled up beside her and started forward.

'Be careful—' Janice put a hand out to stop her. 'It's not safe – you might go through.'

'I can manage.' The police officer twitched her arm away, irritated, but she moved more carefully, treading from joist to joist with hesitant precision.

Janice waited, listening to the sound of the wind whooshing in the eaves, trying not to be impatient. There was a protocol that must be followed, and in any case Molly would be back, of course she would. They'd be able to laugh about it – their first crisis as a family.

Was that a rolled-up tent she could see? Dun-coloured canvas, with something metal sticking out of the end. She couldn't remember going camping as a child, but perhaps they had. She'd have to ask Dan, she thought idly.

She couldn't ask Dan – about that or any of the other things she didn't know. The remembered recognition of his death was as sharp and heavy as a falling axe.

Momentarily disorientated after descending the ladder, Janice had a flash of memory: being ten and coming downstairs after a fortnight in her room with chickenpox. It was summer, and the house had seemed larger and brighter, its atmosphere subtly altered. When she'd asked Ma what had happened, Ma had looked at her curiously and said that everything was just the same, but it hadn't been. What was it that had happened? She couldn't now remember – had she ever actually found out?

She was glad she'd made Molly's bed, but seeing the girl's room through P.C. Wright's eyes made it seem even more impersonal and shabby than before, with its battered plywood furniture and lack of possessions. The police officer evidently thought so too, because she said, 'Are you quite sure there's nothing missing?'

'Not that I can see, but then I wouldn't really know,' said Janice, feeling hopelessly inadequate.

'But you've been in here?'

'Yes, a couple of times.'

'Well, is there anything that you remember seeing that you can't see now? Have a look.' P.C. Wright gestured at the desk drawers.

Janice opened them all in turn, but the contents – a jumble of pens and candy-coloured trinkets – meant nothing to her, and neither did the few clothes in the cupboard. As soon as Molly was back, she'd take her shopping in Norwich. They could get new furniture too, and maybe even—

'Anything?' P.C. Wright's voice cut across her thoughts.

'As I said, I don't really know. The only thing I can't see is her scrapbook.'

'Scrapbook?'

'For sticking things in. Some sort of project, I think, for school.'

'I suppose that might be relevant.' P.C. Wright didn't sound as if she thought it was.

'It might be downstairs,' said Janice. 'She was carrying it around with her this morning.'

'Anything else?'

'I don't think so. As I said, I can't be sure.'

'What about that?' P.C. Wright was staring at the age-progressed photograph of Phoebe Piper. 'There's quite a similarity, isn't there? I didn't realise when we saw that photo on Mr Bell's phone.'

'Coincidence,' said Janice hastily. 'They happen to look alike – or rather, Molly happens to look like that made-up photograph.'

'Did Molly think so? Was it the reason for putting up the picture?'

'I don't really know . . .' P.C. Wright clearly wanted something more, but Janice faltered, unsure what to say next. 'I thought it might be something she cared about particularly because she looks a bit like Phoebe – or how people think Phoebe looks, anyway.'

P.C. Wright's eyes narrowed imperceptibly. 'Molly's ten, isn't she?'

'Yes, she is.'

Janice wasn't sure exactly what P.C. Wright was getting at, but she was sure it wasn't good. The feeling increased when the police officer asked to look at Dan's room, and the moment she opened the door she realised that the copy of the *Observer* magazine she'd been reading, with the photograph of Phoebe on the front – the same image that was on Molly's wall – was lying on his bed.

'That was in the wardrobe,' said Janice hastily. 'There were lots of them – look . . .' She indicated the stacks of newspapers and magazines. 'I was taking a break from tidying and flicking through a couple of them, that's all. It's just a coincidence that that was the subject matter – or perhaps it was an unconscious thing and I picked it because I'd seen the photo in Molly's room.' Shut up, she told herself. You're making it worse. As she thought this, an image came into her mind of the headline in the copy of the *Eastern Daily Press* she'd found in Dan's shed – *REMAINS MAY BE MISSING GIRL* – although that hadn't been about Phoebe Piper, but Lisa Wynn . . .

P.C. Wright was looking at her intently.

'I can assure you,' Janice said, 'that Dan would never, ever, hurt a child.'

The police officer nodded thoughtfully. 'There've been quite a lot of changes recently, haven't there?'

'It's bound to be unsettling,' Janice agreed. 'For everyone, really.'

'Is alcohol an issue, do you think?'

'I'm not sure,' said Janice, feeling obscurely disloyal. 'It's been a very difficult time, with Dan dying and everything. If you were wondering about the bottles in the kitchen,' she added hastily, 'that's not Suzie. My brother seems to have had rather a . . . That is, I found a lot of empties in his bedroom when I was tidying up. But I'm sure,' she added quickly, 'that with Molly it's really just teething problems.'

'Did she mention anything specific?'

'Not really. Just difficulties making friends, but I suppose that's normal, going to a new school where you don't know anybody – girls can be so cliquey at that age, can't they?'

'Did she mention any friends in London? Anyone she's been in touch with?'

'No, nothing like that.'

'Grandparents? Apart from yourself, I mean.'

'Well, as far as I know her grandmother – Suzie's adoptive mother – is dead, and her grandfather has dementia and is in a home.'

'Any other relatives that you know of?'

'Well, she's got an uncle – Suzie's brother –' Janice remembered the static when she'd tried to ask Suzie about him, 'but I got the impression that they aren't particularly close, so I don't suppose he's seen much of Molly. Suzie has had a pretty difficult time, bringing up Molly by herself.'

P.C. Wright stared at her, unblinking, the eyes Janice had thought hazel now a hard gooseberry green. 'Why didn't she contact you when Molly was younger? Or did she try and you were . . . *travelling*?' The slight pause and the sarcastic emphasis on the word freighted it with irresponsible hedonism.

'No, she didn't. I don't know why not, but if she had I'd have helped, of course I would. I'd have been glad to.'

'But she didn't ask for your help. And she didn't contact you when she was here either, not for six months, and then only—'

'Because Dan died. I know. She feels that I let her down, and I don't blame her. I did let her down, and I want to try and make it up to her.'

P.C. Wright stared at Janice for a moment longer, then turned and went back downstairs.

THIRTY-FIVE

No moon, no stars, only the tail lights of the police car shining in the dark. As they disappeared round the bend in the road, Janice closed the front door and went back into the kitchen. Suzie, reanimated by the officers' departure, was pacing about, vibrating with the adrenaline of distress, fumbling for her cigarettes with shaking hands.

'. . . asking all those bloody questions and coming out with all that rubbish about Dan, when it's obvious what's happened. It's one of those nutters hanging round Joe's place – who else is it going to be?'

'I didn't see anyone when I was there,' said Janice, sitting down in the hope that Suzie would follow suit. Mark was leaning against the worktop, arms folded, looking grim.

'Well, you wouldn't, would you? They'd have grabbed Molly and fucked off by then, wouldn't they? They're probably in the woods or something, and the police aren't going to start searching now, are they, when it's dark? God, they're not going to do anything, are they? They think it's Dan or her dad or some shit like that, and they're just going to stick her picture on their poxy website and sit around on their arses when anything might be hap—'

'Wait a minute,' said Janice. 'Those people come here for Joe, don't they? So why would they be interested . . . ?' Remembering something, she stopped.

'What?'

'Something Molly said – about the one she calls the Sneaky Man. She said something like, "He comes here sometimes and walks up and down the road." Of course, it might not be relevant, but—'

'But it might!' Suzie leapt on the idea. 'He's a weirdo. They all are. And who else would it be? He probably saw Joe coming in here this afternoon and followed him.'

'Do you mean Catweazle?' Mark unfolded his arms.

'Who?'

'It was a series on T.V. when I was a kid.' Mark sounded sheepish. 'A wizard who'd travelled through time from the eleventh century or something, and he made friends with a boy and they had adventures. Wild eyes, big whiskers and a beard, all dirty – you know.' It must be the same man, thought Janice. Molly'd said Dan kept telling him to go away, hadn't she? *He smells and he's got a necklace made of horrible things.* She'd said something about a wizard too, except she'd probably meant like the ones in Harry Potter. 'If you mean him,' Mark continued, 'I think I know where he lives.'

'Yeah,' said Suzie, exasperated, '*in the woods*, like I just told the police.'

Janice thought of the dark, solid mass of trees on the other side of the fields – acres and acres of them, stretching right past the next village. How could you find anyone in there in the dark?

'No, he doesn't,' said Mark. 'Not here, anyway.'

'Where, then?'

'Further over. The woods round by the development – you know, where the psychiatric hospital used to be.'

'Crowhurst?' Janice thought of the gates and security cameras she'd seen. 'It looked to me as if they're doing a pretty good job of keeping people out. How do you know, anyway?'

'A bloke I know goes in there sometimes, you know,' Mark tapped the side of his nose, 'and he's seen his camp. Look –' he glanced at his watch – 'it's nearly half ten. If I go now, I can probably catch him in the pub – he's a regular at the Bull in Sparthorpe, and, if he's not there he only lives round the corner – and I'll get him to take me up there. I'll ask the other regulars too, get them to look for her.'

'What's the time now?'

'Ten past one.'

'God.' Suzie lit another cigarette. 'They're not going to find her, are they? I'm going to ring Mark.'

'He turned his phone off when they got to Crowhurst, remember? So they wouldn't risk alerting Security.' When Janice had suggested, during an earlier phone call, that they ask the guards to help find the Sneaky Man's camp, Mark's friend Harry had grabbed the phone and said the guards wouldn't believe a word of it and it wouldn't do Molly any good if they got arrested. 'He said he'd ring when they were out of the wood.'

Although – to Janice's relief – Suzie hadn't started drinking again, they'd had this conversation, or a version of it, approximately every twenty minutes or so since about half past eleven, which was when Mark had phoned to say they'd arrived at Crowhurst. Suzie had wanted to accompany him, but this had been vetoed on the grounds that if the police or anyone else brought Molly home, she'd need to be there. After she had suggested, for the third time, that Suzie go to bed, and had her head bitten off, Janice decided that talking about anything – anything at all – would be preferable to listening to Suzie wearing herself out blaming first herself and then Janice for Molly's disappearance, her denunciations punctuated by attempts to get hold of Tom on his mobile and by throwing the back door open and yelling Molly's name desperately into the night.

When Suzie had finally stopped pacing and sat down, exhausted, at the table, head in hands, Janice said gently, 'Would you like me to tell you about your father?'

Suzie looked up, eyes wide and incredulous. For a moment Janice thought she was going to start shouting again, but instead she said dully, 'Yeah, why not? This isn't doing any good, is it?'

'Well . . .' Janice realised, as she searched for a starting point, that she couldn't actually remember where she'd first met Jeff, or what sort of initial impression he'd made.

Suzie shrugged. 'It's OK. I didn't think there was much to tell.'

'He was very handsome,' she said. 'I'm afraid I don't have a photograph with me. I'm sure I've got one somewhere,' she added hastily, 'but I didn't have time to find it.'

'Dan said he was handsome,' said Suzie.

'Did he?' That was unexpected. Of all the things Janice could have imagined Dan saying about Jeff, 'handsome' wasn't one of them.

'Yeah. He hadn't got a photo either.'

'I can't remember Dan having a camera – not then, anyway,' said Janice. 'Jeff did though. And a cine camera. He was really into taking pictures and filming and stuff.'

'Dan said that too.'

'Oh.' Rallying, Janice said, 'He was charming, and funny, and generous, and he always . . .' Always what? What had she been going to say? She couldn't remember him being particularly charming or funny. She supposed he must have been, at least a little bit, or she wouldn't have liked him, but right now all she could remember were the things that had irritated her: his habitual lateness, the way he smeared his knife over his fork when he ate, and the way he made comments about other women in front of her and then accused her of being uptight if she complained. Janice shook her head. 'I'm sorry.'

'It's all right. I don't suppose you know where he is now, do you?'

'I'm afraid not.'

'I thought you probably wouldn't. When we came here, that was when I explained to Tom about being adopted, and I asked him to try and find my real dad – see if he was on Facebook or something – but there wasn't anything at all, so we thought he might have died. Mind you, we couldn't find you on the internet either.'

'I only use my computer for email really, and booking flights and things. Maybe Jeff's the same, except . . .' A sudden thought made her tail off.

'What?'

'His surname.'

'Jeff Castle. Dan told me.'

'That's the thing. He used to get called Barbara a lot, because there was a politician called Barbara Castle who was—'

'I *have* heard of her.' Suzie rolled her eyes.

'Sorry.'

'For Christ's sake, stop saying sorry,' snapped Suzie.

'Sor— I mean, OK. Anyway, it really got on his nerves, and he used to say that he was going to take his father's name, because it was his stepfather who was called Castle. He was a few years older than me – I think his dad was killed in the war and his mum had remarried. His dad had quite a famous name too, oddly enough – famous back then anyway. Something to do with films . . .'

'A film star?'

'No, they *made* films. Funny ones.'

'What, like Woody Allen or the Coen Brothers?'

'Yes, but older. They were brothers though. They always had that actor – big teeth, making a mess of things, you know . . .' Janice clicked her fingers. 'Died a few years ago – I can picture him – Ian Carmichael, that's it.'

'But that's not who—'

Janice held up a hand. 'Wait! Boulting – that's what it was. The Boulting Brothers. Why don't we see if we can find Jeff Boulting on my computer?'

'What time is it?'

'Five minutes since the last time you asked. Tell you what, why don't you try Mark while I get my laptop? Maybe he's turned his phone back on now.'

When Janice returned with the computer, relieved that she'd managed to salvage at least something from the mess she'd made of talking about Jeff, Suzie stopped jabbing at her mobile and flung it back on the table. 'Why the fuck doesn't he switch his phone back on?'

'It might be a good sign,' said Janice, sitting down next to her.

'How? If this mate of Mark's knows where that bastard's camp is, surely they'd have found it by now, so they'd know if he's got her or not, wouldn't they?'

'Not necessarily,' said Janice. 'It's a big area, and it's dark, and he might have, I don't know, moved camp or something. It could be lots of things. Let's see if we can find Jeff Boulting, shall we?'

'If you want.' Suzie lit another cigarette. 'I just want someone to tell me Molly's safe, that's all,' she said tearfully. 'You hear about these kids who just disappear into thin air . . .'

'That's only in a very few cases.' Janice thought, uneasily, of Phoebe and Lisa Wynn and all the others in the magazine upstairs.

'Well, supposing this is one of them? I can't bear it! Just thinking about what might have happened to her makes me feel sick.'

'Try not to think about it, love.'

Janice put out a calming hand, but Suzie knocked it away. 'Try not to think about it? Is that what they teach you when you go to yoga school in Goa or wherever the fuck it is – "Try not to think about it"? How the fuck am I supposed to think about anything else?'

'I know it's difficult.'

Suzie jumped up, shoving her chair backwards so that it clattered to the floor. 'It's so dark out there! I ought to be doing something, not just sitting here!'

'There's nothing you can do. That's the hardest thing, I know, but—'

Suzie's scream, harsh and sharp, cut her off. Her daughter's flailing hands knocked over the used mugs that Janice had cleared on to the worktop, sending four of them crashing to the floor. Suzie picked up the remaining one, stared at it for a moment, teeth bared, then hurled it at the opposite wall where it shattered, leaving a dent in the plaster and tea streaking down to the floor.

There was silence, and for a moment neither of them moved. Janice, sensing that an attempt to clear up the mess immediately would relegate what had just happened to the level of a tantrum, and that consolation would be even more disastrous, patted the chair beside her and said, 'Let's see what we can find, shall we?'

Typing *Jeff Boulting* into the search engine produced several images, none of which looked remotely like the man Janice remembered, and two Facebook pages that clearly weren't him either. Having drawn a blank with a law firm in Arizona, a self-published poet and a middle-distance runner, she came across Jeff Boulting Photography: Advertising, Commercial and Editorial, based somewhere in Cornwall. Suzie sat beside her, passive but absent, as she clicked through a relentlessly cheerful series of images: cupcakes; dogs leaning out of car windows, ears flapping; smiling pensioners with jumpers slung casually round their necks, pointing at things from the decks of ocean liners . . . No pictures of the photographer himself, but it made sense, Janice thought, for Jeff to have turned his hobby into his job.

'I can't concentrate anyway,' said Suzie. 'I know what you're trying to do, and it's nice of you, but . . .' She shook her head. 'Why isn't something *happening*? Nothing's being done.'

'You don't know that.'

'Yes, I do. They'd have told us.'

'Not necessarily . . . Suzie, Molly's a child. They're not just going to file it away and forget it. I'm sure they're doing everything they can.'

'If that's the case, why haven't they found her yet?'

'Give them a chance, love. I know it's difficult, but you've got to be—'

'Stop fucking saying you *know*! You don't know. You've no idea what this is like for me.'

'No, of course, but I can imagine—'

'No, you can't!'

'All right, I can't. Just stay with me, OK? Let's see if we can find your dad – it's got to be better than just sitting here worrying.'

'Yeah.' Suzie leant over to put out her cigarette in the already full ashtray. 'Whatever.'

Janice clicked on the *Links* button on the Jeff Boulting site and found one for www.jeffboultinggallery.co.uk, which had a variety of prints of landscapes and abstracts available for sale – but again no self-portrait – and a couple of directions to stuff uploaded on YouTube.

The first was a piece of black and white film entitled *Isle of Wight 1969*. 'Yes!' said Janice. 'It is him. It must be – we were there.'

'Bully for you. He wouldn't have filmed himself though, would he?'

'Let's find out.'

'Fill your boots.' Suzie closed her eyes.

Janice pressed *Play*. The handheld camera panned shakily over people swarming up the gangplank of a ferry to a soundtrack of rock music – festival goers mainly, judging from the bedrolls, rucksacks and neckerchiefs, and, in amongst them, a couple of old chaps in caps looking bemused and an elderly woman with stiff curls, pointy cat's-eye glasses and pursed lips.

'She doesn't look very happy, does she?'

Suzie opened her eyes. 'Who?'

Janice froze the film. 'Her.'

'You know she's probably about the same age as you are now, don't you?'

'God, I suppose she is. What an awful thought.'

'Are you on there?'

'Haven't spotted myself yet.' Had she and Jeff travelled there together? Janice couldn't remember. She pressed *Play* again, and found herself looking at the gentle waves of the Solent, and then at groups of people in bellbottoms and sunhats, dancing or sitting in circles on the grass, beer cans and the remains of fires, someone who looked like Pete Townsend emerging from a B.E.A. helicopter and, finally, a bearded Bob Dylan singing 'The Mighty Quinn'.

Janice returned to the original site and clicked on the other YouTube link. Another black and white film, with the title *Joe & Co*, started with a long shot of a group of men in foppish hippie finery, prancing about and mugging for the camera on a grassy slope. The soundtrack was pan pipes – haunting, mesmeric and, Janice thought, entirely unsuited to what she was seeing. 'Oh! It's one of our picnics. Look, Suzie. That's me, there.' Janice froze the film again to show her younger self lying cuddled against Joe Vincent's chest, doe-eyed, long-haired, looking up at him and laughing, extending a hand to stroke his cheek. Joe looked utterly gorgeous – beautiful eyes, impish grin and razor-sharp cheekbones framed by luxuriant black curls.

'Who's that with you?'

'That's Joe Vincent.'

'Really? Bloody hell. He's *beautiful*.'

'Well, we were young,' Janice protested.

'You're beautiful too,' said Suzie. 'It's just that you still look like the same person . . . Didn't Jeff mind you snuggling up to Joe like that?'

'It was before we got together.' Janice couldn't actually remember Jeff being at the picnic, although she wasn't about to tell Suzie that. 'It's quite near here, that place. South, nearer Suffolk.' The same place, she thought, where five-year-old Lisa Wynn, who'd pestered her mother for a kitten, had disappeared. She pressed *Play* again.

'Who are all those others?'

'That's Keith Petrie, on the left. He was the Weather Ship's bass guitarist – still is, as far as I know – and beside him, with the guitar, is John . . . Blakemore, I think, or Blackmore, one of the two. He's the drummer.' Janice thought of the paintings she'd seen at Joe's – the guitar player; the couple on the grass; the person in the corner carrying away something that might or might not be his dead sister, Marie . . . 'I'm pretty sure the other guy was a musician as well. Bob somebody.' The camera panned back to her and Joe for a moment, and then a shadow fell across the pair of them and Joe rose abruptly, throwing her off him. The camera followed him as he ran away, up the slope and out of shot, pursued by another man . . . 'It's Dan, look!'

'Where are they going?'

'No idea. Perhaps Joe just wanted Jeff to stop filming.'

'Looks like someone did anyway.' Suzie pointed to the screen, where the camera angles had become wonky, alternating between grass and treetops, as if the operator were being jostled – and then, suddenly, there was Jeff, standing and flicking a V sign. Despite the grimace, he was more handsome than she remembered. Quite a lot more handsome, in fact.

'That's your dad,' said Janice, pressing *Pause*. 'We've found him.'

'Yeah.' Suzie stared at Jeff for a long moment before she began to cry in deep, gulping sobs. 'But we've lost Molly.'

Janice reached out to put an arm around her, but feeling her daughter's shoulders stiffen, drew back and sat silent, staring at the tea stains on the wall, while Suzie wept.

THIRTY-SIX

'I'll get the blame, won't I? They'll say it's my fault.'

'No one's going to blame anyone,' said Janice. She switched on the bedside light, turned off the big one and sat down on the edge of the double bed. Although Suzie had shrunk from her attempts at an embrace, she had finally, with the dazed compliance of exhaustion, let Janice take her upstairs and help her into bed. 'Molly's going to come back safe and sound.'

Twenty minutes earlier, at Suzie's insistence, she'd telephoned the police station to ask for an update. The woman she'd finally got through to was clearly unfamiliar with the situation, and had said only that neither D.S. Calvert nor P.C. Wright were available, but that she was sure that everything that could be done was being done. Which, Janice thought, was probably – given that it was quarter to two in the morning – not very much. She'd translated it to Suzie as, 'Still making enquiries', which, while not a whole lot better, at least sounded as if something was happening.

Suzie leant up on one elbow. 'She's gone.' In the light cast by the bedside lamp she was a picture of pallid, bruise-eyed wretchedness.

'She'll come back,' said Janice firmly. 'And you need to get some rest.'

'You will keep trying Mark, won't you?'

'I promise. It's a shame we haven't got any sleeping pills, because you really could use a decent night's—'

'There should be some temazepam in there somewhere.' Suzie gestured at the nightstand on what had been Ma's side of the bed.

'Are they yours?'

'Yeah. The doctor gave them to me when I lost my job.'

'You should probably have told P.C. Calvert about them when he came to ask about Dan.'

'I didn't think. In any case it'll keep till tomorrow, won't it?'

The shelves inside the nightstand had always housed, veiled in brown paper bags, the things that had to be hidden away, such as sanitary towels and Ma's Dutch cap. Now, the contents were a jumble of cigarette packets, lighters, blister packs of painkillers, condoms and a cling-filmed lump of what looked like resin.

'These?' said Janice, holding up a white plastic pill bottle marked *Restoril*.

'Yes. But –' Suzie scrambled into a sitting position – 'what if there's some news about Molly, or if she comes back? You will come and get me, won't you?'

'Course I will. But you've got to get some sleep. How many?'

'A couple. I hardly ever take them,' Suzie added. 'Don't know why I kept them, really.'

Janice popped the cap. In the bottom of the bottle were two pink and maroon capsules. Fetching a tooth-mug of water from the bathroom, she thought: This is not the time to discuss it.

Shaking the capsules into her palm, she handed them over and Suzie swallowed obediently. 'Thanks. Do you know any prayers, Janice? We should say one. For Molly.'

'Yes.' She'd said prayers with Ma when she was little, both of them kneeling by the bed.

Janice got down on her knees. 'Our Father, which art in heaven, hallowed be Thy name. Thy kingdom come, Thy will be done on earth, as it is in heaven. Give us this day our daily bread . . .' Line after line popped up in her mind, as if her subconscious were reading the words from an invisible sheet. 'For Thine is the kingdom, the power and the glory, for ever and ever . . . and please look after Molly and keep her safe and bring her back to us. Amen.'

'Amen,' Suzie echoed.

After a moment, Janice got up and sat on the bed again. 'Now, why don't you lie down and close your eyes?'

'OK.' Suzie slid down into the bed. 'But will you stay till I go to sleep? I don't want to be on my own.' Seeing the absolute entreaty on her face, Janice thought: This is what she must have been like as a child.

'Course I will, darling.' For a moment she was overwhelmed, and had to turn away. The devastating power of love . . . I wasn't allowed to feel this, Janice thought. I didn't know how it could be. She felt the touch of Suzie's hand on her back, and looked round.

'It's good, you being here,' Suzie murmured. 'They will bring Molly back, won't they?'

Unable to stop herself, Janice reached out and touched her daughter's cheek. 'Yes, darling. They'll bring her back.'

Suzie closed her eyes, and Janice sat looking at her, thinking of what Lisa Wynn's mother had said in the article she'd read. *Nobody wants to think there's a possibility that their child might still be missing after almost fifty years, do they?*

In fifty years' time, Janice thought, Suzie will be ninety-four – if she's still alive – and I'll be long gone.

She picked up the Restoril bottle and read the label. Underneath the address of a pharmacy in Croydon was typed *Mrs Suzanne Armitage, 12/11/13*. The pub where Suzie said she'd worked had been in Leytonstone, hadn't it? But then it had closed and she'd lost her job and the flat that went with it – that was when the doctor had given her the tablets. Perhaps the B & B she'd mentioned had been in Croydon.

What about Molly's school? Croydon to Leytonstone was a hell of a journey. And then there was the date: 12th November. Suzie must have been made jobless and homeless six weeks before Christmas. And Christmas in a B & B, wherever it was . . . Janice recalled an article she'd seen in one of the Sundays. Single rooms so cramped that meals had to be eaten off the bed. Tiny kitchens, shared with strangers. Belongings in plastic bags. Drunks staggering about on the landings and drug addicts in the toilet. The forlorn impossibility of trying to pretend to a ten-year-old that any of it was an adventure. 'Oh, Suzie,' she murmured, 'I'm so sorry.'

Underneath Suzie's name was typed *56 x 15mg. Take no more than ONE at a time or FOUR in 24 hours. Avoid alcohol.* A high level of alcohol in the bloodstream, Janice thought, remembering Suzie's conversation with the police officer about Dan's post-mortem.

Suzie had asked for two, but she'd said she'd hardly taken any of them, so perhaps she'd forgotten, and anyway, just one extra couldn't hurt. If she'd taken, say, a couple when she first had them, and two had been left in the bottle, then fifty-six tablets minus four was fifty-two, and fifty-two times fifteen milligrams was . . . seven hundred and eighty milligrams. Would that be enough to kill someone, if taken with a shedload of booze? Was that what Dan had done?

Janice watched Suzie for a few minutes longer and then, moving with exaggerated slowness and care, put the empty pill bottle back on the nightstand and tiptoed out of the room. She needed to be downstairs to answer phone calls, and she could tidy up the kitchen while she was waiting. Either Mark would have found

Molly, or someone would have spotted her wandering about, lost, and taken her to a police station. She couldn't have gone far, and the vast majority of missing children were found within a few hours, everyone knew that. It was just a matter of time.

THIRTY-SEVEN

In the kitchen, sweeping up the remains of the smashed mugs, Janice wondered why, if Dan had taken the temazepam, he'd left two of them. It couldn't be that he'd lost consciousness before he'd finished necking them, otherwise the bottle would have been found in his room with the lid open – unless Suzie, or somebody else, had seen it there and replaced it in the nightstand. But if Suzie *had* done that, surely she'd have mentioned it to the police? After all, the drugs were on prescription, so there was no question of her getting into trouble. Perhaps Dan had been removing the capsules in twos and threes, waiting to see if she'd notice – which would, of course, mean that he'd been planning to commit suicide for days, or even weeks . . .

If only I *had* come up here more, she thought. Her relationship with her parents, especially Ma, had never recovered from giving Suzie up, but she hadn't felt actually angry with her until her miscarriage, aged thirty-seven, eight years into her second marriage. The pregnancy hadn't been planned – she'd always shied away from the idea of another child – but Ma, then in her late sixties, had been appallingly solicitous, insisting on coming down to London to look after her. After two days, the endless parade of treats and comforts and the iteration of what a pity it was and how sorry she felt – the contrast with the cold matter-of-factness with which she'd greeted the arrival of Janice's living, breathing daughter – had become too much, and Janice, angry and tearful, had asked her to leave. Her bewildered husband, ignorant of the past, had chalked it up to hormones. When Janice had calmed down sufficiently to be able to think about it, it had occurred to her that guilt might well have prompted Ma's behaviour, but she'd felt only bitterness. Now she saw that because of it, Dan had suffered. But he'd pushed her away too, hadn't he? Perhaps he'd been trying to punish her – although for what, she wasn't sure.

She heard the sound of tyres on gravel as she was emptying the last crumbs of broken crockery into the bin and a moment later Mark burst through the door. He looked dishevelled, as though he'd been in a fight, with one sleeve of his waxed jacket ripped at the cuff and mud-spattered trousers.

'What happened?'

Mark dropped into the nearest chair, elbows on knees, head in hands. 'Oh, Christ. Where's Suzie?'

'Upstairs, asleep. She took a pill. Is it Molly?'

Mark shook his head without looking up. 'We didn't find her.'

'OK . . .' The warm flare of hope in Janice's chest subsided, leaving behind it ashen dread. 'Did you find anything? Any . . . traces?'

'Nothing.'

'Have you heard from any of the others? The ones from the pub who were looking?'

'Shit, I haven't checked.'

'Do it now.'

Janice sat, impatient, while Mark listened to several messages, each time shaking his head. 'Nothing. Sorry. Thing is, we didn't find Molly, but we found him. Catweazle.'

'And?'

Mark stared at Janice, his eyes, baggy with exhaustion, full of remembered horror. 'And he's dead.'

THIRTY-EIGHT

'Can you get me a drink?'

'Sure. Tea? Coffee? Wine?'

'There's a bottle of Scotch inside the piano.'

'The *piano*?'

'Hiding place. Dan,' he added, with a touch of impatience.

Janice found the half bottle of Teacher's lying on top of the strings of the baby grand, returned with it to the kitchen, and placed it, with a glass, in front of Mark.

'Sorry,' he said, pouring. 'I thought you knew.'

'I did know. Well, once I'd seen the empties in his room.' Janice took a seat opposite. 'Where's your friend?'

'I dropped him off.'

'Did you have a fight?'

Mark shook his head. 'We found him.'

'Tell me.'

'Well, we got into the wood easily enough, and Harry – that's the bloke I was with – he took me to where he said the camp was, only there wasn't much there. I mean, you could see he'd been there – the remains of a fire and some other stuff, an old rucksack and a tarpaulin – but there wasn't anyone about, and we thought he might have moved. To be honest, we were thinking, if he was hiding Molly or something . . . So we walked about a bit, trying to see where he might have gone. We must have been looking for a couple of hours at least – Harry knows those woods like the back of his hand, but when it's dark . . . And there's some bits you can't get into at all – completely overgrown, no one looking after it or anything.' Mark gulped from his drink. 'Eventually we got to a bit where someone'd hacked a sort of tunnel through all the brambles and things. Harry said he thought it was recent, so we went in and there's a sort of camp there, one of those wigwam things covered in tarpaulins and plastic sheets, you know, like those environmental protesters have when they're trying to stop new roads and whatnot, only this one looks like it's half falling down. We can't hear or see anyone, and I thought it must be empty because we'd made quite a bit of noise getting past the brambles, and anyone in there would have heard us, but . . .' Mark shook his head. 'There he was.'

'Inside the tent?'

'Yeah.' Mark drank some more Scotch.

'And he was definitely dead?'

'No question. It was fucking horrible. He had some sort of wound on his head – looked like someone had walloped him with something – and his face was all bashed up.' Mark shook his head, grimacing. 'Jesus. I can't stop thinking about it.'

'Did you call the police?'

Mark shook his head. 'Harry's a poacher, Janice.'

'But you were looking for Molly,' said Janice incredulously, 'not lamping deer or whatever Harry does. You've *got* to tell them. Supposing that man *did* take Molly and somebody else was involved as well and they had, I don't know, a fight or something, and this other person took Molly away with him, and—'

'You don't understand.'

'What don't I understand?'

'It can't have been him.'

'Why can't it?' Janice demanded.

'Because he's been dead for at a day at least,' said Mark, in a tone of weary exasperation. 'It was obvious. That was why it was so . . . you know . . . and why we weren't sure about the wound on his head. There was blood on him – at least I think it was blood – and it looked like a fox or a rat or something had been chewing his face. '

'Did he have clothes on?'

'Yeah, he was dressed, and there was a rucksack with some stuff in it and plastic bags with food in, tins and things, all scattered round the back of the tent. We had a look in his pockets, just on the off chance there might be something to do with Molly, because Suzie seemed so sure. Harry said he'd do it, thank God. All he found was a couple of these . . . Hang on.' Mark dug into the deep pockets of his waxed jacket and rooted around. 'Here.'

He held out a business card between his first and second finger. Turning it over, Janice read *Jeff Boulting Photography*, and an address in Cornwall.

THIRTY-NINE

'So you're telling me that Jeff Boulting is Molly's granddad?' Mark downed the last of his Scotch. 'Bloody hell. And you really haven't been in touch with him since Suzie was born?'

Janice shook her head.

'But you just said you were telling Suzie about him.'

'Yes,' said Janice impatiently. 'About when we first met. I was trying to keep her mind off Molly – and because I thought she'd want to know. Look, you really do need to call the police.'

Mark sighed. 'OK. I'd better get hold of Harry first, though.'

'Right. You give him a ring, and I'll be back in a sec.' Janice headed upstairs to check on Suzie.

'Fast asleep,' she told Mark. 'I didn't think I ought to wake her, not till we know a bit more about what's going on. Was Harry OK about it?'

'He wasn't overjoyed, but he gets it all right.'

Janice nodded and handed over her own phone. 'The number's on there, under *Police*.'

'Hang on though, what about the card? I mean, we took it off him, didn't we? Doesn't that count as interfering with a corpse or, I don't know, tampering with evidence or something?'

'Surely it isn't wrong to try and find out who somebody is?

And you said he had a couple of those cards, so it's not as if you removed something unique, is it?'

'I suppose not. All right then.'

At least, Janice thought as she listened to Mark explaining the situation – and, by the sound of things, making not a bad job of it – something was happening. Firmly blocking out of her mind the fact that the direction things were taking was, potentially, very bad indeed, she concentrated on the fact that Mark and Harry hadn't found any trace of Molly anywhere near Jeff – if Molly's Sneaky Man actually *was* Jeff. She got up and went to stand in front of the open window, staring into the enormous darkness. No stars, no lighted windows to be seen from the village, just pitch-black. Molly could be anywhere out there, she thought. Anywhere at all.

If it *was* Jeff, what the hell was he doing living in a wood and mooning about outside Joe Vincent's house? Was he trying to enlist Joe's help in getting his hands on Molly, and if so, why now? And anyway, if Suzie hadn't contacted him, how did he even know that Molly existed?

Perhaps Jeff had gone mad and had no idea Molly was related to him . . . but that much of a coincidence only happened in things like Thomas Hardy novels, not in real life. Molly'd said she was a bit scared of the Sneaky Man, but she hadn't said anything about him pestering her – and she'd said that Joe had hidden from him and that Dan kept telling him to go away . . . And if it was Jeff, surely *Dan* would have recognised him, even if Joe hadn't?

Unless he'd changed so completely as to be unrecognisable, of course. That was entirely possible, because people did . . . Janice went back to the table and, pulling her laptop towards her, switched it on.

*

'Right.' Mark ended the call and slid Janice's phone back across the table. 'I don't know how much of that you got, but they're coming here to fetch me and they want me to show them where the body is.'

'What, now?' Janice glanced at her watch – twenty to four.

'First thing, when it gets light. They're going to get in touch with Harry and ask him to come as well, because he's the one who knows the woods, not me – although he only stumbled on that second camp by accident, so I hope he can find it again.'

'Mark,' said Janice, 'if I showed you a photo of Jeff as a young man, do you think you could tell if it was the same person?'

'I can try.' Mark looked doubtful.

Janice found the *Joe & Co* YouTube footage and moved the cursor along the bar until Jeff, handsome and jubilant, stood sticking two fingers up at them. Was it her imagination, or was his smile full of terrible knowledge, his slightly narrowed eyes gleaming across the years with triumphant clairvoyant vengefulness?

After a few seconds, Mark said, 'Look, I don't know. It might be – I mean, it's not impossible, but I've never seen the guy in the wood up close – not when he was alive, anyway. I'd only ever seen him from my car, going past Joe's place. People change, Janice, and that,' he nodded at the image of Jeff on the screen, 'looks like it was filmed some time ago.'

'The late sixties.'

'Almost fifty years ago.'

Exactly, Janice told herself. It's Jeff, mucking around, almost fifty years ago. Of course Mark can't tell.

'There is an easier way to find out, of course,' said Mark, getting up to put the kettle on. 'Phone him up. There's a landline and a mobile number on that card.'

'I suppose,' said Janice. 'But he's not going to be awake now, is he? If he's alive, I mean.' The idea of speaking to a living Jeff was alarming enough, but the thought of her voice issuing from a phone in a dead man's belongings in a deserted wood had a sickening necrophiliac intimacy.

'There'll be an answerphone, won't there?'

'Yes – and if he's the guy in the wood and he's got a message on his phone from me, the police are going to wonder why, aren't they?'

'We didn't find a phone on him.'

'That doesn't mean he didn't have one. You said Harry only looked in his pockets, not the bags and things. And it'll be the same if I ring the landline – if it's him, the police might think I had something to do with it.'

'Hardly, if he was already dead. They'll know the time of the call, remember? They'll know it was after I rang them – and I told them I was here, with you.'

'Yeah, but they might not believe I'd only just got in touch with him. They might think I'd been involved with him and we were, I don't know, in cahoots or something.'

'Were you?'

'Of course not! For God's sake, I haven't seen or spoken to Jeff since 1970. I told you that.'

'Then there won't be any evidence that you have, will there?' Mark's tone, and his words, were quite reasonable, but Janice felt apprehensive and when he added, 'I'd have thought you'd want to know if it was him,' it made her angry.

'I think we should leave it for the police,' she said stiffly. 'Allow them to do their job.'

Mark looked at her curiously. 'As you wish. Right,' he got to his feet, 'the kettle's boiled. Tea?'

'Thanks.'

'Can I have a couple of pillows and a duvet or something? I'll go in the sitting room. I'm going to try and grab some sleep before the police get here, and I don't want to risk waking Suzie.'

On her way upstairs, having made up a bed of sorts on one of the sofas, Janice paused in front of the closed door of Molly's room. As her hand reached to turn the knob, she was convinced that Molly would be inside, sound asleep in bed, but as soon as her fingers touched the porcelain surface she stopped, gasping as though the air around her had somehow withdrawn itself, leaving her to suffocate. Molly wasn't in bed. She wasn't in the house. She was lost. *Nobody wants to think there's a possibility that their child might still be missing after nearly fifty years . . .*

That will not happen to Molly, she told herself. She will come back. Everything that can be done is being done. We just have to be patient.

She had a shower and went and lay down on her bed. She'd meditate. That was bound to help – and not just her, but Suzie, Molly, the police, everyone. She closed her eyes, started her breathing exercises and, repeating the mantra she'd learnt at the ashram in Kerala, tried to empty her mind.

She failed. Molly, wandering, lost, down a dark lane, struck by a drunk driver and left in a ditch, bleeding and helpless; Molly, dragged behind a hedge by a maniac, raped and strangled . . . After ten minutes, her mind clenched like a fist around a clutch of thoughts about what might be happening or have happened, and misery like a stone in her chest, she gave up and got under the covers. At least it isn't winter, she thought. If Molly is out there somewhere there's no risk of frostbite or exposure – a small comfort, but better than nothing at all.

Staring into the darkness, she realised quite how much she

didn't want to find out either that Jeff *was* the man in the wood
or that he'd had something to do with him, because that would
make it, in part, her fault. She'd chosen Jeff, hadn't she? Only in a
casual sense, of course, because her pregnancy with Suzie hadn't
been planned, but nevertheless . . . *Could* it be a coincidence, Jeff,
or at least his card, being so near? Stranger things had happened
– and she only had Mark's word for it that he'd found the card,
or rather cards, in the man's pocket. Perhaps he'd planted them
there, although of course he'd had Harry with him, so that would
have been difficult . . . Unless Harry had been distracted or something. But why, anyway? What would be the point, unless Mark
had taken Molly – or worse, killed her – and was trying to put the
blame elsewhere? He'd suggested going into the wood, of course,
but then, why take Harry? Unless Harry was part of it – or perhaps
Harry hadn't gone with him at all. No, that couldn't be right,
because Mark had told the police about Harry, hadn't he? Harry
was going to help them.

Don't be ridiculous, Janice told herself. But what if Jeff had paid
the man in the wood to snatch Molly, and then he'd killed him
and taken Molly away – or the man had hidden Molly somewhere,
locked up, and then fallen and hit his head and died before he
could tell Jeff where she was – and what if no one found her and
she died of starvation?

After about an hour, light started to appear round the edges of
the closed curtains. Janice stared at the room as it began to reas-
semble itself around her: the wardrobe and the chest of drawers,
the shadeless, bulbless standard lamp, and the chair where Molly
had sat and watched her unpack, its cushion still slightly dented.
At half past six she heard the front door close and tyres crunch
on the gravel and, kneeling up on the bed, saw Mark get into the
police car and be driven away down the lane.

She went to the door of her room and listened. The silence had a plaintive quality, as though the house itself were wretched with waiting. Suzie is still asleep, she thought. The double dose of temazepam. No sense in waking her if there isn't any news.

Blank with exhaustion, she shut the door and lay down once more on the bed.

FORTY

'So you arrive, and then Molly disappears and all of this happens, and you expect me to believe none of it's connected?' Suzie was sitting at the kitchen table in her nightclothes, vibrating with anger, her mug of tea untouched. 'How stupid do you think I am, for fuck's sake?'

'How could there be a connection?' Woken out of a confused half-sleep by someone moving about below, Janice had dressed hastily and gone down to the kitchen, where she'd found Suzie wrapped in a duvet, standing in front of the window and staring glassily down the lane. Now, more shaken than she cared to admit, even to herself, by the tirade of fury and disbelief that had greeted her account of the previous night's events, Janice spoke deliberately calmly and slowly. 'You rang me, remember? Because of Dan. That's why I came.'

'You were the one who wanted to talk about Jeff last night – the one who insisted on looking him up on the net. All that about not having any pictures was bollocks, wasn't it? You've been in touch with him – you knew he was here, and you were just waiting for your chance, the pair of you. What have you done with her?'

'We haven't done anything! If the man in the wood is – was – Jeff, then I had absolutely no idea he was here. It's like I told Mark,

I haven't seen or spoken to him since 1970, and I didn't even know that Molly *existed* until two days ago.'

'Yeah,' said Suzie. 'So you keep saying.'

'Because it's *true*! I don't know what else I can say,' said Janice helplessly.

'You know –' Suzie's eyes, puffy and raw with crying, narrowed into slits – 'when I was little, I used to tell myself that you were dead and that was why you couldn't look after me. I'd tell myself that because it was easier, because if you were dead you couldn't help not being there, and it was like one of those stories where the kid or the princess or whoever is an orphan but it's nobody's fault, and now . . . now . . . if you were—'

'Suzie, please!' Janice couldn't bear to hear any more. Cold all over, as if something inside her had broken and filled her up with icy water, she cried out, 'Stop! I know you're upset, and I under-stand that, and of course you've every right to be angry, but you've got this so absolutely and completely wrong that it's –' Janice spread her hands, unable to fix on a word that would describe the magnitude or absurdness of the accusation – 'it's laughable – or,' she added quickly, 'it would be if the situation weren't so serious.'

'Yeah, well.' Suzie pushed her chair back. 'Laugh away. Let's hear what the police have to say when they get here, shall we? I'm going upstairs to put some clothes on.'

'Do you know, or know of, anyone by the name of Malcolm Devlin?'

It was almost eleven o'clock when Mark had returned, brought back – D.S. Calvert and P.C. Wright presumably having gone home some hours earlier – by two different officers, older than their colleagues from the night before and both in plain clothes. Having introduced themselves as D.S. Glenville and D.C. Singer and refused cups of tea, they'd announced that they needed to ask Suzie and Janice some questions, and that Mark should absent himself from the room.

'Is that who's got Molly?' Suzie, now dressed in a T-shirt and jeans, leant forward eagerly. 'Has he brought her back?'

'We're trying to establish whether there's a connection, Mrs Armitage. Do you know anyone of that name?'

'No. Why do—'

D.S. Glenville held up a hand. His checked shirt was crisp and his face hard and rosy like an apple, but he looked friendly enough. D.C. Singer, beside him, was younger, and, both in terms of ironing and physiognomy, softer round the edges. 'Do you, Mrs Keaton?'

'I'm afraid I don't.'

'Is it the name of the bloke in the wood?' asked Suzie. 'The dead one?'

'We're trying to establish his identity at the moment, Mrs Armitage. One thing we can tell you,' D.S. Glenville turned to look at Janice, 'is that he isn't Jeffrey Boulting, who we understand from Mr Bell is Molly's grandfather. Our colleagues in Cornwall have been able to confirm that Mr Boulting was at his home in St Ives this morning, alive and well.'

Janice had a falling sense of relief, a safe landing after dropping through space. 'So if the dead man is this Malcolm Devlin, what's Jeff's business card doing in his pocket?'

'As I said, we're awaiting confirmation about the identity. As to the business card, we should know more in due course. We understand that the man in the wood was known to your brother, Mrs Keaton.'

What had Molly told her? *Joe hid from him and Dan kept telling him to go away* . . . Aloud, she said, 'Dan and I had rather lost touch over the years, so I'm not really sure who his friends were.'

'Mrs Armitage?'

'He wasn't his friend,' said Suzie. 'He was always telling him to leave Joe alone, because he used to hang about his house.'

'Joe?'

'Joe Vincent,' said Suzie impatiently. 'We told the other officers all this last night. Surely Mark's explained already? And if this Devlin, or whoever he is, is dead, what's that got to do with Molly? Talking about him isn't going to find her, is it?'

'As I said, Mrs Armitage,' Glenville's tone was placid, reasonable, 'we need to establish whether there's a connection.'

'But there can't be! Not if he was dead before Molly disappeared!'

After a pause, during which D.S. Glenville stared at Suzie intently, he said, 'What makes you think that?'

'I thought . . .' Suzie looked at Janice.

'It's what Mark told me. He said there were signs of, you know, disturbance to the body. Foxes.'

'We haven't yet established when he died,' said D.S. Glenville. 'We're conducting a thorough search of the woods now, and the surrounding area. I know this is difficult for you, Mrs Armitage, but do remember that the vast majority of children who go missing are recovered within forty-eight hours.'

'People keep saying that! Molly's been missing for nearly twenty-four hours already. What if you don't find her?'

Half an hour later, after a lot more questions about Molly's father and her school and about the details of Dan's van and which festival Tom had taken it to and whether Janice had a partner ('It helps us to get a picture of the family, Mrs Armitage'), D.S. Glenville thanked Janice and Suzie and asked if they could please tell Mark to come in.

Sitting opposite Suzie in the living room, while the officers were talking to Mark behind the closed kitchen door, Janice said, 'We could make some posters and put them up.'

Suzie stared at her for a moment before saying, wearily, 'Tom's printer's broken, so we can't. Tom's going to put it on his Facebook page and get his mates to tweet about it.'

'Oh, did he ring back? I didn't hear.'

'He rang my mobile before you came down. He said he'd do the Facebook stuff first, then he'd sort things out with his mate at the festival and drive back.'

Janice thought that this might take more time than expected if the Wiltshire police, alerted by D.S. Glenville, wanted to talk to him, but said, merely, 'Wouldn't it be good to have something local as well? We could do posters by hand, as long as we can scan a photo. I'm sure there's someone in the village who'd do that for us.'

'I suppose . . . They've got a printer in the office at the pub. Simon Curtis called earlier, too – said he'd seen the police car this morning and wanted to know if Molly was back. Said he'd ring round the others and ask them to carry on looking.'

'That was nice of him. I'm sure he'd let you use the printer. Tell you what,' the thought of being able to do something propelled Janice from her chair, 'why don't I go and get some paper? Then we can make one poster and do as many copies as we want. I'll just check that the officers don't need me again, and—'

She was brought up short by the sound of the kitchen door opening and voices in the hall. Mark, his face pale and somehow powdery, like flour, addressed her as she opened the sitting-room door. 'They're taking me to my flat. They want to search it. I've given permission.'

'Oh.' Janice felt herself blink and hoped she hadn't sounded surprised. 'Right.'

'They think it's you?' She turned to see Suzie behind her, staring at Mark. Something about her face made Janice think, with unexpected force: She doesn't love him. She's with him because she doesn't want to be alone. Then, as nobody else seemed about to speak, she said, 'It's just to be sure, Suzie. They have to check.'

'We'll be off now,' said D.S. Glenville. 'Shouldn't take long. You'll be all right here, will you? Best not leave her alone,' he added to Janice, as if he knew what she'd been planning to do. 'If you need to go out for any reason, call a neighbour.'

'Yes.' Janice felt obscurely guilty. 'Of course.'

Neither she nor Suzie made any move to follow Mark and the officers to the front door, but remained where they were, in the hall. Once outside, Mark, standing between the two policemen, looked back. Janice couldn't read the expression on his face. A sort of furtive pleading, she thought, but she wasn't sure.

The word *furtive*, with its weaselly connotations, reminded Janice of what Mark had called the Sneaky Man: Catweazle, the wizard, from television. She didn't remember seeing the programme, but she'd heard of it. *We understand he is known to your brother, Mrs Keaton* . . . How had D.S. Glenville known this? Who'd told him? Had he spoken to Joe? Janice tried to imagine this conversation, and failed. Perhaps Glenville had asked the police in Cornwall to ask Jeff – after all, they must have asked how the man in the wood had got hold of his business card.

Malcolm Devlin. For a moment, it was as if something had whisked round a dark corner in her mind and vanished out of sight, and she couldn't retrieve it. Then she had an idea.

FORTY-ONE

Janice sat on the floor of Dan's room and flipped through the pile of loose photographs that had tumbled out of the large brown envelope she'd found at the bottom of his wardrobe. She'd glanced through the stuff on the desk for the photo of the woman called Marguerite that she'd found tucked into Dan's collection of L.P.s, thinking that she must have missed it before; she thought she might be able to kill two birds with one stone by identifying her, if she appeared in any of the other photos, but the picture had definitely disappeared. Janice wondered, vaguely, whether P.C. Wright might have moved it, although she had no memory of the policewoman touching anything on the desk – and besides, the photo hadn't been there when she'd looked before, had it?

She'd left Suzie in the company of Norma Rocklin, who'd turned up on the doorstep unexpectedly, saying how sorry she was and asking if there was anything she could do to help. When Suzie had – equally unexpectedly, Janice thought – welcomed her inside, she'd judged it safe to leave the pair of them in the kitchen, where Mrs Rocklin had shakily embarked on making a pot of tea and assembling a sandwich lunch.

Putting aside all the family photographs, she concentrated on making a pile of the ones showing a young adult Dan with his

London friends. There were a surprisingly large number of them for someone who hadn't possessed a camera, and Janice supposed he must have asked for, or been given, copies. There were a lot of people she didn't recognise, slouching young men in ill-fitting greatcoats and braless girls with long straight curtains of hair, but the sexily insolent faces of group members were familiar – Joe's kohl-encircled eyes as he stood discussing something with Roger Maynard and Keith Petrie, backstage in some dressing room. Herself in a long black velvet coat, smiling at Eddy Worth of Electric Village, who clearly wanted the camera to know that he wasn't wearing underpants beneath his very tight trousers. She thought Eddy might have died of a drug overdose a couple of years later, but she wasn't sure.

Janice shuffled the photo underneath a pile of others, feeling vaguely guilty that she could remember buying the coat – ten and six from a stall in Petticoat Lane market – but not whether she'd slept with Eddy Worth, and guiltier still for allowing herself to get sidetracked. There were a whole lot of black and white photos of Dan in his roadie days. In the first few he was alone, humping amplifiers across festival-scuffed grass, sunbathing on the tops of scaffolding towers with a can of beer, or behind the wheel of a battered-looking Transit van. Sometimes there were other people in the pictures, but no one she could recognise until she came upon a series of large colour photographs taken inside a barn-like venue, obviously in the middle of some sort of celebration: nine, no, ten guys, grouped together in front of a mural of a huge and anatomically implausible naked woman. Janice remembered some of them, including the skinny chap on the left-hand end who was wearing jeans and an Afghan waistcoat edged in fur, with nothing apparently underneath it, except ... *He's got a necklace made of horrible things.* She peered at the photo and thought she could make out feathers, something furry – a rabbit's foot, per-haps? – and other bits and pieces, including the glassy round disc of a Greek 'evil eye' pendant with its bright blue iris. The man had a moustache and beard – several of the others did too, but his was bushier, less scrubby. The expression on his face was shifty, and there was a half-smoked roll-up in his hand, the unlit end nipped to a pinch between his thumb and forefinger, as though he were trying to hide it.

The Sneaky Man. Yes, he had been sneaky. Underhand. Indirect. Surreptitious. He'd been all of those things, she remembered now . . . but what was his name?

There were six of these photographs: all, so far as she could tell, identical. Nothing was written on the fronts to identify the subjects, but glancing at the back of each, Janice found, on the last, a series of scrawled names. There was *Dan CT*, for Dan Carthy-Todd, her brother, third from the right, and the name at that end was – yes! – *Malc D*. It must be the same man, and she definitely remembered him now: a guy who'd hung around, wanting to be part of it all, leering at the girls. None of the guys had minded, but Janice had thought he was creepy. So had a lot of her friends, but . . . She suddenly remembered a funny conversation, gasps when three of them had admitted they had, and then they'd not believed her when she'd said she hadn't . . . Of course! The drugs. That was it – the missing bit of the puzzle, the thing that had jogged her memory. Malcolm Devlin was Magic Malc. *Magic*. Not himself a wizard, like the ones Molly and Mark had mentioned, but a supplier of magical substances.

She took the photograph with the names on the back downstairs to show to Suzie, and found her sitting in the kitchen opposite Norma Rocklin, who, frail arms stretched across the table, was clasping her by the hands. As Suzie turned her head, Janice saw that she looked calmer, and judging from the plate beside her, she'd even managed a couple of the sandwiches.

'I'll be off.' Mrs Rocklin raised herself from her chair with difficulty, and shuffled round the table to squeeze Suzie's shoulder. 'Remember, dear, I'm just over the way if you want me.'

Passing Janice on the way to the kitchen door, Mrs Rocklin raised her stick a briskly dismissive couple of inches, narrowly missing her shin, and said, 'You don't have to bother; I'll see myself out.'

Ignoring Janice's raised eyebrows, Suzie said, 'That was kind of her. What were you doing?'

'I found this in Dan's wardrobe.' Janice put the photograph on the table.

'That's *him*! The Sneaky Man. That bloody necklace – how old must it be, for God's sake? I mean, this picture's ancient – look at the clothes . . . Oh, God.' Suzie shoved the photo away from her and stared up at Janice. 'What if Molly's dead in the wood as well? What if they find her body?'

'Come on.' Janice, standing beside Suzie, rubbed her daughter's arm awkwardly, unsure how she'd respond. 'You mustn't think like that.'

'That's what Mrs Rocklin said, but . . .' Suzie slumped, slack with despair.

'Did she?' Janice sat down. 'What did she say?'

'She told me about in the war, she'd got married and then Mr Rocklin was away fighting and she and the baby were at home in Kent and a bomb fell on the house and there was a fire. She said she couldn't get to the baby because the ceiling had come down and there was rubble everywhere and everything was burning, but she could hear him crying. Then the rescue people took her to hospital because she was burnt and nobody knew if the baby was alive or dead for ages. She said she kept asking God to take her instead of him, so that he could have a chance.'

Her face, thought Janice. She remembered Ma telling her that Mrs Rocklin's scars came from something that had happened during the war, but not what it was.

'She had to stay in hospital for ages,' said Suzie, 'but the baby was all right. Mrs Rocklin said that when she didn't know what had happened to him – it was about two days, because it was chaos and the people looking after the baby didn't know who he belonged to – she couldn't think about him being dead, only herself, that she'd be happy to die if it meant he could be OK. She didn't mean that I ought to wish I'm dead or anything, just that she believed so strongly that he was alive, and he was. He was fine.'

Janice had a dim memory of the Rocklins' son. Plump. Hair oil. Twenty-one-going-on-forty in a car coat. He must have been the baby Mrs Rocklin had been telling Suzie about, because there were no other children. She couldn't remember him at a younger age but that, she thought, was because he'd been about ten or twelve years older than her and Dan, so they wouldn't have had anything to do with each other. Had he been called Norman, or did she just think that because Mrs Rocklin was called Norma? He'd certainly *looked* like a Norman. 'Well,' she said, 'it's a good idea to stay positive.'

'Yeah . . .' Suzie sighed and pulled the photograph back towards her. 'Did you know . . . ? What's the Sneaky Man's real name again?'

'Malcolm Devlin. Not really. Not *well*, anyway. He was . . . I suppose he was a sort of drug dealer.'

'Oh?'

'Not like now. It was before all the organised crime and everything. It was more innocent in those days, and there wasn't so much of it – only if you were involved with bands and things.

He just hung around with those people, really, and he had stuff. We called him Magic Malc.'

'There's Dan.' Suzie jabbed a finger at the photo. 'God, his hair! He never told me he knew the Sneaky Man from before.'

'Tom said he didn't like talking about the past much.'

'I suppose . . . Not that I ever really asked him about it – well, except about you.'

'What made me think there might be a picture,' Janice said, 'was D.S. Glenville saying about Malc and Dan knowing each other. Not that it's particularly important, but I was just wondering who'd told him. OK, it was probably Mark, but we didn't have the chance to talk to him before he left, so then I started thinking, what if it had been Jeff, when the police in Cornwall talked to him, or even Joe, because they said last night they'd make enquiries, didn't they, and—'

Suzie looked doubtful. 'Joe's not likely to remember, is he?'

'Probably not, but I thought if *Jeff* had told the police about Dan and Malc knowing each other it must mean that it was a long time ago, because Jeff wouldn't have seen either of them in years, would he?'

'We don't actually *know* that none of them had seen each other in years though, do we? And I really don't understand what any of it has to do with Molly.'

'Perhaps it doesn't, but—'

'Then what the fuck are we doing talking about it?' Suzie pushed the photograph away from her in disgust. 'It's pointless!'

'We don't know that,' said Janice. 'Surely it's worth looking into? I'm going to give Jeff a ring.'

FORTY-TWO

The phone was answered straightaway, before she had time to ready herself. 'Could I speak to Jeff Boulting, please? My name's Janice Keaton.' Stomach churning, heart racing, hands shaking. Her body seemed to be taking on a life of its own, her mind somehow suspended above it, so entirely detached that for a second she couldn't remember where she was or what she was supposed to be doing.

Unable to make the call in front of Suzie, or even be in the house, Janice had gone outside to sit on the painfully hot leather seats of her car, taking one copy of the group photograph with her. Rather to her surprise, Suzie had accepted her exit without comment, saying merely that she would use the time to phone the pub and ask about making posters.

'. . . help you?'

Oh, God. 'Is that Jeff Boulting?'

'Yes.' The tone was patient, slightly weary. 'Speaking.' His voice is the same, she thought. Or perhaps it wasn't. She couldn't really remember.

'It's Janice.'

A beat of silence. 'I'm sorry, I don't—'

'Janice Keaton.'

Another beat. Shit, she'd used the wrong name. Of course he

didn't know who she was. 'Sorry, I didn't think. I mean Janice Carthy-Todd.'

'Janice.' Another pause. Surely he knew who she was now? 'What the hell is going on?'

Oh, God, where should she start? 'I'm sorry to bother you – I mean, after so long and . . . you know, everything, but I need to ask you about something.'

'I see. First Dan, then the police, then you.'

'Dan? You talked to *Dan*?'

'Yes. He came to see me. Said he was passing.' Jeff sounded doubtful. 'Anyway, I was sorry to hear he's no longer with us.'

'Who told you that?' Janice had a sudden mad idea that Dan's visit to Jeff had been posthumous, perhaps in a dream.

'The police. They woke me up at stupid o'clock this morning, banging on the door and wanting to know if I was dead in a wood in Norfolk. Then they buggered off and came back a couple of hours later, asking if I knew anyone called Malcolm Devlin and why I had given him my business card.'

'And . . . ?'

'I told them – once I'd remembered who Malcolm Devlin was, which took a few minutes – that I hadn't seen him for around forty years and had absolutely no idea what he was up to, and then I told them that, so far as I could recollect, the only person I knew in Norfolk who might have some connection to him was your brother, and I knew *he* had a couple of my cards because I'd given them to him when he came to see me a couple of weeks ago.'

'Two weeks ago?'

'Around that, yeah. Look, Janice, if it's about Malc, I don't really know what more I can tell you.'

'Did anyone mention Molly?'

'Who's Molly?'

Janice took a deep, shuddering breath. 'Molly's your grand-daughter. She's ten years old, and she's been missing for almost twenty-four hours.'

A long silence, which, this time, Janice made no attempt to fill.

'Wait,' said Jeff, as though to recall something and undo it. 'I thought . . . the child you had . . . you gave it up for adoption, right?'

'*It* was a girl, Jeff. I wrote and told you.'

'Yes.' There was another pause. 'It was a long time ago.'

'Forty-four years.'

'Was it? But she was adopted, wasn't she?'

'Yes. I told you that in the letter.'

'So . . . what? She got in touch with you?'

'Yes.' *The child you had* . . . As if he'd had nothing to do with it. The short version'll do, Janice thought. Why the hell should she give him the details? 'She's been living in Norfolk, and Molly's missing, and it's just possible that it's something to do with this Devlin guy, so if you know anything – *anything at all* – that you think might help, you need to tell me, OK?'

'Dan didn't tell me that. About Molly, I mean, and . . . what's her name?'

'Your daughter, you mean? Suzie – short for Suzanne. It was something else, but she changed it back to the name I gave her.'

'He never said.'

'Yeah, well. I'm telling you now.'

'OK, OK. Just . . . Give me a minute, will you?'

'I don't *have* a minute,' snapped Janice. 'Molly's missing. You can sort out your feelings later. Did Dan say anything to you about Malcolm Devlin?'

'No. It was weird, Janice. He wanted to know about some footage of a picnic we had with some of the guys from the Weather Ship.

It was years ago, just before their first album came out. It's on YouTube, and—'

'I've seen it.'

'Have you?'

'I was trying to find a picture of you to show Suzie. What about it?'

'Like I said, it was weird. The police thought it was weird too when I told them – I'm not even sure they believed me. Anyway, there was a knock on the door one afternoon, and I answered it – I'm a photographer and the studio's part of the house – and there was Dan. He asked if we could have a chat, and I hadn't got a lot on, so I said sure. He wanted to take me to the pub, so I said OK, and we went. At first it was just catching up, although he didn't tell me anything about you or . . . any of what you just told me.'

'Did you ask?' It was out of Janice's mouth before she could stop it.

His silence reproached her. 'I asked about you, and he said you were abroad, travelling. Weren't you?'

'Yes – until a few weeks ago anyway. Go on.'

'Well, he started talking about the past, and then he mentioned that picnic. He said he'd remembered I'd had my cine camera, and asked what I'd done with the footage. When I asked him why he hadn't just looked on the internet, he got defensive and said he didn't own a computer.'

'It's true, he didn't. He didn't think much of the internet.'

'So I gathered. Anyway, I said something about surely he knew someone who could look it up for him, and he got even more defensive and said how was he supposed to know it was there and he didn't want to waste people's time . . . To be honest, Janice, I'd completely forgotten about that piece of film. It was my youngest son who found it, a few years ago – I didn't even know I'd still got it, but Olly'd just started at film school, and he was interested in all my old stuff. So then Dan asked if I'd show him, and we went back to my place and had a look at it, and he asked me several times if it was the whole film, or if there was more – which there isn't, because Olly uploaded everything there was. Then he started asking me what I remembered about the day. He kept going on about it – obviously wanted something significant, you know?'

'Like what?'

'I've no idea. It was a picnic, that's all.'

'Did you get any idea *why* he was asking you about it?'

'No. All I could think was . . . well, since it's been up, we've had a few emails from fans asking about it – did Joe play his guitar? What did he talk about? What did he eat and drink? Did he take any drugs? – that kind of thing. How the hell am I supposed to remember that? I mean, can you remember?'

'Not really, no.'

'Of course you can't, because it's not important. But those people see meaning in everything – trivial shit. I'd no idea there was still such an obsession with Joe, but apparently there is – and I suppose I thought Dan had turned into one of those types and he was after some sort of inside track or something, although why he'd bother coming all the way down here to ask me, I don't know. I mean, Dan was *there*, wasn't he? At the picnic, same as we were. Come to that, why didn't he ask *you*?'

Janice sighed. 'God knows. And you're sure he didn't ask any specific questions?'

'Not that I can remember. He wanted to know who was there – and I wouldn't even have remembered that unless I'd looked at the footage.'

'Was anyone else there? I mean, anyone not in the film?'

'I don't know! Christ, you're as bad as him – if you can't remember, why the hell should *I* be able to?'

'Because I seem to remember less and less these days. I keep finding I've got holes where names and places used to be. When the police asked me about Malcolm Devlin, I had no idea who they were talking about until I looked through Dan's photos and realised we used to call him Magic Malc.'

'I shouldn't worry. Happens to all of us – just as long as it's not the important stuff, like who *you* are.'

'You know Joe lives here, don't you? In this village?'

'In Norfolk, you mean? Yeah, I think I read it somewhere, or someone told me or something.'

'I didn't know until a couple of days ago. Dan didn't mention it, then?'

'No, he didn't. How is Joe? Is he OK? I heard all the stories, but . . .'

'He's all right – I think. Pretty solitary. Quiet. You get these sort of flashes of how he used to be, but there's not much connection. He's completely turned his back on the past. I mentioned something about one of his songs and it was like a shutter coming down. He didn't want to know.'

'Do you think it was the acid that did it?'

'I don't know. To be honest, I don't see how it can have been *just* that – there had to have been something else as well, because lots of people took loads of acid and they're all right, aren't they?'

'Most of them, yeah. It's a shame, though, that he just walked away from it when he was so talented . . . Do you think you're gonna, you know, be friends?'

'I don't think Joe has many friends. Dan used to go to his house a bit and help him with stuff. I get the impression that he doesn't really do other people much at all – although that might be because he's scared they'll turn out to be obsessive, of course.'

'You were pretty hung up on him, Janice.'

Hearing an edge in his voice, Janice said lightly, 'That was all a very long time ago.'

'Yeah . . .' The word drifted into her ear like a sigh. 'This is all pretty bizarre. I wish I could be more help, but . . .'

'I know. Look, Jeff, I realise you'd not seen Dan for a long time, but how did he seem to you?'

'I have to say he did look pretty rough. And, well . . . intense, I suppose. Urgent. A man on a mission, you know? Like he was running out of time, but I suppose that must have been the illness, wanting to do things before—'

'That's the thing. He wasn't ill.'

'I don't understand. If he wasn't ill, why . . . ?'

'Why did he die? We don't know yet. He died in his sleep. There's a suggestion it might have been suicide, but they have to do more tests.'

'And you didn't . . . I mean, he didn't, you know, say anything?'

'Nothing. Not to me, and – as far as I know – not to anyone else either.'

'God. You don't think . . .'

'What?'

'Well, did Dan have any debts or anything like that? Because if he was trying to get hold of cash fast, that might account for why I had this feeling that he was against the clock, you know?'

'I don't understand. He didn't ask you for money, did he?'

'No, but he was obviously after some information, wasn't he? I'm just wondering if he'd got some idea that he could sell something about Joe to a newspaper.'

'Doesn't sound like Dan. And no one's turned up claiming he owes them money. At least, not yet.'

'Just a thought. And anyway, it doesn't explain why my business card ended up in Malc's pocket.'

'No, it doesn't.' Janice was conscious, once more, that she'd made a mental grab at something and come up with a handful of empty air. Scrabbling for something to latch on to, she said, 'That picnic – do you remember what the date was?'

'Not offhand, but the canister's around somewhere and I usually write the date on the label. It's probably in Olly's room. Hang on . . .' The sound of creaking – stairs, Janice thought – was followed by muffled bumps and bangs. After a couple of minutes, Jeff said, 'Here we go: twelfth of August nineteen sixty-seven.'

FORTY-THREE

Janice sat in the car for several minutes after the conversation had finished, eyes closed, mind fluttering between thoughts like a bird unsure of where it might be safe to alight. The noise of a vehicle brought her back to the present, and opening her eyes she saw Suzie at the kitchen window, staring at a car coming up the lane.

Seeing D.S. Glenville in the back with Mark, Janice got out of her car to give him the photograph and an explanation. 'That's Malcolm Devlin at the end, with all the stuff round his neck. He still wore that necklace, or something like it – Molly told me.'

Glenville, who was closest to her and who hadn't moved to get out of the car, raised his eyebrows. 'Not this morning. Did you remove it?' he asked Mark.

'He wasn't wearing it,' said Mark, reaching for the door. 'It wasn't there. All right if I go now?'

Glenville sighed, then nodded in the direction of the rear-view mirror, and the policeman who'd been driving got out and opened the back door for Mark. Of course, thought Janice, you wouldn't be able to do it from the inside, or people would escape all the time.

'You didn't say anything about the necklace last night,' she said to Mark, as they turned to go into the house. 'About it not being there.'

'Probably because I was in shock. Does it matter?' He glared at her. 'And what the fuck do you think *you* were doing, going out and leaving Suzie by herself?'

'I haven't been out. I was sitting in the car to make a private phone call, that's all.'

Mark stared at her for a second, exasperated, then ran past her into the kitchen. Perhaps Malc had lost the necklace, Janice thought. Or, if he'd struggled with whoever killed him, perhaps it had got broken and was somewhere in the camp, trampled underfoot.

'Did they find anything?' Suzie was still standing in the same position in front of the kitchen window, staring down the lane.

'Of course not!' Mark sat down with his elbows on the table, running his hands through his hair. 'Did you think they would?'

'Just asking.'

Mark's arms thumped down on the table. 'I can't believe you said that.'

'Too bad.' Still Suzie hadn't turned round.

'You can't think I had anything to do with it?' Mark's eyes were wide.

Suzie turned with a weary, shuffling motion. 'I don't know what I think, do I?'

Watching them eyeing each other, Janice didn't know what she thought either, but she had the sense of a relationship irrevocably broken. A quick, piercing memory made her blink and draw back: being in bed with her first husband, Sean, on their last holiday together, and him saying, 'I can't get to you. I never could. It's as if you've sealed yourself off.' Later, walking along the beach by herself – in Spain? France? – she'd been struck by the accuracy of the word 'seal'. Like a medieval surgeon, thrusting the pollarded stump of a limb into a barrel of pitch – closing the wound of losing Suzie . . . who was talking to her.

'. . . any use?'

'Jeff? I don't know. He said that Dan had been to see him.'

'When?'

'A fortnight ago, he said. He must have stayed the night somewhere, because you couldn't get there and back in a day. Well, I suppose you *could*, but it'd be at least eight hours each way, probably more.'

Suzie was shaking her head, but Mark said, 'Dan might have gone to Cornwall when we went over to Sheringham to see Clive. He's a friend of mine,' he explained. 'He and his wife run a hotel there, and we stayed the night.'

'I don't understand,' Suzie said. 'Why would Dan go and see him?'

'You know that bit of film I showed you, on YouTube? The picnic?'

'What about it?'

'That's what Dan wanted to talk to Jeff about.'

'Why?'

Janice sighed. 'I have no idea. Neither does Jeff.'

'Well,' said Suzie slowly, as though it was an idea she was only reluctantly letting go of, 'that doesn't sound like it's got anything to do with Molly, does it? Unless . . . You believe him, do you?'

'Yes. I mean, I don't have any reason not to.'

'But when he talked about Molly, you didn't think it sounded strange or anything?'

'No. I mean, he was concerned, of course, but . . .' But only as one might be about someone else's tragedy, thought Janice. *The child you had* . . . Jeff didn't see it as being anything to do with him, except tangentially.

Suzie shot her a look. 'You did tell him about me, didn't you? At the time, I mean.'

'Of course I did.'

'But he didn't know about Molly.'

'No.'

'So Dan hadn't told him about us being here.'

'No – but you didn't want him to, did you? At least, you didn't want him to tell me. And,' Janice added quickly, in case Suzie thought it was a dig, 'the police didn't say anything because they were only interested in establishing that it wasn't Jeff in the wood.'

'That's fair enough, I suppose. It's all right, Janice. You and Jeff – I didn't think it was the love affair of the century. I grew out of that one about thirty years ago, so it's hardly a great surprise and anyway, it's not important. While you were on the phone I rang the pub, and Simon says we can come and use the printer whenever we like, but we'll need to bring paper. And,' she turned to Mark, 'Simon says the shop doesn't sell A4 paper, so someone'll have to go to the supermarket.'

'Right.' Janice palmed her car key, relieved to have something useful to do that wouldn't involve talking to anybody. 'I'll do that now.'

Crossing the landing for her bag, Janice spotted the rest of the group photographs on the floor of Dan's room and, rolling one up, took it with her. She was getting into her car when Mark appeared in the doorway, clearly halfway through a conversation on his mobile, shouting for her to call him when she was on the way back.

She was about to drive off when she remembered about the temazepam. Turning off the ignition, she ran past Mark and back into the kitchen. Suzie had returned to her position at the window. 'Who's Mark on the phone to?'

'Mrs Rocklin.' Suzie looked past her, distracted by a distant, horrible horizon. 'Asking her to come over while he goes and does the poster.'

'That's good. I've just remembered, love, about the temazepam. You said you hardly ever took them.'

'I didn't. Once, I think, or maybe twice – apart from this time, that is.'

'There were only two left in the bottle. I think Dan might have taken them . . .'

'Oh, shit.' Suzie turned to look at her. 'I'm sorry.'

'Not your fault – you'd forgotten they were there, hadn't you?'

'Yes, I had. I wish he'd *said* something. It's like he just . . . *gave up* on life.'

'Yeah, I know.' Janice shook her head, defeated. 'We'd better tell the police about the temazepam.'

'Did he leave a number?' Janice turned to see Mark standing in the doorway.

'Who?'

'P.C. Whatsit, who came round about Dan – about the post-mortem.'

'Calvert. I think there's a card somewhere.' Suzie went to fish about in her handbag, which was hanging on the back of the kitchen door. 'Here you are.'

'Don't worry.' Mark looked at Janice. 'I'll get on to it.' Suzie sank into a chair. 'Mrs Rocklin's on her way.' Mark squeezed her shoulder. 'It will be OK, love. They'll find her.'

'Oh, Dan . . .' The car seemed even hotter than before. Sitting at the wheel, Janice was a husk, drained of energy, so that even turning the key in the ignition felt like an achievement. It wasn't supposed to be like this, she thought, and then, But what *was* it supposed to be like? She couldn't remember. She sat for a minute, trying to summon what was no longer there – had it ever been? – and then, gathering the strength to release the handbrake, drove off down the lane.

FORTY-FOUR

Molly checked that the letter and photos were still inside her plastic bag. She knew it was silly, really, because they had been there when she'd checked a minute ago and no one apart from her had even touched her things, but she couldn't help it. Just to be extra safe, in case anyone tried to take the bag away or she lost it, she transferred the letter and pictures to her skirt pocket, with her money.

She'd been waiting for ages, and she was starting to feel shivery and weird and a bit sick. She wondered if she should tell the lady who'd brought her the orange drink and biscuits, but she was just sitting in the corner and not saying anything, so perhaps they weren't meant to be talking. The lady looked OK, though – chubby, with rolls of fat on her middle that her black top made look like a stack of tyres, and a smile like she must be someone's mum. Well, sort of. Almost smiling, like she wanted to say something friendly but she wasn't allowed to.

None of it was like she'd imagined, with the pink marquee and gold chairs and a special dress and someone to brush her hair and everything – but now she was here she could see that was stupid, because all those things would be for when the television people came and so it could be on YouTube and stuff. This room looked scruffy, like nobody bothered about it. There was a sofa, one of those ones where you could keep adding more bits to make it longer and go round a corner, but it wasn't clean, like a T.V. sofa would be, and it was a yucky blue that wasn't dark enough to hide all the marks where people had spilt their drinks. The beige carpet tiles had marks too, and the little table. The only other things in the room were two paintings of flowers in vases – sploshy, so you couldn't see what sort they were – and a big green plant in a pot in one corner. At first she'd thought it was real, but when she went and fiddled with one of the leaves, it was made of some weird plasticky stuff.

It was hard to imagine anyone as nice and pretty as Melissa Piper being in this room, and Molly was worried about how she looked too. When she'd imagined their very first meeting, the picture in her mind had always been of her looking . . . well, like herself but different. Changed. Better and prettier. She'd imagined how good and *right* it would feel a million times, but now she just felt hot and dirty. Janice's plait was all messy and coming out in wisps – she'd seen it in the mirror when the lady had taken her to the loo.

The lady had retied the hair ribbon for her, in a bow, but now it had come undone again and Molly didn't want to ask her a second time because she'd undone it herself, fiddling, and because she didn't know if they were allowed to say anything.

She couldn't believe how many questions the policeman and woman had asked yesterday, before they took her to a house to sleep. The lady at the house had called her Phoebe, which made her feel funny – although it was bound to be a *bit* strange until she got used to it – and she'd made scrambled eggs for breakfast, and toast, and lots of children had sat round the table like in a book, talking and laughing. That bit was quite nice, even though she didn't know any of them, because one of the boys was really funny. She'd thought that the Pipers might come after that, but then the lady had brought her back here and there'd been more questions from a woman policeman – a different one to yesterday – who got all huffy and cross, and then they'd made her sit in this stupid room. She'd been here for ages and people kept coming in to whisper to the stack-of-tyres lady who kept trying to smile at her but never said anything. Every time the door opened she'd thought that this time it must be the Pipers, but it never was.

They'd given her a box with books and comics in it. Most of them were for little kids, with big pictures, but there was one old paperback book called *Skellig*. It was quite difficult, but she had a try. The Pipers would be pleased if they saw her reading a book, because they had proper jobs in offices where you wore neat clothes and went in a clean car. The book was about a boy called Michael who finds a strange man in the garage. It made her think of the Sneaky Man, and she couldn't decide if Michael and his friend were really brave talking to him, or really stupid, because she wouldn't have.

It was quite an interesting book, but it was hard to sit and read when she kept thinking about what was going to happen. Honestly, what did it matter where she'd come from and how she'd got here? She *was* here, wasn't she? And all they needed to do was stop asking stupid questions and fetch her real mum and dad and everything would be all right. She'd shown them the scrapbook because that was like *evidence* – but not the letter or the photos, because those were special and only for the Pipers – and she'd told them she'd walked here. That was because she didn't want to get Tom into trouble, especially as he hadn't even known she'd been hidden in the back of the van behind Dan's gardening stuff. The other reason was that she didn't want David and Melissa to find out that she'd weed herself while she was in there and had to leave her wet pants behind, hidden under some old sacks. She wished she had some pants on now. She hadn't brought any clean ones with her, and having a bare bum felt wrong, especially because she was wearing a skirt and someone might see and tell on her or laugh or something. It was her best skirt, and now there was a big sticky black mark at the side where she'd sat in the stuff Dan had used for painting sheds and fences, which had been spilt in the van. She adjusted it again, smoothing the material and tucking it carefully under her legs on both sides. Her legs had bruises all over because there'd been no cushions in the back of the van, just sacks, and she'd kept banging against all the spades and petrol cans and stuff. It had taken *ages*. Getting out and running away had been easy enough, because there were masses of things to hide behind when Tom's friend had opened the back for his tent, and then he'd left the doors open while they had a beer, so that was OK. After that it was a bit scary because of all the people and not knowing where she was going, but she'd managed to find a policeman, so that was all right.

Molly felt quite pleased with herself. They'd asked and asked, but she hadn't said a word about Suzie or Tom or anyone. Not many people would be able to do that, but she had.

Obviously, she wouldn't forget that she'd been Molly – after all, it had been quite a lot of years – and nor would she forget Suzie or any of them. In fact, she was going to say nice things about Suzie and Dan to David and Melissa, so they'd be forgiven and not in any trouble and Tom could carry on being her brother; but that would come later, after she'd started being Phoebe really and properly.

What a good job she'd walked past the shop and seen the newspaper when she had and saved David and Melissa from getting divorced. Even if David had found someone he loved more, like Tom's dad did when he left Tom and Suzie, he'd change his mind if *she* was there, wouldn't he? He'd do it for her.

If only they'd hurry up.

FORTY-FIVE

Having delivered the ream of paper she'd bought at the super-market to the Lord Nelson, where Simon Curtis and Mark were busy creating a poster in the tiny back office, Janice went back outside and sat in her car.

Mark had told her that Mrs Rocklin was sitting with Suzie. Better it's her, Janice thought. Gazing at the wheelie bins ranged along the side of the pub car park she realised, with a sort of hopeless detachment, that as far as Suzie was concerned she was part of the problem. There was nothing she could do to change that. There is nothing that I can do at all, she thought. I'm useless.

I didn't think it was the love affair of the century: Suzie's voice in her mind, almost a jeer.

At the end of their conversation, and more to make up for her earlier brusqueness than anything else, Janice had asked Jeff about his life. In return, she'd got a casual-sounding speech about how the advent of digital was making things tough and how he'd real-ised he needed to get out of London before it suffocated him She hadn't judged him for it when he'd said it, and she didn't now: she'd heard dozens of men of her age talk that way, sandpapering over the rough edges of failure. After all, hadn't she given him, in return, a version of her life that was just as practised and philo-sophically optimistic as his own?

256

A tortoiseshell cat leapt on top of the low wall beside the wheelie bins and sat, sleek in the sun, self-contained and absolutely still. Like an Egyptian cat goddess, thought Janice, remembering something she'd read: Bastet, protector of mothers. A good omen, perhaps?

Jeff hadn't asked anything more about Suzie – hadn't commented at all, in fact. Shock, maybe. The suddenness of it. Besides, what could she have told him? She was almost as much of a stranger to their daughter as he was. The only experience she and Suzie had shared, prior to that phone call about Dan, was one that her daughter couldn't remember. Janice couldn't remember much about Suzie's birth either, except that for most of the time she'd been by herself, in pain and scared. The midwife had been brisk and impersonal and, when he'd finally shown up, so had the doctor. There'd been no congratulations from anybody, just awkwardness and avoidance, as if it had been a stillbirth and not a living, healthy child. Only one young nurse, an Irish girl, who'd come in when everyone else had gone, had reached out her hand – Janice had a clear picture of the square palm, blunt fingers and the round, flour-white arm – and, placing it momentarily over Janice's, murmured, 'Well done.' For that short time – ten seconds, perhaps, or fifteen – she had had a glimpse of what it would have been like, had everything been different.

The memory, with the detail of the nurse's arm and hand, surprised her. She was sure that she hadn't shed tears when it happened, but now it engendered a howl in her throat that couldn't be suppressed and she sat, bawling like a child. Scarcely able to breathe between sobs, she rolled her head from side to side on the headrest until the tears ran into her ears and she no longer knew what, or who, she was crying for.

*

Five minutes later, or perhaps ten, or even a quarter of an hour, she managed to stop for long enough to mop up and start trying to repair her face. Driving away, sunglasses firmly on her nose, she noticed that the cat – which wasn't a symbol, or any sort of omen, but just a cat – was still sitting on the wall.

FORTY-SIX

Janice could see the bonfire smoke rising from behind Joe's house as she drove up the lane and she smelt it on his clothes when he answered the door. Seeing her, he shook his head violently and made to close it again, but – 'Please, Joe, stop!' – she stepped forward, preventing him. They struggled in silence for a few seconds, pushing at opposite sides of the door, and then Joe yielded so abruptly that Janice almost fell over. He stood back, blocking the hallway with his body.

'I just want to show you something.' Janice pulled the rolled-up photograph out of her bag. 'I found this, and I thought you might know if it's the same person who's been hanging round your house. Look . . . The one on the end, with the necklace.' She held out the photograph, but Joe refused to touch it. Janice jabbed the photo with a forefinger. 'Him. Malcolm Devlin. We used to call him Magic Malc.'

Joe flinched as if she'd stuck a blazing torch in his face, and backed away. 'He's here all the time. I don't want to see him.'

'He won't come anymore, Joe. He's dead.'

Joe shook his head wildly, and tried to shoo her back outside.

'Please, just tell me, did he say anything—?'

'No!' Joe shouted. 'I told you, I don't do that anymore.'

'Wait! Did he ever say anything about Molly?' Not Molly, she

259

thought, remembering the paintings. He's confused. 'Or Marie? What about when you came for the hair ribbon – was that something to do with him? Did the police—?'

A final headshake before the door was slammed shut. Janice smacked the flaking paint with the flat of her hand. 'Please, Joe! You've got to help me!'

Silence. It was hopeless. Dispirited, Janice traipsed back down the overgrown path to her car. It looked as if Joe was already distressed from the visit from Calvert and Wright, and all she'd done was to make things worse for him – and perhaps none of it was anything to do with Molly anyway.

She'd parked her car too close to Joe's fence. Barking her shin, she peered down and saw that the lifebelt she'd seen before, left by a fan, was still propped there. So were all the other things – the ribbons, the C.D.s, the hopeful letters in transparent plastic bags. Suzie had told her that Joe always burnt such offerings, but he hadn't collected them up for this bonfire, which, judging from the smoke, was well underway.

Putting her car keys back into her bag, she walked down the verge and let herself into the field next to the house, stumbling across the dusty rows of wheat stubble until she reached the hedge that separated it from Joe's back garden. Seen in daylight, it was longer than she'd expected – something like two hundred feet down to the row of trees at the bottom. Standing on tiptoe halfway along and peering over the top of the hawthorn, she could just manage to see the bonfire in the middle of the lawn, the air around it quivering, smudgy with smoke. It seemed to be made mainly of branches, although the ends of a couple of thick, paint-splattered planks were sticking out at the bottom. Joe was nowhere to be seen, but a few yards away from the blaze were six or seven canvases, piled haphazardly on the lawn, and next to them what looked like several rolls of wallpaper. Janice couldn't see what was on the canvases – the top one was face down – but assumed that Joe must have put them there with the intention of burning them. Why, though? Surely they were reuseable, unless they'd been damaged in some way. Perhaps he was in the habit of burning his paintings if he didn't like them, as well as all the stuff that got left by the fence. Remembering something she'd read about Francis Bacon destroying canvases, she thought: Lots of artists probably do it, if they don't think their work is good enough.

It wasn't helping find Molly though. Ashamed of her nosiness, she crossed the field, back to the car, the jagged edges of the wheat stalks scraping across her bare ankles.

Driving the short distance through the hot afternoon, sweaty hair sticking to the back of her neck, Janice, rounding the corner by the Lord Nelson, suddenly found herself wishing she really were going *home*, to the Old Rectory as she'd known it in childhood. At the end of a summer day when she was nine or ten, when she and Dan had been playing outside for hours with the other kids, and she'd felt tired and happy and full of sun, and Ma would give them a lovely big tea and they could do it all over again tomorrow. And everything was ahead of them, and nothing had gone wrong.

No one appeared to greet her. Passing the kitchen door on her way upstairs, she heard the murmur of voices but decided not to interrupt. Soothing her scratched legs and feet with Germolene from an old tin she'd found in the bathroom cabinet, she saw that it was almost quarter to five. More than twenty-four hours, now.

The majority of children who aren't found are killed within . . . No. That wasn't what had happened. Snatched, dragged behind a hedge . . . It couldn't be that. There must be an explanation, a clue, something significant to do with Molly *herself*. Not just a child in the wrong place at the wrong time, a piece of disposable, impersonal flesh. An object. Prey.

It couldn't be that. Janice crossed the landing to Molly's bedroom. Feverishly, she pawed through the contents of the drawers, the cupboard, the few books and games on the shelves, the keepsake box on the window sill and the pink plastic handbag hanging from a hook behind the door. She pulled the bed away from the wall as far as she could and then, shoving it back into place, lay down with the side of her face flattened against the floor to peer underneath it.

Drifts of dust and one wire coat-hanger. Nothing else. The scrapbook wasn't there, and nor were the felt-tip pens. Molly'd been carrying the scrapbook, hadn't she? Perhaps it was part of a homework project about nature or something.

She sat down on the side of the bed and looked around the room, racking her brains. What had happened that morning? What had Molly said or done? What had she missed? From the corkboard above the desk, the artificially aged photograph of Phoebe Piper gazed back at her. In her mind's eye Janice saw a line of such photographs, a year-on-year progression towards crow's feet, turkey neck and the rest. Imagined moments from a life unlived, no memories behind the subject's eyes. Phoebe Piper. Lisa Wynn. Molly.

Not Molly. Molly would be found. *Phoebe hasn't been found*, said a sharp voice in her head. *Nor has Lisa. Lisa's been missing for forty-seven years, since . . . since . . .*

Since . . . ? Frowning, Janice got up and went into Dan's room. The colour supplement was still on the bed. She scanned through the 'Missing' article until she found the relevant paragraph: . . . *12th August, the anniversary of Lisa's disappearance . . .* The 12th August 1967: what Jeff had said was written on the film canister. The date of the picnic.

FORTY-SEVEN

It was her. Really her. Melissa Piper. For a moment, Molly thought she'd actually forgotten how to breathe. Her chest felt as though it might burst, as if she'd been swimming underwater for too long. Heart hammering, she scrambled off the grubby sofa and stood, swaying slightly, not sure what to do next. Melissa was even more beautiful than in the photos, and she was smiling, glowing, full of hope and joy, and it was *the moment* when everything would be all right and she'd be Phoebe again and she stumbled forward and—

She heard a jagged intake of breath above her head. Instead of embracing her, Melissa took hold of her upper arms, gently but firmly, and, kneeling down in front of her on the nasty carpet, looked at her for a long time. Molly stared at the smooth, lovely face, with its perfect hair and sweet perfume, so close to her own. She was trembling, holding her breath, willing Melissa to speak, to transform her back into Phoebe, to make it happen because it was now, it was *now*, it was NOW—

'I'm sorry, but you're not my little girl.'

The voice was so kind, so sweet, that it was several seconds before the meaning of the words sank in. It must be a shock for her, Molly thought, seeing me again. 'I'm not little anymore,' she explained. 'I'm ten years old now. I've grown, and—'

'No, darling.' Melissa's hand was on her cheek, light and soft. 'That's not what I meant. You're not my Phoebe.'

'But I am. I'm her. Really I am.'

Melissa shook her head and Molly saw that the light in her eyes, the gleam of expectation, was gone. The air around her seemed somehow to go flat, taking the glow and the brightness, leaving the pair of them in a scruffy room full of disappointment. 'I am,' she repeated stubbornly. 'I know I am. Please—'

'No, love.' As Molly took a step forward, Melissa stood up and stepped back in a swift, evasive movement. Turning to the lady, who'd suddenly appeared at the edge of Molly's vision, making her jump because she'd forgotten that there was anyone else in the room, she said, 'I'm afraid this isn't Phoebe.'

'I am!' Molly shouted, teetering on one foot. 'I must be. I'm just like the photo.' She had to make it real again, make the happiness and loveliness turn solid and stay.

'I know you are, love.' Melissa looked unbearably sad. 'But it isn't a real photo. To be perfectly honest,' she turned to the lady again, 'I never really thought that's what Phoebe would look like.'

'But it is,' said Molly desperately. 'It is. It's what I look like. And I've got this.' Frantically, she clawed the ribbon from the tail of her plait and held it out.

Melissa stared at the palmful of scrunched pink satin. 'What's that?'

'Phoebe's hair ribbon.'

Melissa frowned. 'Phoebe didn't have a hair ribbon. She hated having her hair tied back, so I never did.' She looked at the lady and said, in a sad voice, 'She'd never let me do anything with her hair apart from brush it.'

'But I am Phoebe.' Mind racing, desperate to stop everything

slipping away, Molly scrabbled in her skirt pocket for Dan's letter.
'Look.'

'What's that?' The huffing policewoman stepped forward.

'It's not for you.' Molly clutched the envelope to her chest.
Turning to Mrs Piper, she said, 'If you read it, you'll know it's me.'

'Well . . .' Melissa frowned, then said, 'I will if you want me to,
but you know it won't make any difference.'

'It will.' Molly pulled the letter out of the envelope and handed
it over. 'Really. You'll see.'

Melissa read the letter several times – Molly could see this from
the way her eyes were moving – in complete silence. Finally, she
passed it over to the policewoman. 'I don't understand. There
seems to be a reference, but . . .' Turning back to Molly, she said,
'What's your name?' Her voice was tight, as if she was really
excited but trying not to show it.

With a wild upsurge of hope, Molly blurted, 'Phoebe. My name's
Phoebe.'

'I see.' Melissa's voice was taut, careful. 'Do people call you
Phoebe?'

Reluctantly, Molly shook her head.

'What do they call you?'

'It isn't my name. I . . .' Molly looked into the luminous, glistening eyes, and faltered. 'Molly,' she whispered.

'Molly. Like the Molly in the letter?'

'Yes.'

'Is that you?'

'Yes, but—'

'What about your other name? Your surname?'

'It's Armitage, but—'

'Mrs Piper,' the policewoman interrupted, 'can I have a word?'

'Of course.' She turned away from Molly, and both of them went to stand on the other side of the room, facing away from her. The policewoman had her hand on Melissa's back.

Molly couldn't hear what they were saying, except that there was something about a test and about knowing something. Whenever they did tests at school she was rubbish, so she'd be bound to fail . . . Unless it was some other kind of test, like a medical one. Perhaps it would hurt.

Suddenly, Molly didn't feel quite so sure about being Phoebe, or at least about wanting to be Phoebe, anyway, but wanting to be Phoebe and thinking she *was* Phoebe were sort of the same thing . . . Or maybe they weren't really, but they'd got sort of stuck together and now they were unsticking again. She'd been so certain before, but supposing – just supposing – she wasn't Phoebe? And what if this test, whatever it was, showed that she wasn't Phoebe or Molly, but somebody else, someone she'd never even heard of? That couldn't happen, could it? *Could* it?

Melissa and the policewoman were coming back now. Molly felt a bit sick. She opened her mouth to ask what the test was, but Melissa held up a hand to quiet her and said, 'I'm glad you showed me that letter, Molly, because it might be important. But you're not my Phoebe, darling, not really.'

'But . . .' Molly faltered, confused and unsure of what she wanted to say.

'Do you know what a coincidence is, Molly?'

Dumb now, Molly shook her head.

'It's when something happens by accident. Like you looking like that photo. It's just chance. There isn't always a reason for things, Molly. Sometimes they just happen.' Melissa shook her head. 'I'm sorry.' She looked so beautiful in her simple summer dress with the gold necklace, like a grown-up princess, and so sad.

Looking at her, Molly wanted with all her might to be Phoebe, to make Melissa smile. Perhaps I can pretend, she thought. I can be the next best thing to Phoebe. 'I want to make you happy,' she gabbled. 'I know I can. I came as fast as I could because I want to make it be all right with you and Mr Piper, so you'll be together again. Please let me.' She reached out a hand, but Melissa made a small tearing sound in her throat and backed away again, this time holding up both hands, palms forward, with a terrible finality. 'I know I can make you happy, because . . .' Molly persisted – then couldn't think of anything else to say. She was supposed to make Melissa happy just by being there, *actually being* Phoebe, and it wasn't working. She'd been hoping, dreaming, praying for this moment for so long and now it had all gone wrong. She'd known deep inside that she was Phoebe and she could make Melissa happy, and if you knew a thing right deep inside like that you couldn't be wrong, could you? It had never occurred to her that Melissa wouldn't believe her, but now it was getting all confused in her head, and—

Wait! She'd forgotten about the photos. 'I've got these as well.' She'd had to fold them to get them into her skirt pocket and now she smoothed them frantically, trying to get the creases out. 'That one –' she pointed to the photograph of the two women – 'has got stuff written on the back.'

'*Ask her who your mother is.*' Melissa was staring at the photos, a look of increasing bafflement on her face. 'I've never seen any of these people before.'

'It's only two people,' said Molly eagerly. 'The one with only the face is the same as one of the women in the other picture.'

'Do you know who they are?' asked the fat lady, who'd been staring over Melissa's shoulder at the photos.

'No,' said Molly, turning to Melissa. 'I thought you'd know.'

'I'm sorry.' Melissa turned to the policewoman. 'I've got no idea.'

'Where did you get this letter?' asked the policewoman.

'I found it,' said Molly. 'In the shed at home.'

'And where's home?'

'Norfolk.'

'OK.' The policewoman muttered something to the fat lady, then left the room, taking the letter with her.

'I am sorry,' Melissa repeated. 'I really am.' She was speaking fast, and the words were sort of curling up as though she were trying to get them out before she started crying. 'You're not Phoebe. You're Molly, and you have to be Molly, because that's who you are. You can't be someone else, even if you want to, but I'm sure you're lovely as you are, and I'm sure you make your mummy – your real mummy – very happy.'

Speechless, Molly stared as Melissa turned away and, after fumbling blindly with the door handle and being helped by the fat lady, left the room. Now the fat lady was talking to her, saying something about who was her real mum and how did she get here all the way from Norfolk, but Molly wasn't listening. The fat lady put a hand on Molly's shoulder, but Molly twisted away and went to sit, huddled up, her feet on the nasty sofa.

Everything was in a mess. She'd been left in this horrible room because she was the wrong girl. She wasn't good enough to be Phoebe or have a mum like Melissa. Of course she wasn't. How could she ever have thought she was?

FORTY-EIGHT

The exact same day. Why hadn't she remembered that? She hadn't been aware of anything at the time – no police, or people searching the area – but then they'd all been tripping, so they'd have kept away to avoid being busted. Besides, it was a huge place – it would be entirely possible to be there and not have noticed such activity, even if one was clean and sober, she thought. She must have seen it in a newspaper or something afterwards, otherwise why would Lisa Wynn's name have seemed vaguely familiar? And why had Dan asked Jeff who was at the picnic?

There must be a clue here, somewhere in his bedroom. Janice started opening drawers. Socks, underwear, T-shirts, a nest of brightly coloured ties like flat snakes ... Ordinary, explicable things. Athlete's foot powder. Throat lozenges. She was glancing about for anything else that might possibly explain Dan's questions to Jeff when she heard Suzie yelling from downstairs.

Yanking open the bedroom door, she heard the words 'They've found Molly!' and rushed down the stairs. Suzie was in the kitchen, beaming and clutching her mobile phone to her chest. 'She's OK! She's safe!'

'Oh, thank God.' Without thinking, Janice threw her arms around Suzie and felt the pressure of her hug returned. When, after a long moment – during which, unable to form sentences, they half laughed and half cried – the two of them disengaged, she asked, 'Where?'

'Wiltshire. That was their police.'

'So she *did* go with Tom.' Light-headed with relief, Janice dropped into a chair. 'You'd better sit down too, you look as though you're about to fall over.'

Suzie did as she was told, then said, 'She told them she hid in the back of the van – Tom didn't know she was there.'

'Why?'

'They didn't say. Some game, I suppose. Perhaps he drove off before she had time to get out. Anyway, it's not Tom's fault.'

'It wouldn't have been difficult to get his attention, though – why didn't she bang on the side?'

'God knows. Maybe she fell asleep. Anyway, who cares? I'm just so relieved she's OK.'

'They definitely said that, did they?'

Suzie nodded. 'She's a bit upset, apparently, but not hurt or anything. Anyway, we'll be able to find out what exactly happened when we get there.' She let out a long, shuddering breath. 'I asked if Tom could bring her back, but they said I need to go and pick her up.'

'Have they spoken to Tom?'

'Not yet. I just tried to call him, but he's not picking up. I thought the police were going to get in touch with him – you know, when Molly was missing – and I'd given them his number and all the stuff about the van, but the one who rang didn't have any of those details. They're going to ring him now, though.'

'Would you like me to take you to Wiltshire? I'll understand if you'd rather go with Mark, but the offer's there if you want it.'

Suzie looked at Janice for a moment, her expression inscrutable.

Then she said, 'OK, thanks. I'd like that. I'll give Mark a call at the pub and tell him.'

Feeling absurdly pleased, Janice said, 'I should think it'll take at least four hours to get there, maybe more, so it might be a good idea to pack an overnight bag, and maybe some stuff for Molly.'

'Yeah, and I'll need some I.D. as well.' Suzie ran her hands through her hair. 'God knows what I'm supposed to do about that.'

'Driving licence?'

Suzie shook her head. 'Don't drive.'

'Passport?'

Suzie shook her head. 'Expired about five years ago, and I didn't bother renewing it. I wasn't going anywhere, so what was the point?' She shrugged. 'I've got a credit card, and that's registered to here, but I don't know if it's enough.'

'That's proof of address anyway, and maybe you could get Molly's school to vouch for you, or the G.P. – if he's seen her, that is.'

Suzie nodded. 'She had a bit of eczema a couple of months ago – you know, what kids get – and head lice, although,' she added quickly, 'that was the whole class, of course – one gets them and they all do.'

'That's good. The G.P., I mean, not the head lice. And of course you've seen the police here . . . Do they know Molly's been found, by the way?'

'The officer in Wiltshire said they'd sorted it – apparently there's a database or something. Do you think that would do it? For the I.D., I mean. It's not as if she's on the 'at risk' register or anything.'

'I suppose so. They probably check all that, and they'd have a social worker for anyone under age, wouldn't they? Assuming it's somewhere near the festival, they're probably inundated with kids who've got separated from their families by mistake . . . What about Molly's birth certificate? That might help.'

LAURA WILSON | 272

'Probably with the other papers, in the sideboard. I gave Dan a bunch of stuff like that when we arrived, for safekeeping. I think the birth certificates were in there.'

Janice knelt on the floor of the sitting room and shook the contents of the large Manila envelope on to the rug – important papers, passports and driving licences, some long out of date; there were even ration books for Ma and Pa, saved from the war. One document was thicker than the rest – several pages stapled together. Unfolding them, Janice saw that she was looking at an official copy of Dan's will. The solicitors were Midgley & Brace of Norwich, and the date was 10th August. Just over a fortnight before he died, thought Janice. Skimming through it, she saw, *I appoint my sister, Janice Louise Keaton, and one of the partners, at the date of my death, in Midgley & Brace to be the executors and trustees of my Will . . .* Janice had no recollection of Dan asking her to be his executor, but supposed the conversation might have taken place quite some time before he got round to actually making a will. There was a lot of legalese following this clause that her eyes slid over, before she came to *I give the whole of my Estate both real and personal whatsoever and wheresoever situate including any ready money subject to and after the payment of my debts, funeral and testamentary expenses to the said Janice Louise Keaton absolutely.*

Nothing for anyone else, not even Suzie or Molly. He obviously thought I could be trusted to look after them, she thought wryly. Putting the will to one side, she found Ma's birth certificate, then Pa's, then Dan's divorce papers – that, at least, put paid to any chance of Marietta turning up with her claws out, thought Janice – and Ma and Pa's marriage certificate. Unfolding the last piece of paper, she found not Molly's birth certificate, or Suzie's, but Dan's. She was about to fold it up again when something caught her eye.

Pa was there all right – Francis Richard Carthy-Todd – but in the next column, headed *Name and Maiden Surname of Mother*, instead of Audrey Jane Carthy-Todd (formerly Stephenson) was written *Marguerite Edith McLaurin*.

Janice stared. It was Dan's birth certificate, no doubt about it: *When & Where born: Fifteenth May 1948, Norfolk & Norwich Hospital, Brunswick Road, Norwich; Name, if any: Daniel Edward Carthy-Todd; Sex: Boy.* Under *Rank or Profession of Father* was written *Professor of Theoretical Physics*, and Pa had registered Dan's birth on 29th May, two weeks after the event.

And – Janice scrabbled for the marriage certificate to make sure – he'd definitely been married to Ma at the time.

Park it, she told herself. Now isn't the time. The important thing is to get on the road and get Molly.

Marguerite.

You didn't even know, did you? Janice heard Suzie's voice in her head, pictured the folded arms.

She'd have to give up on Molly's birth certificate. It had probably got lost along the way somewhere, but it would be easy enough for the police to check, surely? Stuffing everything back into the large envelope, Janice tucked it under her arm and headed upstairs. She looked everywhere in Dan's room, but she couldn't find the photograph of the woman she'd spotted tucked between the L.P.s two days earlier.

FORTY-NINE

'The thing with the Peels wasn't that they were particularly religious, or particularly *anything*, really. Just strict.' Garrulous with relief, Suzie was talking about her childhood. Zipping down the M11, with semi-familiar music – some golden-oldie station Suzie had found – playing in the background, Janice experienced a sudden feeling of gleeful, fizzy joy, as if the pair of them were children embarking on some long-awaited adventure.

'But that doesn't mean they didn't love you.' In her current mood, Janice felt benevolent towards Suzie's adoptive parents.

'True. It wasn't a lovey-dovey sort of family – hugs and kisses and positive reinforcement and all that – but I think they probably did. I never felt they had much ambition for me though – not that I was brilliant at school or anything – but it was more that they just wanted me to stay on the straight and narrow and not go wild or do anything unusual or . . . you know.'

'You mean they didn't want you to turn into me?'

Suzie gave a bark of laughter. 'Yeah, pretty much.'

'What did they do?'

'Dad was a clerk at the town hall. He lost that when they started putting everything on computer, and they gave him a caretaker job. It wasn't what you'd call a career – he'd worked there since he left school. Mum had a part-time job serving in a chemist's, but she wasn't qualified or anything.'

'Where did you live?'

'Croydon.'

That explained the label on the temazepam bottle, thought Janice – Suzie had moved around, but she hadn't changed her G.P.

'They both came from round there. Mum was a shop assistant when she met Dad, but she gave it up when they got married, because she thought she'd have a family – only it didn't happen like that. They'd been trying for about six years before they adopted me, and then Dean came along when I was four.'

'That's your brother?'

'Yeah.' Suzie sighed. 'I don't mean to sound, I don't know, snobbish or whatever, because they were perfectly nice people – decent – and it wasn't their fault or anything, but it was all so *cautious*. Obsessing about what could go wrong, always doing the same things, going to the same place on holiday every year, going on and on about how much things cost – that one was fair enough, I suppose, because there wasn't money to throw around . . . But any sort of change, even a suggestion that there might be a change, threw them into a panic. Mind you,' she added ruefully, 'I'm saying they didn't have any ambition for me and all that, but I should have figured out for myself how to get away and make a different sort of life, and I didn't, not really. I mean, I just drifted through school feeling fed up and hard done by, you know, like I was in the wrong place, and then I left and got a job in a supermarket.'

'Was that when you changed your name to Suzanne?'

Suzie nodded. 'I was trying to change my whole life, really. I figured out I'd *got* to do something, because it wasn't going to happen by itself – and then I discovered I was pregnant.'

All this was recounted without any hint of blame. We're all the same, Janice thought. I ran away to London, Suzie wanted to run away, and now Molly's run away. 'With Tom?'

'Yeah. I was nineteen. The weird thing was, I hadn't told anybody about it because I wasn't going to go through with it, but then Mum found out, and she and Dad started carrying on like the world had ended, and they were on at me to have an abortion, so I thought, Fuck it, at least *something* is happening to me, you know? And when I told Andy, he said, "Let's get married," so that's what we did. It was OK at first.'

'But then it wasn't?'

'Yeah. You know, I was thinking about you saying how it's hard to explain about the past because it's like you just react to stuff at the time, and it's not like most of us have this big plan for our life – and even if someone does have it all mapped out, that doesn't mean it's going to happen, does it? I know I had a go at you when you said it, but you're right, really.'

A pinwheel of pleasure whirring inside her, Janice said, 'You know, Suzie, if you did want to go to college, I'd be more than happy to help with the finances.'

Suzie hesitated, then said, 'I don't know. I always used to fantasise about the wonderful career I could have had if I'd worked harder at school, but that's not real, is it? I mean, lots of people think those things.'

'I don't see why that should stop you going to college, if you want to. Have a think about it.'

'OK. And thanks. For offering, I mean.'

'That's all right. Do you want to carry on living in Norfolk?'

'I haven't really thought. Not up to me, is it? I mean, Dan left the house to you, right?'

'Yeah, but you're welcome to stay on if you'd like to.'

Suzie looked at her, surprised. 'I thought you'd want to sell it.'

'Not particularly.'

Suzie stared out of the window for a moment before replying. 'It's nice of you, but there's no way I could afford the bills and the upkeep and everything.'

Stifling the urge to say she'd be happy to pay for all that – she mustn't just clomp in and take over – Janice said, 'You wouldn't have to. If you want to stay, I'm sure we can work something out.'

'Well, for the moment . . . Like I said, I'm not sure what I want to do really. But thanks, yeah? I appreciate it.'

Janice opened her mouth to speak, but was cut off by the satnav telling her to leave the M11 at junction six and join the M25. Once she'd negotiated that, and they were bowling along past the fields and business parks, she said, 'I was thinking about something you said too, and wondering if maybe you could solve a mystery for me.'

'Oh . . .' The sound was guarded, suspicious. 'What?'

'You know what you told me about Dan looking after Ma, when she was . . . you know, at the end? Did he say anything else?'

'How do you mean?'

'About his mother. Not Ma – his birth mother.'

'I don't understand. Are you saying it was someone else?'

Janice nodded. 'I found his birth certificate with the others, and his mother's name is given as Marguerite McLaurin.'

'What about the father?'

'Pa. He was already married to Ma when Dan was born, so he must have had an affair with someone who couldn't keep the baby for some reason, and Ma must have agreed to take him.'

'And you had no idea?'

'None.'

'*Really?*' Suzie's voice rose an incredulous half octave.

'Really, honestly. None at all.' Aware of how this must sound

– that either she was an idiot or she hadn't been thought worth informing, or both – Janice made no attempt to keep the sardonic tone out of her voice. 'They obviously didn't think I needed to know.'

'Perhaps they didn't tell Dan either.'

'They must have done at some stage, because you need your birth certificate for things, don't you? When you get married, stuff like that. So he must have seen it.'

'Perhaps he thought it didn't matter. Some people don't – they never try and find their birth parents. They're not bothered, or they think it's disloyal to their adoptive family, or something.'

'Was that why you left it so long?'

'Yeah. Well, partly. I think my mother dying had something to do with it, and Dad losing his grip. I had to get enough distance from them first, and then there's that whole thing of trying to make sense of everything – maybe that's to do with having children, I don't know. And let's face it, it's not as if I was having this other wonderful life – I mean, I needed something, didn't I?' Suzie blinked, taken aback by what she'd just said. 'Sorry, that sounds mercenary, but honestly, I didn't just mean money.'

'It's all right. But that was why you didn't do it before, when you applied for the original birth certificate?'

'I did think about it, but it was like I said . . . I mean, my parents didn't put a ban on talking about it or anything, but it wasn't a comfortable subject so I didn't really feel I could ask them anything else, and having the birth certificate answered the immediate questions – you know, who I was and where I was born and all that. I think I just wasn't ready really. And I wasn't confident that you'd even want to see me if I did manage to find you.'

'I would have done.' Although, Janice reflected, it would have been pretty hard for Suzie to find her in the pre-internet late eighties, because she and her second husband, Matthew, had been living in California. Deciding not to mention this, she said instead, 'I think Dan had a photo of his birth mother. At least, he had a picture of a woman called Marguerite who looks as if she'd be the right age. I found it in his wardrobe when I was trying to clear up. I'm pretty sure I put it on his desk, but when I went to get it just before we came out, it wasn't there.'

'Perhaps it slipped down behind the desk,' said Suzie, 'there's so much crap on there. I'm sure we'll find it. It's weird though. Are you sure he never said anything about it?'

'Positive. No one did.'

'Well, he never mentioned it to me. I know this is going to sound horrible, but I'd have said. When I was having a go at you about not knowing your mum had dementia. I was angry, and I'd have said it.'

'Yeah.' Janice grimaced. 'What a bunch we are! I hope you're not regretting all this.' Without waiting for an answer, she added, 'I'm just wondering if that was why Ma . . . When I had you, why she was so . . .' Janice felt the lump of Ma's obduracy, and her own, stoppering her throat like a cork in a bottle. 'If it wasn't something to do with that,' she finished. 'As well as the stigma, I mean.'

'Might have been.' Suzie was looking out of the window again. 'Did you feel ashamed?' she asked, without turning her head. 'Of me, I mean.'

'No,' said Janice. 'At the time, I felt confused. Emotional. And later I felt regret, and I felt guilty, and I was angry – especially with Ma. But I never felt ashamed. Not once.'

FIFTY

'She said she came as fast as she could because she wanted David and me to stay together.' Melissa Piper looked so sad and so brave and had suffered so much that Janice could hardly manage to look her in the face. The meeting had been at Mrs Piper's behest, and Suzie had requested that Janice be present. 'She must have read about us getting divorced and thought she could save our marriage.'

Janice, imagining the Pipers' pain accumulating as the months passed, driving away any possibility of intimacy to leave only a thick, despairing silence, stared down at the scratched top of the interview-room table. Out of the corner of her eye, she saw Suzie doing the same.

P.C. Kenwright, lumpily serviceable in her dark uniform beside Mrs Piper's delicate pastels and taupes and smooth cara-mel-coloured hair, gave an almost imperceptible sigh of empathy. Then, leaning over, she said, 'And you're sure you two weren't aware of this? You didn't read about the Pipers separating in the papers and decide it was the right time to make your move?'

Without looking up, Suzie shook her head. 'I've told you. We had no idea.' The words came out small. Janice knew that they were shrunken in the scalding shame that she was feeling too, the kind of agonising mortification that usually only arrives with a suddenly rebooted memory of some appalling past selfishness.

'Molly does look exactly like those pictures,' said Mrs Piper. 'But those pictures aren't Phoebe, they're projections of how she might look.'

'I know,' said Suzie. 'People would sometimes say that she looked like Phoebe, but we never made anything of it. We certainly didn't encourage her to do this.'

'Two point five million pounds is a lot of money,' said P.C. Kenwright, voice expressionless, eyes narrow.

The texture of the air in the room grew taut, so that it almost seemed to vibrate between them. Seeing Suzie's downcast face suffused with blood to a dull brick red, Janice put a warning hand on her knee. Clasping it so that Janice had to make an effort not to flinch, Suzie raised her head and said, quietly 'Absolutely not. Molly is my daughter and I've never encouraged her to think she's anything else.'

'I don't know if you remember,' disgust seeped through the professional deadpan of P.C. Kenwright's voice and face, 'but some years ago a woman called Karen Matthews faked the kidnap of her daughter in order to claim the reward money. Her *own* daughter, drugged and stuffed under a bed.'

'No. We're nothing like those people.' Suzie's voice, though still small, was firm.

Glancing at Mrs Piper's face, Janice saw baffled disappointment, and the knowledge that the pair of them must be included in it made her cringe. 'We thought she was missing,' she said. 'Honestly. We reported it to the police in Norfolk. There's a database, isn't there, for missing people? She'll be on there – you can check.'

'We've already done that.' P.C. Kenwright looked at her as though she were an imbecile. 'Karen Matthews told the police that *her* daughter was missing. She was given an eight-year prison sentence and her daughter was taken into care.'

'We didn't put Molly up to it,' said Suzie.

'You didn't say *anything* to her to suggest that she might be Phoebe?'

'No. Nothing. Nothing at all.'

'Are you absolutely sure about that?'

'Yes, I am.'

'Then can you explain why this happened?'

Suzie ducked her head again, quickly, as if dodging a blow. After a moment she let go of Janice's hand and started speaking slowly, picking her way through the narrative in a tentative way that made Janice think of someone negotiating a fast-flowing river on stepping stones. 'I think Molly was missing her old school and her friends. We were in London before, but things were difficult because I'd lost my job and we were living in a B & B . . . When I say "difficult", I know it's nothing like—' Suzie looked across the table at Mrs Piper in hasty acknowledgement of degree, 'but it was pretty bad, so when Dan – my uncle – offered, we went to live with him in Norfolk.' Here, Janice saw P.C. Kenwright's eyes flick in her direction and caught her breath in anticipation. 'Molly said she liked it,' Suzie continued, faster now, 'and it was great being away from the B & B, because that was a nightmare – nowhere to cook and no space – but we all missed London. Molly must have been more lonely than I realised.' *I did have a friend at school*, Janice heard Molly's voice in her head, *but she doesn't like me anymore.* 'She had become a bit withdrawn and secretive,' said Suzie, 'but I just thought it was taking her a bit of time to get settled at the new school.'

P.C. Kenwright looked at Janice. 'You couldn't take them in?'

Although she'd been dreading this, Janice would have sworn, a moment before, that it wasn't possible for her to feel any worse, but the puzzled sadness she saw on Mrs Piper's face was as excoriating as acid. How could she tell this woman, of all people, that she'd given her own daughter away to a pair of complete strangers? It occurred to her then that if she had, in the preceding forty-odd years, told either of her husbands, or any of her friends, or her lovers, or *anyone*, in fact, about it, then at least she would have a fluent narrative. Now it was just a rough, raw thing, crude and improperly formed. Closing her eyes momentarily, she took a breath, then spoke, in a rapid monotone, into the space between Mrs Piper's tastefully clad, slender shoulder and P.C. Kenwright's dark, thick one. 'I gave my daughter up for adoption when she was born. I was abroad when Suzie got in touch with my brother, and we've only just made contact. I was very young when I became pregnant, and not married. I wasn't mature enough to know my own mind and I let my parents make the decision for me. I should have fought to keep Suzie, and I've regretted it ever since.' As she came to an abrupt halt, the blood thundering in her ears, Janice shifted her gaze fractionally to take in Mrs Piper's face and saw, to her astonishment, nothing but pity.

'I see.' P.C. Kenwright was staring at her with an expression which suggested that in her view Janice was a fag-paper away from Karen Matthews. 'Do you think,' she asked Suzie, 'that that might not have had something to do with it, you being reunited with your birth mother after all this time?'

Janice opened her mouth to respond, but Suzie got there first. 'I don't see why. I knew that I was adopted from an early age, but Molly wasn't, so it's not the same, is it?'

'Did you know about this?' P.C. Kenwright leant down and, putting a bulging plastic bag – Janice recognised Molly's jacket sticking out of the top – on the table, produced a child's scrapbook.

Janice recognised the cover: a teddy bear sporting a bow tie, with a bunch of balloons in its paw. 'Molly was carrying it around with her just before she went missing,' she said. 'She told me it was something she was doing for school.'

'Have a look.' P.C. Kenwright slid the scrapbook across the table. Inside, the fuzzy-textured, thick pages in their different coloured greyish pastels were covered in photographs cut from newspapers and magazines: Phoebe at every stage of her life, from real baby- and toddlerhood to scientifically imagined girl; Melissa and David Piper comforting each other, facing the press from the steps of official buildings, shaking hands with religious leaders and politicians, sitting on sofas in television studios; Snuggle Pup, the cuddly dog that was Phoebe's favourite toy . . . And at the back, the writing, lovingly practised – Janice winced involuntarily at the image of Molly concentrating, her tongue poking out, as she wielded her purple felt-tip – *Phoebe Amanda Piper, Phoebe Amanda Piper, Phoebe Amanda Piper,* over and over again, page after page, ringed with hearts and orbited with kisses.

'She has a photo of Phoebe in her room,' said Suzie, 'but I never realised that she was, you know, convincing herself.'

'She talked about there not being any pictures of her when she was a baby,' said Janice. 'She asked me if I had any, and of course I hadn't. I think she must have been looking for confirmation.'

Suzie, elbows on the table and palms pressed against her forehead, shook her head and said, 'There aren't any. It's my fault. When Molly was born I was completely on my own and I had post-natal depression. I was barely coping. My dad – my adoptive father, that is – was starting to . . . you know, the dementia was beginning to take hold, and Mum was completely taken up with that, the appointments and tests and everything. Tom was at his dad's most of the time, because there was no way I could manage him as well. Molly had colic all the time, I'd go for days without talking to anyone and I just felt like I was being sucked into this *tunnel* . . . None of it was Molly's fault. She didn't ask to be born, did she? No wonder she wanted a different family.'

'That must have been very difficult,' said Mrs Piper gently, 'being on your own with no support.' She stood up and, fishing in her handbag, produced a small packet of paper tissues, which she held out to Suzie. 'Here.'

'Thank you.'

'I don't think you put Molly up to it, but I wanted to be sure. There have been people, hoaxers . . . I'm sure you can imagine. I know she's out there somewhere, and children do get found, even after many years – Natascha Kampusch, Jaycee Lee Dugard, Carlina White, Crystal Anzaldi . . .' Telling the names as if they were rosary beads. 'And Phoebe's out there, waiting for us to find her, but you have to train yourself, your expectations . . .' In the weary economy of Mrs Piper's brief smile, Janice saw all the relentless cruelty of hope. Feeling as though she'd been struck dumb, she simply nodded.

P.C. Kenwright pushed back her chair, her carefully neutral face failing to hide her disappointment. 'You wait here,' she said, and followed Mrs Piper to the door.

Suzie held out the packet of tissues, but Mrs Piper, half turning, held up a hand. 'It's fine. Keep them.'

'I am sorry,' said Suzie. 'Thank you for being so nice about this. I really hope you find Phoebe, and that everything works out for you.'

'Look after Molly, won't you? You're very lucky to have her.' There was the faintest hint of a catch in Melissa Piper's voice, there and gone. 'She's a lovely little girl.'

FIFTY-ONE

The door closed. Janice stared at Suzie for a moment, and Suzie stared back. Then Janice reached out and Suzie didn't flinch, but let herself be embraced. After a moment, she put her arms around Janice and they stayed like that for a while, not speaking.

'I ought to tell you something,' said Suzie finally.

'What it is, love?' Janice rubbed her daughter's back.

'It's about why we left London.' Janice felt Suzie's breath as the hurried words streamed past her ear. 'It's true about living at the B & B, and everything I've told you, but not the reason I lost my job. The pub didn't close – the landlord sacked me because I was drinking. I'd get rat-arsed behind the bar, and I'd stagger upstairs and have some more, and Molly used to put me to bed – unless I'd brought some bloke up with me. I wouldn't remember it in the morning, wouldn't know who the hell it was in my bed or what had happened or anything. Molly'd try and straighten things out, take herself off to school . . . When we got kicked out, I thought I'd be able to get another job, but nobody wanted to know. Where they'd put us was miles away from Molly's school, and there was a mix-up over the benefits so I hardly had money for the bus fare, never mind anything else. Dean wasn't going to help me. He said if he gave me money, I'd just drink it. He didn't want me near his family, and I don't blame him, not really. It was like this huge wake-up call. I realised that all the people I thought were my friends, they were just people to get drunk with, and I knew I couldn't sort things out unless I got right away from them – from all of it. That was when I started looking really – properly, I mean – and then I found Dan. I wrote him a letter, and he wrote back with his phone number. We talked, and he just seemed to get it – the whole situation, everything – and he said why didn't I come to Norfolk? We had one room with a double bed in it at the B & B, and I remember sitting there in the dark with a bottle of vodka when Molly was asleep and thinking, what have I got to lose?'

'Oh, darling . . . Why didn't you contact me then? I'd have been glad to help.'

Disengaging herself, Suzie said, 'Because I *did* have something to lose: pride. And I wanted you to be proud of me. I thought, if I could turn my life around, then . . . Dan understood that. He told me you wouldn't care about any of that, but he knew how I felt, so he'd say, "Do it whenever you're ready."'

'And then he died.'

'Yeah.' Suzie sniffed.

'You ought to blow your nose,' said Janice.

Suzie gave her a lopsided smile. 'Yes, Mum.'

The sunburst of happiness inside Janice's chest, so intense that it was almost physically painful, was doused by P.C. Kenwright, who, barging back into the room, said sourly, 'You're lucky. Mrs Piper doesn't want to press charges. You're lucky we're not charging you with wasting police time an' all.' The festival, thought Janice. They're busy, and her boss wants to get shot of us. 'We've spoken to the officer who was dealing with you in Norfolk, and to your son and his mate,' she told Suzie, 'and we're satisfied that they didn't know your daughter was in the van.' The manner in which she said this suggested that Tom and his friend were blind or stupid or both. 'She said she hid behind some of your uncle's gardening things and crawled out when they weren't looking, then found her way off the site and down to the White Hart. It was the land-lady who brought her in – they'd found her wandering around the garden and they thought she must be foreign because they couldn't get a word out of her. Then, when she came in here, that's when she came out with her story about being Phoebe Piper. It wasn't until Mrs Piper came in and said she wasn't that she told us the truth.'

Deciding that it would be wiser not to engage with any of this – after all, they could ask Molly about it later – Janice said, 'So Tom's here now, is he?'

'Yes.' P.C. Kenwright's mouth twitched derisively. 'You can see him in a minute.'

'Can we take Molly home, then?' asked Suzie.

'Not quite yet,' said P.C. Kenwright. She went to the door, stuck her head out and, after a few whispered words, a young male officer came in and, without speaking, stationed himself behind her as she resumed her seat. 'Now,' she said, taking a plastic evidence bag from the officer and holding it up with the air of one producing a trump card, 'I need you to tell me what you know about this.'

FIFTY-TWO

P.C. Kenwright and Janice watched as Suzie read the words on the creased piece of paper through the clear plastic. The handwriting was big and loose, with a downward slope, leaving just enough room for a signature in the bottom right-hand corner. Recognising the squiggly flourish of the shape rather than reading the letters, she knew what it said: *Dan Carthy-Todd*.

After a couple of minutes, Suzie looked up and, without speaking, slid the evidence bag across to Janice.

I know what you said about the girl at the picnic is true. Malc showed me the other piece of ribbon, and it's the same as mine. It was because we couldn't remember, we didn't 'see' what we saw because our reality was altered. It was my fault, persuading you not to tell anyone, and then I thought he was harmless when you told me, what he said was part of some fantasy he had, like the girl in 2007. I know two wrongs don't make a right. I wanted to protect Molly but everything went wrong. There's a woman who knows about him, she lives nearby and she's known for years, but I don't think she would ever say anything (what would the neighbours think). I don't want to end up in that place. I can't do it. I'm sorry. I hope you understand this and you know how much I have valued you as a friend.

There had been a suicide note, after all. When Janice looked up, the air between her and P.C. Kenwright felt so tight that it was almost painful, like skin around a boil.

'Well?' said P.C. Kenwright finally.

'Dan is – was – my brother,' said Janice. 'But I've never seen this before.'

'Neither have I,' said Suzie.

'Do you understand the contents?'

'Not really, no.' Janice looked at Suzie, but her expression, as she shook her head, was unreadable.

'Phoebe Piper was abducted in 2007.'

'Yes, but Dan had nothing to do with that. You can see – he describes it as a fantasy. Malc's fantasy, I think. I'm pretty sure that he – Malc, I mean – is Malcolm Devlin. We thought he'd taken Molly, but then he was found dead in a wood near us.'

'My partner found him,' said Suzie, 'when he was looking for Molly. The Norfolk police can confirm it.'

'I see.' P.C. Kenwright sounded as if she didn't see at all. 'And the woman who—' she tilted her head to read the letter, which was still in front of Janice, 'who "lives nearby and she's known for years". Do you know who that is?'

Suzie shook her head. 'We don't even know who the letter is *to*.'

'Molly told us she found it in Mr Carthy-Todd's garden shed, after his death,' said P.C. Kenwright, 'in an envelope addressed to someone called Joe, who I understand is a neighbour.'

'Yes,' said Suzie. 'He and Dan were friends.'

'So you can't tell me anything more about this letter?'

'No. I'm sorry. I can see how this . . . how it looks,' said Janice, 'but we don't know anything more than you do. They're not even sure how Dan died yet.' In the back of her mind, she wondered if she should explain some more about Malc and Joe, but that was a matter for the Norfolk police, and besides, P.C. Kenwright had said they were busy, hadn't she? She didn't want to listen to a lot of guff about ribbons and songs – besides which, any lengthy explanation would mean dragging Jeff into things, and the Norfolk police knew about all that already . . . Glancing at Suzie, she could see that she was thinking much the same thing.

'All right,' said P.C. Kenwright, reluctantly. 'How about these?' She held up her hand, and, like a conjuror, the young police officer deposited two more evidence bags on her open palm.

They stared at the two black and white photographs in the middle of the table. 'That's the one I was telling you about,' Janice said to Suzie, pointing to the signed portrait. 'I found it in Dan's room and then it disappeared. Molly must have taken it.'

'Do you know who it is?' P.C. Kenwright asked. 'The signature says *Marguerite*.'

'I think it may be my brother's biological mother,' said Janice. 'We had the same father, but I wasn't aware that we had different mothers until after he died, when I found his birth certificate.'

'He seems to have left quite a few mysteries, doesn't he?' said P.C. Kenwright – rather spitefully, Janice thought.

'Yes,' she said, as neutrally as she could manage. 'He does.'

'And this photograph?'

'I've never seen it before.' Janice stared at the two women in wartime fashions who didn't look as if they liked each other much, or wanted to be photographed – at least, not arm in arm. Once more, she had the sensation of something elusive, accompanied by the wholly unexpected but very keen memory of being ten once more and just recovered from chickenpox, descending the Old Rectory stairs to bright, empty rooms. Why, though? It made no sense. 'The woman on the right looks as if it might be her,' she said, pointing at the *Marguerite* picture.

'What about the other one?'

'I'm sorry,' Janice said, 'I don't know.'

'Mrs Armitage?'

'Sorry, I've got no idea either.'

P.C. Kenwright turned the bag over, and Janice saw, in capital letters, the words *ASK HER WHO YOUR MOTHER IS*. 'It must have been meant for Dan,' she said. 'Did Molly say where she found it?'

'She told us it was in the shed with the letter – although she said it wasn't in the same envelope.'

'Look,' said Suzie, 'Molly obviously made a mistake. She wanted to believe she was Phoebe Piper, so she jumped to the wrong conclusion. We don't want to be unhelpful, but we just don't know – and if there's nothing else, I'd really like to take my daughter home.'

P.C. Kenwright stared at them both for a moment, then heaved a sigh. 'There's a bit of paperwork to sort out, then you can go. I assume you have some proof that Molly is, in fact, your daughter?'

'I couldn't find the birth certificate,' Janice said to Suzie. 'I should have told you.'

Suzie, elbows on the table, sank her face in her hands.

'Anything with photo I.D.?' asked P.C. Kenwright.

'Such as what?' Suzie jerked her head up. 'Molly doesn't have a driving licence.'

'Passport?'

'She hasn't got one. Didn't the Norfolk police send you a copy of the photo we gave them?'

P.C. Kenwright turned and muttered something to the young policeman, who left the room.

'For heaven's sake,' said Suzie. 'What do you want, a D.N.A. test?'

'I don't think that'll be necessary,' said P.C. Kenwright crisply.

'Mrs Piper said Molly wasn't Phoebe, didn't she? We came because the Norfolk police contacted us – we didn't just come all the way here on the off chance.'

'I know that, Mrs Armitage. My colleague is getting in touch with them. We'll need to keep these,' she indicated the evidence bags, 'and we'll be sending them to Norfolk. I'm sure they'll be interviewing you in due course.'

They spent almost ten minutes in complete silence, during which Janice tried, and failed, to process the information that Dan had not only left a suicide note, but had – apparently – confessed to a crime of some sort as well, and P.C. Kenwright watched the pair of them with an increasingly baleful look in her eyes. Eventually, the young policeman stuck his head around the door. After a muttered conversation with P.C. Kenwright, he left and reappeared with Molly and a large woman with geometric earrings, who Janice assumed was a social worker of some sort.

'Mum!' Breaking away from the woman, Molly rushed at Suzie and buried her face in her chest.

Suzie, her arms round Molly, glared at the policewoman over the top of the girl's head. 'Is that it, then? Can we go?'

P.C. Kenwright nodded. 'You can take those with you,' she said, and jerked her head at the scrapbook and Molly's plastic bag, which were still lying on the table.

'Thank you.' Janice picked up the items. Removing Molly's wadded-up jacket from the bag in order to slide the scrapbook inside, she saw, at the very bottom, the black pinpoint pupil of a round and blueish glass eye staring up at her from the middle of a jumble of feathers, shells and lumps of fur.

Molly had found the Sneaky Man's necklace.

FIFTY-THREE

'I'm not sure that policewoman believed me. I kept telling her I had no idea Moll was in the van, but . . .' Tom shrugged and lit his roll-up.

'I don't think she believed any of us,' said Janice, 'but there was nothing she could do about it. Except tell the police in Norfolk that we're a thoroughly bad lot, of course.'

Tom had given his friend a lift back to the Chipfest site and they'd been waiting for him in the car park next to the police station, sitting in the Fiat with the doors wide open because of the heat. Molly, very subdued, was curled up in the back seat, her carrier bag clutched to her chest. After her initial joyful yelp on seeing Suzie, she'd been hollow with shock, and hesitant, and Janice was relieved that there had been no recriminations or demands for an explanation. In fact, after a hasty, muttered decision between her and Suzie not to talk about the letter and the photos until Molly was out of earshot, most of the past hour had been spent in silence, for which she was grateful, feeling too tired, and too emotionally overloaded, to talk. Suzie was in the passenger seat, head back and eyes closed, apparently asleep, and Janice, perched sideways in the driver's seat, elbows on knees, was staring down at the tarmac. Anxious to get them all out of the police station, and not wanting to get Molly into any more trouble, she hadn't mentioned seeing the necklace in the bag. P.C. Kenwright couldn't have spotted it under the jacket, she thought, otherwise there would have undoubtedly been questions about that too. She'd tell Suzie and Tom about it later, when they'd put a safe distance between themselves and the police station. In any case, there was probably a perfectly innocent explanation: Molly – who could have no idea that Malcolm Devlin was dead, or even, in fact, that he was Malcolm Devlin – must have found it lying on the ground somewhere, stuffed it into her carrier and forgotten about it.

'She's probably sitting in there now,' Janice told Tom, 'fuming and wishing she could clap the lot of us in irons.'

Suzie opened her eyes. 'Yeah, that business at the end – I thought for a second she was actually going to insist on a D.N.A. test.'

'I think it was just procedure,' said Janice. 'Covering her back.'

'Or being arsey.'

'I'm sorry I forgot to mention about the birth certificate. I couldn't find yours either.'

'Not your fault,' said Suzie. 'To be honest, I'm not surprised you couldn't find them. The day we left the pub I was so hungover, I just stuffed everything into bin liners, so they probably got lost – then or at the B & B – or they're in my friend's garage.' She shook her head. 'I told you I was hopeless.'

'You're not hopeless,' Janice protested. 'Anyone can lose a document. It happens all the time.'

'Oh, well. Easy enough to get a new one, I suppose.' Suzie closed her eyes again.

Tom took a few steps away from the Fiat, indicating that Janice should follow him. 'I really didn't know,' said Tom in a low voice. 'When she started talking about how Molly was claiming to be Phoebe Piper, I was just . . .' He shook his head. 'I didn't know what to say. I remember Molly asking me to look for stuff about Phoebe

on the internet a couple of times, but it never occurred to me . . .
I thought she just felt sorry for her.'

'She thought she had the wrong life,' said Janice quietly, remembering what Molly had said.

'I suppose,' Tom lowered his voice, 'I can understand why. She's
never really had that much attention. It was pretty difficult for
Mum.'

'Yeah, I know.'

'I had my dad and his family, but poor old Moll . . .'

'Well . . .' Janice rubbed her hands over her face. It occurred to
her, as she did so, that Pa always used to say 'Well . . .' to indicate
something that he couldn't – or wouldn't – discuss any further. 'It
must have been difficult for everyone,' she finished lamely. 'Are
you sure you don't want to go back to the festival?'

'Nah . . . I've seen most of what I went for. I'll stay with you.' He
grinned. 'Guard Molly.'

'I think your mum would like that.'

'Yeah.' Tom took a last drag on his roll-up and stubbed it out.
'By the way, Mum told me – while you were in the loo, in there,'
he jerked his head in the direction of the police station, 'that you
used to be Joe's girlfriend. You really *were* pretty cool, weren't you?'

'As I said, it was all a long time ago.'

'But will you tell me about him? When all this is sorted, I mean.
It's like I said, Dan never wanted to talk about those days.'

'I'll tell you sometime. The thing is, though, even if we leave
now,' Janice looked at her watch and saw that it was twenty to
eight, 'we're not going to get back until after midnight, and we
need something to eat.' She went back to the car and, leaning in,
put her hand on Suzie's shoulder, 'Love? What do you think?'

'Mmm? About what?'

'If we should find somewhere round here to stay?'

'Not here though,' said Tom. 'This place'll be rammed because of Chipfest. Everywhere round here will be. I suppose we could all sleep in the van, but there's quite a lot of tools and stuff in there.'

Janice thought for a moment, then pulled her phone out of her handbag. 'I think we can do a bit better than that. There's a place fairly near here where I stayed a few years ago.'

'It's not, like, an ashram or anything, is it?' Suzie sounded dubious.

'Not a yoga mat or a lentil in sight, I promise.'

'Wow! Is it a palace?'

Janice glanced at Molly in the rear-view mirror as they drove through a pair of impressively large wrought-iron gates. More confident now that she'd put some distance between herself and the sudden extinguishing of her imaginings in the harsh light of the police station, she was gazing, amazed, across the acres of landscaped gardens at the enormous Georgian pile. 'Are we *really* staying here?'

'We are. Now close your mouth, there's a bus coming.'

'No, there isn't.' Molly's forehead crinkled in a frown.

'Not a real bus. It's just something old people say.'

'Oh.' Molly pressed her nose to the window again. A minute later, as they neared the house and the car crunched over gravel between banks of rhododendrons, she pointed at the discreet signage. 'It says there's a tennis court, and golf, and a spa, and an in . . . infinity pool. What's an infinity pool, Janice?'

'It's one where you can't see the edge, so the water just looks as if it's going on until it meets the horizon.'

'Can we have a go in it?'

'In the morning,' Janice said, adding quickly, to Suzie, 'as long as that's OK with you, of course.'

'She hasn't got a swimsuit though.'

'That's OK – they've got a shop, so we can get her one. You too, if you like. And Tom.'

Suzie stared out at the beautiful honey-coloured stone buildings, golden in the evening sun, then turned to grin at Janice. 'Not an ashram, then.'

'You don't mind, do you? I thought we deserved a bit of a treat.'

'*Mind?*' Suzie rolled her eyes, then said, anxious, 'We're a bit scruffy though. *They* might mind about *us*.'

'Doubt it.' Janice came to a halt in the car park at the end of a gleaming row of Aston Martins, Porsches and four-by-fours. 'Anyway, they've taken my card details, so it's a bit late if they do. And it's not as if we're going to sit in the restaurant – well, not unless you particularly want to – because they've got very good room service. I got a suite with two bedrooms and a sitting room because I thought it would be nicer if we were all together.'

'Great,' said Suzie. 'Bet no one's ever rolled up to stay here in a white van before. I'm surprised one of the staff hasn't come out to tell him to use the tradesmen's entrance. Look,' she added, when Molly, who had clambered out of the car, was out of earshot, 'this is very nice of you, but it's way too much and you really didn't have to.'

'I know I didn't,' said Janice, 'but I wanted to. Come on.'

Janice did feel pretty scruffy next to the florid middle-aged businessmen and their carefully preserved wives who were strolling through the lobby, but the sleek receptionists, groomed to glossy perfection in their designer livery, didn't bat an eyelid. Molly, still clutching her plastic bag – the more Janice thought about what was inside it, the more she wished she'd never spotted the bloody thing – stayed very close to Suzie. As they waited while the booking was confirmed, she stared, round-eyed and silent, at the grand staircase, with its flower arrangements the size of telephone boxes, and the bar, with its dazzle of glassware, rich dark red walls and enormous leather sofas facing each other across low teak tables.

The rooms, which had a balcony and a view over the lake, were every bit as sumptuous and tasteful as Janice remembered. Molly tiptoed about, carefully examining the wrapped soaps and toiletries, the cunning little cloth bags containing combs, razors and shower caps, and the squared-off pyramid of fluffy white towels. Showered, with freshly washed hair, they congregated in the sitting room, dressed in the thick white towelling robes provided, having drinks and studying the room-service menus. Watching the three of them, Janice, having pushed the subject of the necklace, letters and photos into a corner of her mind, suddenly felt absurdly, almost giddily, happy.

'Crispy oysters with hollandaise and caviar?' said Suzie. 'I can't even imagine that. I've never been anywhere like this,' she added. 'Even the hotel where Andy and I went for our honeymoon didn't come close.'

Tom lifted his head from the menu card. 'Janice, what's freekeh tabbouleh?'

'Tabbouleh's a kind of salad. It's usually made with bulgur wheat, but freekeh is green wheat, so I suppose they've used that instead. It normally has tomatoes, onion, parsley, mint, that sort of thing.'

'Bit poncey for me. I think I'll stick with the hamburger.'

'There's steak with fat chips and Béarnaise sauce,' said Suzie.

'Fat chips!' Molly looked up from rearranging the contents of the minibar. It was the first thing she'd said – in Janice's hearing, at least – since they'd entered the hotel. 'Can we have some?'

'Say please,' said Suzie.

'Please . . .' Molly looked up at Janice, who was sitting nearest.

Janice swung a lazy leg off the chaise longue and prodded Molly's bottom gently with her toes. 'All right, then. If you insist.'

When they'd finished eating, and Suzie and Tom had gone out on to the balcony to smoke, Janice wandered about, tidying the debris on to trays and steeling herself to broach the subject of the necklace in Molly's carrier.

'That was the best food ever.' Molly, revitalised by her dinner, was sprawled on the floor, eating crisps and watching cartoons. Remembering what Suzie had said about there being nowhere to cook at the B & B, Janice had an image of dismal meals – pot noodles, microwaveable pies – eaten straight out of the container, sitting on the edge of a bed. 'Good. I'm glad you liked it.'

'Yeah.' Molly grinned up at her. Why had she brought the necklace along? Perhaps it had just been in the bag and she either hadn't noticed or hadn't bothered to remove it.

She didn't want to spoil the mood, but this was the time, not the morning. Tom had only had a couple of cans of beer, and Suzie's intake had been minimal: a small bottle of wine from the minibar and one glass from the ordinary-sized bottle she'd had sent up in an ice bucket. From that point of view, at least, they'd be proof against any paranoia of the what-are-you-accusing-me-of variety. The best place for talking about it, she reflected, would really be the car, tomorrow – not being able to look at the person you were talking to and having to concentrate on something else made it perfect for difficult conversations – but that was no good, because Tom wouldn't be there.

'Soon be your bedtime, Moll.' Suzie and Tom came in from the balcony.

Molly was just starting to protest against the unfairness of this when Janice said, 'Actually, there is something we ought to discuss while we're all together.'

'Oh?' Instantly alert, Suzie's whole body – shoulders, elbows – seemed to sharpen.

Janice felt the happiness inside her ebbing away, like air from a deflating balloon. She picked up the remote and silenced the T.V. 'There's something we need to talk about, and that includes you. It's the necklace,' she told Suzie, 'the one worn by Malcolm Devlin. It's in Molly's bag.'

'What?'

'In her carrier, with her jacket and the scrapbook. I saw it when we were in the police station.'

'Who's Malcolm Devlin?' asked Tom.

'Molly calls him the Sneaky Man,' said Janice. 'We'll tell you the rest of that later.'

Molly, sitting on the floor with Tom and Jerry silently engaged in cartoon violence behind her head, stared at her mother apprehensively.

'For fuck's sake!' Suzie dashed into the bedroom and returned, a moment later, with the plastic carrier bag, which she upended on the coffee table. Janice recoiled as the necklace slithered out like a live thing, the charm-bracelet trinkets winking up from the mixture of rabbits' paws, feathers and the geometric web of a dream catcher, and, in the centre of it all, the unblinking blue eye.

'Must have fallen off,' said Tom. 'Where did you find it, Moll?'

Molly ducked her head and muttered something.

'It's all right, love,' said Janice. 'You're not going to get into trouble. We just need to know, that's all.'

Molly scanned Janice's face nervously, trying to decide whether this was true.

'Doesn't matter, does it?' said Tom. 'We can just give it back to him – after all, he's not hard to find, is he, hanging about outside Joe's place?'

'Hang on a sec.' Calmer now, Suzie put a hand on his arm. 'Honestly, Molly, you're not in trouble. We promise. Just tell us where you found it.'

Molly blinked and stared up at them for a moment before saying, 'It was in the back of the van.'

FIFTY-FOUR

Janice felt a physical jolt, like missing a step and encountering empty space where ground should be, and sat down quickly on the sofa. What was it Dan's note had said? Something about wanting to protect Molly but everything going wrong? *Two wrongs don't make a right* . . . But which two wrongs was he talking about? What had he done? Suzie was staring at her. 'How the hell did it get *there*?'

'Dan probably gave him a lift somewhere,' said Tom. 'What's the big deal?'

'The big deal,' said Suzie, 'is that Malcolm Devlin was found dead in the Crowhurst woods after Molly disappeared. Mark said he had wounds on his head.'

'He's *dead*?' Molly scrambled backwards, staring at the necklace as though it were a severed part of the corpse. 'Did somebody *kill* him?'

The word 'kill' seemed to ricochet round the room as a knock on the door brought the maid to turn the sheets down and Tom, who was nearest, let her in before Janice could intervene. The four of them sat, or – in Tom's case – stood, in freeze-frame, their thoughts deafening in the silence until she had finished. On her way out, the girl glanced curiously at the coffee table, where the jumble of fur and feathers curled on the wood had a definite look of bloodless roadkill. She was, Janice thought, in her twenties and very attractive. 'You want I take it away?' she said. Polish, perhaps, or Romanian.

'No, no.' Janice tried to keep her voice light, as though it were a mistake anyone might make. 'It's fine. Really. It's a present for a friend.'

'A present?' The elegant black eyebrows arched upwards. 'You sure?'

'Yes,' said Janice firmly. 'Absolutely sure, but thank you very much.'

The sense of relief when the door clicked shut was so palpable that Janice half expected her ears to pop.

'*Jesus.*' Suzie raked her hands through her hair.

'Is he dead?' Molly asked, gaping. 'Really?'

'Yes, love.' Janice leant over and gave Molly's shoulder a squeeze. 'I'm sorry.'

'Hang on . . .' said Tom. 'Mum, you just said Mark told you he had wounds on his head. Do you mean *your* Mark? What was he doing there?'

'Looking for Molly,' said Suzie. 'And he told us that the Sneaky— that Malcolm Devlin wasn't wearing his necklace when they found him.'

'Who's "they"?'

'Him and his friend Harry. You must have heard Mark mention him, haven't you? He does a bit of poaching, and he'd spotted Devlin's camp in the woods round Crowhurst.'

'Oh, yeah. OK. So . . . he was murdered?'

'The police didn't actually say that, but it looks like it, from . . .' Suzie hesitated, glancing at Molly, 'the injuries. And he had a business card for my birth father – that's your granddad – in his pocket.'

'Oh, shit.'

'Yes, oh, shit.'

'Why? The business card, I mean?'

'We're not sure,' said Janice. 'I haven't seen Jeff Boulting – that's your granddad's name – for over forty years—'

'Is that his name?' Tom turned to Suzie. 'I'm sure you told me it was something else when we searched for him.'

'He changed his surname,' said Janice. 'Anyway, what with Mark finding him, and now this, it doesn't exactly look, you know . . . That's why I didn't say anything at the police station,' she told Suzie, and then, turning back to Tom, she said, 'I don't suppose you know how that thing got into the van, do you?'

'No!' Tom's eyes widened. 'Mum, you don't think I had anything to do with it, do you?'

Suzie opened her mouth but Janice got in first. 'I didn't say that. I'm just trying to get an idea of how it ended up in there.'

'It was there already,' said Molly in a small voice. 'When I got in.'

'Why don't you tell us what happened, love?' Janice sat down on the edge of the sofa nearest Molly. 'From when you got in the van.'

'That was easy because you were in the kitchen with Joe, so I knew you wouldn't be looking,' said Molly, 'and it wasn't locked, because Dan never locks it. I mean,' she added quickly, 'he never used to, and nor does Tom. It's because if they want to get something,' she told Janice, clearly feeling that this required explanation, 'and it's in the van, then they don't have to go and find the keys. All the spades and things are meant to be hanging up on the sides, but some of them weren't, and they were bumping around, but there were some sacks, and Tom had put his things in before, so it made a place to sit. I waited till he put his bag in—'

'I didn't see you,' said Tom.

'I was hiding, that's why. Round the corner.'

'You must have been really quick,' said Tom, 'jumping in the back before I noticed.'

'No, because you went back into the house. I knew where you were going, because I heard you tell Janice. When your friend opened the door I was scared he'd see me, but I put one of the sacks over my head and he just threw his things in quickly, so it was OK.'

'That was when Tom picked him up, was it?' asked Janice.

'Yes. Then they drove for *ages*,' said Molly, 'and it was really uncomfortable, and then they stopped at a place.'

'That must have been the motorway services at Chieveley,' said Tom. 'On the M4.'

'You got out,' said Molly. 'I heard you. I was worried in case you didn't come back for the whole night, and it was dark and boring, so I found a torch in your bag and I was shining it all round inside the van, and that's when I found it.'

'Where was it?'

'Just on the floor, under some sacks.'

'Was there anything else?'

'I don't know. I mean,' Molly looked doubtful, 'I didn't see anything.'

'We can go and check if you like,' said Tom. 'There's no light in the back, but we can use my torch.'

'In a minute,' said Suzie. 'Did you recognise it, Moll?'

'I knew it was the Sneaky Man's thing. When I saw it, I was really scared because I thought it meant he must be hiding in the van somewhere, but when I shone the torch around again I saw he wouldn't be able to fit behind any of the things. I put the necklace in my bag because I didn't want to look at it.' Grimacing, Molly wiped her hands on her bathrobe. 'He's dead and I touched it, and it's got all bits of him on it.' Janice could see what she meant.

Judging from the photos she'd seen, it had practically *been* a bit of him. 'Can't we put it away again?'

Janice exchanged glances with Suzie and Tom over Molly's head. 'Better put it back in the bag, I suppose.'

'What about fingerprints and things?' asked Suzie.

'Bit late for that,' said Tom. 'I mean, it'll be covered with all the crap from the back of the van, won't it?'

'I suppose so.' Janice picked up the plastic bag and, upending it, scooped up the necklace in the manner of a dog walker picking up a turd. 'There. They didn't ask you about the van at the police station, did they?'

Tom frowned, shaking his head. 'Why should they?'

'Just that the ones in Norfolk asked lots of questions about it, and I thought they might have passed on the details to other police forces, that's all.'

'Yeah, but that was to do with Molly, wasn't it? And she'd turned up, so they didn't have any reason to . . . Hang on, are you saying they think it's connected to the other business?'

Janice and Suzie exchanged glances, and Suzie gave an almost imperceptible shake of her head. 'They haven't said that,' she told Tom. 'No one has. And Molly going off like she did had nothing to do with Malcolm Devlin. Mark finding him in the wood was just coincidence.'

'Yes,' said Tom, 'but the business card in his pocket and his necklace being in Dan's van make it a bit more than just coincidence, don't they?'

'Not necessarily,' said Suzie. 'Dan might have been giving him a lift somewhere.'

'Yeah, right. First off, Dan wouldn't have given him a lift. He hated his guts.'

'That's right,' said Janice, remembering. 'Molly said Dan was always telling him to go away, didn't you?'

Molly nodded. 'He didn't though.'

'And you said Joe used to hide from him.'

'Joe didn't like him. He was scared of him, like me.'

'It used to piss Dan off,' Tom said, 'the way he was hanging around all the time. He'd been there for months, and he wouldn't leave Joe alone. Dan would never have let him get in the van – and anyway, Mum, if you give someone a lift they'll be sitting in the cab, won't they? Not in the back.'

'He might have put his stuff in the back,' said Suzie, 'and the necklace fell out of a bag or something.'

'Except that he never took the thing off, did he? Come on, Mum, when did you ever see him without it?'

'He must have taken it off sometimes,' said Suzie weakly.

'I don't think so.'

Janice didn't think so either. Out of the corner of her eye she could see the television screen where Tom the cat, in hot pursuit of Jerry, had just run headlong into a tree. Janice's brain supplied the sound effect – *splat!* – as Tom slithered down to the ground in a heap, a constellation of bright yellow stars orbiting his ears.

FIFTY-FIVE

The chocolate on the pillow was almost – but not quite – too nice to eat. Molly lay on her back, carefully smoothing its shiny gold and black wrapper and staring up at the dangly crystals round the centre light. She'd begged Suzie to leave it on so she could look at the room before she went to sleep. It was the nicest room – the nicest place – she'd ever been, and she wanted to remember it forever. That was the reason – well, mostly – but it was also because, even though she knew that the Sneaky Man's horrible necklace was safely in the plastic bag, she could still imagine the rabbit paws somehow dragging along the feathers and glass eye and all the rest of it – a deformed, hideous creature, bent on getting into the bed with her. If the light was on she'd be safe from it, and she knew it wouldn't come once Tom, who was outside looking in the van with Janice, was there, in the other bed.

It wasn't just the necklace either. What if the Sneaky Man himself came in, dead and covered in blood, like in the films Tom watched on his computer? Mrs Piper had said she was glad Molly had shown her the letter, that it might be important. Did that mean that the Sneaky Man, or perhaps even Dan, had done something bad to Phoebe? She could tell that when Janice and Suzie were telling Tom about the Sneaky Man being dead they hadn't said everything, because Mum had done that head-shaking thing people do when they are telling someone to shut up but they don't want anyone else to see. And what did the message on the back of the photo mean if it wasn't anything to do with Phoebe? And what was that test the policewoman had wanted her to take?

She didn't understand *anything*. Looking across at the empty bed she thought, Mrs Piper will be in Phoebe's room now, sitting on Phoebe's bed all by herself with Snuggle Pup in her arms. Thinking about this made Molly huddle under the covers, sick with shame, as though she'd killed something small and defenceless through being clumsy and stupid and horrible. She almost wished Suzie *had* shouted at her – it would have been better than everybody being so quiet. Except Mrs Piper had said it was good about the letter, hadn't she?

She couldn't be Phoebe because she had to be Molly. She closed her eyes against the memory of Mrs Piper's face. *I'm sorry, but you're not my little girl.* Molly wriggled down under the covers, but it wouldn't go away, and nor would the memory of the feeling she'd had when Mrs Piper had asked who she was, and then when the other lady had asked again when she'd gone, and wanted to know where she lived and everything. It made her think of how, once, when they were at the horrible B & B and Suzie had been drinking vodka and fallen asleep and she'd had to get out of bed to go to the loo and locked herself out of the room by accident, she couldn't make Suzie wake up and let her in. She'd been outside, banging and banging on the door, and the woman upstairs had leant over the banisters and yelled at her for making a noise, and she hadn't known what to do because her life was inside the room and she was outside and scared. When Mrs Piper and the other lady had asked those questions, it was sort of like Phoebe had filled up all the space inside her and she was outside herself and couldn't get back in again.

She didn't deserve all the niceness – the lovely hotel and the food and Suzie and Janice and Tom being kind to her – but Janice would find her knickers in the back of the van and know she'd wet herself and she'd tell Suzie and Suzie would be cross and everything would be horrible, and—

'Molly? Are you awake?'

Janice. The knickers. Molly wiped her nose with the back of her hand.

'Are you all right, love?'

'Yes.' She squirmed out from under the covers and sat up.

Janice was standing beside the bed, hiding something behind her back. Molly ducked her head, waiting to be told off.

'I've got something for you.'

Molly sniffed. Perhaps it would be OK. Perhaps they hadn't found the knickers after all. 'What is it?'

'Close your eyes and hold out your hands.' Molly did as she was told and felt something squashy and plush. 'You can open them now, love.'

Gazing up at her was a cuddly panda. 'He's lovely! What's his name?'

'Panda. Well, as far as I know. I'm sure you can think of a better one.'

'He's quite big. Where did you get him?'

'Well, we stopped on the motorway for a cup of coffee on the way to get you, and there he was, and I thought you might like him.'

'I *love* him.'

'That's good.' Janice sounded pleased, Molly thought. Happy. 'Do you think you'll be able to go to sleep now, if I turn off the light?'

'Can I ask you something first?'

Janice sat down on the side of the bed. 'Go on then.'

'It's just . . .' Molly faltered. It was hard to say the words, even though she wanted to – they felt too heavy, like a big thing she was dragging along the ground. 'Did Dan do something bad to Phoebe?'

'No, darling.' Janice sounded really surprised and Molly felt stupid. 'Of course not.'

'Did the Sneaky Man?'

'We don't know.'

Molly looked hard at Janice's face and decided she was telling the truth.

'I'm sure the police will investigate.'

'Will they find Phoebe?'

'I hope so, love.'

'What if . . .' The thought made Molly feel cold and sick. 'What if she's dead?'

'She may well be,' said Janice. 'It's been a long time.'

Molly thought of Phoebe not existing anymore, ever, anywhere, and the idea of it was so enormous that it seemed like nothing was solid and everything might just crumble away all around her. Clutching the panda more tightly, she said, 'Do you know who killed the Sneaky Man?'

'We don't know that either.' Molly thought Janice's face looked a bit less truthful when she said this – sort of wobbly and not quite certain. 'But whoever it was they can't hurt you, so you're not to worry about it, OK?'

Molly nodded and snuggled down, the panda still clasped against her chest.

'I'll tell Tom to be really quiet when he comes in,' said Janice, 'so he doesn't wake you.' And she leant over and kissed the top of Molly's head. Even with the bad things that had happened, being here in the lovely room with the panda was so much like how she'd imagined being Phoebe would be that it almost made her start crying again – except that she wasn't Phoebe, and she might not even be herself anymore.

'Jan-ice?' she asked.

'Ye-es?' Janice mimicked her, but in a nice way.

'I am Molly, aren't I?'

'Of course you are, darling.'

'Really and truly?'

'Really and truly.'

'The policewoman at the station wanted me to do a test, to see if I was Phoebe or Molly or someone else. I won't have to do it, will I? I'm always rubbish at tests at school because I'm stupid – I thought if I was Phoebe I wouldn't be stupid anymore, but I'm not, and—'

'Oh, darling . . .' Janice's eyes glistened and Molly thought she was going to cry, but she didn't. Instead she stroked Molly's cheek with the back of her hand. 'You *are* Molly, and you're *not* stupid. You've just had a very difficult time, that's all. You won't have to take a test, I promise. Now, you go to sleep, and everything will look better in the morning, honestly it will. OK?'

Molly nodded, and Janice stood up. 'Good. Night night, love.'

'Thanks, Janice. For the panda, and coming to get me and everything.'

'That's OK. Sleep tight.'

In the darkness, Molly stroked the panda's soft nose. 'Go to sleep now,' she whispered. 'It'll be all right. Everything'll be all right.'

FIFTY-SIX

'There's something else we need to tell you,' Suzie told Tom, when Janice was back in the sitting room, 'so you might want to get yourself a drink.'

'That sounds worrying.'

'It is – especially as we don't really know what's going on.'

Tom turned away from the minibar, a can of beer in his hand. 'How do you mean?'

Seeing Suzie hesitate, Janice said, 'Well, after you'd gone, we had a visit from a policeman about Dan.'

'Oh?'

'It was about the post-mortem – they wanted to do more tests because they found a lot of alcohol in his system—'

'There's a surprise.' Tom flung himself on the sofa.

'It wasn't just that. They seem pretty sure there were drugs as well, and they think he might have taken an overdose.'

'On purpose, do you mean?'

'It's beginning to look like it. He left a note – your mum didn't know about it because Molly took it from the shed. She thought it was connected with the business of her really being Phoebe Piper, and she brought it down here.'

'So . . .' Tom frowned. 'What did it say? Can I see it?'

'No, because the police kept it. They're sending it back to

315

Norfolk. It was addressed to Joe – his name was on the envelope –
and, the thing is, it was pretty . . . well, *odd*. There was a lot of stuff
about Dan knowing that something Joe had said was true, with
the implication that Malcolm Devlin had done something terrible,
although we're not sure what. Dan also said that he'd wanted to
protect Molly, but that everything had gone wrong.'

'And then,' said Suzie, 'there was something about a local woman
knowing about it, and "not wanting to end up in that place".'

'What place?'

'I'm not sure,' said Janice.

'Do you think,' said Tom slowly, 'that it might mean prison?
When he said he'd wanted to protect Molly but everything had
gone wrong, he might have meant that he was trying to protect her
from Malcolm Devlin, and what went wrong was that he wound
up killing him. That might explain the necklace being in his van.'

There was a pause, during which Janice was aware that Suzie
was watching her carefully before saying, 'What do you think?'

'To be honest,' said Janice, 'I've been trying not to think at all –
about that, I mean. Mark said Malcolm had been dead for at least
a day, didn't he?'

Suzie nodded. 'He said some animals had, you know, got to work
on him, so it might have been longer than that,' she told Tom.

'Which means that it's possible that they had a fight and Dan
killed him by accident,' Janice said. 'I can't believe he would have
done it on purpose – and that might be what he meant about
wanting to protect Molly but everything going wrong, if he'd
thought Malcolm Devlin was a threat to her . . . If Malcolm really
had done something to a girl before, I mean, and it wasn't just
some weird fantasy he'd told Dan about.'

'But there was a bit at the beginning about knowing something
about a girl was true, wasn't there?' said Suzie. 'It sounded to me

more like he'd thought Malcolm was making something up and then found out that he wasn't.'

'Yeah . . .' Janice sighed. 'I suppose I don't want to believe Dan killed anyone, whatever the reason was.' I want to keep *my* Dan, Janice thought. My memories. I don't want them spoilt.

'You did say you'd lost touch,' Suzie said.

'I don't know.' Dan had always been practical, Janice thought. As a roadie, he'd needed to be: problem solving, jury rigging, palm greasing, doing what it took. Smoothing the path for rock stars. 'Perhaps I never knew him that well in the first place.'

'But people are different with different people, aren't they?' said Tom. 'Whether it's your mum or your friends or your teachers or whoever, you act in a different way with all of them. Nobody ever knows the whole of another person.'

'I suppose not,' said Janice. 'But I don't want the bit of Dan I didn't know to have killed anyone either, any more than I wanted to believe he was a pervert when the police were asking us all those questions back in Norfolk.'

'Well, he didn't do anything to Molly,' said Tom, 'and maybe he didn't kill anyone either. We don't know, do we?'

'There was something else they showed us at the police station, that Molly'd given them,' said Suzie. 'Two old photos. One was of two women and the other just one of the women – or we think it is, anyway. Molly said she'd found the one with two women in the shed, with the letter—'

'But not actually inside the envelope,' put in Janice.

'It had something like "Ask her who your mother is" written on the back,' said Suzie, 'so of course Molly assumed it had something to do with her being Phoebe, because that's what she was looking for. The other photo was in Dan's room. Janice dug it out of his box of vinyl and left it on his desk, and then it disappeared.'

'The police kept those as well, so we can't show you, but did Dan ever talk to you about someone called Marguerite?'

'That wasn't the name of the woman he was married to, was it?'

Janice shook her head. 'That was Marietta. This photo had *Marguerite* written on it, like a signature, and I'm pretty sure it was taken sometime during the war, because she's wearing a uniform of some sort.'

Tom made a face. 'Sorry, no idea.'

'Janice thinks it was Dan's mother,' said Suzie.

'What?' Tom looked confused. 'I don't understand.'

'Neither do I,' said Janice, 'but when I was looking through all the papers for Molly's birth certificate I found Dan's, and in the column for mother it said *Marguerite McLaurin*.'

'What about the father?'

'That was my father – your great-grandfather. And he was definitely married to Ma – your great-grandmother – at the time Dan was born.'

Tom raised his eyebrows. 'Must have been a wartime thing, then.'

'Except that Dan was born after the war, in 1948.'

'Did your dad . . .' Tom faltered. 'Look, I don't mean to be rude, but was he one of those guys that's always got someone on the side?'

'Affairs, you mean?' After the chickenpox, Janice thought. The air in those downstairs rooms, hard and bright and somehow dangerous, and no one there. 'I don't think so. But – and I know this makes me sound Victorian, and I'm sorry – kids understand more now. They grow up much faster than we did, and people didn't talk about those things so much . . . Or at all, in some cases. And, as you just said, people are different with different people. So the answer is that I don't *think* he fooled around, but I don't actually know that he didn't.'

'The woman in the photo couldn't be the same woman who knows about the stuff in the letter, could she?' asked Suzie.

'They're two different things, aren't they?' said Tom. 'Janice just said that the photo Molly found in the shed wasn't actually *with* the letter, so presumably Dan didn't mean Joe to have it – and the stuff in the letter is nothing to do with Dan's mother being this Marguerite woman, is it?'

'No, it's not.'

'Hang on,' said Suzie. 'I don't see how the stuff in the letter can be anything to do with the photos either, but there's something else. You told me –' she turned to Janice – 'that when you phoned Jeff Boulting, he said Dan had been there asking questions about some filming he'd done at a picnic, didn't you? I didn't take it in properly because I was too worried about Molly, but there was a picnic mentioned in the letter – something about a girl at a picnic and "knowing it was true". *And* there was something about a ribbon, and you said, when Joe came round to see Molly he mentioned a ribbon, didn't you? But you didn't say anything to that policewoman.'

Janice opened her mouth, then shut it again.

'I didn't put it together when we were at the station,' Suzie continued, 'because the whole thing was just so confusing, what with Molly and everything . . . Look, Janice,' she held up both hands in a 'backing off' gesture, 'I'm not accusing you of anything, but if there's something you're not telling us . . .'

Tom and Suzie were both staring at her with – despite what Suzie had just said – something a lot like accusation in their eyes.

Janice took a deep breath. 'I really don't know what I could have said to her – or to you, for that matter – because I don't understand it myself.'

'Wait,' said Tom. 'Tell us from the beginning.'

Janice explained about Joe coming round to the Old Rectory to see Molly about a ribbon, but referring to her as Marie, and about Marie being Joe's sister, killed by a car when she was little. Then she recounted what Jeff had said to her about Dan visiting him and wanting to know about the picnic, and the picnic being in the same place and on the same day that Lisa Wynn had disappeared. As she was speaking, Joe's lyrics from 'Ribbons in the Wind' played in her mind: *All the colours are running away / Streamers on the wind, one step ahead of me / See, round the corner, behind the tree / You're here, you're not here* . . . But that was about Joe's sister Marie, wasn't it? And anyway, the lyrics sounded as if they might be about some sort of game – hide-and-seek or tag. Maybe that wasn't the explanation at all . . .

'The thing is,' she finished, 'Malcolm wasn't at that picnic. He wasn't on Jeff's film, and Jeff didn't remember him being there, and neither do I, and Dan mustn't have remembered him being there either. Dan's letter said he thought the bit about "the girl at the picnic" was true – something Malcolm told him, I suppose – but he also said Malcolm was a fantasist, didn't he?'

'That was the thing about the girl in 2007, wasn't it? The police-woman thought it was a reference to Phoebe Piper.'

'*What?*' Tom stared at Suzie, incredulous.

'That was the year she disappeared.'

'Yes,' said Janice, 'but I imagine quite a lot of other girls went missing too – Phoebe's case just got more attention. It's all specu-lation. And we don't know how Jeff's business card came to be in Malcolm Devlin's pocket either.'

'I've just thought of something,' said Tom. 'Nothing to do with Phoebe Piper, but . . . when we were looking in the back of the van just now, I didn't see Dan's coat.'

'What coat?'

'An old overcoat. He always kept it in the back of the van in case it started raining when he was out on a job. If that necklace thing was in the van, that must mean that Malcolm was in there – or, anyway, that he *could* have been in there – at some point. Perhaps he nicked it.'

'Perhaps Dan just took it into the house,' said Suzie impatiently.

'Perhaps. But it's been so hot recently that he wouldn't have been wearing it, would he?'

'We'll have a look when we get back,' said Suzie. 'It's probably hanging up in the cloakroom with all the other stuff. And I think you should definitely talk to Joe,' she added to Janice. 'After all, you were both there at the picnic, weren't you?'

'Yes, we were, but I don't know how much sense I'll be able to get out of him. You didn't see the state he was in when I went round there with the photo of Malcolm.'

'When was that? You didn't tell me.'

'After I'd dropped the paper off at the pub, for the posters. He was really frightened, Suzie. And he'd been burning paintings in his garden.'

'Dan said he often did that,' said Tom, 'if he didn't like them.'

'It's just that the ones I saw when I went round to see if Molly had gone to his house were all pictures of people in a landscape, dancing and playing guitars and stuff, with a figure in the corner carrying something that looked like a child. I thought it was Marie – that he'd somehow conflated the picnic and her death in his mind – but perhaps it wasn't. Or maybe it wasn't a child at all, and I'm reading too much into it. Now do you see why I didn't say anything? I just don't know.'

'But didn't you tell me,' Suzie screwed up her face, remembering, 'that Joe had said something about how he hoped it would be all right this time?'

'Yes, and you said that you didn't know what he was talking about because no other child had disappeared.'

'I thought he meant recently – since we'd come to Norfolk. You've just told us that Lisa Wynn disappeared in 1967.'

'I found a magazine with an article about missing children when I was clearing out Dan's room,' said Janice. 'Ones who'd never been found. Phoebe Piper and Lisa Wynn were both mentioned.'

'Dan had a ton of magazines in his room, Janice,' said Suzie. 'And newspapers. That doesn't prove anything.'

'I know, but . . . Oh, God, what am I saying? I don't know anything.'

'Are you *sure* you can't remember anything else about that picnic?' said Tom.

'No. I've been trying, but there's nothing . . . Dan's note said something about how they didn't see what was in front of them because their reality was altered – but it wasn't just them, it was all of us.' *You're here, you're not here*, she thought. 'Everyone at that picnic. We were tripping, dancing, doing our thing, and all the time . . .' Janice shook her head in disgust. 'You said I was pretty cool, Tom, but I wasn't. None of us were. We were a bunch of idiots.'

FIFTY-SEVEN

'That is *really* bizarre – I don't know what to say – but thank God Molly's OK, anyway. Sounds like she's pretty mixed up, though.'

'Yeah . . . I hope she's going to be all right.' It was almost midnight and Janice was standing alone, on the balcony. Suzie and Tom had gone to bed and she'd been about to follow them when Jeff had rung and Janice had found herself telling him everything. The conversation with Suzie and Tom about what might or might not have happened had gone round and round in circles until, admitting defeat, they'd decided to call it a night.

'I shouldn't worry,' said Jeff. 'Children are pretty resilient, you know.'

'I suppose so,' said Janice. Or that's what we tell ourselves, she thought.

'She'll be fine. Listen, I don't suppose you've had a chance to look at a paper, what with everything that's been going on, but there was a piece about a girl's remains – a partial skeleton – being found in woods near Thetford, which they've identified. It's a girl called Lisa Wynn, and she disappeared on the day of that picnic – the one Dan was asking about.'

'Oh, God, really? I'd figured it out about the date, after we talked. I didn't know they'd actually managed to identify the bones, though.'

'Well, given what you've just been telling me, I think you need to hear this.'

The night was warm, but Janice felt a physical chill of apprehension, tight and clammy. 'What?'

'I remembered something. A few days before that picnic, Joe Orton was killed by Kenneth Halliwell. We talked about it while we were there.'

'OK . . .' Janice remembered seeing a film about the playwright and his lover, years later: blood and brain tissue spattered on the ceiling and on the elaborately collaged walls by the bed where Halliwell had caved in Orton's skull with a hammer. She pictured Halliwell lying on the floor in the middle of the small room, his bloodstained pyjama top hanging on the back of a chair, a glass of fruit juice and an empty bottle of Nembutal by his side. Something small and disturbing scuttled down the edge of her mind like a rodent, half glimpsed, across the corner of a room, there and gone. 'What's that got to do with anything?'

'Just bear with me, Janice, OK? I heard Joe and Dan having a conversation a day or so after the picnic, and there was a paper on the table with a photo of Joe Orton, so that's who I thought they were talking about. I wasn't paying much attention – I think I walked in in the middle of it and I was probably too busy feeling jealous of Joe because of how much you dug him . . .' There was a slight pause, which Janice decided to ignore, before Jeff continued. 'Thinking back, I'm not sure why I thought they were talking about Orton, because it didn't really make any sense, but anyway . . . Dan said something like "You didn't see that", and Joe said he did see whatever it was, and then he said, "You were the one who picked it up." That's all I can remember. I looked at the footage again, after you rang – that bit with Joe suddenly running out of shot and Dan following . . .'

'When Joe said Dan had "picked it up",' said Janice, 'do you think he meant he'd understood something, or that he'd literally picked something up?'

'I thought he meant the first one at the time – about Orton and Halliwell being gay, you know – but now I'm not so sure.'

Janice thought of Joe's landscapes: the person in the corner, carrying the child away, that single pink blob at the bottom of the painting that she'd thought was a flower . . . But the flowers that grew on that sort of grass weren't multicoloured meadow flowers, they were daisies, buttercups, dandelions – yellow flowers, or yellow and white, not the antiseptic pink of Germolene. Could it have been a ribbon?

She had a sudden mental picture of herself standing on the half landing the first time Joe had come, calling Molly's name. *You never see girls wearing ribbons in their hair nowadays. Not like when I was Molly's age.* She remembered thinking it.

All the colours are running away | Streamers on the wind, one step ahead of me | See, round the corner, behind the tree | You're here, you're not here . . . Marie and Lisa. Here and not here. The chances were that Marie, who'd died sometime in the mid-fifties, aged seven, had had ribbons in her hair, because little girls did in those days. But also Lisa, in the photograph in the magazine, gazing across the years with her worried eyes, had her hair in two plaits, each tied with a ribbon. What was it Dan's letter had said? Something about Malc showing him the other piece of ribbon, and it was the same . . . Hair ribbons came off easily enough ('You're always losing things –' Ma's irritation, still fresh after more than fifty years – 'why don't you take more care?') if they weren't slotted underneath the elastic band at the end of the plait. In the photo, the ribbons on Lisa's plaits looked too dark to be pink, but that was because it was black and white, a school photograph. Pink, at least in those days, had been for special occasions, not school. Janice pictured the ribbon lying on a dusty track in the huge expanse of parkland, still knotted in a bow to secure an invisible girl's hair. Was that what Dan had picked up?

'Janice? Are you still there?'

'Yes. Sorry, I was just thinking.'

'You said you didn't tell the police about the picnic.'

'No, because there didn't seem any point – I mean, I didn't really *know* anything, did I?'

'Have you told anyone else?'

'Only Suzie and Tom.'

'Is that her partner?'

'No, her son. Your grandson. He's twenty-four.'

'You didn't tell me.'

'No. I was more concerned with Molly at the time.' And exasperated by Jeff's apparent indifference to Suzie, Janice remembered.

'Would you mind if I told someone?'

'About Tom?'

'About the picnic. It's just, I've been thinking about it a lot since we spoke before, and I rang up Bob Harling.'

'Who?'

'The singer with Armadillo – they were around at the same time, remember?'

'Yes, just about. Oh, OK – was he the other guy at the picnic?'

'Yes. Apart from you, he's the only one I'm in touch with who was there. He told me he couldn't remember much at all about the day itself, but I thought there was a good chance that he'd remember Magic— Malcolm Devlin, I mean, and he did. He's a chiropodist nowadays, believe it or not. In fact, he's here now – we've just been talking about it all. Is it all right if I tell him what you've just told me?'

'I don't see why not.'

Holding the phone to her ear, Janice went to get herself a glass of wine. She could hear the murmur of voices as Jeff and Bob had a conversation, and then Jeff came back on the line. 'D'you want a word with him? I'll put it on speakerphone.'

'Sure.'

There was a pause, and then, 'Hi, Janice. Sorry to hear about your brother. He was a good guy.'

'Thanks,' Janice heard herself say. 'I'm going to miss him.'

'Glad your granddaughter's OK though,' said Bob Harling. 'Jeff's just filled me in about what's been going on. Pretty weird.' His voice was deep, with a slight West Country burr. As he spoke, the black and white image of him from Jeff's film acquired colour – ruddy, square-chinned, mid-brown curly hair – and resolved into a real memory of an entire person, broad-shouldered and athletic, helping Dan hump some gear down the stairs at the UFO Club and across the ballroom. Why had she been there? It was the only time she'd ever seen it with the lights up, the shamrocks and the parquet floor, the smallness of the stage.

'. . . because I didn't know Malc all that well,' Bob was saying. 'He was just someone who used to hang around, sell a few drugs . . . He was just sort of *there*. What I remember most about him from that time was that he had all these plans; he was always telling you how someone had asked him to be in a band, or he was going to do some theatre piece at the Arts Lab, or, I don't know, he was writing some article about the underground for one of the papers and it was going to stir everything up, blow the lid off, really stick it to the Man, you know? Never did any of it though. Then I heard he had some sort of breakdown. That was in sixty-nine or seventy. I saw him a few times after that, and there was something – well, this is what I thought at the time anyway – *calculated* about it, like he'd tried to break into singing and acting and writing and whatever else, and it hadn't worked out, so he was going to try being mad instead. Like it was another form of self-expression – you know, the whole schizophrenic thing – just so he could have a place at that table, you know?'

'You mean you think he was putting it on?'

'Not exactly, but . . . Well, maybe at first, but even if that was how it started, you couldn't keep it up, could you? I don't know – perhaps it was in his family.'

'Do you know what happened to him after he had the breakdown?'

'I know he was in a psychiatric hospital for a while, and then he lived with a relative – his aunt, I think. I had tea with them once. Totally surreal. He'd phoned me up out of the blue – I suppose he must have got my number out of the book – and begged me to come and see him. He said there was something he had to tell me, and he was really freaking out, so . . .'

'When was that?'

'Must have been sometime before the middle of 1975, because I was still living in London. The aunt's house was this little box on one of the new estates in Hertfordshire, full of china ornaments and antimacassars, really *fussy*, you know? There was this bone china tea-set, sandwiches with the crusts cut off, the lot, and she was so genteel, all this polite conversation and how was my journey, and . . . that's right, I remember she asked me what I thought about Mrs Thatcher becoming the leader of the Conservatives, so that was, hang on . . .' His voice faded as he broke off to talk to Jeff, then came back: 'Jeff just looked it up – February 1975, so that fits. But all the time we're talking, and she's asking me if I've got enough milk in my tea and would I like some more cake, Malc's just sitting there, holding this old tennis racquet like it was a guitar and sort of plucking at it, and he didn't say a single word all the time I was there. Not one. I was thinking that perhaps he didn't want to talk in front of her, so when she went out of the room for hot water or something I asked him what he wanted to tell me, but he just sat there. Nothing, you know? Just this lobotomised, sort of . . . *black hole* stare, right through you. When I was leaving, the aunt kept saying, "Oh, I'm so glad you came; nobody else would, and I know it's meant a lot to him," but I had the impression he didn't even know I was there.'

'Was that the last time you saw him?'

'That's right, yeah. Somebody told me the aunt died about ten years ago – I'd say she was around sixty when I saw her, so she must have been pretty old. I don't know what happened to him after that.'

'Well, he eventually fetched up in Repshall. He was living in a wood, camping.'

'Yeah, Jeff said. Sounds like he wanted to be near Joe.'

'Do you remember *anything* about that picnic, Bob?'

'I remember Joe and Dan running around chasing each other, but that's about all. Oh, and Keith Petrie said it was the first time he'd ever had champagne – that was because their first L.P. was coming out. He didn't like it – spat it out and said he'd stick to beer. But I was pretty . . . you know. We all were.' *Our reality was altered*, thought Janice, remembering Dan's letter. 'It sounds to me,' Bob's voice was hesitant, as though he was picking over which words to use, 'as if Joe saw something that afternoon and Dan persuaded him to keep quiet about it.'

'Saw someone take Lisa Wynn, you mean?'

'I don't know. Perhaps.'

'Well, it can't have been Malcolm, because he wasn't there.'

'He wasn't there *with us*, no.'

'I've been looking on the map, Janice.' Jeff was speaking. 'It's a bloody big area. It was summer – there would have been dozens of people there.'

'Yes, but if Malcolm got near enough for Joe to see him . . .' said Janice.

'Joe probably didn't know *what* he was seeing,' said Jeff. 'Come on, Janice, you've taken acid. You know what it's like.'

'I suppose so. It's just . . . Oh, I don't know. And why would Malcolm follow us out to the country and do that anyway?'

'Because he's a pervert?' said Bob.

'But he wasn't,' said Janice. 'He was into girls – grown-up ones, not kids.'

'You didn't, did you?' said Jeff.

'You must be joking! A couple of my friends did, but I wouldn't have touched him with a bargepole.'

'All right, fair enough. So, OK, we don't know the reason Malcolm did it, but assuming that we're right, do you think when Dan realised he'd been wrong and Joe really had seen Malcolm with Lisa Wynn – that Malcolm had, I don't know, boasted to him about it or something – Dan thought he was a threat to Molly, and . . .'

'. . . and killed him?' supplied Janice. 'And then put your business card in his pocket?'

'Well, yes – to the first bit, anyway. You said he wrote something about wanting to protect Molly but it went wrong . . .'

Kenneth Halliwell's pyjama top, thought Janice suddenly. Hanging on the back of the chair, in that film. Bloodstains. What Mark Bell had said, when he came back after finding Malcolm Devlin's body in the wood at Crowhurst. 'Jeff?'

'I'm still here.'

'You know when I phoned you, before? You said that Dan looked rough, didn't you? What did you mean?'

'Well, generally. Scruffy, you know?'

'Can you remember what he was wearing?'

'Yeah. It was a really hot day, but he had this old coat on. Pretty rank, to be honest. It crossed my mind that he might have been sleeping in his van or something.'

'So when you gave him your business card, he'd have put it in the coat pocket?'

'Probably. I don't remember.'

'It might explain why Malcolm Devlin had your card in his pocket, mightn't it? If Dan had lent him the coat – all right, that doesn't seem very likely – but if he'd pinched it out of the van or something?'

'I suppose so. Doesn't explain the rest of it though. Perhaps Dan felt he couldn't, you know, live with himself – or perhaps he was afraid of being sent to prison.'

'I don't know, Jeff.' Janice stared out into the darkness. 'I just don't know.'

FIFTY-EIGHT

Suzie's regular breathing told Janice she was asleep. Turning to look at her, Janice could just make out the curve of her cheek on the pillow, white against the cloud of dark hair.

If what Jeff and Bob had suggested was right, *when* had Dan made his discovery about Malcolm and Lisa Wynn? Had he persuaded Joe not to go to the police back in 1967 because he was afraid of being busted? It had happened to Mick Jagger and Keith Richards earlier in the year – their prison sentences had been dismissed but everyone, Janice remembered, had thought they were lucky and that whoever was next wouldn't get away with it.

Perhaps Dan's not wanting to see her was because she was part of the past, and he didn't want to think about it ... Then again, he'd been OK about seeing Joe, hadn't he? Maybe that was because they'd shared a secret. Had Dan been worried that she might somehow worm it out of him? What was it that Tom had said about Dan bottling stuff up? *It was like he was going to explode and take the whole village with him*, that was it – and he hadn't liked Tom asking him about the past.

Maybe that was why he'd looked after Ma for so long, by himself – unless that was some sort of self-imposed punishment, a form of penance ... And taking Suzie and Molly in like that, without telling her ...

Perhaps it wasn't any one of those things, but a mixture of all of them – or none of them, and she was inventing things because she was tired and confused. Trying to turn her mind to something happier, she thought about the swimming costumes she'd buy for Molly and Tom from the hotel shop, so that they could use the pool in the morning. She and Suzie had agreed earlier that – for Molly's sake, if nothing else – everything should be kept as normal as possible, and that there was, in any case, no point in haring home at the crack of dawn.

She was glad she'd bought the panda too. Realising, belatedly, that it had been a mistake to turn up in Norfolk empty-handed, she'd been on the lookout for something for Molly when she and Suzie had stopped at the motorway services, and the bear's benevolent expression had appealed to her. She'd put the carrier bag that contained it in the boot before Suzie had got back from the Ladies', and she'd forgotten about it until she and Tom had gone down to the car park to search the van after dinner, while Suzie put Molly to bed. They'd found the sacks and gardening tools that Molly had described, but nothing else apart from a pair of damp knickers and a whiff of urine mixed with the sharper odour of fertiliser. Tom had dropped the pants into the car-park bin. 'Must have had an accident, poor kid.'

She'd worried, when she bought the toy, that Molly might find it too childish, but she needed something reassuring – a friend, even if it was only a stuffed bear. An image of all the toys clustered together in a pile in the bright, noisy shop, their arms open, ready for whoever wanted to take them home, was overtaken by one of the National Trust car park after Phoebe disappeared, carpeted with soft toys and bouquets, sodden in the rain . . . All that vegetation would soon have started to rot, to smell, and the plush teddies and puppies would have become abject, disturbing – a reminder of the despoiling of innocence.

Poor Melissa Piper. The memory of her face made Janice burn with shame, a feeling that she knew would be inextricably inter-mingled with her other memories of today, of Suzie feeling that she could talk to her, of Molly's squeals of delight at the hotel, her own confused feelings about Dan . . . She pictured it as a grid reference on a private topography of memory, an imaginary trans-parent sheet hovering over a real Ordnance Survey map.

The following morning, after Suzie, Molly and Tom had splashed in the pool and breakfast had been consumed – Molly gasping at the range of foodstuffs on offer and refusing to relinquish the panda, who was given his own chair by a nice waiter – they drove home.

Both Suzie and Molly had nodded off by the time they'd reached the M11, Molly slumped sideways, cheek against the window, so that Janice, looking in the rear-view mirror, could see only the panda, upright and benign on the back seat. Malcolm Devlin's necklace, still curled in its plastic bag, was in the back of Tom's van, because Molly had insisted, fearfully, that she didn't want to travel with it in the car.

After an uneasy, restless night – yoga breathing hadn't helped at all – Janice felt weary. 'You mind you stay awake, pal,' she mut-tered, exchanging another glance with the bear in the mirror. Next to the panda, crudely refolded, was the newspaper she'd bought and flicked through over tea while the others were swimming. Just as Jeff had said, the partial skeleton discovered at Thetford had been confirmed as the remains – or at least some of them – of Lisa Wynn. It was a small item: no colour, nothing from the family, just the facts and the headshot.

Janice had decided to keep Jeff's call to herself until she could get Suzie and Tom on their own – no sense in upsetting Molly further. She'd have to be told about Lisa at some point, but this wasn't the time. At least the Wynn family *know* now, she thought uneasily. That has to be better than nothing.

She wondered if Melissa Piper had read the story, or perhaps seen it on the news, accompanied by the same photograph of little Lisa as in the paper, with her plaits and her snub nose and her worried expression. She imagined Mrs Piper turning away, pressing the *Off* button. What would she be thinking?

FIFTY-NINE

Janice added the herbs and the stock, then turned down the heat under the saucepan. She'd volunteered to make dinner – spaghetti Bolognese, something she could do almost without thought – while Suzie, Tom and Molly strolled down to the Lord Nelson to meet Mark and say thank you to Simon Curtis. Not wanting to remind Molly about Malcolm Devlin's horrible necklace, she'd waited until they'd left before retrieving it from the back of the van, and now it was sitting on the end of the Old Rectory kitchen table, still in its plastic bag. She'd get it out of sight now, before she put the water on for the pasta – they'd decided that nothing further should be discussed before Molly was in bed, and so far there'd been no communication from the Norfolk police. They're probably even more confused than we are, Janice thought, picking up the plastic carrier and shoving it into her handbag.

The phone rang as she was setting the water to boil, and after a few seconds' confusion – it wasn't her mobile, but the landline – she went into the sitting room to answer it.

'Janice?'

'Yes. Who is it?'

'It's Joe. Joe Vincent. I'm glad you found Molly. Can you come?'

'Come? Over to you, you mean?'

'Yes. I have to talk to you.'

'Now?'

'Yes. Please. It's important. About Dan.' His voice was tense, the words clipped. He sounds far more *there*, she thought. Present, lucid. I'll get more out of him if I go now, she thought, before he gets abstracted again.

'All right. I'll just be a few minutes.'

'But you're coming?'

'Yes. I'm on my way.'

He *did* remember her! He'd said her name, hadn't he, with no prompting, when she'd picked up the phone. The police must have talked to him, she thought, otherwise he wouldn't know about Molly being found. They must have shown him a copy of Dan's note – after all, it had been addressed to him – and asked him about it. And now he had something to tell her – her in particular. He'd reconnected with the intimacy they'd had.

She allowed herself a moment's jubilation as she dashed upstairs to brush her hair and redo her make-up, and then, pausing only to turn off the gas and leave a note for Suzie – *Joe phoned, wants to talk to me about Dan. Sounds quite together, just a bit odd. Supper nearly finished – only needs pasta. Back soon, J x* – she grabbed her bag and went out to the car. It might be dark when she came back, and she didn't fancy walking down the lane, even with a torch.

It was nearly half past seven, and twilight was just beginning to soften the edges of the landscape, making the tributes ranged along Joe's fence look more forlorn than ever. Poor man, she thought, remembering what Suzie had said about people getting into his garden and trying to take photographs. What a way to live.

The house appeared to be in darkness, but as soon as she knocked on the door she saw light behind the frosted glass panels and a second later Joe was standing in the doorway, looking apprehensive.

'It's OK,' she said. 'It's only me. There's no one else out there.'

'That's good.' Joe was wearing jeans and a shirt – unironed, but clean. Had he changed especially? His smile was nervous, almost shy. It would be hard for him to open up to anybody after so many years, she thought, feeling a warm, keen sense of pleasure that it was her he'd chosen.

Joe cleared his throat. 'I was at the back,' he said. 'In the studio.'

'It's this way, isn't it?' As she went down the hall, Janice heard the click as he closed the front door. I must be calm, she thought, and allow him to go at his own pace – and in those few seconds her mind flew ahead as she allowed herself to imagine, not sex, but *knowing* him again, sharing, being part of his world. There was a smell of frying – onions, perhaps, or bacon – and she wondered, with another warm rush, if he were going to invite her to eat with him.

She sniffed. The studio smelt slightly acrid too, as though Joe had had another bonfire and the smoke had drifted in through the French windows. She could see, as she stood in the doorway, that only a few paintings were left, and she wondered how long it had taken him to burn so many. She was turning to ask him why he didn't reuse the canvases, when a flicker of movement – a grey, ragged thing, all but obscured by the open door – caught her eye.

An unexpected image of the tattered, trailing shape she'd glimpsed on her walk on that first night here flung itself through her mind before resolving itself in front of her. And that smell – how could she have thought it was cooking?

A scruffy grey greatcoat on a scarecrow, skinny and filthy. Weather-beaten skin like bark, as though a man had grown out of a tree. Malevolent, red-rimmed eyes. Teeth like rotting fence posts in the hole between the straggling fungi of moustache and beard. Knobbly, ochre-coloured fingers ... And a long, sharp kitchen knife.

But he's *dead*, clamoured a voice in her brain. He can't be here, he can't, he's—

'Remember me, Janice?' said Malcolm Devlin. 'I haven't forgotten you.'

SIXTY

Gasping, Janice turned. Joe was standing behind her in the hallway. 'What's going on? What's he doing here?'

Joe's face was entirely blank. He's retreated into himself, Janice thought. He doesn't know what's happening. In desperation, she flew at him – 'Joe, it's Malcolm! We've got to get *out*!' – shoving him to get him outside, into the car, away, anywhere—

She was yanked backwards as Malcolm grabbed hold of her arm, and she felt something cold and hard against her neck – the knife – and twisted away, screaming.

'Shut up!'

Malcolm's breath blasted her face, and she could feel her heart thudding against her ribcage as they struggled soundlessly for a few moments – his grip was iron – before he jerked her arm painfully upwards behind her back and, thrash as she might, she couldn't break away. Joe's face bobbed, expressionless, in front of her. *He's not going to help me*, she thought in despair. *He's not going to do anything. He got me here, he—*

'Let's be cool, Janice,' said Malcolm into her hair.

Janice drove her free elbow into Malcolm's stomach and heard him grunt. For just a second he loosened his grip and the knife jumped against the flesh of her neck, but then he was back, as close and unyielding as before. 'Be cool,' he repeated. 'You'll cut yourself.'

Janice felt as though she might suffocate. Instructions flash-flooded her brain: *breathe-through-your-mouth-don't-try-and-fight-him-go-limp-calm-him-down—*

'What do you want, Malcolm?' she panted.

For answer, Malcolm jerked her arm upwards so sharply that for a few excruciating seconds she thought it might snap.

'Joe,' she moaned. 'Please . . . What does he want?'

For a moment all she could hear was Malcolm's breath, ragged in her ear, and then Joe said, 'Music.'

'*Music?*'

'He wants music.' Joe's face and voice were toneless. 'My music.'

Janice gritted her teeth. 'Then play him your bloody music. Just do it, before—' She gasped as Malcolm jerked again. 'Before. He. Breaks. My. Arm.'

'I can't.'

'Please, Joe.' Janice forced her head higher, away from the blade at her throat. 'You must have a C.D. player, a record player . . . a guitar. *Something.*'

Joe shook his head. 'That's not what he wants.'

'Then what—?'

'Music.' Janice flinched as Malcolm's voice rasped in her ear. 'The *sound*, Janice. Consciousness expanding. It can happen again. We can make it happen.'

'Make *what* happen?'

'The most important thing in the world.'

'I told him.' Joe spoke as if Malcolm wasn't there. 'I don't do that anymore.'

'But there's other music,' said Janice desperately. 'Lots of music.'

'Not *that* music. Not the same.' Janice felt the blade's sharp edge scrape her neck. 'We can make it happen.'

Try-and-relax-make-him-think-you're-on-his-side— 'How?'

'I can't do it alone.'

Keep-him-talking-play-for-time— 'Then why don't you let me help you?'

'You're too old.'

'That's a shame.' Janice tried to keep her tone light, as if this were a perfectly normal conversation.

'When Joe told me about Marie, then I understood what had to happen.'

Her arm was agony. The pain seemed to dance in little spots in front of her eyes, pixelating Joe's face and the hallway behind him. Marie, Joe's sister, she thought. Hit by a car. Dead. That stuff on Wikipedia about how her death had had a profound effect on him . . . 'I don't understand, Malcolm. Will you tell me? Then I can help you.'

'Acid freed me,' said Malcolm, as if she hadn't spoken. 'Made it possible for me to act.'

What had Bob Harling said? Something about Malcolm wanting 'a place at that table' – madness as just another form of self-expression, except that Malcolm really was mad. He wanted to be *part* of it, Janice thought, so much that he was prepared to kill.

'It took away my fear,' said Malcolm. 'I had no attachment. I just did what needed to be done.'

My arm's dying, thought Janice. Why doesn't Joe *do* something? 'What was that?' she gasped. 'What needed to be done?'

'Sacrifice. I wanted to do something, but I didn't know what it was until I really listened to the music, and then I knew.'

Lisa Wynn, thought Janice. A week before 'Song of Sixpence' was released.

Malcolm was talking again: 'The first one was right – everything was right – the world changed.'

The Japanese soldiers, thought Janice. What Suzie had said? In the jungle for years, not realising that the war was over.

'I wanted the wisdom of acid,' Malcolm was saying, 'but I couldn't get it back. I knew there must be a way, but we couldn't do it without Joe.' He carried on, but the words seemed to be dissolving in her ear. She tried to snatch them out of the pain, snatch at breath, snatch at— Where was Joe? She couldn't see him anymore, just the dots in front of her eyes. *Keep-breathing-don't-black-out—*

'The other girl ... thought it could bring it back ... didn't work ...'

My-arm-oh-God-my-arm—

'My head was in a bad place ... I wasn't free ...'

Other girl? Was he talking about Phoebe?

'Dan Carthy-Todd, thieving bastard, he knew—'

He knew? Dan's letter – what was it? Something about a fantasy, *like the girl in 2007* – but that was years later, so how could it be—?

'Wanted it for himself but it's bigger than all of us—'

'Let go of me,' Janice whispered. 'Please ...'

'We have to try again—'

'Please ...'

'It's as big as the cosmos itself—'

'Please ...'

'The destruction of ego—'

'Joe ...'

'Beyond life and death—'

'Oh, God, please help me ...'

'Give her to me—'

There was a crash and as Janice was flung forward she had the warm, slithery sensation of an enormous egg being broken over her head. The side of her face smacked into the wall of the studio and the world went silent as she slid down to the floor, engulfed in solvent fumes, viscous liquid puddling and trickling in her hair. Her right arm felt like a dead thing, a lump of solid, boneless meat, not part of her but somehow attached, and she scrabbled furiously with her left hand, trying to turn herself round, away from the wall. The room appeared to be melting around her in thick streaks of white. Her eyes stung and she clawed at her face, trying to see, and, opening her mouth to shout tasted something chemical, tacky and mucoid. There was a faint pop somewhere in her left ear and a whoosh of air and she could hear again – incoherent shouting and movement – and she heaved herself on to her knees, retching. She could see Malcolm lying on the floor in front of her, the side of his head obliterated in a thick white pool and Joe above him, yelling, something large – not a weapon but a shape, cylindrical like a drum – swinging from his hand.

She tried to blink, but her eyes refused to stay open. There was something heavy on them, gummy, holding them closed, and a burning, burning pain. As she staggered upright and half walked, half crawled the few paces down the hall to Joe's kitchen, she heard the sound of glass breaking somewhere behind her. She flailed and batted along the work surfaces until she found the sink and then, dimly aware of a confusion of crashes and bangs in the next room, she lunged for the tap and leant forward, shoving away the clutter of dirty pots and pans until she felt water gush on to her face and the pain begin to subside.

Blinking down at the milky swirls swilling around the plughole, Janice realised that it was paint. Not artists' paint, but house paint – the big tins she'd seen lining the hallway. Joe had thrown it at them. Shaking her head violently, like a dog, she grabbed a tea towel and mopped her face.

*

'Are you all right?'

The voice wasn't Joe's or Malcolm's. Janice took her head out of the tea towel and saw Tom standing in the kitchen doorway.

'What are you doing here?'

'We saw the note and Mum was worried because you'd put that Joe sounded odd, so I said I'd come and see if you were OK. When I heard all the shouting I came round the back and smashed a pane in the French windows.'

'Where's Malcolm?'

'Next door. It's all right, he isn't going anywhere – Joe's sitting on him, and I've called the police.'

SIXTY-ONE

'I'm sorry,' said Joe. 'It was all I could think of.'

'At least it was water-based,' said Janice, 'or I'd reek of turpentine by now.'

'You don't mind me being in here, do you?' They were upstairs in the bathroom, and Joe was sitting on the edge of the bath, watching, while Janice, kneeling on the mat, shampooed the rest of the paint out of her hair.

'Not at all.' Janice groped for the shower attachment and lifted it to rinse her hair, wincing at the pain across her shoulders.

'I'm sorry about your arm,' said Joe. 'And about the smell.'

'It's only mildew.' It was a sad little room – clammy cold, even in summer, with a cracked basin and grouting that bloomed with mould – but at least they were alone now.

The police had turned up in whooping cars that strobed the bruised-plum sky with bands of blue and white. They'd taken Malcolm away, crunching across the carpet of glittering smithereens from the French windows, stolidly oblivious to his shouts and curses.

D.S. Glenville and D.C. Singer had remained behind to take preliminary statements from Joe, Janice and Tom. They'd politely deflected Janice's questions about the identity of the corpse in the wood and then they too had departed. While Joe had swept up the glass and cut up a cardboard box to patch the broken panes, Janice had given Tom a hasty rundown of what Bob Harling and Jeff had told her on the phone the previous evening, and then Tom had left too, saying that Suzie would be worrying and he should get back and tell her what had happened. Janice had been on the point of telling Joe that she was going too, when he'd appeared in the kitchen doorway with a dustpan full of shards and said that he was going to make tea and would she like some.

I misjudged him, thought Janice, struggling to rinse her hair. I believed what everyone told me – myths and exaggerations, things to keep people at bay. The man in the room with her now, the patina of his fame long rubbed away, was an older and – yes, all right – *slower* version of the one she remembered, charming and diffident.

'Shall I help you?'

'Thanks.' Gratefully, Janice handed him the shower attachment and bent her head over the bath once more while Joe, solemnly and with great attention, rinsed her hair.

Towelling her head afterwards, she said, 'Did you actually want to talk to me, or did Malc make you call?'

'I did want to. The police came this morning and showed me Dan's letter. They wanted to know what it meant.' Joe frowned. 'The girl at the picnic, and the other things. They showed you as well, didn't they?'

'Yes, the ones in Wiltshire.'

Joe leant over to put the shampoo back in the cabinet. 'They told me Molly'd been found – oh, and they showed me a couple of old photos too, but they didn't mean anything to me. I was going to ring you but I only had Dan's number, not yours – they said you'd gone to fetch Molly and I wasn't sure when you'd be back.'

'So was Malcolm here when you phoned?'

'Yes. But would you mind if I told you from the beginning? It's easier – you know, keeping it all straight in my head.'

'Sure.'

'Do you want to do your hair first? I'm afraid I haven't got a dryer.'

'That doesn't matter.'

'Or a brush.'

'That doesn't matter either. There's one in my handbag.'

'You've still got a few spots of paint on your face as well.'

Janice wiped the steam off the glass front of the cabinet with her sleeve, revealing a paint-smeared madwoman with hair standing out in a demented halo. 'My God, it's the Witch of Endor.'

'She was OK.' Joe handed her a flannel. 'She summoned Samuel back from the dead to help Saul. It's in the Bible.'

Janice stopped rubbing her face and stared at him.

Joe grinned. 'I have to do something with my time. I've read the Bible and the Qur'an, all the way through.'

'I'm impressed. Did they make sense?'

'Not really, but you take out what you want, so . . .' Joe shrugged. 'How's your arm?'

'Not too bad now.'

'Why don't you go into the back room?' said Joe. 'There's nowhere to sit downstairs. I can bring you some more tea – or something stronger if you want.'

'I think I do. Can you bring my handbag up too? I think it's still on the floor in your studio.'

'I had to find a way of living that worked for me,' said Joe. 'That was the thing.' They were settled in the back room with glasses of wine, Janice on the armchair and Joe on the sofa with his feet up on the toolbox.

'And does it work?'

'Up to a point. The problem is that people want things. It's as if I owe them something – and I don't, Janice. Even if I did, I haven't got anything to give them.'

'You once told me that you'd run out of thought,' said Janice.

'Did I?' Joe gave her a sheepish smile. 'That was right – well, sort of. I felt as if I'd dropped off the edge of my own mind, if that makes any sense. People always think there's got to be something more, and there isn't.'

A place at that table, thought Janice, remembering Bob Harling's words. A connection. Nearness, so that the magic might rub off. She remembered the girls who'd made Joe and the others beautiful hand-sewn shirts, and the gifts laid reverently outside the door of his flat in Earls Court. *I'm your biggest fan. I love you more than anything else in the world. I'd do anything for you.* The weight of expectation. 'Was that why you . . . retreated?'

'Not at first, but then it was just . . . Well, *easier*, I suppose. That makes it sound like a strategy, but it wasn't, not consciously. I didn't want to go back to that place.'

'I think I understand. Tell me about Malcolm.'

'He was the worst of them. From right back . . . after that picnic, that poor girl . . .' Joe shook his head.

'Lisa Wynn,' said Janice. 'It was him, wasn't it?'

'Yes. He came to me afterwards, kept telling me he'd done it for us. For me, for the album, so it would be a success.'

'A sacrifice.'

'Yes. I didn't believe him, and neither did Dan when I told him. Dan had picked up the ribbon though, and I'd thought it was a good omen – a message from Marie, because she'd had pink ribbons in her hair when she died, and I'd put a song about them on the album.' Joe grimaced. 'I *know*. Stupid. But everyone was looking for *meaning*, remember, and you persuade yourself it's important or significant or whatever you want to call it . . . And we were all tripping, Janice: I thought I saw Marie, and this man, carrying her – in the distance, like a mirage. Shimmering, really alive, intense . . . That whole acid thing.'

'Why did you think it was her?'

'Because when she was killed one of our neighbours carried her back to our house. She was hit by a car at the corner of the road where we lived. Mr Cochrane saw it happen, but he didn't realise how badly hurt she was – I don't know if she was dead when he picked her up, but she was by the time he brought her in . . . We were having a party and Mum needed something from the shop, so she'd sent Marie. The guests had just started arriving, and there was all this food on the sideboard, plates and plates of it, and then Mr Cochrane came into the middle of the room with Marie in his arms and just stood there . . . I don't know if that's what actually happened, but it's what I remember. And at the picnic I was suddenly back in that place, only it was fractured in my head . . . I wanted to get to Marie so I started running towards the man, but Dan stopped me. When we talked about it afterwards, he told me he hadn't seen anyone carrying a child, and if I went to the police I'd probably get busted. It was all so confused, Janice. I was confused . . . and with the album, and people telling us we were going to be stars, and the drugs . . . It was a complete head-fuck.'

Joe fell silent, leaving Janice wondering if Dan *had* seen anyone carrying a child in the distance, but said he hadn't because Joe was as high as a kite and he needed to stop him running off. Had he been high himself? *She* certainly had been. Perhaps Dan wasn't sure *what* he'd seen, but something Malcolm said had made it prey on his mind – which was why he'd gone to see Jeff to ask about that little piece of film. 'So what happened then?' she asked.

'I was really messing myself up, Janice, and Malc was there all the time . . . It felt as if he was trying to climb inside my head.'

'Was that why you left the Weather Ship?'

'Part of it. I wasn't functioning – just . . . *not there*, really – and I don't blame the others for deciding they could do without me, which is pretty much what happened. But even then Malc wouldn't go away – he used to come and visit me when I was in Crowhurst. He wouldn't stop talking about it, what he'd done for the Weather Ship. He said the others had betrayed me, kicking me out of the band – betrayed the music . . . I didn't want to talk about any of it, I just wanted to be left alone. I told the staff I didn't want him to come, but they wouldn't listen.' Joe grimaced. 'He always tried to be really, you know, *straight* with them, and they bought it – they thought it was good for me to get reconnected with my past. They'd keep giving me a guitar, encouraging me to play, and I couldn't, because I was in a different place.'

'Did Malc talk about Lisa specifically?'

'Yes – not by name, but it was all that shit about the cosmos and the rest of it . . . I don't remember telling him about Marie but I suppose I must have done, or someone did – he'd got this idea that her dying like that was, I don't know, *connected* to the Weather Ship's music, some sort of driving force . . . I was falling apart; I didn't know what was real anymore. I was just – mentally, emotionally – hand to mouth, keeping going from day to day. And then I got a bit better, and I went to live with my mum for a while, and I didn't hear from him. Or maybe she kept him away – I don't know – but, either way I didn't see him.' Malc would have been living with this aunt then, thought Janice, remembering what Bob Harling had told her. 'I was always in touch with Dan – he really was great, by the way – and after my mum died he found me this place.'

'And then Malc came back?'

'Not for a few years, but then it all started again. I couldn't go out of the house without seeing him, and he'd leave notes . . . Sometimes he'd be gone for a few months, but he'd always come back.'

'You could have moved.'

'No point. He'd have found me. They all would, because they always do. And I *like* living here, Janice. I like this house – being here and doing things.' Joe tapped the toolbox with his heels. 'Projects.'

'Dan's note said something about a girl in 2007.'

'Yeah, the police asked me about that, but it didn't mean anything. Malc might have told me, but . . .'

'Not something you'd forget, is it?'

'I don't mean "told me" like that, because I wouldn't talk to him. I had the phone disconnected because he'd got hold of the number – Dan got me a mobile – but he used to leave notes and things, out there on the fence.'

'And you burnt them?'

'Yeah. I never read them. Like I said, I just wanted to be left alone.'

'But Dan knew about it.'

Joe frowned. 'Yes, he did.'

'In the letter,' Janice said, 'he said something about a woman who knew about Malc too. Someone who lives near here. Do you know who that is?'

Joe shook his head. 'The police asked me about that – I suppose it's one of your neighbours, but I don't know who. I think Malc must have told Dan about her. Dan did speak to Malc sometimes, to warn him off. He'd usually go away for a bit after that. Malc's never broken in before, by the way – not when I've been here anyway. I'm pretty sure he wouldn't have dared while Dan was around.'

'Well, he must have convinced Dan that he'd done something to Lisa, and that he was a threat to Molly. She's the only female child who lives round here . . .' And, she thought, she looks exactly like Phoebe's age-progressed photo. If Phoebe, back in 2007, had been Malc's next 'sacrifice', and it had failed to produce any music from Joe, Molly must have seemed, to his deranged mind, to be a heaven-sent opportunity for another go. 'We thought the girl in 2007 might have been Phoebe Piper,' she said. 'Molly looks like her – or like everyone thinks she looks now anyway.'

'I suppose the police will ask him about it,' said Joe.

'It might be nothing to do with him, of course,' said Janice. 'But what if it is? What if he refuses to tell them?'

Joe took his feet off the toolbox and leant forward, elbows on knees, raking his hands through his hair. 'He won't care, will he? He might not even remember where he buried her.'

'You mean, because it didn't work out? From his point of view, I mean.'

'Yes – so he wouldn't have a reason to remember, would he?' Joe groaned and buried his face in his hands.

'We probably shouldn't jump to conclusions,' said Janice. 'Can you explain to me about what's happened in the last couple of weeks?'

Joe looked up, his eyes weary. 'Where do you want me to start?'

'You came to see Dan the day after I arrived, remember? When I told you he was dead.'

Joe nodded.

'You asked to see Molly – except that you called her Marie – about the ribbon.'

'I suppose I was confused,' Joe said. 'Dan told me what Malc said about the ribbon – they must have compared the two pieces afterwards – and I wanted to see it for myself. And you being there, because he hadn't told me—'

'He didn't know I was coming,' said Janice. 'Suzie phoned me when he died.'

'OK . . . I thought I remembered you, but I wasn't sure. I don't always remember things. Gaps . . . I don't make the connections.'

'That's fair enough,' said Janice. 'It must have been a hell of a shock, hearing that Dan was dead.'

Joe nodded. 'Hard to take it in. I don't think I really did until this morning, when the police came. But Dan'd always said, if he wasn't around and I wanted something – for the garden, or anything like that – that I should ask Marie—'

'Molly—'

'*Molly*. Dan said she was so nosy she knew where everything was – and I thought maybe he'd given her the ribbon . . .' Joe put his head in his hands. 'Oh, God, what a mess . . .'

'There's something else,' said Janice. 'When we thought it was Malc in the wood, when we thought he was dead, we – Suzie and Tom and I, I mean – thought perhaps Dan had . . . well, that he was responsible.' She thought for a moment. 'But you knew Malc wasn't dead, didn't you? When I tried to show you that photo of Malc, and I told you he was dead, you said, "He's here all the time."'

'He was. He'd been in the garden. I saw him. That's why I was so freaked out.'

'But there *was* a body in the wood at Crowhurst, Joe. Mark – that's Suzie's partner – he found it, and he thought it was Malc.' The wound on the head, thought Janice. The foxes tearing at the flesh of his face and neck. The darkness, with only a torch to see by, and the shock – and, she supposed, the fact that Mark and

Harry were expecting to find Malc and not someone else. And then they'd thought it might be Jeff because of the card, and when it had turned out not to be, they'd simply assumed . . . Mark had said that the camp where Harry thought Malc lived was empty, hadn't he? 'I think whoever it was might have been wearing Dan's coat,' said Janice. 'Tom said it was missing from his van, and—'

'Dan had a fight with Malc,' Joe said suddenly. 'He told me. Perhaps he thought Malc had pinched the coat. He used to leave the back doors of the van open if he was working, so he could get at his tools and things.'

'When was that?'

'I don't know. Last week or the week before.'

'Was that when he told you about Malc and the ribbon?'

'I'm not sure. Afterwards, I think. A different conversation anyway. But there are a couple of other people who hang about here sometimes, who look a bit like Malc,' Joe added. 'They don't usually cause trouble, but one of them might have taken the coat.'

Janice heard Suzie's voice in her head: *a couple of old trampy types left over from the sixties*. 'Do they live in the wood?' she asked.

'Maybe, I don't know.'

'Dan's note said something about everything going wrong,' said Janice. Dan the roadie. Dan the fixer-upper. Dan, who wanted to protect Molly, in the woods at Crowhurst, in the dark . . . 'Perhaps that's what he meant,' she added bleakly. 'He killed the wrong man.'

SIXTY-TWO

'Oh, *fuck*.' Joe put his head in his hands and groaned. 'All of this is my fault. That little kid and her family . . . And I was just stuck in this big fucking empty space inside my head . . . And if there was another one too, and I just turned my back on the whole thing – I couldn't . . . couldn't . . . ' He started crying, shoulders heaving, deep, gulping, painful sobs.

Janice put down her glass and went to sit beside him on the sofa, rubbing his back. Joe, Dan and the guilt he must have felt, the Wynn family and the Pipers grieving and hoping through all those years, Suzie and Molly: the raw enormity of it all left her numb and stupefied, so that she didn't know where, or how, to begin to process it. 'But you stopped Malc hurting Molly, didn't you?' she asked. '"We have to try again" – that's what he said – and that's why he came, isn't it? Why he made you ring me – he wanted me to fetch Molly.'

'Yes.' The word was a howl. Janice clutched his shoulder and turned him towards her so that their foreheads were almost touching; his eyes were two bottomless black pools. 'He wanted Molly.' The words came out wet and swollen. 'I told him – if you came and he explained it to you first, you'd understand. It was the only thing I could think of to stop him. He had the knife, and he was standing there . . . I didn't know what else to do. I thought, if I didn't, he'd go and take another girl and it would all happen again.'

'But it won't happen again, because you stopped him, Joe. You did that.'

'Yes,' said Joe. 'But fifty years too late.'

'We can't change the past, love.'

'That girl – Lisa – her family . . . I have to tell them it was my fault that she didn't have a life.'

'It wasn't your fault, Joe.'

'But I'm responsible.' Joe pulled away from her. 'I have to do something about it.'

'OK.' At least, Janice thought, it was something that he could do – that *they* could do. It wouldn't bring Lisa back, but it might help the Wynn family. 'We'll have to think of the best way to do that. I'm sure the police'll be able to help if you ask them, but right now I think you ought to blow your nose. What did you do with my handbag?'

Wordlessly, Joe reached over the arm of the sofa and handed it up to her.

Janice realised, as she fished inside, that she still hadn't brushed her hair or sorted out her face. She found a packet of tissues, handed it to Joe, and was about to pull out her make-up bag when her fingers brushed against the bunched-up plastic carrier, with its soft and lumpy contents, and she yelped in shock.

'What?'

'I'd forgotten that was in here.' Bending forward, Janice shook out the plastic bag until, flopping and jerking like something alive, the necklace disgorged itself.

They both stared at it in silence for a moment, and then Joe said slowly, 'That's Malc's. What are you doing with it?'

'We found it in the back of Dan's van.'

Joe nudged it with his foot. 'Perhaps it came off when they had that fight – if Dan grabbed it or something.'

'Do you think that was why he said Dan was a thief? He called him a thieving bastard, remember?'

'I don't, but that thing must have meant a lot to Malc because he'd had it for years. Every time I saw him there seemed to be more of it. Looks as if it could grow all by itself, doesn't it?'

'Yes. It's revolting.' Picking up her handbag, Janice took out her hairbrush and make-up and set to work.

Joe poured them both some more wine, then squatted down to look more closely at the necklace. He doesn't want to touch it any more than I do, Janice thought. 'He's got some dog tags on here,' he said. 'Wonder where they came from.'

Janice lowered her pocket mirror. 'Where? I can't see any.'

'See these?' Joe pointed to two pieces of what looked like fibre, one red and circular, the other green and octagonal, lying in the middle of one of the bundles of feathers.

'I thought dog tags were metal.'

'Not always.'

'Maybe they were his dad's or something.'

Janice picked up her bag and looked inside. 'I haven't got my reading glasses.'

'Hang on.' Joe left the room and returned a few seconds later with a pair of his own.

'You need them too.'

'So did Dan.' Joe gave a what-can-you-do shrug. 'Age.'

'Tell me about it,' said Janice. 'I hardly recognise myself anymore.'

'You look OK.' He said it neutrally, as if confirming that she still had two arms and two legs. Serves me right for fishing, thought Janice.

Joe took a screwdriver from his toolbox and, hooking it through the necklace, held it up beneath the room's single unshaded light bulb. 'Belonged to a WAAF. She was C of E, and there's a service number, and an O – that's separate, must be the blood group – and . . .' he turned the red disc round with his thumb and finger 'a name. Hang on . . . M, C, L, A, U . . . *McLaurin*. And two initials – M and E.'

SIXTY-THREE

McLaurin, M. E. Marguerite Edith McLaurin. Her identity tags, worn around Malcolm Devlin's neck, next to his heart. Driving back from Joe's with the two discs, cut from the necklace, in her handbag, Janice had a nervous, teetering feeling, as though she were on a high ledge somewhere, looking down into a void.

The Old Rectory was dark and silent, its front door locked. Janice let herself in and, turning on the kitchen light, found a note on the table from Suzie, written on the reverse of the note she had left – how many hours ago? She'd lost all track of time, but the clock on the wall told her it was almost two o'clock in the morning.

She'd left Joe after giving him a cautious kiss on the cheek, which, to her surprise, he'd returned with easy affection, saying, 'You will come back tomorrow, won't you?'

Now, too tired to speculate about what this might mean – if anything – she simply felt glad that there was not to be an entire separation. The name McLaurin had obviously meant nothing to him, and when she'd explained about Dan's mother and the probable connection with the *Marguerite* photograph, he'd just nodded and looked perplexed until she'd told him not to worry, she'd figure it out somehow. Clearly exhausted, he'd said, 'This is the most talking I've done in a long time. I've used up about a year's worth of words' – as if they were rationed.

I learnt not to love him, she thought. *What happens now?*

She wouldn't allow herself any expectations. Besides, for the immediate future there was plenty else to think about. Suzie's note read: *Tom told us what happened. We waited up till one but he thought you might be spending the night at Joe's. See you tomorrow. S xxx*

Lying in bed, the arm that Malcolm had twisted up her back ached in a way that it hadn't since he'd let go of it. Her legs ached too. Tiredness, she thought. And being old. There was enough light coming through the thin curtains for her to make out their rows of stylised yellow and orange flowers, the skeletal plant forms rendered in spidery black lines. They must be over fifty years old, she thought. Vintage. Everything comes round again.

Getting up the stairs and into bed had felt like climbing a mountain, and even now, lying down, her body felt like a dead weight. I must sleep, she thought. Sleep, and sort it all out in the morning.

She heard a scuffling sound on the landing, and then the door creaked open a few inches and Molly's head appeared. 'Janice?'

'You're supposed to be asleep.'

'I wanted to see if you were OK.'

'I'm fine.'

'Can I come in properly, just for a minute?'

Janice struggled into a sitting position. 'Come on, then.'

Molly inched round the edge of the door and Janice saw she had the panda tucked underneath her arm. She perched on the edge of the mattress and sat the bear on her lap, facing away from her, one arm around its stomach. The top of its head was the same height as hers. 'I *was* asleep, but I woke up when Tom came back. He was talking to Mum and Mark, and I listened. On the stairs. They didn't know I there, but I could hear them because the kitchen door was open. Tom said the Sneaky Man killed a girl a long time ago, and nobody knew, and he's not dead at all, like you thought, and he tried to kill you. And Joe.'

Janice opened her mouth, failed to marshal her thoughts into any kind of coherent sequence, and closed it again. 'He didn't kill us,' she said. 'We're all right.'

'Tom said Joe threw paint all over you and the Sneaky Man, and the police came.' She peered at Janice's face. 'Was he making it up? I can't see any paint.'

'I managed to wash most of it off.'

Molly looked anxious. 'It wasn't like that picture you showed me, was it? You didn't have any clothes on.'

'I did this time.'

Molly nodded, and nuzzled the back of the panda's head for a moment before saying, 'Why did he kill the girl?'

'Because he's mad, love.'

'And horrible.'

'Yes. Mad *and* horrible.'

'And the girl was called Lisa?'

'Yes.'

'How old was she?'

'Only five, I'm afraid.'

Molly sat in silence for a moment, stroking the panda's ear. 'She didn't have any life at all, hardly.'

'No, she didn't.'

'Will he go to prison?'

'Yes, I should think so. For a very long time.'

'So . . . will we be safe?'

'Yes, darling. We'll all be safe. Why don't you come and give me a kiss, and then I can come with you to your room and tuck you in, if you like.'

Molly considered this for a moment, then said, 'No, I can go by myself.'

'Just the kiss, then.'

'All right.'

The panda got in the way a bit, so Janice kissed him too. 'Have you thought of a name yet?'

'Well, I thought . . .' Molly hesitated, then said, in a rush, 'Is it OK if I call him Dan?'

'Of course it is, love.'

'I thought you might not like it.'

'I think it's lovely. Dan would have too.'

Molly digested this, then said, 'I'm going now.'

Halfway to the door, she stopped and turned round. 'Lisa's mum . . . She must have cried and cried.'

SIXTY-FOUR

Janice turned off the tap and set the kettle to boil. It wasn't quite quarter past six and the sun was still rising, pale light creeping towards the windows. The rest of the house was silent and heavy with sleep but after a restless, uncomfortable night, she'd decided to come downstairs for some tea. Her whole body seemed to be aching now and she had the cement feeling again, so that reaching into the cupboard for a mug and bending to get milk out of the fridge seemed as effortful as weightlifting.

She'd dreamt about the unknown man in the wood. She could see his legs and feet, but his upper body was hidden under the furry bodies of foxes that had converged to eat his face. They tore at his flesh, snarling and ripping, and she tried to beat them away but the air resisted her as though it were water, and the animals ignored her.

Seeing a fox trotting down the lane, she shuddered involuntarily. The pack in the dream had evaporated into russet ripples, leaving her staring down at what looked like a cutaway model of a human head with a cross section of cream-coloured folds of brain and one visible eyeball, bulbous in its socket. Shiny pink plastic skin on one side, sinewy bands of muscle and blood vessels coloured blue and red on the other. Waking with a sense, not of horror but despair, she'd thought: No one will recognise him now.

Fragments of this came back to her as she stood in front of the window drinking tea, together with scraps of thoughts about the day before, bobbing along on the surface of her mind like flotsam. After about a quarter of an hour the fox came back, neat and purposeful, as though it were returning from an errand. Unless, of course, it was a different animal altogether.

He walks up and down the road. Molly had said it, hadn't she? Malcolm Devlin didn't come to this house, but walked up and down the road. Going to see someone? The road the Old Rectory was on led out of the village, and there were hardly any other houses.

Janice pottered around the kitchen, scraping leftover food off plates, wiping surfaces, thinking. After a while she sat down at the kitchen table and stared in the direction of the sink for a bit.

The mistake Mark made in the wood. Her dream – *No one will recognise him now.* That cutaway plastic head . . . Early skin grafts looked like plastic. Pink and shiny, shirred skin around them. *There's a woman who knows about him, she lives nearby and she's known for years.* The twisted mouth. *I don't think she would ever say anything.* The glaring eye with its too-tight lid.

He walks up and down the road. Of course he did, thought Janice. He was visiting her.

The tea was stone cold now. Looking at the kitchen clock, she was surprised to see that almost an hour had passed since she'd come downstairs. She needed to fill Suzie and Tom in about her conversation with Joe, and she must talk to D.S. Glenville too – but she doubted that anyone else in the house would stir for another hour at least, and Glenville could wait. There was something else she needed to do first.

Invigorated, she washed her mug and went upstairs to shower and get dressed.

SIXTY-FIVE

'I'm pleased to hear your granddaughter is safe, but as far as the rest of it's concerned, I have no idea what you're talking about.' The words issued sideways from the good corner of Mrs Rocklin's mouth.

'I think you do.'

Leaning on her stick in the doorway of her cottage, dressed in corduroy trousers and a sweater, Norma Rocklin, with her short, wispy hair, looked like a wizened schoolboy.

'Please wait.' Janice put a foot over the threshold.

Mrs Rocklin jabbed it with the end of her stick. 'Go away!'

'No. Not until I've got some answers.'

'I've got nothing to say to you.'

'Yes, you have. But first I'd like you to look at these.' Janice took the dog tags out of her pocket and held them up.

Mrs Rocklin waved them away with a scrawny, impatient hand. 'I've never seen them before. I don't even know what they are.'

'They're military identification tags for M. E. McLaurin. Marguerite Edith – Dan's mother. She was in the WAAF during the war.'

'I don't know anything about it.'

'Yes, you do. I may as well tell you this, because you're bound to find out sooner or later, but my brother committed suicide. He left a note, and you're mentioned in it. You knew about Marguerite McLaurin, and about Malcolm Devlin. There was a photo of you with Marguerite too.'

Mrs Rocklin stared at her for a long moment. Please, Janice thought, let me be right. The old lady closed her eyes and for a second Janice thought she was going to keel over, but when she opened them and spoke, her words were as firm and hard as stones. 'Where did you get those dog tags?'

'They formed part of a necklace worn by Malcolm Devlin.'

'Perhaps he found them in a junk shop.'

'Bit of a coincidence if he did, don't you think? There's no doubt about Marguerite McLaurin being Dan's mother, by the way – her name is on his birth certificate. I assume she must have met my father when he was in the R.A.F. in Norfolk. Dan had a photograph of her signed *Marguerite*, and there was another photograph showing her standing next to you. I didn't recognise you at first, because it was before you were burnt. I think Malcolm Devlin gave it to Dan.'

'Show me those things.'

Janice dropped the tags into Mrs Rocklin's outstretched hand and watched as she fumbled a pair of glasses out of her trouser pocket and held them up vertically, inspecting the little discs one by one through a single lens.

'Well?'

Mrs Rocklin closed her eyes again. This time, when she opened them, she looked at Janice with the weary resignation of one who has lost a long and exhausting argument. 'McLaurin was my maiden name. Marguerite was my sister.'

SIXTY-SIX

They sat on opposite sides of the table in Mrs Rocklin's kitchen, drinking the tea that Janice, acting on her instructions, had made. The room was stuffy, with curtains drawn despite the bright morning. In the harsh, flickering light from the neon strip on the ceiling Janice saw the supports of old age: medicine bottles and boxes of pills ranged along the shelf above the kettle, the packet of incontinence pads on the top of the fridge, the walking frame ready by the back door. This is the next step, she thought. How it ends.

'She was younger than me by a few years. Very clever, but . . .' Mrs Rocklin turned her head, appearing to stare at the calendar on the wall – Janice thought she recognised Scafell Pike – and muttered something under her breath.

'I'm sorry, I didn't quite catch that.'

'She was nervy. Excitable, easily upset, and always one for the men. She met your father towards the end of the war. I suppose she'd have been about twenty then. Frank was older, of course.'

Darling Frank . . . Janice remembered the cache of letters she'd found in the spare room. 'My parents got married in September 1945.'

'Yes. Marguerite was . . . Well, I suppose you'd say she was devastated. Very unhappy. Although – and these aren't necessarily the facts, because I didn't know your father in those days, so what I'm going to say is only my impression of what happened – I think the affection . . . the relationship, I suppose you'd call it, was always rather more on her side than on his.'

'You mean Marguerite was keener on him than he was on her?'

'I think so, yes. She would get very . . . *overcome* by men. She'd fall in love with them and become convinced that they were going to propose to her.'

'And they didn't?'

'Frank didn't.' Mrs Rocklin sighed. 'I remember her being very excited one day – I was married by then, and living in Kent, but she'd managed to telephone – and she said to me, "Tonight's the night," meaning that he was going to ask her to marry him. But he didn't. Instead, he told her that he was going to marry your mother.'

'So he was engaged to one woman and seeing another woman on the side.'

'It was different in those days.' Mrs Rocklin's tone was sharp. 'None of this dropping your knickers in the first minute.'

'Well, she must have dropped her knickers at some stage,' snapped Janice, 'because Dan came along in 1948.' Mrs Rocklin stared at the calendar some more. 'So what happened?'

Mrs Rocklin sighed. 'It was all a long time ago.'

'Yes, it was. And I do know that things were "different then". I ought to – I've had enough explaining of my own to do in the last few days, to my daughter, who I haven't seen since she was born, and to my grandson and granddaughter, who I'd never seen *at all* until this week. I realise that you're not responsible for what happened between my father and Marguerite, but I would like – *all of us* would like – some sort of explanation.'

'Yes. I realise that. I can't tell you precisely what happened, but I'll do my best. We came back to Norfolk after the war – my husband and I were both born near here – and Marguerite lived with us for a while, but she never seemed to settle. I suppose, with Frank and your mother living so close, it was like a slap in the face . . . She got herself a job, and she tried seeing other people, but it never seemed to work out because she was still thinking about your father. She . . . Well, she pursued him. There's no other word for it. And eventually . . .'

'He succumbed?'

'Yes. When she told him she was pregnant – expecting his child – she thought he would leave your mother and marry her, but he refused to. The child – your brother – was born and for a while she and the baby lived here with us, and then, when he was a few months old, she had a breakdown. She went to the hospital – to Crowhurst.'

'Did Pa visit her?'

'He used to go and see her, yes.'

The paraldehyde, Janice thought. That's how he knew about it.

'And what about Dan?'

'Your mother agreed to take him – to bring him up as her own son.'

'When did she find out about him?'

'When Marguerite discovered she was pregnant she went to your parents' house. Your mother refused to believe it at first; she came to see me . . . It was dreadful having to tell her it was true. I was very fond of your mother, and to see her like that – so upset – was terrible. There were rumours, of course – the village – but these things always die down after a while, people forget . . . The normal thing would have been for *us* to keep him, of course, but I let it be known that we couldn't afford another baby – and the truth was that it would have been quite a struggle – so people thought that your parents were being kind, and, as I say, they soon forget – they have their own business to worry about – and so . . . Well, there it is.'

Which explains – at least in part – Ma's reaction when I got pregnant with Suzie, thought Janice. 'So when did Dan discover who his real mother was?'

'That I don't know. I suppose – because of the birth certificate – that he must have found out at some point, but . . .' Mrs Rocklin shook her head. 'One forgets these things, but they are important after all.'

'Yes, they are. What about Malcolm Devlin? Dan's letter – his last letter – said you knew about him and you'd known for years. What did he mean by that?'

Mrs Rocklin took a deep breath, like someone preparing for a dive, then said, 'Marguerite had another son.'

'So Malcolm was Dan's half-brother?'

'Yes, although I don't think Dan knew. At least, not until much later.'

'Older or younger?'

'Younger. It was after she'd been at Crowhurst. She met a man called Bill Devlin. She got pregnant, and he agreed to marry her. Malcolm was born in 1950. They lived in Surrey, and she went to Cane Hill for a time—'

'That's a psychiatric hospital, is it?'

'Yes – not that it did any good. She was in and out – Bill stood by her, but it can't have been easy. She used to get obsessions about people – men – and she'd construct fantasies about how she was going to run away with them, things like that.'

'Malcolm was obsessed with Joe Vincent and his music.'

'Yes . . . I suppose he must have got that from her.'

I don't want to end up in that place. Joe had said it too – something about not wanting to go back to 'that place'. Not a literal place, because Crowhurst was closed now, but a metaphorical one: madness. It hadn't been Ma that Dan was afraid of ending up like, but Marguerite and Malc. Janice had a sudden memory of his wife, Marietta, telling her, around the time they'd split up, that Dan was emphatic about not wanting children. Maybe that – knowing about his biological mother, if not, at that stage, his half-brother – had had something to do with it.

'What happened to Marguerite?'

'She committed suicide in . . . 1960, I think. No, 1961. In the summer. We'd just been to see a film: *Whistle Down the Wind* with Hayley Mills – odd what one remembers – and when we came back the phone was ringing, and it was Bill. Peter spoke to him, and when he put the phone down he said, "That's it, then," and I knew . . . Then he told me she'd jumped in front of a Tube train, in London. Perhaps they could have helped her now – drugs or something – but not then. She wasn't even forty.'

I was ten that summer, Janice thought. Chickenpox. Comics and calamine lotion, lying in bed . . . And when I was allowed downstairs, something in the house had changed; all the *things* were the same – no new furniture or curtains – but there was something else that I couldn't explain. Ma looking at me in an odd way when I asked what had happened, asking me what I meant, and I couldn't tell her. I didn't know what I knew, but I knew. Had it been then?

'Bill tried his best with Malcolm, but it was always difficult. Malcolm was going down the same route, and he couldn't cope. His aunt – Bill's sister – helped a lot, and she ended up looking after him after Bill died.' The aunt in Hertfordshire, Janice thought, remembering what Bob Harling had said. Sandwiches with the crusts cut off. Insanity and Dresden china.

Mrs Rocklin's skin felt dry and papery when Janice leant across and touched one of her hands. 'Do you know about Malcolm?' she asked gently. 'Do you know what's happened?'

Norma Rocklin's mismatched eyes were fearful and watery. 'Has he done something?' She made no attempt to disengage her hand from Janice's, but put the free one up to her mouth as if to prepare herself.

'He's been arrested. Last night, at Joe's house. He tried to attack us both.' Janice wasn't sure what she was expecting, but the expression on Mrs Rocklin's face was unmistakably one of relief. After a strange moment, during which the air in the room seemed to gather itself around the two of them, Janice said, 'You thought he'd done something worse than that, didn't you?'

Mrs Rocklin batted the air in front of her with her hands as if Janice's words were a cloud of flies. 'No, we didn't . . . It wasn't . . . We did our best. We didn't like him coming round here – Peter would get so upset – but what could we do? I didn't know what was happening; I couldn't help—' The flood of words, hasty and querulous, stopped only when Janice grabbed one hand out of the air and held it.

'What *did* you know, Mrs Rocklin?'

'I never knew any of the details. Pat – that was his aunt – she mentioned something to me once that he'd told her, but I never knew if it was true – he was like his mother, making things up . . .'

'Was it about a little girl called Lisa Wynn?'

'I don't know.' Mrs Rocklin's free hand did a frantic, twitchy dance on the table, the nails clicking on the Formica, and her head turned agitatedly from side to side, as if to rid herself of a memory buzzing around it. 'And he'll go to prison now, won't he? It's over, finished . . .'

'Did you think he might have done something to my grand-daughter?'

'No.' The word came out in a wail. 'I don't know what I thought.'

'That was why you went to see Suzie when Molly went missing? Because you felt guilty?'

Mrs Rocklin fumbled with a box of Kleenex, one claw-like hand pulling out a sheet of tissue paper. 'I don't know,' she said, folding it to dab at the glistening corners of her mouth. 'I thought . . . I don't know what I thought. It's no good.' She turned to stare at the calendar once more. 'I can't explain. It was all so long ago. And if there was anything else – later on, I mean, after that girl you mentioned – I never heard about it.'

There was no point in pursuing it, Janice thought, as Norma Rocklin fumbled her way back down the hall to the front door. A narrative remade – convincing herself, over time, that she didn't know the details about Lisa Wynn, that Pat had been mistaken, that Malc had been making it up – so that now, nearly fifty years later, it had become the truth. It was an adult version of the games we play as children – if I don't step on the cracks, this will happen; if I shut my eyes, the bad thing will go away and everything will be all right again. Rituals, hoping against hope. Melissa Piper saying, over and over, 'I know she's out there somewhere, and children do get found, even after many years . . .' as the age-progressed photographs took Phoebe, year on year, further and further away from the child she knew. And eventually, Janice added to herself, looking into Mrs Rocklin's nonagenarian face and seeing a shroud, everything recedes in the face of the inevitable.

She'd tell D.S. Glenville what she knew and hope it was enough.

'Thank you,' she said. Then she opened the front door and stepped outside, into the sunlight.

ACKNOWLEDGEMENTS

I am very grateful to Irene Baldoni, Tim Donnelly, Marcella Fidiles, Stephanie Glencross, Katie Gordon, Jane Gregory, Sue Hall, George Harding, Trudy Howson, Maya Jacobs, Therese Keating, Ruth Murray, Joel Richardson, Hannah Robinson, June Wilson and Jane Wood for their enthusiasm, advice and support during the writing of this book.

I have taken some minor liberties with the geography of Norfolk. Repshall, Yelton, Gorleigh Green, Sparthorpe, R.A.F. Ventham and Crowhurst Psychiatric Hospital do not exist, and neither does Chipfest in Chippenham, Wiltshire.